WYRD GERE

BOOK 2 VALHALLA AWOL

STEVE CURRY

Steve Curry, Author

Lubbock, TX 79413

https://www.facebook.com/MyWyrdMuse/

https://MyWyrdMuse.com

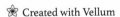 Created with Vellum

ACKNOWLEDGMENTS

Acknowledgments: To my usual crew, "The Crows", Chuckie, John, Christhon and others. Julie Marie, Mr. Kellan, and Ms. McCridhe for their editing and proofreading. A hearty thank you goes out to Sheila for onerous rereads to check my instincts and scoff at my second guessing. To everyone in my circle of friends, critics, confidants and drinking buddies; thanks for the support, gentle nudges and drunken brainstorming sessions. Also thanks to "germancreative" on Fiverr.com for the amazing cover-art that helps me get the words out in front of people. Also on Fiverr, JAClement sculpted my document into a book. And finally, a huge thank you and appreciation to Cindy for pushing prodding and encouraging me with only the occasional reminder that I should have started writing twenty-years ago when she first told me I could write.

GERE~

pronounced as the Anglish gear. "The Ravenous" in old Norse, Gere was one of two wolves who could normally be found at Odin's side to do his bidding.

1

I was trying hard to keep on the lookout for Border Patrol, Lake Patrol, hostile gang members, immortal watchers, and a boat I'd never laid my eyes on. Hel for all I knew the NSA or Coast guard might be watching me in that gigantic lake on the Mexican border. I couldn't see more than a stone's throw away in the miserable drizzle. I called it miserable because the resultant trickle of near glacial water down my neck was increasingly annoying. The persistent rain had the added benefit of making me impatient and irritable at the driver's seat.

I looked down with a glare for the icy water swirling in the bottom of the tiny rental boat. I distinctly remember leakier boats and worse weather. Those had been bigger boats with lots of other men around to help bail or row or whatever it took. This wasn't a bad leak, but it was enough to bother me in the middle of a lake this size. I wouldn't be able to see shoreline from out here even if it was broad daylight and clear weather. All of those factors were enough to make me ask how the Hel I got myself into this situation.

Of course, I knew how I got here. After decades of

keeping off the radar, I popped up in a big way. The start of it all wasn't my doing. I was just the lucky winner who discovered the first body. After that, one thing led to another and I ended up with the attention of a spook from one of the alphabet agencies, and the much more welcome attention of a beautiful redhead from the Emerald Isle. I also caught exactly the kind of attention I had managed to avoid for so long.

I guess I should explain the reason for my evasiveness. I've been around for a while. In fact, off and on, I've been around since sometime before the ninth century. Yeah, I said off and on. In the span of all of those years, I've spent an unknown time in Valhalla and can't count all my deaths. It's an unknown time for more than a single simple reason.

First off, even a life full of wine, women, and brawls palls after a few years. You can get bored enough to lose whole years at a time. Secondly, death loses some of its fearsomeness if it's not permanent.

I have a theory that most of the fighting Einherjar do is because they're just that bored. We spent a huge amount of time training. More often we were kept in a kind of stasis. Oh, I have vague memories of good-natured competitive dismemberment. Remember, when one of us dies he just wakes up later back in the feast hall. Depending on your own group leader, aka Valkyrie, you might wake up in time for the feasting on the very day you died, or you might wake up when she decided you could be useful again. The worst part is, when she finally decides to wake you up it's as if no time has passed. Someone else might mention that they hadn't seen you in a while. Otherwise, you'd think you were back immediately.

The best part was missions. Every so often one of us or even a whole bunch of us would get tapped for duty.

Usually, it was a quick covert op. Drop us in at a key place to shift the odds in a battle. I know I took part in some events that were in the history books. I just can't remember all of them. It's my guess that whatever they do to keep us in stasis also affects our memories and freewill. Some of my brothers in arms were little more than mindless zombies.

The best of us though were allowed more free thought. A zombie is only of limited use in any type of fight. That kind of troops main value is in how cheap they are. A zombie who just goes back to the fold is easy to waste. On the other hand, sometimes you needed more experienced boots on the ground. The fight that needs discretion is where those of us with a little more free will shined. Mine were some of those smarter boots. Or maybe I was just too stubborn for their brainwashing to stick.

I was still suffering from certain effects that popped up after one of our discreet little missions back in Vietnam. Maybe I lost my memories in the thunder and fire of battle. Maybe I owed a certain manipulating old god for the lost years of my life. All I remember is the job we did that day and who was behind it. After that, I woke up in a MASH tent. I'm not sure whether old One-eye had a stake in the fight himself or was paid by someone else. Hel, he may have just liked the idea of a new type of airborne troop being used. Whatever the reasoning was; we were dropped in to provide some extra firepower in a bad situation.

A new idea in the American Army had been to quickly move some real tough troops into position. The indigenous people in those jungle mountains were good at fast hit and run strikes against the entrenched American bases. So some bright chair polisher came up with Infantry that moved fast in helicopters. These Air Cavalry could hit the ground within minutes or hours rather than the days it might take to respond by marching or trucking troops through the jungle.

Well, they responded fast alright. They got there ahead of any real Intel. I heard later that the first scout caught was asked how many of the VC were up on the mountain. His reply was supposedly "All of them."

That was all gossip, but there were certainly enough of the little bastards to go around. Kara, our Valkyrie, got us into position beside a dry river bed. For the first half of that battle, we moved around the perimeter providing some secretive assistance wherever it would do the most good.

Everything came to a head later in the fight. The little guys with black pajamas made a massive push and broke into the troops we were assisting. Kara popped up out of nowhere and yelled "Charge".

When a Valkyrie yells, any soldier or individual with even a spark of the old warrior spirit is carried along with her will. So compelling was her power over us, that only a handful kept using our more modern weapons. The rest of us charged in. I clubbed my rifle at darting smaller figures. Beside me, one of my brothers stabbed and ripped through those same bodies with the bayonet from his rifle. Past him, I saw an entrenching tool chop a hand off just as effectively as our axes centuries ago. Those of us still mobile were shooting, hacking and chopping right up until the super-sonic birds streaked overhead and slowed just enough to drop napalm on us.

I'm not going to try and tell you what napalm is like. But I'm pretty sure the guy who invented it had seen visions of the Christian Hell. I went from shooting and brawling to darkness in a scarlet thunder and screams of anguish. Dozens of people were screaming around me when I lost consciousness. Kara must have thought I was one of the dead ones. She never left one of us just hanging out after a mission. We either went back with her or were dead and just woke up later.

I woke up briefly in a helicopter with bullet holes everywhere you could see. I almost tossed my breakfast from the stench of overcooked meat. I didn't figure out until later that some of those smells were coming from me. I quelled the puke by focusing on the other sensations around me.

I felt hard steel against my back. The steel plate surged and bucked with the wind and the will of the pilot. I also heard a continuous litany of sulfurous profanities coming from the cockpit. I knew just enough English to know the pilot was beyond furious about something to do with orders and other choppers. The ride was bumpy enough that I didn't mind passing out again.

The next time I woke up it was to a cheerful nurse with a fake smile asking how I was doing. It was the first time I woke up in mortal care since before I died first a thousand years ago. There was more to it but it's too much to tell all at once.

Short version is, I stole a dying soldier's dog tags and ID and got shipped stateside. It was Hel keeping anyone from looking under the bandages at first, but once I was en route people just looked at my orders and took them at face value.

Queue forward half a century.

I still looked like a military veteran. I sport short hair most of the time. People tell me I've got pretty good posture whenever anyone notices. I even have the scout's tendency to keep my eyes moving to spot "them" before they spot me. Anyone seeing me would guess I'd spent time in the middle east "sandbox", rather than Vietnam though.

For one, I've been told I look to be in my thirties or maybe a very, very well maintained forty-something. That's always a little embarrassing. I mean, I was in my mid-twenties when a spear took out most of my left lung and did some pretty unpleasant things to my heart in passing. That hardly shows though except for an ugly scar on my chest. Kara didn't fix that when she brought me back from the fight that first time. Some Valkyrie like their troops all flat muscle and scar-less. Kara liked us to keep the ones we got before she chose us. She also let us keep any we picked up against her wishes.

My short faux-hawk hair is a tawny brown. In contrast, I wear a goatee of slightly darker brown or auburn with bits of coppery red showing through. I keep my tattoos covered by long sleeves as much as possible. No scars or brands are visible unless I have some clothes missing. I don't even show much jewelry unless I happen to be wearing one of several earrings I've made for special occasions.

Perhaps the most notable aspect of my appearance is what I prefer calling an atypical height to width ratio. My shoulders are as wide as most football players even with their pads on. Unfortunately, I also have to look up to even a moderately tall woman.

I'm pretty sure my appearance isn't what gave me away to get me out here on Lake Amistad in the middle of the night though. The very large and intimidating biker I met had "sniffed out" the little oddities of my origin more than saw them. He helped me avoid some legal entanglements through creative fraud and moving/mutilating a corpse.

The problem was, he isn't exactly a man. He tends to spend a lot of time at the right hand of one of the most powerful beings I didn't want to see. And worst of all, he wanted a favor from me.

THAT is what got me stuck out in a freezing rain in the middle of a ponderously large lake on the Mexican border.

I was interrupted mid-muse by the murmur of a boat motor idling slowly closer. I cranked my head around looking for lights but never found them. What I did spot was a bobbing shadow that resolved itself into a decrepit old pontoon boat. The slow-moving beast was fitted with what seemed like an excessive number of fishing poles in metal pipes welded to the rails. Other than that it consisted of a single flat deck with some beat-up old bench seats and a pedestal from which a barely visible wiry looking silhouette steered. I watched the stern lights and bow light alike sort of flicker and then dull to a glow so wan and sullen that the driver's watch dial was more visible.

"Hey Jefe...toss me a line." I got a glimpse of the driver of that unsafe looking boat when the flare of his match lit a narrow face within his hooded raincoat. He ducked his head down and looked at me sideways through the smoke that spiraled up from his fresh cigarette. The eyes were partially squinted, maybe from the smoke but I was betting from a cold calculating stare. What I could see through the slits of his eyes was dark enough to be black in the darkness. I was guessing at dark brown. His thin and somewhat sparse moustache, however, looked black and a little oily as did the small soul patch and sharply pointed beard under thin and colorless lips. The lips themselves were curved in a cunning little smile. "I mean you better be the fellow ole Lobo got Pedro Perro out here for on a shitty night like this."

I shrugged and then thought about the fact that he might not be able to see me. That also meant he probably couldn't see the pistol grip shotgun I had hanging down beside my leg. In daylight, the shotgun might have been a little too visible. In that case, I'd have brought a pistol. At night on a moving boat though, the shotgun with its barely legal length of barrel was the obvious choice. I might not be able to sweep the deck of the other boat, but it would spread big enough to clip two men if they were standing close together. With boats bobbing on waves I probably needed the pattern just to efficiently nail one guy.

"I'm the guy that was supposed to meet you in Doc Holiday's two nights ago. Which begs the question, why send me a note and drag *me* out here on such a shitty night?" I did toss him a line with my left hand. The gun-toting right hand I kept somewhat behind me and out of the light. A sharp glimpse and nodding grin from "Pedro" told me he wasn't that oblivious.

"Big gringo I saw getting out of his border patrol car. We was um, acquainted. Didn't really want to get reacquainted when he was drinkin with his buddies." His grin was less calculating this time. He was probably trying for open and charming. I got oily and manipulative out of it.

He nodded at the gun while tying our boats together. "You ain't gonna need that bro. Ole Lobo told me you was a VIP. Handle with kid gloves, full cooperation, and all that crap. Ok, I'm tied off. You got a compass up there then head off at twenty-two degrees west of north. Otherwise, just head that way." His indicator for direction was nothing other than the cigarette in his cupped hand as he jumped from his higher deck into my smaller if sturdier-looking boat.

I shrugged and turned the wheel as directed. We were just about to a reasonable speed when he tapped me with the same cigarette laden hand. "Ease up on the throttle. We don't need to get too much attention. I got the fuel tank rigged up on the pontoon boat. If anyone stops us you're just giving a poor old Mexican fisherman a ride for gas."

Well, I was pretty sure that a clandestine meeting somewhere in the middle of the night hadn't been planned for the scenery. I just hoped he wasn't engaging me in some crime I'd disapprove of. My bet was drug smuggling. He was referred by a guy who looked the part. My only glimpse of the old "Lobo's" crew said they were probably major contributors to the consumption if not the distribution of drugs and alcohol in the states or wherever else they might be at any given moment.

Ok, don't get too judgmental. I don't do drugs. I don't even like most recreational pharmaceuticals. I damned sure don't like the idea of pushers getting kids hooked in schools. But in my own personal experience, most of the people buying their "candy" from distributors were old enough to know better. Sure it was poison but rarely did someone hold down the victims and force them to partake.

Did I feel bad for their families? Sure. It's never good for the honor of your bloodline to be stained with the kinds of things drug addicts did. In that instance, it was probably the family's job to deal with the addict.

I hadn't met anyone from my bloodline in a very long time though. These other poor fools, the ones who burned up their lives with needles or pipes didn't mean much to me. Come to think of it, it was unlikely that this Pedro Perro was doing anything worse than I had been part of more than a few times before.

I kept my thoughts to myself as we puttered at a stealthy crawl across the lake. I thought maybe old Pedro Perro was drunk or lost when we got to his destination. For a while, it was kind of touch and go about whether we were going to make it at all. His boat was low in the water when he jumped back over the rail. I caught his gesture to cut my engines and did so. He reached under the dashboard and played with some wires then fired up the rusty old outboard motor and drove the boat right up into the shallows near the shoreline.

It wasn't a particularly distinctive piece of shoreline either. I didn't see anything to indicate where exactly along that massive lake we might be. Apparently, my guide did though. He managed to get the decrepit old pontoon sideways to the overgrown shore with one whole edge of the pontoon over dry land while the other side grated and bumped in the surge of waves. I was impressed that he could drive that well with my boat a deadweight on the side away from the shore.

"Hey Gringo, drive around that point over there and tie up at the dock." He pointed with his chin and cigarette while both hands were busy untying his boat from mine and then ran towards the side on the shore. "If it's empty then turn on the light at the back of the dock. Tall pole with a bulb on it. Nothin fancy. Switch on the pole."

I started the engine, threw it in reverse and started to maneuver away from the shallows. In front of me, the wiry "captain" of the other boat was leaning over and futzing with the pontoons resting on the shore. Just as the darkness swallowed them from my sight, I saw him swing the top of the pontoon open. He smiled and leaned down to lift out a teenage girl. I was still stunned and staring when he went to turn the fake rivets on the next pontoon. Before I saw what else, or who else, his cargo contained, the shoreline dipped between us and hid the other boat from view.

Human trafficking? That one was of a little more concern to me than other types of smuggling. I'm not a big fan of slavery. When I was young, we had thralls and it was a matter of little concern. Everyday lives from that time were not truly recognizable by today's standards.

Truth is thralls or what you would define as slaves formed the second largest population of the three classes.

The smallest of the groups, like today, were the nobles or

what you would call the one-percenters. The nobles were exemplified by a Jarl or sometimes a king. In fact, we held both in about the same regard. If they were strong warriors and admirable leaders then we followed them. If they were neither of the above, well, we often ended up with a new Jarl fairly soon. Sadly this usually occurred after the abrupt death of the weaker leader.

The entire thought of a Royal or Regal quality was foreign to us. There was a story of some Danes confronted by a retinue of the Frankish King. The Franks insisted that the Danes kiss the foot of their Royal personage. The leader of the Danes was not in favor of the idea and delegated it to another member of their band. The second Dane fulfilled the request but in a typical Viking manner. He knelt and grabbed the kingly foot then lifted it up to where he could kiss the questionable appendage at head height. It was assumed that the Frankish king's royal bearing was not enhanced by sprawling on the ground at the foot of the Danes.

Below the Jarls were the Karls or freemen. This was the main layer of society with landowners and tradesmen lumped together. There were, naturally, different layers with that main body of peoples. Godi or chieftains often fulfilled a local leadership role but were also quite frequently the religious leaders of the community with a connection to the gods.

And then there were the Thralls. They worked with little or no pay to hopefully gain their freedom. Some were "property" brought back as spoils of war. Others were debtors sold into their lot until they could repay debts. Most of them, young and old alike, were treated well enough to maintain their health. A thrall was only worth the work he could do.

As I said, those times were little like today. Much of the time we were just trying to survive. We rarely grew or caught enough food to drive hunger away. We just discouraged it a little. You couldn't hunt up a repairman whenever the roof leaked. Goods and clothing must be made or traded for. People were judged for the value they added to their holding.

To be a Thrall was still not a position anyone strove to achieve. They did the worst of the unskilled labor. Food and living conditions were pretty miserable sometimes. Some were taken as bed slaves, nannies or milk mothers. These usually had a gentler lot than a field hand or a woman grinding grain or salt by hand. It was not common nor was it illegal for a thrall to be treated badly by the freedman above him. Such abusers rarely kept more than a few slaves. One is wise not to anger slaves that outnumber your own men or family.

My own taste of slavery was at the hands of Wends or Vandals. My Scandinavian brothers and I traveled much of Europe and even as far as Asia and Africa. Sometimes we traded. Sometimes we raided. We were, however, by no means the only raiders in our time. The Rugi were a band of Slavs, we called them Rugi, Vandals, Vind, Wend or those goat-loving motherless dogs of the east.

One of their longboats captured me after a little naval disagreement. They carried me from Denmark into the Slavic lands. From there I was sold a number of times, usually by Jewish traders who could move freely in both Christian and Muslim lands. I ended up rowing a ship around the Mediterranean and Atlantic for a trader from Cordova. His rules for slaves were unpleasantly different from those I'd known. Fortunately, I was not his type. He was probably put off by my height. Some of the other men were not so lucky.

It was the Cordova ship that ruined me for slavery or thralls. We still had them on some of the ships and lands where I lived. After my own time in the collar, I always made sure their lot was never harsher than it had to be. And I never yearned to own any myself.

That's probably why I was much more concerned with the sight of my guide's "cargo" than I might be over the smuggling of drugs or other goods. I've also heard a few stories about the kind of things a young girl can expect once they're part of the human trafficking operation. Maybe my kind had a reputation for ferocity and cruelty, but I was never part of a scenario like the stories you hear these days. That wasn't very likely to change for some weasel I just met.

When I rounded the point it was readily apparent that there was nobody around the rickety dock. I hesitated to tie up at the ramshackle affair. At least the tires were likely to float. The rest of the thing was the best illustration I'd ever seen of the term flotsam.

Other than the tires and decaying slats of the dock, there was a rusted tin shack with no doors or glass in the windows. It was open enough to the elements that nobody over three years old could have been hiding. Or maybe a small dwarf. I guess some of the fey might hide there but they're so good at hiding they wouldn't need the building. But I digress.

The only other sign of people was a rugged looking block of rust that slowly resolved itself into an old utility van with filthy windows. Just on the off chance, I dug a flashlight out of my tackle-box and cruised by to check through the van windows.

No ninjas or irate border patrol jumped out at my light so I went ahead and looked through the dirty window. No people lurked inside but there was a dirty blanket atop what looked like a couple of milk crates. Fair enough, there didn't seem any immediate threats so I crunched through dried weeds to turn on the light with the switch on the aforementioned light post.

I had fished my thermos full of coffee out of the boat and started pouring a cup when a cheerfully whistled "Tijuana Taxi" alerted me to the approach of my supposed guide. What surprised me most was that he came out of the weeds alone and walked straight to the van.

I tried not to be obvious while I looked for his trafficking merchandise. He wouldn't have noticed anyway. Without giving me more than a quick glance and a smirk he produced keys and unlocked the van to climb behind the steering wheel. "Well, get in Gringo. If we hurry I can get you back to your room to grab a few hours of sleep before checkout."

I was curious. Maybe he had a partner that took possession of the young girl before he came over to the van. If that were the case though, why involve me or drive a second vehicle like this van himself?

I shrugged and climbed into the passenger seat. "What's the deal with the boat then? I paid a hefty cash deposit since I didn't want to use a credit card. I'd rather not buy even a cheap used boat and leave it on the lake for whatever reason."

He flashed me his sharp grin again. "No worries. We won't need to do anything for a while. I'll make a call. One of my associates can turn it back in at the marina. Until then it can wait right where it is. Nobody comes over here anyway."

The engine sputtered once but then coughed into life

with only a few clicks and whistles that you wouldn't expect to hear from an automobile. The sounds did, however, go with several spots of visible rust on the sides and rear of the van. Even the doors had what looked like Bondo repairs that hadn't been sanded or painted either one. If the engine was on a par with the rest I was worried we might not make it back to my room in any reasonable amount of time. I was worried about nothing. He dropped me off half an hour after we got out of the boats.

It was already after midnight. I contemplated a drink or two. Even more than a drink I wanted to call Maureen. It had only been a day since I left her lying in a tangle of silk sheets and lithely golden thigh. The thought of that last glimpse of red hair and carelessly exposed legs had me reaching for the phone. Before I finished dialing though, I reached back across the cheap bedside table and put the handset back on the receiver.

I wasn't very comfortable about how much I missed this particular girl. I was pretty sure giving in to call her after midnight would not win me any favor points. Or it might. My always sketchy knowledge of women and relationships was not exactly current. In fact, I often tripped myself up between expectations from the seventies and expectations from a thousand years ago.

I felt pretty confident the late call would score on the lower scale of her favor. Nor would it score very high in the autonomous male department. It was too late to call anybody anyway. I told myself that several times while I tried to fall asleep.

2

ONE OF THE main perks from my previous one-eyed mostly-niscient employer is the whole healing and recuperating thing. We don't fall over from the most serious of injuries. If something doesn't kill us we tend to recover rapidly and we can run the ragged edge of exhaustion and then recover with barely a short night's rest.

I wasn't feeling the least bit tired, so after just a couple of hours, I woke as refreshed and revitalized as your average trophy wife after a spa weekend. The revitalization factor has never bothered my appetite though. Sometimes I think our higher vitality requires a higher calorie intake as well. Or maybe we're just the ravenous out of control barbarian brutes people like to imagine. Whatever the cause, I usually enjoy a healthy breakfast.

That meant I was up, sampling the hotel buffet when Perro walked back in. He spotted me right away and walked straight across the foyer without an apparent care in the world. At least he didn't look like he was trying to avoid attention.

Perro was apparently of the opinion that hotels were lax

about who was and was not a guest entitled to their complimentary perks. He piled a plate with assorted breakfast meats and eggs then topped it off with a gooey hot cinnamon roll of some sort. When he got to my table he slid the plate down across the table from me. Before he sat down he fished out a bundle he'd tucked under his arm while juggling with the prodigious stack of food.

Tossing the package to me he sat down with a grin and dug into the free grub with a fascinating amount of energy and obvious enjoyment. Between mouthfuls, he pointed at the package I had reflexively caught.

"When you're done eating go put that on. We got a little time but not enough to screw around all morning. Glad you're up though. Otherwise, I wouldn't have had time to stoke the furnaces like this." The sentences came out in bite-sized phrases only slightly muffled and distorted by the oversized chunks of sausage and bacon he consumed steadily and rapidly. It was enough to make me wonder how he kept that lean whipcord physique.

Despite my intentions to eat a hearty morning repast, the sight of gobs of mixed and mashed meat as he talked did a number on my appetite. I shrugged and pushed a half-empty plate away. We might as well get on the road and I was more than a little curious about what was in the package.

I headed back to the room while Pedro got up for another run at the free food. What I found in the package was pretty much a standard uniform for lots of first responders. Ambulance drivers or ER techs even trauma nurses often wore the same thing. Black trousers with a kind of combat fatigue look were matched with a black polo-style shirt that had a caduceus and some stylized letters on it. I wondered what the AMTMA stood for. Then again I doubted it was going to matter. I had to assume that the uniform was just for disguise.

Don't get me wrong, I have more than a little experience as a combat medic. While it's true that our Valkyrie handlers weren't especially thrifty with our replenishable lives, they always wanted as much profit as possible before one of us died. We were tough enough to survive wounds that would put other men down. Yet, we were just as vulnerable to massive trauma or slow depletion of our resources as other people. It just took *more* massive trauma or longer periods of time for us to bleed out or lose our endurance.

That meant somebody or everybody had to learn how to plug up holes and splint broken bones. It wasn't uncommon to see someone that you had no doubt was sporting a broken bone still clubbing a rifle like some kind of medieval maul. We were supposed to give our bosses the most bang for the buck after all.

Perro shouldn't know that much about me though. Or if he did then I was going to do some research and have a long and brutal talk with a seemingly immortal wolf. Freke was supposed to make sure he erased anything about my current existence from his memories. Come to think of it he'd never promised not to tell anyone else first.

Wolves aren't usually quite that damned deceptive though. I mean cunning and stealthy yes. They were great at camouflage and misdirection but usually, you could depend on their odd sense of honor to keep them from telling outright lies or forswearing themselves by breaking an oath. If this one had broken his sworn oath then there was probably a way for me to exact some revenge. The universe seems to have its own code of honor when it comes to things like that.

I came down from the room in my newly acquired

uniform and my own comfortably broken in combat boots. Since I was traveling light, my own clothes were in a gym bag. An old army issue duffle slung over my shoulder held some other clothes and gear. The room key I left on a bedside table in plain sight. Housekeeping would turn it in for me. It meant I might lose the cash deposit from checking out properly. On the other hand, nobody would know exactly when and where I was going or what I was wearing now.

The wiry little guide for my odd little tour of south Texas crooked a finger at me from the door and jerked his head to indicate the exit. We came out under an awning that shaded a vanilla looking white van with the AMTMA logo on sides and doors as well as various other markers that OSHA would probably approve of.

I was still looking at the van with a nagging feeling in my gut when Perro took my duffel and hefted it with a grin. "Gear in here too? Maybe something we don't want to explain to Law Enforcement Officer types?"

His chuckle told me he wasn't particularly distressed about deceiving an LEO or two. "Probably best if we don't have those on us just yet. I'll take care of it. Here take this for now and hand over anything else that might make some-body suspicious."

The bundle he handed me contained a few clip-on holsters with pepper spray and an EMS multi-tool. I checked the multi-tool and discovered that one of the blades had been replaced with a locking tanto style blade. The new attachment was about five inches long and looked deadly as well as durable. There was also a plain and cheap looking cell phone.

I expected him to put the duffel into another hidden compartment or such. If the boat had been any indication then this fellow knew smuggling better than most. So I was surprised when he waved and summoned a rider on a large thunderously loud motorcycle. The biker stopped for Pedro to strap my duffel behind the seat with handy cords. Before I could protest, the bike rumbled away.

Pedro walked back to the van and gestured for me to get in the passenger side. It wasn't until I opened the door that I knew where that nagging feeling had come from. Rather than sit down I took a few steps back and looked over the vehicle. The thick layer of dust was gone which made the windows look old but not cracked or falling apart. Likewise, the rusted spots and primer paint was covered with new logos and safety signs.

I ran a hand over the "artwork" on my door and discovered it was a thin and very well made film of some sort that looked like it had been painted on. I was willing to bet that it would peel off and stick back on with very little effort. Our decrepit wreck from the night before was now a worn but serviceable and more importantly recognizable medical transport.

When I got in I started to speak to Perro behind the wheel. Except Perro wasn't behind the wheel. Instead, I saw a small and very pretty young girl anywhere from seventeen years old to thirty. She had a petite but attractive figure and large dark eyes that were much too innocent for the world I'd assumed she was part of the previous evening. She was also wearing a uniform similar to mine.

"Elena, this is Moose. Moose, Elena." The voice was familiar but the frail-looking old man in the wheelchair behind us resembled Pedro Perro only in size and weight. He was still lean but that appeared more a lack of muscular development than the whipcord physique he usually displayed.

His was one of three wheelchairs locked to the floor in back. One was empty. The other held a dozing older lady wearing a floral patterned ankle-length dress or robe of some sort. She had the wan olive skin that some of the older Mexicans get from their Spanish ancestry. Her hair was a cascade of silver with just threads of the dark brown mane she had probably once used to lure the young men. Even half-asleep her bearing was erect and proud looking. Her head bobbed but her neck would never bend.

"That's Senora Dolores Mr. Moose. She's probably gonna sleep most of the way. Last night was tough on her. She'll be ok by the time we get to Arizona though."

Arizona? I thought I was supposed to be headed down south. What the hell was I going to Arizona for? I started to ask. The oily little weasel of a man beat me to it though. "We just gotta drop these two off. Got us a hotel room in Sedona tonight. We cross into Mexico tomorrow. Your guy ain't there right now anyway. Might as well take care of my two birds with one trip eh?"

Perro probably thought his smile was charming or maybe disarming. To me it was just annoying as Hel. Or maybe I was just irritated at being kept in the dark deliberately. His introduction in English had convinced me that the little cutie driving the van was fluent enough that I didn't want to discuss our "business" in front of her. Probably because I still had no stinking idea what our business was.

The trip was long enough that I got bored with fuming before we had to stop for gas. Somewhere in New Mexico Pedro spoke his rapid-fire Spanish at the girl driving and she pulled over into a truckstop just a few miles down the road. As far as I could tell there was very little town except for the truck stop itself. There were signs for casinos and other entertainments everywhere. The casinos themselves seemed rather few and far between.

Somehow when you hear the word Casino you expect something like Caesars Palace or Treasure Island. Half of these places just looked like fairly well maintained large adobe or stucco hotels. They were surrounded by lots of sand and cactus with some easy to maintain gardens of the same materials as well as volcanic looking chunks of rock here and there. Each of them seemed to have some link to Native American lore.

There were Buffalo, Horses, Eagles, Wind, and Thunder in most of the titles. Logos often had some form of Kachina or Dancer on them if they weren't overwhelmed by south-western wildlife like stampeding buffalo. Las Vegas, this was not.

As drab and uninspired as the casinos were, our truck-stop was worse. It bordered on dilapidated. If a building could look both aged and weary, this one managed it. Old man Pedro reached between the seats to hand me a credit card. "Use that for gas. Use cash for food or anything else. Everyone take a few minutes. Get some food. Stretch your legs and use the facilities."

He repeated in Spanish what I assumed were the same instructions. Likewise in Spanish, the little old lady spoke to our driver Elena. The girl nodded and then said something to Pedro that I didn't catch. He must have understood though since he produced a handful of cash and laughed again as he passed it to the girl.

I got out and pumped the gas while he maneuvered his chair down the ramp with a couple more phrases that seemed to reassure or placate Senora Dolores. As I was finishing he rolled up for the first explanation he'd really bothered to give me.

"They pay me to get them across then got no money for a bag of chips or a coke." He shook his head and chuckled again. I wasn't sure if he was amused by them or by me. Maybe he was chuckling at giving money back to his clients.

"Is that what we're doing? Smuggling illegals across?" I watched his reaction. That didn't mean I missed the arrival of the bike bearing its heavily muscled Hispanic rider and my duffel bag. Without looking in our direction the motorcyclist rode up and dismounted to fill his own tank. Apparently, he had some of his own money because he didn't bother coming to beg from my fake wheelchair-bound companion.

"No, we're smuggling an Illegal across. Just the one. Elena has all the right papers and stuff but I made her mail them back home to Arizona. For now, she has a different name and IDs. No use giving anybody information that might get someone arrested or deported eh?" He irritated me with that smug grin of his again. He also nodded cheerfully and started to wheel himself away.

"Wait up and I'll give you back your card. Gas is almost done." I was still waiting for the click of the pump that would tell me we were full.

"No worries. Not my card. I'd probably get rid of it if I were you." He said it over a shoulder and barely loud enough for me to hear. I just shook my head and folded the stolen card over and dropped it into the trash. Before I got rid of it though I read the name. Pedro Perro definitely did not look much like a Tyrone White.

The biker walked in right beside me. We kind of thumped shoulders without him bothering to even acknowledge my presence. Maybe he was just taking his job serious about not knowing any of us. Maybe he was a world-class asshole too and meant to prove how tough he was by shoving me aside.

That's fine. I was here on a job. No need to prove I could fold him and his bike up into a compact block for disposal. There was plenty of temptation, just no need. He wasn't carrying any bags so I looked back at the bike. Sure enough, there was my duffel sitting strapped to a motorcycle by nothing more secure than bungee cords.

I felt the steam under my collar. Maybe it wasn't his worry. That gear had been put in his care though and I didn't really want to have to replace two or three firearms and a few odds and end of other combat-ready gear. About the only thing missing was my new tactical vest with the thin chainmail shirt stuck to its underside. Ballistic plates are great for bullets but a knife can slip right through some of the stuff they use these days. The chainmail was good enough quality to turn aside most blades...or claws.

I had taken two or three very heavy strides back towards the door on my way back to the bike outside. That was far as I got before the little scoundrel in his wheelchair darted out and blocked my path. This time his voice was still quiet but intense enough to make up for any lost volume. "No sir. You don't know him. He don't know you. And you got nothing to do with that bike. Got it?"

I started to push past the chair but the long thin fingers that wrapped around my bicep were stronger than I had imagined. I looked down at Perro and flexed my arm in preparation for ripping it out of his grip. I don't much like being pawed at or grabbed. Probably has something to do with making a living grabbing people and restraining them.

Before I could jerk away he released his grasp but kept his eyes locked on mine. "Look I get paid to get people where they go. I'm a coyote. That's what people call guys that smuggle other people around. Most of em are pretty bad guys. Just take the money and do as little as possible. Maybe let some people cook or choke to death in a train car or the back of a truck or something. Some of the real assholes take a little bonus from the cuter girls and women. Maybe even sell them to other dudes. I don't do that. A little cash is all I take and I don't leave nobody locked up anyplace to die."

He gestured for me to push him around the grocery section which was mostly empty. I pushed while he continued in his rapid and intense explanation."Elena paid me to get her Abuela, her grandma, to someplace near Sedona. Elena been working for some rich people here for a few years. She earned enough money to get her own place. Now she wants her grandmother over to take care of. Makes some more money and talks to some people and bingo...she finds me to get Abuela Dolores across. The old lady is kind of special and the little girl can make you wanna do stuff for her just by blinking those big eyes so I take the job."

We were almost still alone so I slowed stopped in one of the aisles to look at some beef jerky. I didn't really want any of this processed salty crap. But it gave Perro time to finish. This was more info than I'd gotten from the secretive little weasel since I'd met him. "That's all I get paid for. No fake IDs or social security or nothing. That costs a lot extra. They just paid me for grandma."

He jerked a thumb towards the bike outside. "This asshole is her cousin from down near Matamoros. I ain't paid to get him across and I don't like him. But asshole knows some people I don't wanna cross comprende? So walk soft and stay away from him. He's trouble we don't gotta mess with. Just deliver the old lady and then we head back down to start working on your deal ok?"

It took some restraint, but I jerked my chin down in a sharp nod. At least I knew the bag was warded to a degree. If it was turned inside out the runes painted into it would have been visible. Somebody who studied and understood the potential of the elder futhark would have been able to guess at their purpose.

Ok Runes might need some explanation. Historians will tell you that they're a germanic permutation of an older alphabet from the Mediterranean. That's probably true as far as it goes.

Runes are much more than that though. In the North, back in the days of Beowulf and Sigurd Snake-in-the-eye, we had a lot of beliefs that have faded to a degree. Written language probably seemed like magic to the first of our people to encounter it.

Before that our histories always came down through skalds who memorized the tales and stories that helped us identify important people and events. When people could make marks on a hide or cloth or even carved in stone, then come back and tell you word for word what the marks said; well that seemed like magick.

Already we had a respect that bordered on fear for the power of language, song, words of any sort. For centuries it was illegal to compose a love song or poem and then utter it aloud. Words can be strong enough that such an act could be considered a form of enchantment. I'm pretty sure we lost more than a few bright and creative fellows with romantic intentions over what now seems like such an innocent act.

Fathers and brothers were careful of their womenfolk in my time. A woman had rights and responsibilities just like a man. Sometimes an especially good marriage would elevate not only the newlywed, but also his or her family depending on the match.

Anyone jeopardizing such a pairing with their own suspect incantations or creative performances could expect a thorough beating at the least. There was also the distinct possibility that an indiscreet romantic poet might find himself bleeding to death on a mountainside or locked into his hut while it burned.

I guess what I'm saying is, we already had a respect for the spoken word. The runes just gave us a handy tool to use in enhancing the fear and faith into an actual tool of magic and power. Most of us used them in certain ways and could recognize the meaning of runes created by another.

Everyone had their own personal perceptions about the meanings and uses of each of the twenty-four runes. At least there were twenty-four of them in the system I used. Some systems used runic alphabets from other places and times to achieve fewer runes or rarely more of them. Each of those letters though had centuries of lore behind them that helped shape what each was capable of. The practitioner just put his own spin on them with his will and his perceptions.

Anyone who used elder Futhark runes would probably guess that my duffel was made to be durable, fire resistant and tougher than normal cloth. A very astute Runemal or wise man of the runes might also notice that there were runes made to shift the eyes and thoughts of others away from the duffel and its contents. It wasn't foolproof by any means. Given a choice between that bag and looting someone else's property though, most people wouldn't even pay attention to my stuff.

Maybe that would be enough. With a second nod that lacked some of the initial irritation, I turned away and took the necessary angry strides to reach a long hallway that advertised all of the necessary facilities up to and including hot showers and laundry machines. Behind me, I heard the fake quaver of Perro. "I'll keep an eye out til you can push me back in the van Mister Medic."

More fake nonsense like that did little to improve my mood. Maybe if I hurried I could get back and have a chat with Old Pedro before the ladies rejoined us. In my experience, modern womenfolk (and frankly a majority of women from other places and eras) took considerably longer than men in situations like truck stops and restaurants or almost any endeavor that might include some grooming opportunities.

I'd taken care of some necessities and grabbed a dozen tamales with an energy drink. That made it a bit of a juggle to push the wheelchair and handle my lunch all at once. Perro took the bag from me though and held it on top of the blanket that covered his lap and legs. In that fashion, we made it to the van without mishap. We didn't get to have my private conversation though.

When I opened the rear of the van, Senora Dolores was already back in her place and looking around with just a hint of confusion. Ahead of her and back in the driver's seat was the petite Elena. They were talking quietly when we got there but stopped their soft whispering as soon as the door opened. I hadn't heard more than one or two sentences from the cute little Elena. Most of the time if she spoke it was to Pedro Perro or her mother and it was in a soft but very pleasant sounding Spanish. Pedro supplied the only explanation I was likely to get for their current conversation. "Abuela doesn't remember much since I let her out of the boat. It was hard on her and she's old. She's just wondering where we are."

He turned back to the two ladies and spoke in the rolling tones of Spanish. I recognized Santa Fe and a couple of other names that I knew from some maps I'd seen here and there. From what I gathered we were just a little south of Santa Fe and were well on our way to their destination. The cousin on his bike must have been in a bigger hurry than we were. He blew past the van in a roar before we were out of sight of our last stop.

None of us made it much further though. Less than half an hour after we left the truck stop there was a roadblock with a state police cruiser and two or three of the familiar green border patrol trucks. Leaning on the hood of one of the trucks was our biker buddy. He looked terribly uncomfortable with his hands holding him at an awkward angle and his legs wide apart.

Elena was breathing noticeably faster as she pulled in behind a short line of cars waiting to be cleared. I didn't know how to help her anxiety. I was having a hard time controlling my own. In addition to the biker being handcuffed, I saw my duffel open on the back of the state trooper's car. As much as I wanted that gear back, there was no way I was going to put a claim on it while I was sitting with at least one illegal alien and one smuggler who specialized in people.

I was still looking at my gear with a feeling of remorse or maybe just longing when a tap on the other window signaled the approach of one of the officers at the roadblock.

"I'm going to need your license and registration ma'am. Everyone else please get out a picture ID to..." His pleasantly bored drone of words was cut off by a deep voice with the hint of a British accent behind me.

"These aren't the Drones you're looking for." I looked back to see Pedro making a mystical gesture with his hands while the blanket he'd had on his knees was now over his head like a hood or shawl or something.

"Right. These aren't the DROIDS we're looking for...asshole." The mixed native American and Mexican looking cop peered expectantly at both Elena and me before giving up with a sigh and turning back to the Coyote. "How about you Viejo? You got the right paperwork?"

"Viejo? I ain't that damned old you jackass. The wheelchair is just a disguise. Tell you what, tell that cute young bride of yours to expect me next week. I'll let her tell you how much of an old man Viejo I am." Pedro was glaring but I suspect he might have been inwardly delighted by the exchange with the jaded old border cop.

"Yea, well we ain't sure you're going anywhere yet are we Perro? I ain't seen any paperwork on anybody in this junk heap. Three to one I can book you for the old lady. Maybe the young one too. You're probably ok with the gringo though. Unless you're importing some of those Russian spies or terrorists or something we get fliers about every few months. So how about it? You got my paperwork or do I bust all of you and start doing some digging?" He still looked bored, but that might have been one of those Indian stereotypes at work. Maybe he was just being stone-faced and phlegmatic to go with his heritage.

That stern scowl curved abruptly the other way though when our cruise director tossed a brown envelope over Elena's shoulder. She jumped at the impact but picked the envelope up very gingerly and offered it up in a hand all but trembling with her anxiety.

The cop showed no hesitation at all. He practically snatched the brown paper out of the girl's hand and opened it to show a stack of green bills. Good old fashioned American currency ensuring the fine and revered tradition of corruption at the local level. "Yessirree bob. Those aren't the droids we're looking for alright."

He leaned back out of the window and rolled his arm from the shoulder in the international cop signal for "get your ass on down the road". At the same time, he barked over a shoulder for the benefit of the other cops around. "This one's clear. Paperwork in order and an old guy looks like he better see a doctor quick...smells something awful in there."

That last bit was spoken just loud enough to get a laugh from the nearest cop, and plenty loud enough to get a smile from Elena and a scowl from Pedro. As we started to pull away he stuck his head back into the window for one brief second. "Perro I catch you sniffing around my wife and the only thing you're sticking that little pink thing in is going to be a shotgun barrel. Think about that."

Despite the threat, the cop smiled and waved as we drove off. I waited until the assorted border guards and cops couldn't see me before I waved forlornly at my guns and gear receding into the distance.

3

It took me almost to the Arizona border to finish grieving. The shotgun was easy to replace. There was a knife in that bag though, that had hours of work in modifications and runework invested. Just as bad, my favorite little quirky revolver that fired .45 slugs or .410 shotgun shells was now the property of the state of New Mexico. Once the grieving was over though, the brooding and the stewing commenced.

Perro had told me he didn't like the bike guy. He wasn't being paid for that guy's passage and thought the arrogant thug was an asshole. Maybe Perro didn't want to hassle with whatever weight his former escort could employ. If the guy was stupid enough to get pulled over without proper ID and carrying a load of weapons of suspicious origins then that wasn't the coyote's fault was it?

Sure it wasn't. And I had a bridge for sale in Arizona. That grinning snarky little son-of-a-bitch had used my gear to get rid of someone he both feared and disliked. Which meant somebody needed to replace my stuff before things got out of hand. I mean come on, I was sent down to get a freaking divine wolf out of trouble he couldn't handle alone.

If this was something an immortal dire wolf couldn't handle, there was no way I was going in waving a toadsticker like the one at my belt.

It was no time to talk about this stuff in front of the ladies though. Just a couple of miles from the checkpoint she'd pulled over and burst into tears. Pedro and I both looked around and shrugged rather helplessly at each other. Seemed like Mr. Charming Smirk didn't handle feminine outbursts any better than I did. Finally, I settled for patting her shoulder until she stopped gasping for breath.

Once she had some of her poise back, Elena slipped off her seat belt and sniffled a couple of times before asking me, "Mr. Moose you wanna drive, please? I'm just so tired of being scared. You drive and I'll try to catch a nap. Wake me up if you need me por favor."

I didn't even have the heart to correct her about my name. Instead, I nodded and climbed out of my side and around to hers. She was small enough she just swapped seats without exiting.

By the time I'd adjusted seats, belts, mirrors and steering wheels the girl had curled up sideways in her seat and was nodding already. Rather than risk waking the worn and weary young lady I drove us on into Arizona and turned off to get us down near Sedona.

If you've never been in that part of the country it's pretty special. You come out of the tawny plains of New Mexico into some bluffs and volcanic rock. Then those bluffs get higher and higher until you're into high hills or small mountains. At first, the trees and plants stay about the same. High desert with lots of buffalo grass and mesquite gives away to timberlands with evergreens and mossy rock. Around about Flagstaff you turn south and come out of the mountains into someplace envisioned by older beings that were more about beauty than rules and right and wrong.

Pillars and whorling spires compete with rocks shaped as if sculpted by the hands of gods into fantastic beasts and ships and buildings. Hel there's even a rock that looks like Snoopy laying on his dog house. And the colors are full of reds and pinks. Scientists tell you it's because there was so much iron deposited in the rock back when water covered the land.

The Yavapai people native to the area tell other stories. New age psychics and ancient stories alike speak of the red rock area. A well of warm mineral water from a now known source is rumored to come from the very heart of the earth. Another cave was supposed to be the birthplace for the "first people with medicine". The red of the rocks could be the blood of the earth itself or painted by the desert sunsets to bless the tribes of that enchanted land.

When you come down from the tall green mountains into that sculpted and raw painted landscape any of the stories seem believable. The people that live and visit there all seem to agree. There are more psychics, mystics, new age bookstores and crystal shops in that little village than in most of California, the land of kooks and dreamers.

We drove through at the perfect time of the evening to get the full impact of that sunset. When I asked about pulling over for food though Pedro shook his head. "Resort prices, man. Food's not bad but expensive as hell. We get a few miles down the road and I'll get you some pozole and tamales for a few bucks. Taste better than that shit in Sedona too."

We stopped and had dinner with the ladies. Elena calmed down in the shabby little railroad car with cheap plastic tables and chairs. Maybe it just felt familiar or maybe it was the way the old couple that ran the place fussed over her. The food was everything promised as well. By the time my belly was stuffed I wasn't even that mad anymore.

I was half dozing with my belt loosened while Perro and Elena talked. Their conversation was a mishmash of Spanish and English, what people call Spanglish. If I hadn't been so comfortable and tired I might have paid more attention. As it was I woke up when the girl shook my shoulder to say goodbye.

"Thanks for helping us, Mr. Moose. I'm sorry about my cousin and I don't blame you for getting rid of him." I'm not very tall at all, but the girl was so petite she had to tiptoe just to reach my cheek with her kiss. I even got a hug from her grandmother while I was piecing together what she'd said. I guess maybe since it was my guns that got him arrested she thought it was my fault. I just shrugged and enjoyed the pleasant sensation of having met some nice people and getting to part with them before anything bad happened.

They caught a ride from a son of the restaurant owners. He piled them up in a beat-up old F-150 pickup and drove on their way. When I looked up, Pedro was gone as well. The old man brought me a cup of coffee in styrofoam and handed me a handwritten note on a napkin. He also gave me the ticket for fifty bucks. I'd had worse food and service for more money though. Besides they were kind of a sweet old couple. I dropped four twenties and left the change.

The napkin with its note wasn't even clean. There were pink spots where someone had cleaned up salsa with it before Perro wrote his note. "You got a room at the Best Western in Sedona. It's on this end of the main street through town. Get some sleep and I'll meet you at the breakfast bar."

I wasn't sure if he had more business that was going to

delay my own trip, or if he just wanted to avoid the little "talk" we were scheduled to have just as soon as I could arrange it. He still owed me for the duffel bag full of comfort and reassurance.

Without many options, I went and checked into the Best Western. They put me in a ground floor room with parking about forty feet from my room door. Since the closest parking place was empty I locked up the van and left it there. With my gym bag in hand, I entered the room.

It had been a long day so I went straight for a hot shower and some clean clothes. Within half an hour I was clothed and sitting at the table. My first task was a phone call.

"Shoot". That was Bill's typical response on this particular line. He had another for normal business and as many as two or three other phone numbers for various personal and private reasons. The "hot-line" as he called it only went to a few select clients. I was one of them.

When I first got to Austin, William "Wild Bill" Woolly had done me some favors. He was, without exaggeration, one of the best hackers and technophiles anyone around could refer me to. He'd provided me with identification and documentation for decades back that had kept me covered and out of trouble for years.

That faltered a little when a spook from one of the Alphabet Agencies got interested in my little...idiosyncrasies. Bill had discovered that certain government prototypes were better than even the stuff he had put together on his own. Once he was hacked, and extorted into giving up some info on me, that same spook had compensated Wooly with some new toys and blueprints for his own super-secret spy type stuff.

Now Wild Bill ran "Woolly Electronics and Geek Room". As advertised he sold computers and parts and assorted techno gear. He also did software and repairs for high-end gaming units and such.

His unadvertised services were what I needed though. "Woolly, it's Mouse. I need a few files inserted wherever they need to go. Get me an EMT license with the school records etc. Use my current IDs and stuff. Shoot it back several years and give it to me as soon as possible."

He took a few notes, asked some questions and then shot me an estimate. There were times I appreciated having some funds from more interesting times. Say what you will. If a mercenary doesn't mind taking some risks and living in some rough conditions he can make some money.

For the first dozen years after Vietnam, I wasn't really current on modern morals and beliefs. Living in the bush for months at a time with people of very questionable morals hadn't really helped me with more progressive thinking. It had, on the other hand, padded my bank account and left me some contacts that most people don't have in their friends list or Rolodex.

I dickered halfheartedly but Woolly knew if I wanted it ASAP that I was going to be ready to pay. I ended up paying more than I wanted to and less than I'd expected.

When I hung up there was a minute of pondering. Part of me wanted to get out of the hotel and find someplace where nobody would look for me.

I could always walk down the street and find another hotel or just another room in this Best Western. Nobody should suspect that with the van parked by this room as a decoy.

Another part of me wanted to just go to sleep and wait for the morning developments. And a third part was listening to that little voice that doesn't trust many people.

That voice had been yammering ever since Pedo threw that first measuring sideways glance.

It was the voice that settled me. Rather than head out the door I sat down and started working to reassure myself that I wasn't bugged or being tracked. First I piled up the gear he had given me. Then it was just a matter of checking over all of the pouches and pockets and gear as well as even the stitching of the clothes. I didn't find any hidden bugs or mikes or anything. As close as I got was some weird patches of cloth stitched into the holster for the cheap throwaway cell phone. Of course, the phone could be used as a tracker all by itself for that matter.

While I had it apart I did a little work on the knife and even inscribed a couple of runes onto the high carbon steel with a permanent marker from my bag. It wasn't ideal. Such a cheap means of putting the rune on tended to limit any real power you might want to put into it. In this instance, I figured the knife would be just a touch sharper and maybe twice as tough as normal. That ought to last for a couple of minutes or maybe just a few good swings once it was triggered.

While I was putting everything back together there was a knock at the door. When I looked out, it wasn't to see some sexy little maid ready to fulfill any penthouse letter fantasies. What I got was a very angry and stubborn looking guy decked out in hair, leather, and tattoos. If I wasn't mistaken, the "colors" on his back would probably match the denim vest worn by my brief companion of the road before he was arrested.

Dammit, I knew better than to dawdle with showers and such. The gear inspection was necessary but a change of clothes could have waited. While I was trying to decide what the best course of action would be, the knock came again. It wasn't a pounding as one might expect from angry bikers. It also was not a timid or polite knock. If one could interpret a knock at the door I'd say this one was insistent but not raging.

With my luck that meant the guy outside was royally pissed but had enough discipline and self-control to keep it in rein. I prefer when they lose that bit of self-control. Raging wild and thoughtless individuals aren't as dangerous. This time a low rumbling voice carried quite clearly into the room after that knock. "Look asshole. We know you're in there. You can come out or we can come in. Either way, we're gonna talk to you. Fact is we're probably gonna beat your ass. If you don't piss us off anymore though you'll probably live through the night and get a little smarter."

That snippet of conversation earlier came back to me. Little Elena had forgiven me for her cousin. What the Hel had the little smuggler told the ladies about my guns and their now incarcerated relative? More importantly at this point, who else had, he told the same shit? If I lived throughout the evening I'd address that with him at the first opportunity.

The top priority right now was surviving. I took a few minutes to look around the room and positioned some furniture as quickly and quietly as I could. The third set of knocks was a touch more boisterous than its predecessors. Good, maybe these guys were less self-controlled than I thought. To try and keep that bit of imbalance I put the chain on the door and opened it a crack.

I backed a couple of strides away before I said anything. "Hey, guys I'm trying to sleep in here. What the hell's all the noise about."

The flimsy little chain and sliding bar pulled right out of the door by the screws. That same door banged open to be followed by the red-faced biker in his denim and leather. This guy looked like a larger version of myself. Like me, he had a chest and shoulder spread a little wider than really fit his height. The problem was that he had almost a full foot of height on me. That made his shoulders wide enough to fill the door. In fact, I'm not sure he didn't turn sideways and duck down a little to come through the door.

The first obstacle he encountered was the low bench I'd placed just where he'd find it underfoot. For an instant, I had to wonder if he was just going to stomp it flat and continue forward to run me over like a sweaty and profanity-laden bulldozer. As some of those Texas old-timers would say, he was cussing up a storm. The language didn't get any cleaner when the bench tangled up his shins and allowed gravity to choose a side in our confrontation.

Falling from that high, with all that extra heft on a body, had to be pretty painful. It probably didn't help that I'd swung the arching floor lamp around to where it would clear my head but not by much. He caught it right at the hairline on his way down.

This guy was a brute. I decided he needed to stay out of the way while I dealt with the two guys starting into the room behind him. Before he'd even hit the ground I jumped forward with both feet and used him like a diving board.

My heels drove him face-first into the thin hospitality carpet. The padding underneath must have been thin as well. It barely muffled the solid wooden sound of flooring on facial bone. Since I'd known my footing was pretty unstable, I kept my knees bent for balance while my body weight drove him down and out of the fight. That little bit of balance let me launch forward almost instantly and still on a nice even keel.

The two guys behind him were tangled up in the doorway. Their clear intention had been to rush in and spread out. A heavy armchair I'd spun around the small round table prevented them from going to the right while the left side of the door was covered by a wall and the low dresser with a tv on top. That narrowed down their options and gave me a second to deal with the foremost threat at the moment.

My head hit right under his sternum with all of my launched mass behind it. The rush of air sounded like a speeding car or something above me. It also cut off his litany of slang and obscenities in mid "SHI". Since he was bent over, and I was down on all four after catching myself, my head was conveniently under his contorted face. I lunged up and smashed the back of my head into his face with a crunch. I think it was nose, might have been some teeth in it too. Whatever the crunch was it likely to put him a little further out of the damage dealing business. If it hurt his face as much as it hurt my head he was pretty damned discouraged.

The first guy was barely moving at all and the second one was up almost on tiptoes above me with blood sheeting down his face. His eyes weren't focused at all. In fact, he let them flutter closed before folding over the back of the armchair in slow motion. That left the third guy in the doorway. He was almost as big as the behemoth moaning on the ground behind me.

With the odds back to even, except for a serious imbalance of size, I felt an urge to make some room. I lowered my head and charged again. Behemoth number two had seen this move. He sidestepped and prepared to deliver a stomping kick to my neck or head or maybe even my modelesque face. I was prepared for that eventuality.

Using the door as a brace I adjusted my angle and drove forward and down rather than straight at his midsection. I hit his knee at the same time his other foot clipped me at the point of the shoulder with a crushing amount of strength behind it. A few inches to my right and he'd have missed me completely. Conversely, a few inches to my left would have broken a collarbone and put me at a distinct disadvantage for further negotiations.

We went down in a tangle with him sprawling all over me while I cranked his lower leg around like I was starting a world war one biplane. Another unpleasant sound accompanied this activity. Actually, it was a few unpleasant sounds. His bellowing changed from raging to anguished, and some really nasty crackles and pops came from the vicinity of his knee. I rolled to my feet outside. I was facing the third downed assailant with his back to my door and my back to the parking lot.

He tried to roll up to his feet but discovered that his foot wasn't willing to point the direction he wanted it to. His knee seemed kind of loose and floppy too when he pitched back to the ground. I was busy choosing between a boot to his head, or maybe breaking the wrist he was supporting himself on.

My choices were interrupted by a sudden eruption of voices behind me all clamoring one or another version of "What the Fuck?" That didn't sound promising. In fact, that didn't sound even neutral or tolerant. No, that sounded bad like cardiac arrest sounds bad, or maybe amputation. They all had a similar ring of unpleasantness to come.

Well, I still had a job half done in front of me. My old Da' had always said don't stop until your work is done. A stomping of my combat boot ended with a wet snap of wrist bone and a muffled scream when the guy's face fell unimpeded onto the concrete. I turned around at the rush of bodies moving behind me.

Turned out they were behind me, and beside me, and all around me. I didn't have time for a headcount but it looked like close to a dozen. In fact, I was willing to bet that the guys sprawled in and around my hotel would have brought the number to an even dozen or maybe even thirteen.

A lot of people these days consider thirteen an unlucky number. I'd been one of the ones hunting Templars that Friday in thirteen hundred and seven so it had only seemed unlucky for DeMolay and his troops. Standing there surrounded by pissed off bikers suddenly made me think thirteen was probably not a great number for me either. At least it was painfully unfortunate for me that evening.

I caught the first guy coming in with a jab of my stiffened knuckles at his throat. The "bear paw" punch missed cracking the cartilage that would have killed him. It did, however, cause a gratifying and instant look of panic followed by grunts and whistles as he tried to get enough air in to prevent the blue from coloring his face.

I didn't have time to see if he succeeded. A boot to the back of my knee came close to making the same sounds as I had made cranking on number three's leg. I was lucky enough to catch it more on the back than the side of the knee. The leg still went numb from that knee downward. Maybe a numbed knee doesn't sound all that horrible unless you're dancing or playing football.

Let me assure you, it is also horrible when any of your four limbs become non-responsive in the middle of a parking lot surrounded by leather and denim and bad breath. I managed to slip a punch at my head and grab the arm thus offered. That became a pivot to push me towards the edge of the circle. I thought for an instant I might get to the outside and make a fighting retreat.

I was wrong. While I was busy pivoting, one industrious

soul was snapping an odd weapon made from a padlock and a bandana at me. You don't live through the middle ages and the old west without seeing a few whips and flails. I got my free hand up far enough behind the arcing lock to wrap the bandana around my wrist a couple of times. The lock still hit my forearm painfully but most of the force was lost in that instant.

The other makeshift flail didn't lose any force before it collided with my thick skull just behind the ear. I didn't go completely out. I was not, however, aware of much more than the immediate press of bodies. I still dished out my own shots but I was taking as many lumps as I got.

Maybe the sheer number of attackers was the only thing that saved me at least momentarily. I saw some of them hitting and stomping each other in their attempts to get to me. I was hitting and stomping them as well. There were probably multiple fractures in addition to my own. I know I broke three collarbones. In fact, I'm pretty sure two of those clavicles belonged to the same guy. It would be a while before he held onto any handlebars to ride a bike. Who's the bitch now buddy?

One of the last guys to come for me had a chunk of his tongue snipped off when my uppercut slammed his teeth together. Another one went down to a fairly vicious shot to the ribs. From the feel under my fist and the panicked breathless look on his face some rib fragments probably got a lung.

After that everything faded into a swirled blur of color, sound, and pain.

4

IT IS QUITE true that once we are Chosen by a Valkyrie and
transformed into one of the Einherjar, we gain a great deal
of innate ability to shrug off near mortal wounds and
continue fighting. We can absorb damage like one of the
world war II panzer tanks. We can go for days without sleep,
food or even water. We can not, however, endure enough
blood loss to qualify for exsanguination. Likewise, we can
suffer enough trauma to overcome even our divinely
enhanced toughness and recuperative powers. If we suffer
enough damage or endure enough drainage of our
resources, we die. Death just isn't quite as mysterious for us.
We know where we're going to wake up...eventually.

I'd pretty much figured this was the end for me when I
caught sight of all the enraged two-wheel warriors out for
my blood. I wasn't very far off. There was definitely more
trauma and blood loss than any pure mortal could have
endured. To add insult to injury they stripped me naked and
tossed me in the van. I guess someone searched the room
and found the keys.

A couple of them stayed in the back of the van with me

to keep the night entertaining as they drove me for what seemed like days. It was probably only hours later though when they pulled over and tossed what was left of my body out of the side door. It was too dark to see. From the amount of rolling and falling and impacting with trees and cactus and rocks, I'd guess they left me in the mountains.

When I rolled off a ledge and fell for an undetermined time I was sure it was mountainy. I couldn't tell if it was twenty feet or two hundred feet. All I know was it felt like a terrifying long fall. It didn't help that there wasn't even any air to scream. The impact with whatever surface was at the bottom of that fall drove even that last bit of air out of me. It also drove any kind of awareness away.

I have no idea how long I was out. I know the sun rose at least once and set again because I would wake up just long enough to start to recall where I was. Then the pain and toll taken on my body would suck it back down into oblivion. Time kind of stopped having any meaning while my Hugr, my inner self, tried to decide which side of the veil it would land on.

Finally, my mind and body seemed to quit trying to choose. They stopped debating and decided to let matters fall as they would. I woke up in agony and well aware that matters were very far out of my hands. I just had to hope the Norns were in a kindly mood.

This time I didn't automatically fade back into unconsciousness. Instead, the pain settled in to sap my strength and send me on my way. That was not something I was willing to just lie there and take though. I tried to catalog the injuries, but an overall agony kind of muted one injury into another.

I know I had cracked ribs, a flailed chest, and probably bone fragments in several fairly important organs. There were open wounds that had stopped gushing and switched to seeping as fluids drained to nothing. I couldn't tell if the difficulty in my vision was from damage to the eyes or just a side effect of all the blood loss and stresses to my system. I was pretty sure I had a foot and most of the attached leg already across the line separating life from death.

In fact, I pretty much expected to wake up to a nightmare of pain and retribution for the years spent hiding away from the proverbial fold. Odin is not particularly forgiving or benevolent. His time spent nailed to a tree wasn't to save mankind from any kind of sins. He did it to gain a tool. He sacrificed himself on Yggdrasil to gain the runes as tools to see and shape the future. Just like he gave up an eye to stay abreast of events all over the cosmos. Hel he even sacrificed himself to...Himself.

No Odin isn't forgiving or fair-minded. He's pragmatic and cunning, manipulative and focused. Above all, he's eager to secure and keep any power he can grasp. The einherjar were just more tools and fairly powerful ones in certain situations. I didn't anticipate a fond welcome home when I finally died and returned to Valhalla.

Beside Odin's lack of forgiveness, my Valkyrie Kara was a turbulent angry dark mass of passions. She was not going to be happy at all when she finally found me. I can't guarantee it, but I'm willing to bet she'd caught her share of grief over losing one of us. I suppose if I was a good loyal little automaton I'd have ensured an early return to the fold by whatever means necessary. It wasn't like I didn't have ample opportunity in Vietnam or afterward.

I just didn't want to go back to those fuzzy days of tedium again. Don't get me wrong. The fighting can be entertaining. But without the bite of the final grim specter to worry about, it was just a little like masturbation. Fun but without a lot of purpose. Between fights, we might get some interesting training or practice some new stuff. They gave us all sorts of training as weapons and fighting systems evolved. But if you weren't training or on a mission you might as well have been at an immature and boring frat party.

There was mead. There were lovely girls and boisterous "bros" along with a few super cool older frat brothers like Uller or Thor. But we weren't given access to anything to stimulate our thoughts. Thought stimulation was exactly the opposite of what they wanted in their nice docile sheep with the highly evolved martial skills.

So, yea, I wasn't looking forward to waking up back in Valhalla with a span of torture and humiliation likely to precede my reinduction into the boys' club. I was wrong about waking up to that though. The first thing I remember after the frozen night ravaged my blood-drained body, was Eachan. The old professor woke me up with a nudge of one of his old world cavalry boots. He was dressed in breeches tucked into the polished boots as well as a loose sleeved poet shirt encased in a paisley vest of autumn colors.

"Well, this is a fine mess you've gotten into Ollie." At least he didn't try an impersonation on top of the misquote. I lay there and ached too much to even muster a glare for the wise old educator.

"I dare say you might have forestalled this if you kept your wits about you, my boy. Surely you should have expected some retaliation against the occupants of that van for the incarceration of someone with your biker "friend's" background. Obviously, your tour guide anticipated such an event and made sure it fell on someone other than himself. Of course, if you were even faintly perceptive you would have expected that as well. I would think that even a thick-skulled neanderthal like you, Magnus, should be able to identify a trickster spirit in close proximity for hours at a time." He shook his head in a weary negative as he sat and sipped at a glass full of tawny amber liquid.

"Well, if you don't die maybe you can start keeping your eyes open for a little while eh? I know it might strain your brain but you might strive to be functional and observant at one and the same time. However, it seems to strain your physical limits to take the abuse that comes along with failing to remain vigilant." He leaned over to look at me more intently. Except he didn't just lean over. He came rushing forward and would have slammed his forehead into my face if he hadn't dissipated back into the dreamworld first.

The fear of that impact on my already tortured face jarred me awake. The night was still icy cold when I came up from the dream. It was probably better being asleep. If I stayed asleep though, I would probably continue to dream my way right into the vengeful arms of Kara the stormy. That was not an encouraging thought.

I needed to focus and decide what I could and could not accomplish. With a few goals, I might have a chance to avoid that homecoming for a while longer. To that end, I put every effort into figuring out what all worked or was out of order.

It was still hard to isolate every broken bone and open wound. Trying to stand told me I wasn't likely to accomplish that. Both legs were beyond weak. One ankle was a leaden lump that didn't obey any commands at all. The other leg was one constant muscle cramp of pain from mid-thigh down. I was pretty sure that femur was broken. Walking was apparently not an option at all.

The legs weren't my only problem though. Air only seemed to be moving in one side of my chest and only one of my eyes would focus where I pointed it. Someone had even taken the time to return the favor and break one of my collarbones. Broken bones might take a normal person several weeks or even months to heal. A healthy Chosen warrior can usually start using the injured bone within a few days. With the help of my own runic knowledge and some basic materials, I could usually fix the same damage within a few hours or maybe a day or so at the most.

I was neither fully healthy nor possessed of any materials for rune work. Already the cold was sapping my strength even further. When all of that energy was gone, I'd go to sleep and wake up elsewhere.

That didn't seem like a good plan at all. With one good arm and most of a leg that functioned I started crawling inch by awkward inch towards a fallen tree just a few yards away. Beneath the tree was a hollow just about big enough to get my body into. There was a mat of dead grass and leaves in the bottom of the hollow that might provide some insulation. With a little effort, I might even be able to use some of that as fodder for a fire. Provided I had the energy to make even a spark or two.

With my luck, I'd catch the damned forest on fire and burn to death crawling around in the flames. That didn't seem like much of a gamble when I was laying there hurting in every part of me still reporting any sensation at all. If it wasn't pain or numbness it was a life-sapping cold that clamored for my attention. I ignored all the clamoring long enough to reach the crude haven of the dead tree with a dirty scooped out the hole.

Before I scooted into the hole I scooped out a few handfuls of the dried weeds and grasses. Some sticks broken off of larger trees were near enough to sweep into a rough pile half atop the kindling. That still left enough vegetable matter to cushion and insulate my torn flesh. I took immediate advantage of the filthy natural mattress. Just rolling out of the wind cut the cold down to mere wintery rather than subarctic. My body ached to go back into the pleasant dark fog of sleep. That still seemed likely to be a final sleep though. It was a bitterly cold wind sweeping down the mountain I was starting to see outlined in the faint light of dawn.

I fought off sleep. The cold was a more insidious foe. It didn't just threaten to knock me out. It threatened to rob me of strength and dexterity long before I lost consciousness. The efforts of building a pile of kindling and another stack of small dry sticks had taken a heavy toll. I couldn't even lever myself up on an elbow for the next task. Instead, I lay on my side in the dry stabbing grass. Good thing everything else hurt so much or I'd have been really annoyed with the scratchy jabby vegetation.

I got my hand within a few inches of the kindling and put every bit of focus and willpower I could into the effort. My hands were grey and shaking before I finally saw the dull glow appear and shoot a spark about halfway to the kindling from my fingertip. The spark glowed in my faltering eyesight before fading away and taking my awareness with it.

This time it was Kara jabbing me awake. She didn't use a cavalry boot polished to a high shine either. Kara jabbed me with a spear. She always favored the spear. I'm pretty sure she was one of the models for a fairly famous picture of Valkyrie riding amongst clouds and lighting with their spears and winged horses.

Her horse probably hadn't been winged. You know how artists are. Kara truly loved that spear though. Sometime, centuries past, her spear had been enchanted so that it either reflected light in an enigmatic eye-catching manner or else lightning raced up and down it. Hard to tell without touching it and I'd never met anyone stupid enough to try and lay a hand on Kara's spear.

The jolt of pain in my shoulder was enough to make me flinch away. It was also enough to make my broken clavicle scream its counter-protest. Maybe I was just that sore, or the spear was just that mean, but I felt like she had indeed shot a little bit of lightning into my whole arm and most of my chest. "Have you finally tired of your pathetic hiding? Has the cowardly running finally turned even your weak resolve into something more honorable my Chosen?:

Her voice was dripping with honey and concern. That didn't exactly go with the way she twisted the spear point in my shoulder and sent another bolt of agony that arched my back and drew a rasping moan from between clenched jaws. I wanted to answer her. I tried to spit some defiance and indignation at the malicious wench that held my leash for centuries. I just didn't have enough energy to even speak much less put up a fight.

"Oh, my poor chosen." She crooned her pleasure at my plight without ever saying she was pleased. She also crooned my name. It was not Magnus but an older name and one I had not heard in decades. "You've led a great chase, my love. And you've put up a great fight against returning. But here we are with the journey home just a few breaths away. You can let go. Or you can let me help you. Which do you prefer kjaereste?"

Kjaereste? That was a real pill. Nobody was "dearest" to Kara except Kara herself. Oh, she could be loving and passionate and all-consuming. She had...appetites, that would reduce even an einherjar to a weakened and over-worked mess of raw nerves and exhaustion. But truly tender feelings were not something she'd ever shown. The closest would be her moments of passion, or maybe during the throes of one of her "discipline" sessions with a satisfying victim.

I wanted to spit in her face. Cast my defiance against her in an explosion of wills. If I was lucky maybe she would destroy me completely. She was fully capable of that since I was one of her own Chosen. Alternately she could end my pain or prolong it. She could even put me straight into a form of stasis where I was barely aware of any kind of existence or even the passage of time. She'd done that to others.

I'd seen her torture one of our brothers for a whole week before she let him die. Then she'd left him "down" rather than wake him for the feast or training or even the pointless fighting most of the others seemed to enjoy. We hadn't seen Sven for years and then one day he showed up and apologized to her as if the whole thing had just happened. Maybe if I was lucky she'd lose her temper and either end me permanently or put me down in a rage. Maybe she'd even decide to leave me on ice so to speak.

I couldn't do it though. I was too weak and too out of breath to make even a sound. I tried though. I struggled to even whisper my rage and hate. Nothing came out. She lifted the spear and aimed it at my heart. She aimed right for the scar that showed where a spear had earned me her first attention over a thousand years ago.

I tried to brace myself for the pain. Which left me open for a whole new source of pain. My broken femur twisted and tore its way out of my leg when something grabbed my raw bloody ankle and jerked at it. The pain in my shoulder was nothing compared to the surprise and agony of this new assault.

My own scream woke me from the nightmare. I aimed a

clumsy kick with the other leg and felt my numb foot and ankle connect with something that snarled and let go of my more ravaged appendage. When I twisted weakly around, I found myself face to face with a wolf or large dog. It snarled and seemed to cower back from a second feeble kick. It didn't run away though. Instead, it circled just out of reach of any further kicks. Even weak resistance seemed to bother the canine.

With a surge of adrenalin, I shoved my hand those extra few inches and with my fingers buried in the dry grasses coughed "Kenaz!" in a spatter of blood and spit. The spark was no stronger than my first attempt. It was right in the heart of the kindling though. Within seconds flames were licking up and pushing away the darkness.

A look around made me think I must have slept through the whole day. Snuggled down in my improvised tree shack, I'd managed to survive despite the severity of my injuries. There was fresh blood though from my newest wound. With the latest attack added to my previous toll, it didn't look good for the home team at all.

I turned my head on a wobbling neck and looked back at the wolf. Except it wasn't a wolf. The legs were wrong, and the ears were very wrong. The posture was much too cowering and uncertain as well. No this wasn't a wolf. This was a cowardly carrion-eating coyote. As long as I kept awake and able to show any resistance at all he shouldn't attack.

A wolf might have come for me as weak as I obviously was. Most animals are at least cautious around Man. Wolves are no exception but they're also no cowards. If a wolf discovered me in my weakened state then I was just another meal or two for him and his pack. Coyotes and jackals were more discreet. They tended to want every shred of resistance gone before they started eating. A wolf would help me finish struggling if he had to.

I waited as long as I dared for the kindling to catch into a stable if small fire. Once that was crackling, I poked a few of the smaller sticks into the flames. When those caught some slightly bigger ones went on. The whole time I fought the shakes from the cold, the weakness and the blood loss.

While my fire grew, I kept an eye on the coyote. He hung around circling my little shelter and the tiny fire. The fire seemed fully capable of keeping him at bay. That was a good thing because I could feel my eyelids getting heavier by the second. With the last bit of time I had, the remainder of the sticks got tumbled in a pile on the fire. It might not last all night but there wasn't much I could do about it.

5

――――――

SOMEHOW I WASN'T dead by morning. I woke up unable to move. Every muscle was an unbending bundle of agony. The wounds felt inflamed. Even my good eye was now hard to lock onto any target. I might have had one foot over the line the previous evening. But right after waking up I was almost certain that everything was over that line except one clawed hand trying to keep me from going into that dark night.

The fire was down to coals but still gave off enough smoke to tell me it hadn't gone out very long since. I lifted my head on a neck as wobbly as a newborn colt's legs. Peering through the smoke I thought it was another dream. Actually, I hoped it was another vision.

What I saw was a raven gliding quietly on spread wings. Underneath those ominous black wings, a hooded figure walked clutching a tall staff. Or was it a spear? I dreaded that vision more than even my nightmare of Kara.

The one-eyed god never came for one of us. I'd heard stories of him coming to Midgard to deal with a Valkyrie who had disappointed him. There were plenty of stories of his arrival disguised as a wanderer or vagrant to test a follower's hospitality. Even those tales usually ended with a curse or a punishment on those who did not meet his high standards. I'm pretty sure escaping from my lot in the after-life was not up to his normal standards. I believe I already mentioned, Odin is not a God of forgiveness.

I was barely able to speak. My tongue felt like a piece of jerky in my mouth. The lining of my mouth felt like sand-paper grinding at that piece of jerky. But I was damned if I'd go back without spitting some defiance. Come to think of it I was pretty much damned anyway I guess.

I rolled over onto my side and had to try several times but I managed to hiss out a barely legible word. "NO!"

It was a start. If I could say one word then chances were I could say more. My head lifted on muscles made of spaghetti. The spaghetti was probably overcooked too considering how flaccid the muscles were. I couldn't focus with all of the rolling around of my head on those limp noodles. Come to think of it my head itself was probably something of a limp noodle.

"NO!" See? I got it out again. No stopping me now. I was on my way to chattering. "I'm. Not."

A bloody cough and series of shuddering breaths broke my flow up a little. "Not dead yet! Can't. Can't take me."

"Well, what bloody use would you be to me dead mo chroi? I didn't go to all of this trouble to come and bury you so I guess you better decide to live eh? It would be unforgiv-ably rude to die on a lass now." The voice was not Odin's. It was not even male. It was delightfully female and colored with an absolutely enchanting Irish brogue.

"Dumbass" The last word didn't match the others. That last word was harsh and mocking and not very human. The previous speech had been anything but harsh. It had resonated from the hood with a warmth and healing that made me think I was dreaming again.

The hood came back to reveal red curls and a face that actually went with that lovely lilting Irish brogue. It also had a tenderness mixed with some humor and just a hint of tears. In other circumstances that tender regard might have set off my little antisocial alarms. I was just so eternally grateful it wasn't Odin coming to call that I didn't have a single concern about romance or tender feelings.

Maureen reached behind her and pulled out her satchel style purse or bag or, well, satchel. She laid her tall staff atop my log shelter and bent over to peer inside. Beside her, I saw the beady eyes and gaping beak of my old crow Rafe.

That bold little rascal was on her shoulder. He looked like he belonged there, clinging to her cloak with red locks curling beside and behind him. He also looked smug as Hel. He leaned forward and cocked his head this way and that as if looking over the various wounds visible on my bare-assed skin. His appraisal was probably more accurate than I cared to believe. Once he'd made a decision he looked over as if conferring with an esteemed colleague. He made a couple of odd clicks and whistles then gave his verdict with a bobbing head. "Dumbass."

It took a few minutes for Maureen to convince me it wasn't another dream. I mean c'mon, the talking crow didn't lend any credibility to the situation. There was also no reason to expect the girl I'd left in Austin to suddenly appear in the middle of a desert when not even I knew where they'd tossed me. Then you had the fact that I'd already been having visions and visitations and hallucinations from being that close to death. It was the tears that finally convinced me. Maureen had tried to be encouraging and light-hearted. As her chemical light revealed more of my wrecked and battered body she stopped pretending.

"Magnus I can't move you. I...I'm not sure what's safe to move or even what all is still attached." She bit her lips and bent low to look at the awkward heaving of my broken bones. I felt the splash of warm raindrops, except they were salty enough to sting in my wounds. In the wan green light of her chemical sticks, I could just barely see the tracks of tears falling down on my bare chest.

"Hey now. No tears. You'll scare the patient." I'm not sure how much of it was intelligible but that's what I tried to croak out in my ravaged voice.

"Shush patient. You're talking way too much for someone that should be dead. Or should you? Eachan and I have talked about it but I don't think either of us really has a clue what you can and cannot overcome. Unless you tell me differently, I'm just going to treat you like any other person that's almost dead." At least the need to be professional and competent had pushed the tears to a back burner. She might cry later but for the moment she was busy.

I didn't try and tell her what to do. Truth is I wasn't sure she could save me anyway. I wasn't even entirely sure how long I'd been hanging on. "How long?"

She must have known I couldn't ask much more and guessed what I was asking. "It's been most of a week since we talked. I was patient for the first couple of days. I thought you might call and I was hoping you would. But I also knew you might have your hands too full with whatever stupidity you were getting into next. On the third night though, I went to sleep feeling a bit of a wreck, and the bird woke me up. Remind me to ask you what exactly he is when you're up and about Magnus dear."

The look she gave me was one part stern reproach, one

part curiosity, and three parts professional detachment as she continued gently wiping dirt from some of the wounds and checked various bruises and swollen areas. "First though let's get you cleaned up and warm."

She turned away and whistled once before unloading a second pack I hadn't noticed. This one had been on her back padded by the folds of her cloak. It was a serious backpack too. The kind you see worn by professional backpackers and outdoorsmen. While she was unloading a great yellow bundle of excessive canine enthusiasm came bounding towards me.

I braced for the impact but Grimmr was apparently as confused and concerned by my condition as the bird. He slid to a halt and just poked his nose under my hand and flipped it on top of his head. It took a major effort not to cry out as cramped and torn muscles objected to the rough treatment. I wasn't going to do that to my dog though. I choked up a little myself about then.

Maureen pretended not to notice and kept working. She drew a thin metallic-looking thermal blanket out and laid it over the opening of the log hollow. I had just enough opening in the blanket to watch her further preparations. She was apparently no neophyte to roughing it or survival backpacking. First, she moved the coals of my fire a little further and babied it back to life.

With a light collapsible mess kit, she started heating water from a bottle along with some bouillon powder. More of that same bottle of water went into a couple of paper cups she sat right into the edge of the fire. She was clever enough to know that the paper would only burn down as low as the water level. The water inside would heat up but until it started evaporating it would suck the thermal energy right through the paper and into the liquid inside.

"I know you're thirsty love. And I'll help in a wee bit. Can't just give you water though. We need to find a way to replace the blood instead of just wash it away with water. The bouillon I'm making has some proteins and salts and other minerals. It also has some special ingredients I added that your Yankee AMA would not approve of. Once it's good and warm we'll get some of that in you eh?"

I was too weak to comment. I wouldn't have drank much of the water if she'd given it to me though. I knew better. Of course, my will power was nowhere near where it should be and just the thought of fluid was enough to make me cry too. If I had the fluid for tears.

While the fire took forever to warm up the broth and water, Maureen was busy with other tasks. She dragged a few long evergreen boughs over and then used part of my dead log to prop them up as a surprisingly sturdy lean-to. She tied the whole structure together with some paracord she kept unbraiding from a bracelet. With that done, she spread out a bedroll right beside me. "You should know, we're several hours of hiking from any kind of help. There's a dirt road up the slope but it wasn't even on any maps I could find. I just stumbled across it looking for you. Probably would have still been looking if that dog of yours hadn't chased a coyote over here somewhere. We practically fell right over you then."

That begged more questions. I'd have given anything to be able to ask some questions. Ok, anything except a drink. I was so dry now that I could barely think for want of water or broth or something of that ilk. But think I did. For instance, I still didn't know how many days I'd been out. Near as I could guess she started this direction the same night the Bikers got me. That didn't tell me how long it took her to find me though.

And that was another *HUGE* question. How exactly had she found me? She couldn't have tracked my clothes or used a GPS from my phone. I was completely naked and alone where I was trying to die in the high desert. I was beginning to wonder some things along the same line as Maureen as well. What exactly was that damned bird?

First, he'd started speaking. It seemed randomly applicable to a situation. But it was almost always applicable-random or not. He and the dog had even teamed up to kill a very dark and malicious Bruja or Central American witch that had snuck up and neutralized me and most everyone I cared about.

The dog didn't bother me as much. He was a good mutt. Just a big doofus golden-coated Catahoula Leopard dog with beautiful eyes. One was blue and grey granite while the other was burnished bronze. Bi-color eyes are pretty common in Catahoulas but I'd rarely seen one of the dogs with prettier eyes than my Grimmr. Now the coyote he'd chased was a different story.

Had it been a dream or reality when the lean scavenger had been slinking around all night? If so it was very unusual. They don't tend to have the patience or courage to wait out a moving human. Then again I barely qualified as mobile. I had to hope that this one wasn't rabid and that neither I nor the dog had received any bites. I could check Grimmr over when I was able, *if* I recovered. But there was probably no way to tell if any of my wounds had a bit of rabies slobber in them. There were just too many places oozing blood.

While I'd been musing and trying not to think about dying, Maureen had been busy and productive. Under the limited shelter her lean-to offered, she fished the metal container of broth out and added more herbs a pinch or palmful at a time. "Here. This is not exactly blood but it should help you get started making some more of your own. If you get stronger I can try to get you to my rental car on the road. It's probably not more than a mile or two away."

She helped me lift up on my tortured neck muscles just far enough to sip down some of the fluid. "Moving you may be the worst thing I can do. But not moving you seems as dangerous. So once that elixir takes hold I'm going to clean you up and move you to the sleeping bag. I'd move you first but who knows what manner of infections you would carry over onto the clean material. Even with the herbs, this is probably going to hurt. If we get you stable enough to leave alone. I'll see about going for help."

I could tell she was talking more to keep her thoughts on topic than to reassure me. If she let go of the tasks, then she would probably go off into a dark and frightening place. She obviously had some training, formal or otherwise, that told her how badly injured I was. That means she probably had a guess at how likely a human was to recover even partially from the damage they'd done to me.

I almost wanted to tell her I'm not human. I tried not to make any noise or jerk as she cleaned wounds and straightened limbs. Several times I felt bone scraping on bone while she tried to move me about gently as possible. At least once or twice I felt bones snap back into place. It might have been one of the most intimate days I'd ever spent with another human being. It was *not* the most pleasant.

Whatever she'd put in the broth was effective enough to make the experience better than it might have been. I can only imagine what it would do to a normal metabolism. For me, it quickly put a nice warm fuzzy glow on everything. The best part was how it stayed with me. Most drugs and other mind alterers tended to fade away pretty quickly. The exception is probably mead from Valhalla. They probably put stuff or magick or whatever into it to keep us merrily buzzed and less likely to ask questions. Whatever she gave me just kept things nice and pleasant all things considered. I mean everything still hurt like hell, but it just didn't seem that important.

I even managed to fumble with one arm and the leg that wasn't too busted when Maureen finally tried to move me. That particular task made everything that had gone before seem like a tender massage. I'm pretty sure I cried out more than once.

When my vision cleared a little bit I saw that I was on the clean bedroll. Above me, my redheaded savior was hunched with her arms crossed beneath her breasts to hold in shuddering sobs. I felt the warm salty tears splash on my upturned face and followed those tears back to Maureen's tear-stained face. In those eyes, I saw real fear and a shadow of hopelessness.

That wasn't' right. Maureen shouldn't be crying. She was my angel. Hadn't she saved my life again? Maureen should never cry. I reached a fumbling hand towards her hair. More than anything I wanted to wipe the tears away and tell her it wasn't as bad as it looked. With the help she'd already given my chances had dramatically improved.

The sight of my hand swollen and purple was bad enough. The fact that it flopped only halfway in control was even worse. My numb and disobedient fingers missed her face and fell against my love's shoulder to slide down her chest and flop on the ground. She grabbed the hand and picked it up to press a kiss against the purple sausages that were my fingers. "No mo chroi, you save your strength."

She pressed my hand back down beside me and turned away. I was still befogged enough not to be aware of time. I know some time passed but not how long before she turned back around and helped me up to sip more of the rewarmed elixir. "Now just rest. I'll do some more work on you but it's going to hurt."

She wasn't exaggerating. I closed my eyes to reassure her, but I felt it when she grabbed my ankle and started twisting my leg to get the bones lined back up right. I felt it from my toes to my crotch as if someone were running a strand of molten barbwire under the skin in a back and forth sawing motion. That was about the last memory I had before the darkness rolled back up and pulled me in.

Whether it was the broth, or just the toll of everything added up, I fell into an easier sleep than I'd known in a very long time. No dreams disturbed that rest. If Maureen did more to me, I was blissfully unaware. Compared to the last couple of times I "slept", this was pure heaven.

I woke up with Maureen's arm under my shoulders lifting me for more of her potent little brew. This one had a taste of coffee but still held some of the same herbal medicine flavor. I had only thought yesterday's broth was heavenly. Enough had happened and enough time had passed that I'd almost forgotten what manner of magick lies in a cup of hot coffee. It helped that the girl remembered how I liked mine. She'd managed sugar and dried creamer even if there was no fresh milk or cream.

She followed that with a morning gruel of some sort made out of what she said was wheatgrass juice. The wheatgrass apparently had chlorophyll which she said would replenish red blood cells. Then she told me about the other stuff she'd been giving me. Folic acid, iron, waters and minerals and sugars and all sorts of stuff in her little mixtures. There was even coconut water in some of it. I'd heard that in extreme cases people in the pacific islands had used coconuts for intravenous fluids and other more outlandish solutions. It probably couldn't hurt. I was still pretty broken, but for the first time, I started to think I might actually come through this alive. The problem was, I didn't have time to just sit there and recuperate.

If I'd been a little more whole, and had my own supplies with me, I could probably get everything cobbled together with some of my own special skills. It wouldn't be pretty and I'd not be good as new. I'd be mobile though, and if I didn't get mobile quick then a damned immortal wolf was likely to whisper some words in very unforgiving ears. As far as I was concerned those words didn't ever need to be whispered.

A second problem was Maureen. She was obviously good at roughing it. Left on her own she would be perfectly competent to stay healthy and make her way out of the mountainous desert. She had her jaw set in that manner though. Even without asking I knew that she wasn't walking away until I was mobile enough to accompany her or fend for myself.

That meant she wasn't foraging as much as she needed to for her own needs. I had little doubt she carried a few dehydrated meals or military surplus MREs. She obviously brought a little water and even some coconut water. Water isn't light though. Every ounce of water volume weighs an ounce as well. So every sixteen-ounce bottle weighed a pound.

From somewhere she'd produced a heavy-looking pack, and bedroll plus her big satchel full of mysteries. With a few other pieces of survival gear in there, she just wouldn't have room for a great deal of water and food. The bird and the dog could probably forage for themselves. Ravens and owls lived on small rodents and carrion. I imagine Rafe could make the switch from his preferred prey of domestic cats.

Grimmr was agile and fit enough to run down some larger prey. Back in Louisiana where the Catahoula is the state dog, they are noted hunters. The curs are known for tracking, treeing, herding and even climbing trees after prey that ranged from raccoon to wild boar. He'd be fine.

Maureen would have to hunt for herself though or else go get supplies and help for me. That too would take time I didn't have. As it turned out, I didn't have any choice. Maureen made do with supplies from her pack and came back from a few forays with scavenged edibles. I never asked her where she got various roots and plants or berries. Even the eggs made perfect sense. I did however have to ask where she kept getting small game for our protein.

I wasn't sure whether to believe her or not when she grinned at me and pointed to where Rafe was hopping up and down on my slumbering hound dog. "Your wee companion and the not so wee one yon. They're a rare treat to watch. Now hush and eat the quail."

That went on for at least several days. I kind of lost track of time. Every day was more "therapy" with the holistic talents of my own personal witch, followed by my under-powered attempts to speed things up with some minor runecrafting. I was too weak to attempt anything major. Fortunately my innate recuperative powers began asserting themselves. It was looking like I might make it.

The less "dead" I started to feel, the more I started worrying about time passing. Maybe she had some skill to rival my own runic magick? It was time to ask.

"Maureen, I'm getting stronger." My voice was still a rough croak but at least it wasn't a whisper anymore.

"Not fast enough though. Gotta get mobile and" *cough*, " combat effective ASAP."

I might be stronger but it still took a second to cough up

just a little blood and catch my breath. " If I had...my gear. I could do in hours... what a hospital does..in weeks...Got anything like that?"

At my first couple of sentences, she frowned. As I continued the frown just got deeper. "Combat effective? You're almost dead already. What other combat is important enough to risk even more? The last thing you told *ME* was that you had to run an errand for a friend and would be gone a week or two. An errand that leaves you for me to find half-dead in the desert? And now you want me to slap a bandaid on your multiple fractures, punctured lung, bruised kidney, internal bruising and possible bleeding? I wouldn't do that even if I had everything I needed to make it happen."

I knew she was taller than me but helpless on my back with her standing above me clenching her fists straight down at her side made me uncomfortably aware of how very physically formidable she actually was. I'd seen her go toe to toe with a nigh immortal tree witch. She hadn't won but she'd held her own for an impressive few minutes. It wouldn't take that long for her to finish the job the bikers had flubbed. After all, the last time we'd fought she had shot me with my own gun hadn't she?

While I waited for her to stomp off or stomp the life from me, we were both made aware of a visitor to our impromptu little campsite. Off to the east, a heavy throb-bing beat of drums and bass and electronic instruments reached out to us and proceeded to grow rapidly louder. Whatever or whoever it was had to be closing fairly quickly. In minutes an old beat up half cab pickup bounced into view. The half-cab was boxy and ugly as sin. It barely had enough room for two or three fairly thin and pretty close friends. The dust coated on it helped conceal color but it seemed to be a rust color or else completely rust covered. The ugly truck wasn't traveling on any trail but making its own path through the rocks and stubby trees or cactus.

Despite the dust kicked up by the venerable vehicle's passage, a trio of teenage or slightly older kids could be seen in the front seat. Behind them, music piped out of a battered old "ghetto blaster" stereo straight out of an eighties sitcom. The stereo itself was perched on the shoulder of an ageless looking man with golden brown skin and a t-shirt that said Trance in inkblot letters on one shoulder and upper chest. The name Armin was written on the opposite side of the shirt along with a man's face whom I assumed to be Armin himself.

As they got closer I saw the guy in the back stand up and slap the top of the pickup cab. He must have had some of the best balance in the world. The way that truck was bouncing I'd have bet on him being bucked off faster than an amateur bull-rider on his first trip out of the chute. Somehow he stayed on his feet and made it look easy. When he slapped the roof, the driver rolled his window down. With the electronic music vibrating the air around us we couldn't hear whatever was said.

Apparently, the driver of the window had better ears. I saw his head swivel towards us followed by the erratic course of the truck. Fortunately, they weren't quite as thoughtless as I would have guessed. The truck slid to a stop well short of where it would toss gravel and dust on our little camp. Instead, the techno music aficionado hopped out and handed the music in for his driver. "Mantener este en."

"Keep it on?" My Spanish was rusty but I felt pretty confident of that interpretation. He approached slowly with a glance at everything from the animals and people to the fire and downed log.

"So you is my little bird eh?" He stopped several yards away and looked over the entire campsite again with careful deliberation.

"Well, grandfather pinon said you were a courteous guest. He's old and napping but you did not disturb that rest much. Even the flames are happy that you didn't put a bunch of sticks in mad about being broken off. I guess that means you ain't the ever day asshole wedo." He dropped on his haunches and tilted his head aside to look at each of us in turn. Of course, he used a different order than most would have expected.

First, he looked at the bird and gave him a carefully respectful nod. The dog received no nod and an even more cursory inspection. Maureen and I were tied for attention and silent expression after the fact. Well, maybe not tied. She received a smile and raise of the eyebrows that made me want enough strength to crawl over and smack the newcomer right in the mouth. I just got an appraisal that lasted awkwardly long before he nodded and spoke again.

"Yea the weird Wedo gonna be ok. We just gotta do a little work. But I ain't doin a damned thing with that Espiritu bird watchin." He looked first to Maureen and then to me.

I wanted to tell him several unpleasant things. Unfortunately, I try very hard not to make challenges or threats I can't back up. I just nodded and then looked to Rafe. "Fara, Utsendari."

I wasn't entirely sure how much the bird understood or even how much he would obey even with comprehension. *Go and scout.* Seemed harmless and useful enough that *if* he was smarter than a bird should be, he'd comply.

I wasn't sure if it was more reassuring or awkward for me when he cocked an eye my way then flew up to start a wide arcing circle hundreds of feet above us. Exactly how smart was that damned bird? Or was he even truly a bird? I was still thinking about that when the fellow from the truck approached with a bit of a dancing jerky step.

"Ok Viejo, let's get you on your feet. I ain't even gonna ask who you pissed off this much. Might ask if you learned your lesson though." As he worked he glanced up at my face. I thought my responses were pretty neutral considering I had a complete stranger jerking on recently broken legs and turning my rather painful body this way and that.

Apparently, he could read neutral expressions better than most, " Nope, you ain't learned a damned thing."

He kept talking but it wasn't in English or any language I could identify. It wasn't even Spanish or any version of tex-mex I'd ever heard. That took me a little by surprise. It wasn't half the surprise I felt though compared to when Maureen answered him in the same unfamiliar tongue.

Not only did she answer him, the two of them squatted down just a yard from me and engaged in a long conversation that excluded me entirely. Well, maybe I wasn't completely excluded. Both of them gave me a glance periodically but that usually ended when they turned back to each other and continued their dialogue. Finally, Maureen turned back to me.

"Well Magnus mo chroi, your luck is amazing. Not only can these fine people give us a ride, but you've also fallen into the hands of a certified Yaqui medicine man. Apparently, he's been looking for you almost as long as I was. It wasn't until last night though that he had a dream that told him where to look. Something about a sick bird that led him here." She cocked her head to the side and then nodded when he corrected her.

"Not sick, wounded. The wounded bird bring me. Like the mother bird brings hunters from her chicks." He flashed a wide grin with rather perfectly capped teeth. "Except this time mother bird brought me right to the nest."

His grammar was hell. His accent, however, was almost negligible when he spoke English. It went well with the high dollar dental work and the basically perfect tan. His clothes were even clean and wrinkle-free despite his time in the back of a presumably dirty truck kicking dust up all over the desert. This was one man it would be easy to dislike.

From the delighted smile and animated way she kept jabbering at him in the other language, Maureen did not share my judgment. In fact, I wasn't really keen on the idea of her laughing and clutching at his arm in such a familiar fashion.

I wasn't entirely comfortable or sure about this "relationship" of ours. In fact, it confused the hell out of me. On the other hand, we'd only known each other for a couple of weeks. Sure we'd spent some pretty amazing time together. But was that any reason for me to be getting all proprietary? For that matter, I'd been avoiding any entanglements for decades. This one had been a little harder to avoid than most, or even any others. But I had no say in who she spent time with or clutched at or smiled so winningly towards.

I stopped grinding my teeth and laid back against the soft pad she'd made for me earlier. It would be better for me to quit worrying about this whole relationship thing anyway. I kept repeating that to myself while I was lying there trying not to hurt.

6

IT FELT like sleep was never going to come. Not that I generally require sleep. I do however tend to heal just a little quicker when all of my energy could be directed at repairing damage. In this instance, I'd have welcomed sleep if I could have just put those laughing voices and soft conversation out of my mind. At least I managed to divert my attention from it long enough to do some critical thinking.

The first topic for thought was how the hell I got here. The second topic was going to have to be how the hell did *She* track me down here?? My mind, and maybe those damned voices, kept wanting to make that the priority thought. However, I managed after some tricky wrestling to put my mind back onto the previous problem.

Ok, so Freke sent me down to meet a guide. So far I couldn't say much for his choice in travel agents. The sneaky little twerp had led me around like a prize dupe though. Late-night boating trips to help him smuggle people had led to obvious chicanery with a fake ambulance and a criminally minded and armed biker escort. In all of that time, he'd managed to give me not a single clue concerning our destination or what the hel I was supposed to do when I got there.

In the end, it had been his mistakes or maybe they were supposed to be jokes? Well, his little tricks and jokes had gotten me more than half-killed and abandoned in the middle of a mountainous desert. Probably Sonora or maybe the Chihuahua Mountains. I was a little vague about the geography in the area. In fact, I'd barely touched on Chihuahua since I thought I was crossing into Mexico at Acuna or Del Rio.

I knew that west of that range would be the Sonora and I was guessing it was close to Sedona. The problem was I had no idea how long or what direction I'd been driven across the border other than southish. It could have been a couple of hours and it could have been most of the night. It had certainly been longer than I wanted to spend having a good chunk of my skeletal system and internal organs rearranged. From what little I'd understood between Maureen and her new buddy, we were definitely south of the border. Other than that I had only guesses.

The next problem was, even if I knew where I was, I had no idea where I was supposed to go. In fact, the only directions I'd had were to meet my guide. He was supposed to get me to the theater of action and hopefully give me some more information. All Freke had said was "disrupt my brother's plans." How in Hel's name was I going to disrupt plans I didn't know at a location I hadn't been told?

Somewhere in the middle of that thought my mind shut down and let all of that energy work on my battered body. At least I didn't have to lay there and listen to the two people who had taken their "discussion" into one of two tents someone produced from the disreputable-looking truck.

Instead, I drifted off into one of those semi-aware sleeps.

The desert was still around me. I could hear normal night sounds and the muted buzz of conversation from the tent. I just couldn't make out any words or even be certain who was speaking. I was just faintly aware that someone WAS speaking. Laying there in a haze of slowly diminishing pain, I barely registered the shadows when they first crossed between the moon and my half-closed eyes.

I know part of my mind wanted to investigate those shadows. The bulk of my awareness though was quite content to lay there passively and let the pain subside. That was probably why I found it so annoying when something started rustling around in the haversack at my feet.

Finally, it was too much to sleep through. I cautiously raised on an elbow and looked down to find myself facing a large and somewhat menacing polished black beak. Before I could overreact thought, I remembered that Rafe had been with my unexpected savior nurse. "You scared me half to death Bird. I forgot you were with Maureen. And I can't help wondering *WHY* you're helping her."

Of course, no bird would answer such a comment or musing. Then again Rafe had done some decidedly odd things lately. It seemed unlikely that his use of Icelandic commands would just by coincidence save my dog's life. But it had done just that when a zealous cop had come close to putting several nasty gunshot wounds in old Grimmr. So I could probably be forgiven for wondering whether he might answer even obscurely.

Swift of wit and known for savvy,
Stout warrior and fearsome thinker.
These were why you spurned thoughtbane,
Threw off shackles, knew your own will.
Where has gone the thinking warrior,
When did those brains turn to pudding?

For a minute I half thought those words in skaldic poetry were just in my head. After all, skalds used that weird alliteration instead of rhyming when I was just a young man. Always in couplets, always in an even meter, and always the first letter alliterated with the next to last of line one as well as the first in line two. Why would my aching head revive a centuries dead poetic style?

But then the beast stepped out of the shadows. This was not Rafe. Rafe is a Brown-necked Raven...really more of a large crow in some respects. He's a great pet and I probably owe him my life, him and the aforementioned dog Grimmr. A Brown-neck is larger than most crows but smaller than some of the true ravens. The beast that hopped over to peer eye to eye with me would have made two or maybe even three of Rafe.

I found myself "rabbiting" as I'd heard it called by a master sergeant back in Ia Drang. Rabbiting is something that tends to happen when new recruits freeze under fire for the first time. Then again I suspect that facing a supernaturally large and intelligent Raven can qualify as a new experience despite having been in more fights than a full platoon of Marines usually counts. This is undoubtedly truer if one has spent a few decades trying to avoid the attention of just such a being. This one seemed to have more than its fair share of abilities and boosts. It picked my thoughts right out of my surprised rabbity brain.

"RIGHT YOU ARE *I'm no pet Raven.*
Wroth should I be for the mistake?
Forgotten have you all you fought for?
Friend nor foe can you call Hugin.
Though perhaps I'll aid you this time.

Think you well, can you remember?
Gifts you had that once were greater.
Gone are memories that were once yours.
My raven twin some call Munin.
Made to stay far out of your reach.
To succeed you must clasp to you
Times and lives that you lived ere now.

I was about half-convinced it was all a dream. Even though it was fairly detailed, it might have just been my subconscious using symbols. Far behind and above the bird talking, was an equally large looking shadow silhouetted on the moon behind. That must have symbolized Munin or Memory. So somewhere in the spotty memories from other missions was there help for me? Something to show me where and what I needed to do? That was the logical conclusion if this was any kind of prophecy, communication, or just a clue from my slumbering subconscious.

I saw the representation of Hugin bounce his head eagerly as that thought crossed my mind. So I guess I was on the right track. Then again, a minute later he drove his ominous-looking beak down at my leg and flew off with that irritating humanlike laugh/caw of his.

I came off the ground swearing in the darkness and almost fell all over a few thorny bushes nearby. It was probably mesquite but it was hard to tell in the shadows cast by an almost full moon. They definitely felt like the rugged and painful architecture of mesquite.

For those of you who have never experienced it except as a smokey flavoring, mesquite is a cross between cactus, a tree, and some kind of weird metal. Chopping it takes a strong-willed man and a sturdy tool. It does burn hotter than a Tijuana fan dancer, but it's hell to cut for the fire. And finally, a mesquite tree is possessed of long nail-like thorns. I'm not talking about fingernails either. Every few inches a three or four-inch long piercing piece of hell sticks out of each branch. And the thorns are almost as tough as the tree itself.

You would think that so soon after a brutal beating and a near-death experience at the hands of vindictive bikers, I'd be immune to a few little thorns. Well now, I think I'd rather have fought the bikers again. At least with the big leather-jackets, you can get your own licks in. That damned mesquite didn't care if I fought back or just lay there and bled. The more I thrashed the more thorns magically appeared.

In minutes I had undone about a quarter of the healing that had been accomplished. Which did nothing for my mood. I guess it made a little noise too because by the time I was untangled, there was a small crowd. Ok, only four people and a dog.

"Wow! Dumbass." Ok, make that four people a dog and a smart assed raven. Apparently, Rafe had returned to camp while I was receiving dream visitors from either myth or my subconscious. I was still a little curious where the bird was picking up his vocabulary. I rarely use that particular term. Now the Icelandic/Norse he'd spoken a time or two makes sense. He'd seen me talking to the dog in old Norse which is pretty close to Icelandic. That's what I tend to pass it off as when anyone gets curious.

Dumbass just isn't one of my personal favorites. It had, however, become the bird's phrase of choice in the last few weeks. The worst part was, he usually used the term at all too apt a time. Like now.

I could see Maureen was going to some effort to repress any mirth. That was probably easier since she saw so much of her work undone in torn and bloody bandages. Her newest friends didn't even make the attempt. Despite the darkness and a certain amount of blurriness from a manly watering of the eyes, I could clearly see the younger arrivals laughing out loud. Their older and supposedly wise companion restricted himself to dry chuckles and a shake of the head or two.

Then again I hadn't liked him much even before he started laughing at me. Maybe I should have just brushed it off and indulged in a chuckle or two at my own embarrassment. Some days I might have done just that. However, with the various aches and pains and trials and tribulations I'd been through, my temper was not at its most restrainable.

"Oh yeah! Laugh it up at the feeble old man ripped up by mesquite. Hel is this stuff toxic or anything?" Ok, that last was a bit melodramatic. I'd yet to see a thorn with any kind of venom that could keep up with my metabolism. There are certain perks to being an escaped Einherjar, even if you have to watch out for supernatural spies. Of course someday I'd slip up and find my way back to Valhalla. Then there wouldn't be Hel to pay, just Odin and his pets along with some really vengeful Valkyrie.

"Oh c'mon senor wedo! You ain't as old as me." Now, what was the likelihood this guy was over a thousand years old? Then again I cheat. I rarely have to work out and I never worried about Crepey skin or any of those anti-aging commercials you get on tv after the bars all close.

"We ain't been interduced. I'm Tio Guillermo. You don't gotta worry bout them mesquite thorns either. Mesquite's practically a sacred plant to our people. Eat it, burn it, build with it, cure anything from diarrhea to migraines and makes a passable coffee. We do gotta get the thorns out though. They say mesquite thorn lasts longer than any flesh it's buried in. Not sure how true that is but I do know I ain't never seen a thorn fester and disappear on its own. So we'll get some pliers while yer lady friend makes some more of her poultice."

He might have said "your lady friend", but his glance sure spoke a different message as he all but caressed her with a wistful gaze and some pretty praises. "She knows a few things, that pretty redhead. Taught me a couple of things to put in my own poultices. Once we get all the bits out of ya that ain't s'posed to be there she'll slather ya down. Then maybe we can talk about that messed head of yours eh wedo?"

That probably should have mollified me. Then again I can't say I'd been very rational for the last few days. Instead, I let my mouth have free rein. Instead of directing any vitriol at this new character though I spouted off at Maureen. "What's so damned funny to you? I thought you were here to help, not to laugh at me for being half dead. Is that why you came? To laugh at whatever new predicament the stupid bouncer got into?"

In retrospect, I might have wanted to tone that down a little. That thick mane of red hair was no lie. Her eyes flashed and her face flushed as she turned a curiously emotional eye towards me. I can't say that I'd ever seen eyes flash with heat and yet regard someone with such an icy disdain. I'd also never heard her develop quite so severe a broguish Irish accent. "I came because I thought we'd started something special belike. Yon freakishly smart pets started having worrisome fits. When I asked that villainous bird what was wrong I thought I was talkin' t' meself. Imagine my start when the black ruffian answered. Och yea and it was just "Dumbass! Trouble! Go!" but it was all too apparent that he knew more than nary a bird should ken."

By the end of her tirade, which by the way sounded

amazing in her lovely Irish brogue, Maureen had started stalking towards me with a certain amount of mayhem inherent in her expression. I mean it really was somewhat captivating to listen to her. That did not mean I was unaware of the threat of violence. The sad part was, deep down I knew I deserved whatever she delivered. I could no more have stopped her from undoing all of the bandages and poultice work than I could have stopped the world from spinning.

On the other hand, my ego still had control of my tongue. "So you got the bird to track me down because he's special or magical or something? And the dog helped too I suppose. I'm not buying it, lady. I've spent a lot of time and energy making sure I can't be tracked down by some pretty powerful beings. So how'd you do it? And don't try and sell me on my own bird and dog tracking me down across state line... NO, make that international borders!"

Oh, I was in the groove. Accusations and insults were flying faster than I could keep track. "You know what? Forget it. Take the animals if you want to and go shack up with Uncle Bill in his Yaqui hippy hut. You two can chew on some peyote and do body shots with mezcal or something. I've got too many real problems to worry about."

It's hard to stalk away indignantly when you're limping and tangled up in both ragged bandages and a thorned bush from the depths of hades or muspelheim or some other fiery inferno of the damned. I started to give indignation my best effort though. She never gave me the chance.

I've probably mentioned it, but Maureen is taller than my modest height. She had broad enough shoulders to intimidate a lot of men. On the other hand, I've never been too concerned about whether a woman was taller than me and I've got broad enough shoulders to intimidate the guys she can't.

All of which means, normally I'd have either brushed her off or just gone stoically immovable when she yanked on my shoulder. That apparently did not work the same when I was half my normal strength, bleeding rather impressively and hallucinating about divine carrion birds. I'm not sure if it was her intention, but rather than just spin me around to face her full ire, she spun me around and dropped me on my sprung and bloody ass.

The sudden jarring of assorted semi-healed injuries and barely closed wounds had the bonus of earning an involuntary grimace along with groans. It also caused a few arteries or veins or something to spurt more blood onto my bandages. At least some of them quickly got a little redder.

Rather than invoking any level of sympathy, Maureen seemed to take the additional injuries as a personal affront. Standing over me with one hand on her hip and the other shoving my shoulder back and forth she set me straight on a few...misperceptions.

"Ok smart guy, first things first. I found you..." She ripped a bandage off of my chest and pointed to a spot I could barely see without going cross-eyed trying to look down. "Because I added a little something of my own to your colorful collection of tattoos and scars."

That wasn't fair. I didn't have *that* many scars. Very rarely did Kara leave me with a scar after she started running my group through various missions and forays. Oh, she could be a little vindictive if she felt like her "boys" embarrassed her or needed a reminder. For the most part, though, we all uniformly woke up with any damage from our latest adventures all healed up and easily forgotten.

Compared to scars I had a lot more ink. A few had

personal meaning or were put on to lend "color" for my disguise back in various third world boonies. Most of them were rune workings that I had carefully and meticulously added.

Each tattoo had more than ink added to my skin. There were rare plants, minerals, metals, and other things I won't mention. All of them had been infused into the dyes on my flesh at one time or another. Cleansing and rituals were followed by chanting or drumming. Finally, a truly potent piece could take hours or even days to complete.

I also had a number of less permanent bits. Henna dye and other markings were adequate for short term bolster-ings and runic work. Whatever energy was stored in the markings tended to eat them away and destroy them in the process of being activated and doing their work.

Apparently, Maureen had taken a page from my book. The spot she indicated was almost bare except for a faint, almost invisible tracing of some Celtic figures and knots. They were done in henna but with some vines and other marks in brighter colors. In fact, they were dimmed but had probably been bright enough that I wondered how I'd managed to miss the addition every time I looked in a mirror. I suspected that part of their "job" had been to remain hidden.

"What in Hel's name was that?! And how'd it get there?" I was not angry so much as just surprised. How had she managed to put enough time and energy into a sigil like that without getting caught? I mean I'd felt a touch thick-witted of late. But that had been the work of a recently deceased Bruja witch. Right?

"Well, you probably remember our little late-night picnic before you left town? You always get sleepy after we...enjoy each other so enthusiastically. I just waited until you were asleep and made sure there was a way to locate you if needed. Not like a stalker or anything..." She couldn't quite hide the blush that made that a little less credible.

"It was probably a good precaution as things turned out." At least her voice had lightened from semi-homicidal to mere frosty anger.

"You're telling me you managed to *tattoo* me in my sleep?" My own tones were much more reasonable than hers. I could hardly hear any hint of anger or hysteria. I mean if I had been feeling any anxiety I personally didn't hear it in my voice. By the look in Maureen's eyes though she seemed to imagine something like fear (which I was NOT subject to) came forth in my speech.

"Not a tattoo at all mo chroi, just henna and some other herbs I had in my bag. You can tell it's already fading, unlike a tattoo." That goes to show how much she knew about tattoos. My own runic ink can fade in days or even hours if I use the magick stored in them recklessly. The more I use the enchantments cast into such runes, the quicker they burn out and fade away. The kind of healing I needed would require some decent tools and focus and would probably erase the markings from my skin in a matter of days.

That wasn't as immediately important to me as the decreased hostility from my mercurial redhead though. I found myself wondering how to retreat without sounding like either somebody's meek mare or a complete douchebag. While I wondered, I remained silent. It turns out that perhaps I should remain silent more often.

" Ok, so we're mad at each other." Not only had her tone softened but the curve of her full soft lips had grown rather warm and intriguing as well. "We'll work that out later. You need to hear what Guillermo has been telling me."

She had definitely lost the worst of her anger. Maureen

gently lowered me back to the blankets I'd been resting on. When I was settled and at least more comfortable than incoherent from pain she continued.

"I don't know how much I believe about his methods and philosophies, but he's amazingly accurate in his divinations and dream work. You don't need to know what he saw that convinced me. Just know that he did indeed convince me. Which is important because he told me a couple of things about you that explains some things I'd been wondering. Like why you never talk about your past or your family or anything really personal. I'm not even completely sure why you're so damned tough and hard to kill. Eachan and I decided to assume it's part of those tattoos and whatever energy work you do."

She paused long enough to brush a thick lock of hair from her forehead and give me her most earnest look. "Oh, I thought you were just being all stoic and masculine at first. But even an old British soldier breaks the stoic mold every once in a while. You had me wondering if I'd misunderstood the nature of our...well, of us. You could have told me you had amnesia. Of course, you probably don't know how you got it. Guillermo said you've, let me think how he said it. You've got many doors locked in the houses of your past. But he thinks he can help you learn to unlock them."

I was about to discount dear uncle Guillermo entirely when the sense of that last statement hit me. Was there something there? I mean I'd been assuming it was the Brujah from weeks ago that had scrambled my melon. But was there some other magick related effect dulling my senses and shrouding memories? I had to admit, that would fit in with some other stories about old one-eyed Ygg.

Maureen had continued all but gushing about her new

buddy's discoveries while I mused. When the deeper voice of the native shaman broke in it caught my attention again.

"I said I'll try to help him. Without a journey together though I'm not sure." His shrug was fairly eloquent. I hadn't decided if I was going to believe the smarmy runt yet though. "No sign anything in his head's broke. More like somebody locked pieces away. Maybe he got some memories he ain't too keen to remember too. Not much I can do about that without breakin some rules I take serious."

It took about half an hour of her pleading while the medicine man looked on impassively. To be honest though, I never had a chance. Between the weakness, pain, and guilt from my accusations, she had too many tools to work with. Add my reluctant curiosity to the mix and I might as well have saved time and given in right from the start. When I acquiesced the shaman and his buddies produced some worn clothes that didn't exactly fit but they were lots better than running around in the buff.

As a reward for my agreement to whatever this guy did on a "journey", I had my bandages changed by gentle hands and was made as comfortable as I'd felt in days. The feel of clean clothes even if they were drab an ill-fitting was its own blessing. I got dressed bit by bit as my lady fair finished her work on bits of anatomy. A grey cotton sweatshirt with its sleeves cut off joined some pants that were probably baggy on Guillermo but fit me like yoga pants. Finally, I was given some sandals that looked like they were made from old tire rubber.

Maureen explained to me as she worked. "Don't think this means you're forgiven. But if you're distracted by all the wounds and pain you'll never be able to focus and follow his instructions."

Whatever her reasons, I couldn't stifle a moan or two as

she tended the various hurts my flesh had endured. And of course, the combination of her presence and those gentle hands made me recall other more pleasurable moments we'd shared. Despite the general weakness and sundry aches and pain, I felt an almost predictable response to her touch on my skin.

By the sudden catch in her breath, I knew she felt it too. It hurt when I turned under her attentions to see what I hoped was in her eyes. My searching gaze never found those eyes though. Instead, I was met with her mouth coming down to lock onto mine in a writhing volcanic jolt of need and desire. I did my best to jolt her right back. Despite pains here and there I managed to roll over and pull her down beside me. When my lips found her neck she arched her back against me. My own desires found their answer in a breathless growl of need as she ground herself back against me. I held her with one arm while the other hand slid around her waist and rose to cup a full and tautly tipped breast.

That of course was the exact moment when a dirty old charlatan of a medicine man snapped his tent flap open and called out into the darkness. "Come wounded warrior, let us open the closed places in your thoughts."

I MIGHT HAVE HAULED the girl into the brush all caveman style. Except she went from pleasantly sinuous in my arms to awkwardly stiff and uncomfortable. In my many many years of life, it has become clear to me that only one person in such a situation should strive for stiffness, and it usually isn't the girl.

With an almost inaudible growl, I slowly released my clasp of the young lady. It might have been my preference to ignore the old man and continue with our own cures for my maladies. Unfortunately, it was quite clear that she had other priorities. My Maureen rolled to her feet and lifted me to stand beside her with little assistance or enthusiasm on my part.

With a quick and almost chaste kiss, she turned me around and gently pushed my shoulders towards what I assume had become a medicine tent. "Good luck mo chroi."

In many rituals and forms of magick or religion, people are advised to rid themselves of negative emotions and energy before they enter the "sacred space". If that were the case in this particular instance, then we were probably going to summon an eldritch god of jealousy, hate, and agony. Not only was I bearing an inordinate amount of pain., but I also had a huge helping of salted ass for my "guide" on this journey. Given the opportunity, I'd merrily show him exactly what it felt like to brush his nethers clean with the aforementioned mesquite thorns. And just to make sure he got the message I think a nice antiseptic tequila bath for his punctured danglies would be in order.

I kept entertaining myself with those images and similar entertainments while good ole Bill chanted a little and waved sage smoke around the tent with an eagle feather, or maybe a turkey feather dyed like an eagle. Whatever he was doing, it didn't rid me of my excess "energy" from a week full of miseries and disappointment.

I was pretty thoroughly smoked and fuming myself by the time he got around to offering me some concoction that contained alcohol and maybe a few hallucinogens. In my experience, it's usually a bad idea to imbibe mood-altering goodies when you're in a negative state of mind. Then again, such goodies rarely affected me for more than an hour if even that long. I slurped his goop down and set the wooden bowl or cup or whatever it was on the blanket beside me.

My head didn't start spinning at first. In fact, I was expanding on mental images of mayhem centered around my temporary spiritual guide when he flipped on the portable radio. Once more it erupted with the thumping or some techno racket that had a heavy bass drum beat infused with the typical electric instruments. When the rapid-fire lyrics started I tilted my head and temporarily forgot my formulae for torture. "That Yaqui or apache or Aztec or something?"

I saw a fuzzy-edged face swim into my peripheral vision. In the middle of blurry outlines were obsidian black eyes sunk between leather cheeks. Oh, and there were those obnoxiously pristine white teeth. "Would you believe Frenchies speakin Hindu? Looks o' yer pupils it's about time. Take a look at that snake hole in front of ya."

I almost jumped right out of the tent when I lowered my head and saw a forked tongue flickering in and out of a small hole right at the base of the fire. I didn't exactly remember such a big fire either. I tried to reconcile this man-sized bonfire with the smallish tent and the clay dish full of coals and small blazing twigs. The memory and the current image didn't match but that didn't seem too important.

My head shook slowly from side to side. It probably looked like I was impersonating a confused buffalo or a stumbling bear. The truth was I couldn't seem to put very much energy into thinking or shaking away confusion. Once more I thought I saw a forked tongue flicker in the shadows of that small hole. If I'd been thinking normally that would have been a signal to get the hel out of the tent. The problem was, my head wasn't really working that well. So, of course, it seemed like a good idea to lean over and take a good look at that hole.

I must have underestimated the potency of Old Bill's tequila or herbs. No sooner had I leaned over just a few degrees than my entire center of balance went. I found myself falling face-first at the ground as that little hole loomed larger and larger. I guess I shouldn't have been surprised when the shadows reached up and pulled me in.

There was an awkward moment or two when the earth seemed to convulse around me like a hungry maw sucking me deeper into the darkness. Except it wasn't the earth. The entire hole for one brief instant felt like the gullet of some gigantic snake, or maybe a wyrm. Yea that felt right. An ancient wyrm gulping me down its fiery maw. At the thought of it, my skin began to itch then burn as if being digested. Unable to scream as my breath was robbed by the convulsing muscles lining that maw I writhed and was consumed by the acidic crushing walls of what modern people would call a dragon. To me, it was an Ormr, the greedy, rapacious and evil great serpent.

The thick ribbed walls of its gullet never relented long enough for me to catch my breath as flesh was ground away or burned away by acidic gases and bilious liquid. Then there was the sizzling of flesh from an occasional gout of flame as he belched or roared. I felt skin sizzle and bubble then peel away with chunks of muscle and sinew.

Unable to die, I was helpless as the very bones of my body were crushed apart to fall not into his giant stomach, but into a natural-looking cavern. The shadowy space was dominated by a small fire under a filthy black cauldron. A ragged old hag in disreputable rags used her stirring paddle to bat my bones into the cauldron as they fell from above.

Most of them fell freely into the pot, but none of them got away from the old lady and her paddle.

Finally, she reached into the piled remnants of my corpse and drew out a singed and cracked skull. I found myself looking her eye to orbital socket. She started to toss an evil grin and a cackle at me. That suddenly changed from a malignant grin to a look of indignant surprise. "You be no dreamwalker! How does sich a fine empty-headed young bairn end up here?"

Just like that her grin was back happy but just as evil. "Young brainless boys have good marrow though. Let me find a good long bone to crack eh boyo?! I'll just suck a wee bit o' marrow while yer bones make me soup."

She'd just grabbed what looked like a femur and bent it to the breaking point when a familiar voice echoed out of the shadows. "No old mother. He's with me. No marrow for your soup tonight."

I saw "Old Mother" turn to face a shadow that seemed empty. "Ah! Medicine Bill! Ye've come to warm granny's bed of a night have ye? We'll have a cuddlesome time and then slake ourselves with rich bone soup eh?!"

The bone was creaking. Despite being crushed and dismembered I could somehow feel the sharp agony as if my thigh were splintering. Before it exploded though I saw the Yaqui medicine man appear from the shadows to bow at the hag. An instant later he was gingerly removing my bone from her hand. He spoke to her in a language I could not understand. In a rhythmic almost crooning tone he spoke while his hand almost tenderly brushed the hair back from her face. One side remained covered by brittle grey tangles. The side he cleared though showed the time ravaged visage of a woman who might have once been beautiful. She had once possessed strong features that still stood out in a hawk-like nose and high wide cheekbones. Maybe strong features was a more apt description than beautiful.

It was almost uncomfortable to watch this strange intimacy between the shaman and the witch figure. I closed my "eyes" and tried not to listen to the whispering conversation. That is probably how I became aware of the trance music lingering along the edge of my consciousness. In fact, it almost seemed as if the music had replaced my heartbeat now that I was without muscle and organ to surround my singed bones.

Those singed bones were being moved as well. I peeked again to find Bill had stopped talking to the hag. She now sat in a rickety old rocking chair to clack knitting needles at each other while humming a tune that somehow reminded me of a young girl in the bloom of her youth and romance. Don't ask me why. That's just the feeling of her song.

While she hummed, and Bill sang softly in that exotic language, my bones were being gathered. The shaman carefully laid my bones out as if they were still articulated. Scooping a handful of earth and ash from around the cauldron he blew the mix on the bones. The dusty cloud of ash made me blink and I dearly wanted to cough. That's rather hard to accomplish without lungs though.

As the cloud cleared around me, I heard a rasping wet cough in response to my own urges. Looking down I saw my body. Not the same corporeal flesh that I had worn in his tent. No this was my form in the prime of youth. I only had a couple of tattoos and none of the scars accumulated over several lifetimes of violence. It was if I had never found my way to Valhalla and the battles since then.

A distant part of me howled that it was false. But the sudden peace, the absence of such small familiar aches they were almost unnoticed, those things made it hard to deny this dulling of the senses. There was no pain, no worry, no stress. Just the crackle of the fire and the rhythmic creaking of her chair. I could have stayed there easily and just forgot how to feel or think or even remember.

"You gonna sit there with a stupid look on yer face or we gonna go find those memories?" I really hated his voice more than ever. But the shaman was right. If I stopped for even a minute too long here, I might never wake up. Don't ask me how I knew that. It was just there summoned from the back of my thoughts by his obnoxious comments.

"Yea, I had to get grounded. This is all new to me...medicine man." Even that much of a concession stuck in my throat. I mean I really did not want to admit that this guy had anything in the way of mojo. But it was hard to deny my surroundings and everything that had happened. I mean maybe he was just a good hypnotist. But maybe that and dreamwalking had more in common than people would like to think.

Now that I was here though, it seemed like a good idea not to antagonize the "guide" too much. I mean hel, even if it weren't real he could probably poison me in my stupor and claim some mystical dark force snuffed me out. Maureen seemed pretty convinced about the guy and would probably buy whatever story he came up with. Besides, I wasn't sure he was faking this. It seemed pretty damned real.

"Ok. So what now?" I found myself whispering as well. Some of that same instinct about staying here too long warned me against gaining too much of the old lady's attention. It was probably best for everyone if she sat there humming and knitting.

With his own cautious glance at the bedraggled figure in the rocker, Bill led me off towards those shadows he'd appeared from. He even went so far as to motion me to silence with a finger across his lips. Like I said though, I already had the gut feeling that the quicker we got away from her the better.

We entered that inky blackness at one side of the cave and walked through it for a while. I don't know how long. It felt like several minutes. After some time though I began to see a faint glow that became brighter until we came out of a cave mouth or tunnel of some sort to face a huge bonfire.

Around that bonfire were a number of structures. The majority were made with mud and straw though there were a few sturdier structures of wood and sod. In the middle was a familiar longhouse using an old ship's hull as part of the roof. It had a large A-framed front and sod covering the walls thick enough to hold grass and moss still living along its length. Inside just such a structure one of the old Jarls or chiefs of a powerful clan would live as well as house their most loyal thegns and warriors.

The jarl or chieftain would sleep with his wife, wives or concubines on a high platform or in a small room on the end farthest from the door. Twin rows of pillars would reach from the front to the back of the long narrow structure. There would be a platform that ran around the outer edge to provide bedding and storage for everyone but the landowner and his family. Rooms on the platform would be divided by hide, cloth or thin wooden partitions for minimal privacy.

This particular longhouse looked massive enough to hold dozens of such partitions. Maybe even scores upon scores. In comparison, the other buildings were smaller and more ramshackle. They were wattle and daub huts and half-dugout dwellings for slaves or the lowest of freemen. There were also some crude stables and barns about. In the middle of the village was the giant bonfire that illuminated all of the doorways. Rather it should have illuminated all of the doorways. Instead, each entrance was filled with impenetrable darkness or shadow. Across some of the doorways lay indistinct figures while here and yon a massive wolfhound sprawled to guard.

"Boy, when you get your teeth in a theme you go all the way don't you?" I had been conscious of listening to Bill and answering him with just the smallest fraction of my attention while the scene built in front of me.

"What are you saying, old man?" Still, he got much less than half my attention. Something about those dogs and even more-so about those lumps across doorways held my attention. Maybe it was my imagination but they radiated a cold remorseless danger.

Okay, yea they were all in my imagination. Bill made that pretty clear in the next instant. "I'm saying you built this as the place your memories are hiding. Never saw the likes of such a place myself so this is all you boy. Now...where should we look for the memories? I got my own ideas but that's the fastest way to turn a dream quest into somethin silly and meaningless. You gotta figure this out yourself boy. But listen for my voice. I can maybe pull you back out if you get someplace too dark."

His flow of thoughts or vocalization or whatever faded for a minute. Then came back sharp and clarion clear for a brief second. "In fact, here boy. I've planted a couple of thoughts for ya. Just a tether to yank you out if I can, and a little nudge to keep you whispering about what all you're seein."

Just like that, I was alone. In my own head. Or maybe in my room at the asylum. The way things had been going I wasn't entirely sure anything was real lately. "Thanks, Ole buddy Billy boy. I knew I could count on you."

As far as I could recall this damned "journey" thing hadn't been my idea. I hadn't believed in it. I certainly did not expect it to get quite so palpable in short order. Nor was I certain I could wake up unassisted until his damned psychedelic concoction had worn off. Just on the off chance, I tried to will myself awake. The bonfire never even faded in brightness. So yea, I seemed to be stuck.

Well if I couldn't get out, might as well do some digging around. I walked on proverbial tiptoes to the first hut. This one had a simple Irish wolfhound sleeping at the door. He wasn't sleeping for long. As soon as I got within a few yards the damned thing flowed to its feet as if made of smoke. This was a huge specimen of the breed. His back would have reached higher than my waist. I was pretty sure he'd be able to get my entire head in his mouth if he bothered to tower over me on legs that I suspected were longer than my own.

A low growl rumbled toward me strong enough to shake what passed for ground in my dreams. I realized that I was growling back before I could help myself. A heartbeat later we launched at each other and clashed together in a whirling but a strangely silent blur of violence. Teeth flashed and struck my forearms. Instead of blood though, I saw wisps of smoke or fog rise from my wounds. At each snap of those jaws, a little more strength faded from my muscles and a little more chill seeped into my core.

By contrast, even my first full-strength blows thudded harmlessly into a rib cage seemingly made of oak and iron. The most I got from the beast was a grunt or two as I pounded hardened fists into it. One roundhouse swing turned its head halfway around on its neck. On a normal hound that would have snapped vertebrae. This beast just got angrier.

I felt my knees turn to water. Looking down I saw gaping wounds where the grey wisps curled up from my thighs. Bits of that same wisp clung to the hound's rear claws where it had apparently been raking my lower body. There were similar wounds up from my thighs and groin into my mid-torso. Out of all of them, my essence seemed to pour forth leaving me weaker and less substantial. I had to start wondering, what happens when you're reduced to mists and fog across the veil?

If, as many shaman believed, they were accessing the spirit world, or perhaps A spirit world, would that mean my return trips to Valhalla would end? That might be worth it. What would take its place though? Oblivion? Or some other afterlife I'd never seen or imagined? I tried to yell for the shaman to pull me back out. He said he'd tethered an escape somehow right? The weakness and chill from this battle had left me too weak.

The most I could generate was a low moan of fear, pain and the soul-searing cold. That was all the answer I needed about my possible fate in this shadowland. The aching cold of oblivion awaited. I'd not rest peacefully or see my loved ones again. I would fade away as if I had never drawn a breath. Despair tried to steal into my most innermost soul as my form became more wisp than solid.

None would remember. There would be no one to sing songs, lift a horn, tell the stories of Magnus and his life. All of the wyrd of my family before me would be wasted. I stifled a gasp and fell even further to both knees and a hand reached out for feeble support.

The shadow hound circled out of reach of any futile swing I might take. Without a weapon of some sort, it seemed immune to my attacks anyway. My hands rebounded. Kicks slid harmlessly along its body. It couldn't be afraid. By extension that meant, the damned thing was gloating over my weakness and despair. And that sparked something new and fierce in my heart.

Kill me if you can. Strike me, taunt me, torture me in increments. But I will not be mocked and gloated over by some stinking creation of my own imagination. It sensed the change in me. With a snarl, those finger-length fangs slashed to sever my head from the rest of me. It got my fist instead.

No helpless mewling punch this time, I grabbed for its tongue. With my last strength, I got a grip on the slimy thrashing appendage deep in the beast's maw. Grasping the tongue back near its throat I jerked it towards me. My other hand fought for purchase and finally locked fingers in the thick curls of a hairy shoulder. With one final spine wrenching effort, I lifted the beast from its feet. Rolling over on my own back I got my bent knees under it and kicked out to send the beast spilling over me...right into the bonfire.

There was no crashing sound. No crunch of logs breaking under its weight. No explosion or sparks. Just a faint "whump" of sound as the creature vanished in its own puff of wisps and vapor. Gloat on that carrion spawn.

I lay there wondering if I had the strength to even get up much less carry on this insane quest. The answer came in a faint perfume of cinnamon, strawberries, and Maureen's own special scent. I felt her hand on my forehead and heard her murmur something concerned and sweet but too distant and low to be understood. Then warmth spread from that contact on my head. The aching cold was chased away and I saw substance fill back into the spaces that had been ripped away from my essence. Even from across the veil between life and death my Celtic priestess could reach out and heal me. In that moment I loved her as fiercely as I'd felt anything in my life. Love and pride and desire all coalesced as my Maureen poured life energy into my weakened being and gave me the choice to carry on or follow Guillermo's tether back to my body.

How could I turn away after a gift like that? I turned to the shadowed doorway and stepped through it over the space where the hound had lain. I found myself in a small barracks room with two or three squads of men. Each of us was armed in our preferred mix of leather, chainmail rings or plates, and studs. There were even a handful of the crazy bastards that run in all but naked. Maybe a dozen warriors carried bows. The bows ranged from sturdy longbows to the exotic composite recurves of laminated wood and horn. The latter bows some of us had picked up in Constantinople while others found them on later forays in places we didn't rightly belong.

I felt a hand on my upper arm and turned to find Kara the stormy gazing at me possessively. She grinned sharp and hungry before giving me a kiss that fired my blood like no mead or ale ever could. "Yours is the Honor Chosen. Sound the call."

I lifted my spear and slammed the hard ash shaft against the metal boss that centered my circular shield. "HONOR!"

Four score or more voices roared it back at me. "For HONOR!"

"Odin All-father!" I tried to outmatch all of their voices with my lone cry.

"For the All-father!" Oh, they were my brothers. Each ready and eager for the fray.

"KARA the Stormy!" Our Valkyrie lived up to her name. Stormy, tempestuous, unpredictable and fierce in her passions, Kara was our leader, our priestess and for more than a few of us our lover.

"For KARA!!" If Odin had heard the exuberance and devotion in that final cry he might have been wroth with jealousy. The one-eyed can be almost as unpredictable as Kara herself. But he was not there and we had to hope he was not watching from the high seat.

On the dying echoes of her name, Kara shouted a trio of runes in her eagerly sharp voice. The back wall of the room burst into rolling clouds that parted to reveal roars of artillery and the howls of men dying and being killed. Rifle fire thundered from one edge of a narrow valley to the other while a mass of men in Scottish plaid tried to maintain an orderly retreat despite the vastly larger army pursuing them. Into that maelstrom we poured.

For a change, we were not disguised as contemporaries in whichever engagement we fought. The forces below us all carried rifles and other fairly modern weapons. A few machine guns barked their incessant defiance before their team would uproot the guns and fall back to another position. Time and again the lines would fall back and then reorganize to fire withering fusillades at their enemies in stone grey woolen tunics and breeks.

We, on the other hand, were clad as many of us had for battle before ever being chosen to bide in Valhalla. I had a sturdy byrnie of rings and leather that left most of my arms bare but covered the rest from throat to mid-thigh. Around my neck, a twisted iron torc rested to help divert blades that might take my head. A heavy round shield backed with leather and strengthened with an iron boss rested on my left arm while my right arm bore the heavy boar spear I preferred. At my right hip, a short heavy ax hung. At my left, a lang-seax or longer sword-length seax was sheathed. Its smaller cousin the seax rode horizontally from the belt across my backside.

From behind us Kara's pearly steed thundered up. The Valkyrie launched herself into the saddle without letting the horse break stride. She darted ahead and I could swear she bounded up and into the sky above us as my brothers poured forth.

Arrows hummed from all around me. They struck down and pierced the useless woolen cloth of our foes. Men fell by the dozens while others stood transfixed. I saw more rolling clouds to either side erupt and spew forth more of my brothers. We flooded onto that battlefield between the scots and the Danes on one side, and a quarter-million bewildered Germans on the other.

Had they kept their wits the Germans could easily have mown us down. True we were fierce and strong but we were even more outnumbered than those we came to save. Most of us were armored but what armor can turn away a hail of bullets? Finally, though we are hardy and preternaturally tough, every single one of. us had died at least once. Most of us had fallen in battle dozens of times. We knew we could be blown into pieces but we also knew that Kara would gather us back to her and we would rise in Valhalla to boast of our deeds on this battlefield.

That was perhaps the secret of our success that day on the banks of the Mons-Conde Canal. We knew no fear and we were not surprised by the foes we faced. The Germans were ill-equipped for our attack though. To them, we were a supernatural or even divine force that was possibly immune to their mortal weapons. They stood stunned as I led my own force explosively into their ranks. It was shield and spear against bayonet and firearms. Some few rounds were deflected by armor or shields.

My own arms had been prepared with the help of a Lapland sorceror. Between his arcane arts and my own, admittedly inexpert, understanding of runes, my armor was far superior to anything made up to that day and time. I remember one bayonet catching my shield arm. But that man fell tripping over his own entrails that spilled from a lateral slash of my heavy bladed spear. I pinned a machine-gunner to a tree with a toss of that same spear and then went to shield and sword.

More than one skull cracked under the rim of my shield, and more than a few faces were crushed by that same shield's iron boss. At the same time, my sword whipped out and around to remove hands at the wrist or legs at the knee. Once a wooden stock shattered under that masterwork of a bladesmith.

I lost the sword when a bullet took off two of my fingers. An explosion caught my shield and ripped it away but the Lapland sorcery stopped that same force from laying me low.

Missing fingers made the ax too heavy. I lifted it from my belt and tossed it to the shield hand while my maimed right swept the seax from its sheath behind me. Perhaps half of my brothers remained. We fought like wolves though. Crashing into pockets of Germans in groups of two or three we circled and slashed until they fell or fled. Occasionally they simply overpowered us with their modern weapons. More often they fled before our fiendish battle-fever.

I stabbed a clean-cut looking youngster wielding a pistol and shouting orders. He must have been a freshly promoted officer or perhaps someone had purchased his commission. That mattered little as his lifeblood arced up from the severed vessels in his throat. When I spun around from that kill, I found myself surrounded by a tithe of our original force. Glimpses of mail and broken shields marked where some of them lay. Others were sunk in the bogs or too entangled with a foe to spot easily.

Kara's horse walked towards us with an almost dainty step. The steed looked as fresh as a summer morning and bore no mark of fire or blade. Kara herself radiated a visible glow as her battle fervor fed the magic of the wolf-maidens. I felt my feet slide out from under me. The ground jarred into my butt and I had to grit my teeth against the unexpected pain radiating from my middle.

When I looked down, maybe that young officer hadn't been as bewildered and frightened as I thought. It looked as if he'd emptied the pistol into my gut with the barrel pressed up against my armor. Cherry red links bore evidence of the contact fire while blood welled bright and heavy through those holes and streamed down my legs. I saw Kara coming closer. Her eyes were fever bright and she licked her lips as if hungry or aroused.

"Oh, what have you let happen?"(Magnus was not the name she used, but even in my dreamworld I dared not think the other name that might bring attention that could compel me back to Valhalla again.) I knew what was coming. It had happened before. Normally she did a better job of dulling our memories first. I recalled a couple of instances when she'd been sloppy or perhaps sadistic and let the memories remain. Next, she would find some blood-thirsty manner of ending my struggle, and I would awake in Valhalla.

Over Kara's shoulder, I saw the Valkyrie Gondul riding away from her own troops. They too were resting. The Germans we'd faced were long gone but others were plainly moving against other troops of the British Expeditionary force. Gondul the Wand Bearer rode into a dense woods that sheltered a ragged looking bunch of Brits from the quickly approaching Germans. I saw her gesture to the weary men and then silently lead them into a narrow cleft that would circle away from the Germans and allow the Brits to escape.

Then there was a sharp pain at the base of my skull.

7

I "WOKE UP" standing in a doorway facing an empty sod hut. Something like that's enough to make you question your sanity. I mean it's not every day you wake up and you're still in a dream. Guillermo didn't give me time to dwell on that though. His voice buzzed near my ear like an old crackly radio. "Boy, you gotta be more careful. Can't say much this way. But you were in trouble there. Yank on my anchor if I need to drag ya back."

The "radio" interference disappeared as quickly as it showed up. I found myself alone in a dark landscape again. Suddenly the buildings and their guards took on new significance. I wasn't sure if the "guards" were some construct of my own psyche or a machination from Kara or the Allfather. It was apparent that the buildings all held secreted memories. I couldn't figure out what was in that last battle though that needed to be kept from me.

With a shrug, I moved deeper into the circle of huts while my eyes kept straying to the larger building on the other side of the bonfire. Somehow it seemed even larger now than when I first saw it. Was it possible that the build-

ings themselves were mutable and morphing as I understood more about whatever this quest was?

On the other hand, I was just guessing. Who knew
whether I was right about any of this. I *thought* I'd been
volunteered into this whole damned mess with a supposed
shaman guide. The fact that I suspected he was a charlatan
didn't matter. What mattered was, I was stuck in this crazy
situation without even the dubious support of said shaman.

Okay then. I'd been in worse situations. Not many this
outright nuts, but plenty of corners just as tight. Maybe I'd
died in most of those corners but...Nevermind. Focus on the
quest Mags.

The ratio was about one dog to every three other figures.
Maybe the doorways without dogs weren't as important.
Then again maybe I had no idea what the Hel was going on.
There was only one way to tell.

I deliberately chose a doorway that only had a small
snow-covered hump in the doorway. Edging forward I could
see into that shadowed interior no better than I could any of
the others. With a shrug, I parted the worn rags covering the
door. Under my fingers, the material was both coarse and
oily. It felt like a burlap bag soaked in motor oil, or a wool
cloth treated with linseed to make it waterproof.

Memories of pushing aside just such a weatherproofed
door came to my mind. I tried to recall. It had been my four-
teenth or fifteenth year. We counted our years differently
then. It was close to the same as modern calendars. Instead
of twelve months though we had thirteen moons or the days
that it took our lunar neighbor to go through all of its
changes of appearance. This had been late in the lean cold
months.

With spring about to return, there was talk of crewing a
few ships and heading out to gather some goods to make life

easier during the next long winter. The decisions were two-fold. Would our money be better spent on trading ships or raiders? And which direction would they sail? The memory was clear enough that I felt the crispness in the morning air. Icicles shot a rainbow of beams out to dance along the lattice of frozen snow coating the smokehouse with the waterproof cloth over its door. I could even smell the smoke and the rich welcome scents of a few hams left with the fish and other meats hanging in the shed.

As I stood transfixed by the clarity of a memory from a thousand years ago, the hump of snow at my feet stirred. I looked down in surprise. There was no fear. My mind was too bemused by other things at that moment. When the waist-high little girl writhed her way out of the snow though, there was a brief spike of confusion and maybe just a touch of fear. I didn't feel concerned until she locked her rigid fingers *into* a chunk of firewood as large as her entire torso.

She stared at me through cold dead eyes of blue almost pale enough to be white. They were set in a face that was a mottled mixture of greys, blues, and mauve or purple. The ease with which she swung the log at me told me that this was a veritable nightmare again. She opened a mouth to scream. Instead of a scream though, the blackened ruins of her mouth exhaled a putrid stench of decay and vileness that made me want to drop to my knees and heave away whatever spirit food might be in this phantom gut of mine.

The weakness from the previous fight coupled with my nausea probably saved my...umm, life? My knees buckled and as a result the chunk of lumber barely glanced off the top of my head before splintering against a stone standing nearby. If she'd caught me squarely, it would have popped my head like an overripe grape between stone and wooden cudgel. Even the near-miss left me reeling. Which was time enough time for her to kick my legs out from under me.

I was terrified that to hit the stone-hard frozen ground would stun me worse or give her another opportunity to use that inhuman strength to crush something near and dear to me, like a limb or head, or my nethers. I simply knew, I did not guess or surmise, I *KNEW* that if I hit the ground at full force I was done.

For some reason though, that never happened. Maybe it was all of the adrenaline. I've heard people in wrecks discuss a similar phenomenon. Time quite suddenly slowed to a snail's pace. My fall became leisurely and not at all frightening. In fact, I had time to brace and shift my weight all while considering my diminutive but powerful attacker. I obviously couldn't meet her strength for strength. She swung that log sized bit of firewood like a wand or an orchestra baton. Somehow I didn't want to play her tune though.

As I hit, I rolled. The chunk of wood was down to about the length of my forearm. That was still enough to ruin my day if she managed to connect. Apparently, she expected my roll because she lunged forward to hit me as I rolled to avoid her attack. Which means it was a good thing that I rolled towards her rather than away. With the supernaturally strong arm stretched over me to strike down, I was in a perfect position to use my greater mass and a little leverage.

The terrifying but relatively tiny figure arced over my hip with a little assistance from a judo style maneuver we'd learned long ago. I jerked on that extended arm to give a little more momentum to the Draugr as she left the ground. After that, it was just a matter of shielding my eyes from sparks when she hit the bonfire a few feet away.

Hey, when I was a youngling everybody knew that fire

was the best cure for a number of undead and fey creatures that might come calling. Zombies like Draugr were definitely at the top of the flammable foes list. She went up like her clothes were soaked in kerosene.

This time I hadn't taken any serious wounds, but for some reason, I felt just as weak and even more insubstantial than when I finished the hound. That was something to worry about. Guillermo had said I was in danger. He hadn't mentioned the fight necessarily though. Was the danger less "physical" than I'd been assuming? For that matter, what would happen even if I did get wounded or die in a place that only existed in my own mind?

Would the shock kill me? I'd heard that tale hundreds of times. To die in a dream was to die for real. I'd also heard that we have more control over our dreams than that. Some analysts claim that the dream will shut down before we witness our own deaths even symbolically. But did any of this apply to the work of what I had to admit was a pretty convincing shaman?

I wanted to wake up. If I went on with this, would I wake up in the desert, or in Valhalla though? Finally, I decided it didn't really matter. If you learn one thing in a life as long as mine, it's that you can't start giving up. Once you start something, you finish it. Maybe you have to regroup and plan some more, but you don't stop just because you're scared or confused.

One of our frequent martial arts instructors quoted Confucius at us. The one that really stuck was, "It does not matter how slow you go, as long as you do not stop." So I didn't stop.

When I flipped the cloth out of the doorway this time I found myself standing outside that smokehouse in my youth. A fat goose hanging from my fist was a rare and lucky find for the time of year. After I hung it beside the hams and rows upon rows of salted fish in the smoke, I walked back out into the cold morning air, and saw her for the first time.

Her name was Frejarefn. She must have been born already showing the lustrous black tresses she'd grown into by the time we met. That was the first thing I noticed. Dark brown and red hair was not uncommon in our village. But hair as black as midnight with a shine as if the moon and sun always followed her, that was rare. She was of an age with me, perhaps thirteen or fourteen, perhaps a year or two older. Already her young figure was developing the shape that would draw men to her. I saw almost every young man and more than a few of the older ones pause to give her an appreciative glance or a slight smile.

I fell on my face rather than go with a smile. It wasn't necessarily an intentional display, however once committed I fell with gusto. It started with one foot catching on the other and ended several stumbling steps later. Of course, by then I'd managed to find a fairly expansive puddle of muck and mud to land in. That was how I met Frejarefn. I knew she would be mine sometime after that first meeting. There standing alone in the chill village of my mind though, I stared at the darkened doorway and yearned to see her again. Perhaps the worst part was not remembering her well at all. I just knew we were important to each other.

It might have all been a mental construct, but I was glad to be alone. I couldn't explain my tears to myself. It would have been even more difficult to try and explain to Maureen or that pearly smiled old Indian.

With a roll of the shoulders, I pushed the melancholy away. So far I'd learned that many of my memories were clouded and guarded. I still didn't know who was responsible or why it had happened. But it seemed like a good time to get to the bottom of it all.

Disregarding the other buildings for the moment, I centered my attention on the carved doorway of the longhouse. It seemed even more massive and more forbidding than ever. However, it surprised me that there seemed to be no guards at the door. That took some thinking. Then again I wasn't sure how much time I had for thinking. Hadn't I been in this place for a long time already? The battle at Mons alone had lasted several hours. So how long could one spend on a spiritual journey without doing some kind of psychic or even physical damage?

I had to trust Tio Guillermo to pull me out if that started to be a concern. For now, there were questions to answer. Like why weren't there any guards on the biggest "house" in my mind? Size and complexity alone suggested that this would be the place to look for whatever secrets might be important. Which would have suggested that whatever shrouded my memories would have taken more precautions with it.

Dropping down to my haunches I took a careful look around the ground and steps leading up to that doorway. It wouldn't do to be surprised by another zombie child or something worse. When no obvious threats jumped up and screamed for my attention, I directed it towards the doorway itself. That's where I found the first little surprise.

The delicate scrollwork that decorated the wooden crossed beams was not made of a single line but instead was a long ribbon of runes. Like most, it could be interpreted and read as a story or maybe some kind of directions. But it also held a few surprises. I saw runebinds to ward away intruders and another that was some kind of shock or fire. There was one that I thought would probably paralyze or short circuit someone's nervous system. Since I was not only the intruder but the battleground as well, it made sense that any short circuits would be in my neural network. That was something I thought might be better to avoid.

Sitting there I had to do a little more thinking than I like to engage in. Eachan probably could have blown right past those runes. Maureen even had a better understanding of the way things like that worked than I do. But Eachan and Maureen weren't there.

But wait a sec. I was in my own head. This was like a dream and we all have some input into our dreams. So just maybe...I rose to my feet and spread them about shoulder width. With my arms at my sides, I turned palms forward and extended each finger individually until I could envision anchoring lines between my spread hands and the ground. A similar visualization grounded my feet and allowed me to "clear" my thoughts enough to try something a little interesting.

I invoked only a single rune but used it over and over. Ansuz, the rune of communication seemed appropriate. After the ninth repetition, I summoned an image of Maureen to my thoughts and then willed her to appear in front of me.

The image in my mind was of her soft smile as she pushed me towards the tent to begin this odd odyssey. What showed up though was something unexpected. She was still in the same clothes, but she looked almost as worn and beaten as I had felt after the bikers got done with me. Her eyes were red and puffy. Her complexion was sallow even in the limited light of the bonfire. The sound of her breathing was heavy and wet even above the sounds of harsh winter winds around that fire. Worst of all, her hair was hanging in limp disarray.

In all the time we'd spent together, I'd seen her hair a shambles from loveplay or outdoor activities, but I'd never seen it limp and listless. There was no shine to her normally glowing and fiery mane. It was dull and lifeless enough that for a moment I thought it was another Draugr.

When she spoke though it was obviously not an evil undead creature. "Mo Croi? How did you do this? Is it something Guillermo did to help you?"

"No elsket, I just needed your insight." I pointed towards the doorway. "I can read the runes but I can't figure out how to get past the traps."

To my consternation, she did not look up at the crossed beams standing a good twenty feet high. Rather she knelt and ran her hands over the steps or maybe just a foot or so above them. "I ken what you mean. The Ogham staves on this are well-wrought. Were ya to trigger them I'd say you might turn your brain to porridge."

That startled me enough to lean over and look myself. Try as I might though, the steps were bare of any sigil or sign to me. "I don't see anything there. I was asking if you could help me sneak past the wards on the door."

Again I pointed at the beams crossing above that doorway. This time the look of perplexity was on her face. "What door? I see wardings on yon box that must contain your memories. But I see no door."

She looked around for a minute and turned back to me. "We're in a large room like the feast hall in a castle or summat. There's a table there in the middle with all manner of phials and containers. I see lots of herbs and crystals lying around the tabletop candle too. There are boxes all over the room." She pointed to the nearest of the sod houses and huts to show me.

"There seem to be some little folk standing guard

around some of the boxes. But I dunnae see wards except here." She pointed down at the steps right below the runed crossbeams.

"Ok, that's not what I see. I think we're both shaping the experience around our own expectations. That's not necessarily that important. I need to get past those runes and sigils. So what I suggest is, I'll tell you what I perceive, and you tell me how you would go about getting around the obstacle." At her nod, I began. First I pointed to various aspects of the environment and told her about the Bonfire, the huts, the hounds and the mounds I suspected were various creatures.

Once she had an idea of how my mind was working we began on the runes. The size of the longhouse got a peculiar or maybe just skeptical look from her. The runes themselves, however, got her full attention. I caught her nodding her listless locks as she seemed to come to an understanding.

"I think I've got it Luv." She bent to peer at her own runes again while she thought about what I'd said. "Aye, this is Uath, the Hawthorne, it's tied to defenses and fire both. And over here is Tinne the holly, also a defensive plant associated with weapons and warriors. Yon is Straith the Blackthorne which bodes ill in many cases. Yes, I think I see the knot. But can we unravel it?" She stepped away from the "box" she was studying. A few quick steps brought her to the table where she began gathering goods while she coached me.

"You'll need a way to cleanse the energies around the wards. I would go with Ruis since the elder tree makes an admirable force for purification. There's some lavender. Obsidian and bloodstone should do for the rest." She quickly gathered her bottles and bags and returned to kneel by the box.

While she spoke I could actually see the table beneath my own perceived flames. She gathered the various wispy containers and materials until suddenly I could see them solid and real looking. When she placed her finds down near the wards though, all of it just turned to dully glowing coals. I got the gist of it anyway.

Laguz, water, the rune looks a great deal like a golf flag today. I tried that first to wash away the protections. Maureen looked annoyed enough that I considered whether I should have told her about her goods disappearing as soon as she let go. That would have interrupted my runic cleanse though. So with a niggling hint of foreboding, I maintained my galdor and tried to wash the magic away from those runes.

Once more I felt the energy leaking away. With every surge of weakness, it felt like my "flesh" became lighter and less substantial as well. When I looked over at Maureen, she no longer stood but sat on something invisible to my eyes. If she'd looked worn and ragged before, she looked positively haggard now. Her hair had faded to a mere hint of its former color and luster. Her shoulders slumped and her spine bowed with the effort of just staying upright. I could see the puff of mist in the air as she exhaled one laborious breath.

Whether it was harmful for me to wait or not was no longer the issue. I had to get her out quickly.

"Maureen!" I moved closer and wrapped an arm around her shoulders. My cleansing of runes had accomplished so little anyway I was about to give up. Maybe there was some-thing in these memories to help me, but I could not risk that fiery redhead to find out. "Come on, Guillermo left me a way out. We just need to go back a few steps and find his energy anchor. We get his attention and he'll drag us out."

I had actually taken a step before I noticed that she was fighting free of my arms. "No! You have to keep trying. I know you, Magnus, better than you think. If I let you leave now, we may never find out why you've so many secrets."

"Look I've got some secrets ok. Apparently some from myself as well. But that's not worth harming you, Maureen. You don't look well at all so let's get you to the old medicine man." I couldn't understand why this was so important to her anyway. Maybe it was just because she herself was so worn down she'd like to know it wasn't all for nothing.

"Magnus you don't understand dream journeys. Leaving now could prove traumatic or even impossible for one or the other of us. We're both invested now and attached to the journey. Maybe we could get out, but it would come at a cost. I will be fine. You just need to get in there and fulfill the quest. Preferably quickly." She offered a wan smile to encourage me. But the next instant she wavered on her feet and I had to reach out and steady her.

Fortunately, a chopping log was nearby. I led her over to sit on it and turned back to look at the door with rather more frustration than I'm good at containing. Suddenly I had a thought. Those ingredients she'd amassed had come from a table where my bonfire was right? So maybe what I needed was the same thing but from a different perspective!

Almost certain I was on the right track, I hurried over to the fire and retrieved a burning stick about as thick as my wrist and a couple of feet long. Brandishing the burning torch like a sword I ran back to the crossed beams with their runic traps. Maybe I hadn't found the right rune to wash away the traps. But there was one rune that might do it in a hurry.

Thurisaz is the runic version of a nuclear option. It is one of the strongest runes of the futhark. Shaped like a hammer, it represents Mjolnir the hammer of the thunderer. There are few items to match it in power and sanctity in the Norse belief system. Thor's hammer is a force of chaos created and constrained to fight the ultimate forces of chaos. As such a representative, Thurisaz held enormous power. Like all chaotic symbols though it held an element of risk. The energy was hard to control and often you released it and hoped for the best.

So, hoping for the best, I took a charging step and shouted the rune at the top of my lungs just one time. At the same instant, I bashed the flaming torch down at the first of the dangerous symbols on the door. "THUR-EEE-SAZ!"

The nuclear option was an uncomfortably accurate description. The energy released rushed out and left me drained and falling to my knees. Of course, I probably should have considered that this was all happening inside my own rather thick skull. There was a scorched meat smell and tearing sensation as well as a cacophony of sound that lifted me from my slumped position and tossed me back some distance into darkness and oblivion.

Score one point for Maureen. I didn't wake up in the desert tent. Instead, I came to awareness again with my head cradled comfortably in a sweet and inviting lap. Maureen looked down at me with a crooked grin and a shake of the head with its dangling flaccid hair. "I dinna mean THAT much of a hurry mo chroi."

"Shit, we're still in the dream." I could dimly see a tumultuous grey sky past her head. Or maybe it was just a swirling fog my imagination had made. "Guess maybe that was a tad impetuous on my part."

"Hard-headed, heedless and utterly pigheaded. What

did I do to deserve you?" At least she was laughing with only a tear or two to show. "On the other hand, you did it."

She turned my head to see the cross-beams gone and the doorway completely open. There were no scorch marks or any sign there'd been any crossbeams. Then again the front face of the house would likely sag and fall without those supports. At least they would if normal physics applied.

"You blew up not only my Ogham staves but the box itself." It almost sounded like a hint of pride in her voice. "And made a grand wide hole."

She lifted me up by the elbow and pointed right at the door to the longhouse. But hey, if she saw a hole that worked for me. Trying my best not to limp I took a couple of steps and pierced the shadows of the doorway to see what was inside.

"Ok mo chroi, I see your bonfire finally. And a circle of menhirs each with a portal such as Taliesin himself might have described." This time her voice was colored more with awe than pride.

That worked as well. Though what I saw was a long pit of glowing embers and a platform with individual "rooms" marked off by hanging hides and cloths. It was what was between me and the rest of the room that brought me up short. There with a hand on the ax at her cocked hip stood Kara the stormy.

"Warrior you should not be here." Her voice was stern and crackles of lightning seemed to flicker in her eyes as well as rippling down her mail. "This place is secured from you for a purpose. Secrets dire, secrets dangerous, secrets hurtful all rest beyond. Do not tread where a Valkyrie and the All-Father himself have forbidden."

8

YOU WOULD THINK that the ax, the lightning or power rippling around her armor would have been the scary part of that scenario. Failing that, well, I've been pretty damned wary of the All-father for longer than most redwoods live. But the REALLY frightening thought was, if I was "traveling" inside my own head, were they in there somehow too?? That was enough to make a grown man soil himself no matter what the time period.

I had one "hand" on that tether to pull myself out of the dreamworld. But there was a whole part of me screaming defiance. Kara had taken my free will. She'd used us and discarded us like toys until she felt like breaking the little soldiers out to play with again. For all I knew this was another one of her little games in my head. After all, nobody had more access to our thoughts and souls than the Valkyrie in charge of our destiny. For that matter, even if old one-eye was involved, what right did an old god have to reside uninvited in my head?

Turns out my spine may be slightly stronger than my bowels are weak. I stood to my full if modest height and pushed through the stormy one as if she wasn't there. Which of course in a place like this meant she no longer *was* here. There was a faint tingle as if I'd hit my funny bone except this funny bone was the size of my whole body. Maybe I imagined that feeling though as well as the scent of ozone.

The disappearance of that guardian showed many more doorways inside the longhouse. Not exactly doorways I guess. More like partitioned sleeping areas. Along the fire, a quartet of pillars was carved with more and brighter runes now. They glowed in a myriad of colors from pearlescent white to glaring polar blue. Most disconcerting though, was the great scaled torso like a giant snake that stretched between the farthest two of the pillars.

The beast writhed as I watched and muscles as thick as my own torso rippled along serpentine ribs. From the girth of that torso, I had to imagine a head capable of swallowing a small cart along with the horse and driver. Unfortunately, I was proven correct a bare breath or two later. While I watched, that enormous scaled body writhed until a truly monstrous looking head curved around the pillar to peer at me through the smoke above the firepit.

Somehow even a simple Viking warrior knew better than to peer too long into the eyes of the wyrm. I looked away from that dread visage and found more disturbing views to survey. With my attention firmly on the beast's torso, I was able to see that many of the gleaming scales also glowed with their own runes akin to those on the pillars. These also pulsed not only with light but with the movement of the guardian beast they adorned.

A little voice inside my head said that the really juicy secrets were past those pillars. A much more reasonable voice told me that those secrets could remain hidden for now. If a snow-covered child-sized guard had caused me some grief, then that glowing monstrous apparition would probably consume what little sanity I had left.

An uncommon bit of wisdom took over. I pushed aside the cloth covering the partition closest to me and stepped out into a camp of tall cone-shaped tents dusted in snow. Under the white powder, each of the tents was decorated with simple but graceful bands of artwork. The ground was hard and cold even through the thick soles of leather boots. Flurries of snow swirled around the tail of my heavy canvas coat and the unforgiving cold hard metal of a Springfield rifle cut through thin yellow gauntlets.

I found myself pulling a blanket away from some native American boy, what we had called skraelings centuries ago. I say boy because not only was he young, he was painfully thin and small. The kid might have been sixteen or seventeen years old but he was barely taller than I myself had been at twelve. The fact that I was never particularly tall compared to my Norse cousins just made the kid's stature more significant. For maybe a second or two I hesitated. There were others nearby and I could pick one of them for the mission.

I was interrupted in that thought by the other Einherjar standing nearby. Lorcan was a true brute. If he missed being six and a half feet tall, it wasn't by more than a few hairs. His face resembled a side of raw beef. It was raw, red, ugly and painfully textured from some sort of skin condition. One eye tended to wander which made it difficult to be absolutely certain if he was looking at you or something across the room. As ugly as he was though, it was his nature that made him truly repellent.

Lorcan was the type to pull just one wing off of a fly to watch it spin in tortuous circles. I'm pretty sure he burned his own parents to death and probably ate any younger siblings. He was just that kind of guy. We'd never had much use for each other.

The first time we met had been on the field in Valhalla. Without even knowing his name I hated the brute. Rarely do Einherjar take notice of each other in the middle of battle. We're usually too busy killing or being killed to look around for entertainment. When Lorcan and I met though, well, it took a few seconds but slowly a ring of warriors around us stopped fighting just to watch.

Lorcan was bellowing like some primordial beast and stabbing at me between wild swings of the shaft of his spear. In turn, I was smashing my shield between us and slamming it into him anytime a weapon wasn't headed my way. In my other hand, a foot-long seax darted and slashed at his legs and belly. I don't think I was screaming at him like he was roaring at me. All I recall is the grunt as I put everything possible into each shield bash or rip of the blade.

In short order I had an ear dangling, at least one bone was broken in my left wrist, and one of his spear swings had done something painful and problematic to my eye socket. I hadn't been able to focus well but I could see the splash of crimson all over his legs and groin. I'd hit something that was sending a fresh surge of blood down his front every time he lunged. On the other hand, it was increasingly hard to see where his spear would come from next.

With a death blow all but inevitable I decided to take a chance. This time I saw his spear darting at me. Instead of weaving aside or interjecting my shield between us, I rushed. The spear hit my mail and parted it to find meat at my shoulder. The pain was searing and all but stopped me. I'd expected it though. I swallowed the pained cry and pushed further into the spear, trapping it between my body and the heavy shield dangling uselessly from that arm.

With my eyesight fading, I fell onto the ugly giant and started ripping the blade into him like a sack of wheat or side of beef. We never did discuss which of us blacked out first that night. In fact, we never discussed anything at all except on a mission.

I didn't know why we hated each other, but it had been a hot and violent hatred that didn't end on the battlefield. Most such fights are forgotten by the time we wake for the next fight, or feast, or training session. Our hate never faded.

We were both trained enough not to let it affect a job though. At least we usually were. While I was still looking for another Cheyenne brave to use for my part of the job, Lorcan piped up in that guttural accented bestial Norse of his. I looked to where he was pointing at a particularly well built teenage Cheyenne girl. "Look at that fetching squaw, she reminds me of your little wife with the midnight hair."

Just like that, the Indian in front of me didn't matter. His age, his size, the mission, none of it mattered in that long breath of a moment. I didn't think of my pretty little raven-haired Freja every hour of every day. But I missed her desperately when I did recall our life together. I also never recalled Lorcan meeting Frejarefn.

I found myself looking at Lorcan over my shoulder with the Indian kid locked in place by a hand as cold and hard as stone. "What about my wife? How do you know about her?"

Lorcan laughed at that. Oh, his eyes were filled with the hate we carried. But there was also cruel triumph there. "HA! You don't remember, do you? Did old All-Father take those memories or was it smoldering dark Kara? I wonder why they took those memories eh hero? Well, let me give you some of it back. You know about the spear scar in your chest, but do you think about the smaller scar between your shoulder blades?"

I hated to admit it but he had a point. I rarely thought of the handful of scars I kept after taking the spear in my chest. There was a small one just inside my left shoulder blade though. I'd assumed it was a shallow knife wound or some accident. Kara liked running her fingers across it when we were alone together.

"Aye dwarfkin, that was my arrow that took you in the back. It found your heart even before the spear sundered it. I was always proud of that shot. Always figured that's why you hated me as much as I hated you. I'd planned to give that little wife of yours some special attention too. We had her trapped in the house behind us when you came back home. My fellows took you while you were still outside. They kept you busy until I got my shot. Oh, it was sweet. You folded like a doll and just sat there on your knees as the spear came in to finish a job already done."

His gloating became less smug and much angrier in a flash. "And then that little midnight bird of yours fileted me with my own seax. Oh, she was quick she was. Pulled it from my back and drove it to the hilt in my right kidney. Ripped it out sideways and took the other kidney. She was a fiery thing. Loved you to the last. I could see it in her eyes as my hands closed on her throat. You didn't deserve a woman like that midget."

The blowing snow and the sound of angry men around me faded to nothing under a new roaring that I barely knew was my own blood pounding within my head. In an instant, I recalled my death vividly. I saw it as if from another's eyes. The two men fighting me outside my own home, the flash of a feathered shaft. I'd never remembered the arrow before but his words unlocked the entire scene. I knew that the reason I fought all but barehanded against two armed men was to protect the woman in the house behind me. And I knew that I failed.

Suddenly there was too much going on in my head. A memory within a memory inside a dreamworld, it was too much. I lost control of my own actions and watched helplessly as my own hands twisted the rifle into the youngster's hands and put his fingers through the trigger guard. I switched from the Norse we'd been speaking to a phrase I'd learned from Madoc years ago. "Mae chwarae'n troi'n chwerw wrth chwarae hefo tan."

Lorcan understood. "*Things can turn sour when you play with fire.*"

Today they might say. "*You mess with the bull, you get the horn.*" or even more to the point, "*Sucks to be you.*"

I jerked the rifle inside the Indian youth's hands with the barrel pointed at Lorcan's lower belly. He had turned more towards me when I spoke. At the time he'd cornered a pair of Indians who kept telling him that one of them couldn't understand what he was saying about giving up any weapons.

The shot caught him by surprise and I saw the agony in his face as the ugly .45 caliber lead ripped into his intestines and possibly tore up his groin in the process. I barely registered the Indian kid as my own revolver came up and took off part of his smooth brown jaw and dropped him like a puppet with cut strings. My eyes were locked on Lorcan as he dropped to his knees and tried to control the waves of pain, or at least control his gut. He wasn't up to it. Blood and breakfast came spilling down his coat front at the same time his bowels emptied.

An indisputably masculine voice that belonged to no man bellowed out an order. "Kill them all!"

I hadn't even known Kara was around. But when your own Valkyrie calls, it jerks your soul in whatever direction she wishes. I fired two more shots into the kid as I ripped the gun out of his hands. It took a second to thumb the next cartridge through the trapdoor. It wasn't easy. Kara's voice had twisted me into a near berserker frenzy. I wanted to club and chop my way with the heavy wooden stock and triangular bayonet. I got the cartridge in though. My job wasn't done.

Well, part of the job wasn't done. My part was clear. I had to start the fight with some level of deniability for the 7th cavalry. I knew Lorcan was supposed to kill someone in particular though. He obviously wasn't going to do that from a puddle of his own entrails and the contents of said entrails. That meant I had to find his target and finish the job. After that, I could chop merrily away until we were done and all went to get a beer. That wasn't very likely though. It was much more likely that I'd fall biting and clawing to the end.

I clubbed down a handful of warriors between me and the old man still dancing and yelling encouragement to his braves. Yellow Bird he was called. A Sioux medicine man should know better than to start dabbling with the God of the Cross. Yellow Bird and some of his Sioux brethren had begun what they called a ghost dance. They thought that if they kept the circle going and sang their songs right then the Indian way of life would be restored, the buffalo would return and there would come a time of plenty.

Old Yellow Bird never found out if he was right. I saw him dancing and yelling at the young braves who had managed to sneak a handful of rifles along. They flung aside their blankets as the soldiers inside their camp started firing blindly into the natives around them.

Old Yellow Bird got one lucky shot in. I saw his belt knife almost remove the nose of one of the soldiers nearest him. The medicine man grabbed a rifle from the ground. I don't know if it was his hidden there or if the soldier had dropped one. It didn't really matter. My .45-70 round took him before he could even get the thing shouldered.

After that, I was released from the mission. Once more Kara's will had used me for a job as if I was no more than a marionette and her the puppeteer. The job was over, but Kara's bellowed orders still burned marrow-deep in my very bones. I clubbed down a blanket wrapped figure before me and stabbed into someone coming out of one of the shadowed tents. All around me there were shots and the sounds of battle as well as the confused and terrified cries of other natives. It lasted from seconds to minutes before the light artillery pieces on the hill opened up. Explosive shells hit amongst the tents and blew up into shrapnel. One whole teepee simply disintegrated into shreds of cloth riddled with fingertip-sized holes.

Behind that tent, I saw a Sioux warrior calmly drive a spike into the ground. The spike anchored one end of a long sash that he uncoiled from around him until a few feet were strung between him and the spike. I'd seen similar things in my own time. This was a warrior. A fighter of honor and conviction making a statement. And that statement was; *This far and no further. I make my stand here.*

Around him, a couple of soldiers charged. One of them fired his revolver as fast as he could thumb back the trigger. Either he was a helluva bad shot or that was one tough Indian. The other trooper executed a textbook butt-smash with his rifle followed by a downward sweep of the bayonet and another textbook stab with the same weapon. The warrior rode the buttsmash as if it was a gentle pat. He twisted so that the slash missed him by inches and then twisted the other direction so that the triangular bayonet barely hooked meat along his ribs.

The rifleman took a crudely made handaxe to the face. The same ax took away the pistolero's revolver as well as the hand holding it. With an absolute lack of expression, the warrior shattered his disarmed opponent's breastbone with the same ax. That was my kind of fight. I barked a grunting challenge that caught his attention and then scooped up a fallen spear to engage this brother warrior. He didn't deserve to die at the guns of these berserk cavalrymen. His would-be a clean death at the hands of another warrior.

He seemed to smile and gestured for me to join him in a dance only one of us would finish. My spear thrust wasn't textbook. When I learned to use a spear we didn't have text, or books, or even much in the way of written words. What we did have was generations of justifiably feared warriors who almost all used a spear for most of our fighting. When he weaved aside from my thrust I was ready, I drove the shaft of the spear at him horizontally. There was no way to twist aside from the strike. Maybe a limbo champion could duck under it but that was about the only escape.

I say about the only escape because he showed me a new one. My two-handed smashing blow met his raised palm with a meaty splat. Without any sign of major effort, he redirected the attack so that I found myself stumbling past. Out of the corner of an eye, I saw his ax raised again. About then I decided I was on my way back to Valhalla.

Instead of the skull-crushing blow I expected, I received an almost gentle tap of the oddly adorned stick he held in his off-hand. " *That means something. Something about touching a live foe without harming him.*"

A genuine if completely incongruous smile split his face

beneath a headdress stylized as an owl. It took a second to truly realize that the grinning idiot had just counted coup on one of Odin's own chosen warriors. I was pretty glad Lorcan was too dead to notice. I just had to hope Kara was oblivious as well. Dropping flat I swung at his legs with the spear but he hopped over as lightly as if we were playing some rope-skipping game.

This time I didn't give him time to embarrass me with the damned coup-stick again. I kicked at a point behind and *through* his ankle, then rolled to my own feet expecting him to be down nursing a broken leg or at least a severely sprained ankle. Instead, he was weaving back and forth in a shuffling gait as a low chant started to rumble out of his deep chest. What the Hel? I knew I felt that ankle twist and snap under my kick but there he was moving as if he was at a pavilion dance.

This time I was a little more careful, thrust, sweep, counter his ax, head strike with the butt of the spear and another brutal stab that hit him in the gut and lifted him from his feet. I pulled the spear out and let him fall to the ground. Except the lunatic didn't. With a shiny purple-gray loop of something hanging out of his shirt, he danced his little shuffle step and then broke my spear with his ax and kicked me several steps backward without even a grimace.

I landed on my back and looked up to see Kara smiling down at me. Before I could even begin to be embarrassed, she smiled and gave me a hand up. "You think we're a monopoly? That's a Mandan. Sacred warrior. He's just about as special as any of your brothers and a great deal more holy. Let me take him."

I saw her turn to face the Mandan warrior and then a giant hand reached down and lifted me from the ground. I flew a dozen yards with bits of metal ripping into me in mid-air. The thunder of the exploding cannon shell was incredibly painful but only for a second. After that second I heard nothing.

The ground was iron hard and colder than the depths of Hel. I'd have gotten up if I could but something inside me was broken. As a matter of fact, I imagine lots of things inside me were broken. I saw the blood spreading around my shoulders where I lay almost nose to nose with one of the Sioux women. Her eyes never moved, even when a snowflake landed on one and a piece of shrapnel tore a furrow in her cheek.

The child half underneath her moved though. I saw coal-black eyes looking at me questioningly as the babe tried to find some nourishment or at least warmth from the cold, still mother he suckled. A spasm jerked my whole body and font of blood erupted from my mouth. A bare instant later I felt the life jerked from me to leave just the image of that mother and babe burned into my memory. I doubt even the All-father himself could ever take it away again.

The ground was still hard but at least it wasn't cold when I opened my eyes. I saw eyes as dark and deep as night again and could almost feel that chill wind ripping through me. But the eyes resolved not into an infant Sioux or Cheyenne child but those of old Tio Bill. I tried to talk but my tongue was too large for my mouth and seemed to want to stick to anything it touched in there. The old Yaqi lifted my head and started to pour a cup full of something into my mouth. I was all but helpless to stop him.

I tried though. A hand waved weakly at his in front of my face before he frowned down and brushed my hand aside to offer the cup again. "It's just water. You been down too long boy. Dehydrated and probably half crazy."

I relented and let the most delicious delightful and refreshing thing ever pour down my throat. It was easily a match for Odin's own mead. At least it felt like it. With the old man's help, I struggled to a sitting position and took another cup in hands that barely worked. I drained that one too before looking around. We were back in his little tent on top of a desert mountain. "Where's Maureen?"

He shook his head and shoved a bundle of clothes under my head when he lowered me back down. "Later. You gotta sleep now. You been gone too far and too long. You rest and make sure your whole soul makes it back. We'll talk when ya wake up."

I wanted to protest, but the words died on my lips as the strain of my "journey" overpowered even the vaunted stamina of a chosen warrior. Fortunately, there weren't any dreams to interrupt that deep drained sleep. I'm not sure I could take another view of the kid I'd shot or babies and children brutally slain as they ran. Maybe I was just doing a job. Somehow that seemed like a weak excuse. Even for someone brought up in a harsher time with a less social conscience, that day in the snow seemed needlessly cruel and merciless.

It was the first thing I remembered when I woke up. The bile rose in my throat as guilt came pouring forth from my gut and my newly restored memory. Did all of those rooms in that longhouse contain such grim reminders of something I can't believe I'd ever been? Or rather reminders of something I didn't want to believe? Maybe I'd been around modern morals and standards too long but the very thought of what had happened, of what *I had done*, left me retching into the dirt floor of the tent.

I gasped and vomited and tried to catch my breath for an interminable time. Finally, there was nothing left to toss and no strength to toss it anyway. I lay back away from the stink and the mess and let other thoughts slowly creep in. I remembered my wife.

My little blackbird had meant the world to me. It had always been her great regret that we didn't have children. Of course, we'd only been married a few years and I'd spent a good part of that away from her for one reason or another. Still, most couples in our village welcomed little ones every couple of years. Her belly had never quickened with a new life. A quick calculation made me even sadder. She would have been in her early twenties when I died. When we died.

But why had Lorcan and his allies chosen to ambush me at my own home? I never recognized any of them that I could recall. Or was that another convenient slip of my mind? Had Kara or her secretive old boss taken that from me along with the entirety of my life with Frejarefn?

Well, I had some of that back now. The few memories broken through had opened others. I didn't recall everything. But at least I remembered the broad strokes around our life together. That was something else to think about. Were there other friends and family I did not remember?

From scared and confused I found myself getting angry. Is that why so many of the Einherjar were mindless zombies? Had they been scrambled too often until there was nothing of the man left inside the soldier? God or something else, what gave one the right to take away a man's memories? to erase whole sections of his life and use him for their own purposes?

Again, why had I been targeted? Was Lorcan already one of the Chosen when I met my untimely end? If so, what was the purpose? I was no king or jarl to lead men. I had no money or political power. Everything I could recall indicated I was an uncommonly strong and tough young Northman. I had a small bit of land and a boat for fishing. I had a few weapons gained through fighting for my people and our leaders. But no such power or acclaim to attract what was essentially a pre-gangland "hit".

That was all something to think about. But another thought pushed those considerations aside. Where was Maureen? Had she been injured trying to help me? I know she looked bad the last time I'd seen her on the other side of the dream veil. Had I stayed too long at her cost?

Struggling to me knees took some effort. Making it to my feet was almost beyond me. I managed though. It took two attempts to open the tent. Outside I saw the old man tending a battered and blackened pot of coffee and a cast-iron skillet on the coals of a campfire. The smell of bacon and fry bread almost brought me to my knees again.

"Sit." He pointed with an equally battered and blackened coffee cup. I managed to flop heavily down onto the rock he indicated. Even numb and exhausted I felt the jar all the way up my spine.

"This here's your coffee. Already had mine." He handed me the cup followed by a tin plate with toasted fry bread and a generous helping of the bacon. "Fried the bread in the bacon grease. Best thing for it. Get wrapped around that and then we'll talk."

I didn't question whether we were sharing dishes or even if they'd been wiped down a little between uses. I just did my best to inhale the food between imprudently large draughts of hot black coffee. Normally I like some sugar or maybe a little cream. Today the caffeine was in high enough demand not to ask for anything else.

"Girl's gone." He'd barely waited until I was halfway through the rough campfire sandwich. "Not coming back I reckon."

When I looked up with a sharp jerk of the head I saw
him nodding. "You prolly shoulda mentioned having a wife,
son. She heard you say it in your vision. Tired and weak as
she was you'd have thought even a redhead couldn't get any
paler. You'd be wrong. She turned about as white as them
clouds up there. Muttered something I couldn't catch a
while later and just left."

He took the empty cup from my hand and refilled it. The
coffee replaced the plate of food I was holding. Suddenly
the bacon and the bread didn't seem so delicious. In fact,
about all, I could taste was ash and the bile left over from
my earlier heaves. "Heard her this morning. Asked for a ride
back up to the main road. The boys drove her up a little
while back. Took the dog and the bird with her."

I carefully avoided his gaze. It wasn't easy. The old man
was looking at me like he could see right through me.
"That's only part of it though son. I saw part of your vision.
Should have been in control of it but sure wasn't expecting
you to go over that fast or that far. Best I could do was keep
an eye on ya and toss you that tether. Surprised hell out of
me when you got the lady inside. Don't think I ever heard of
the like. Maybe you was some kind of shaman too before got
your magnesia."

He squinted up at me as he lay back on one elbow.
"Here's the meat though. I saw stuff in there that scared the
crap outta this ole injun. Saw some other stuff too. Other
stuff was pretty normal. Things we don't wanna remember.
Things we just plain forgot cuz it ain't important. But your
scary stuff puts a whole new color on the spooky meter. For
me, it was mostly colors and energy. I could see what kind of
effort was put into things and what kind of energy came out
when you pushed too hard. To be honest I was just as glad
to be out here once I saw what you were finding on that

journey. But son, there's a lot more in there. Lots and lots of secrets locked away. I'd say almost all of em were hid back there by somebody other than you. Less you're one of them schizoid frantics people talk about. Anyway, I'd give it a little time before I went back in there. But I'd go get some of them memories about ever chance I got if I was you."

This time he rose and dusted off his pants. I saw him put the plate of food down on a log lying near the fire. "Eat that when you can. I'll be packing my stuff. Boys will be back this afternoon. We'll give you a lift back to the border or at least to the road if you're going the other way."

Sitting by the fire I considered that very carefully. Did I want to just go back across and make my way home? It sounded like I owed a certain redhead some explanations and very heartfelt apologies. If I was lucky I could get there before she emptied her stuff out of my house. Compared to that, I had a vague and elusive mission from a wolf masquerading as a man.

It wasn't as if I owed the wolf anything yet. I wasn't very impressed with his boss or associates at the moment either. Old Ygg and Kara had sent me to do some pretty dirty things in my time. I wasn't sure what all had happened, but if that last memory at Wounded Knee river was any indication I'd been one of the cruelest and most vile beings even I could remember meeting.

So I didn't like what they'd made of me. It didn't necessarily follow that I could do anything about it. Even in the memories that were still intact, Kara could play with my neurons like the light show at a concert. So my best bet was to keep on the job. Get the wolf off my back and avoid an early retirement back to Valhalla and the mind wipes. Right?

For a few minutes, it was hard to make myself agree with

that. Then the vision of a suckling child and a dead mother
came back. I did that, maybe I didn't shoot that exact native
but I'd pulled the trigger that started the whole thing. Did I
even deserve a woman at all much less someone like
Maureen? More importantly, did she deserve better than an
ancient serial killer?

BY THE TIME the kids arrived with transportation I'd made
my decision. When they left me off it was far from the
border along a dusty and barren stretch of highway.

"Take a couple of bottles of water Gringo." One of them
passed me a pair of one-liter bottles still attached by plastic
rings around their necks. "Don't take the road all the way.
Cut around that hill you see just to the right of the road.
You'll miss a border checkpoint. Once you're around that,
cut back in the arroyo there and you'll find a truck stop a
couple of miles down the road. Should be able to get a ride
from there to wherever you're going."

That, of course, brought me up short. Where exactly was
I going? I'd lost my guide back in Sedona. All I knew was
that my job was to get Gere, freaking Gere the immortal
wolf out of whatever trouble he couldn't manage himself. It
wasn't exactly like Mexico was small enough to walk around
asking people where I could find a wolf disguised as a thug
or whatever costume he was using. His brother had been
playing a biker of titanic proportions. Nobody had told me
anything about what part Gere was playing though.

I had an option. I could try and call the number Freke
had used to set me off on this roller coaster ride. I'd been
wise enough or lucky enough to write it down and stick it in
my shirt pocket. My shirt was gone now, but in the intervening days, I'd snuck a peek at the sticky note enough that

I thought I could remember the number. If I called back there maybe he'd give me the info to do the job.

With a plan in place, I made my way past the hill that supposedly screened me from any nosey checkpoint police. As directed, I found a narrow wash or arroyo and followed it for a good mile or more before it emptied out onto the road. The checkpoint was still hidden from view but to the south, I spotted a truckstop beside the dusty blacktop. If I'd been back in Texas I'd have suspected that very little traffic came this way. In the part of the world I was traveling though, just the presence of asphalt indicated there was probably a decent level of traffic.

Indeed there were close to a dozen vehicles of all shapes and price ranges in the parking lot of the battered and weathered old building. The older cars gave me hope. The trio of nice and fairly new looking Cadillac SUVs was something else entirely. If we were in Vegas I'd assume there were a rockstar and entourage inside. But this close to a checkpoint on a fairly decent route from Central America to the States? I was almost willing to bet there were cartel bigwigs around.

Three carloads seemed a little more than I wanted to confront even on my best day. Just a day or two from the brink of death, with my head twisted inside out, a world-class guilt trip and absolutely no gear or weapons? That just seemed like suicide. Still, nobody down here should recognize me.

That was obviously an erroneous assumption since I didn't even get in the door before someone hissed a warning at me through clenched lips. "PSST! Don't go in there, Gringo! Are you nuts? You go in there now and he'll kill you before you even know what the deal is."

I looked over to where my long lost guide Pedro Perro

was waving me frantically into the bathroom he had hidden in. Well, I really wanted a talk with the little dog turd anyway. It seemed a reasonable conclusion that he'd been responsible for every misery, mishap, and misunderstanding I'd experienced in several days.

All he had to do was guide me to my objective and tell me what the job was. I'd handle the rest. But instead, the little maggot had lost my weapons and gear, sidetracked halfway across the entire southwest, and gotten my ass royally pummeled by no less than a dozen angry bikers. Toss in my little delirious interlude in the desert and some sketchy introspection that ended my relationship and...well. I guess it probably didn't help that I was already mad.

I was pissed about Maureen. I was furious about the memories I'd had stolen. And I was torn to emotional or moral tatters by the actions that I now remembered cost hundreds of people their lives. The fact that fully half of those lives belonged to women and children just made it worse.

Good ole Perro barely cleared the door enough to let me in before he realized the mistake. I kicked the door shut with my heel and slapped the deadbolt closed with my left hand while my right locked like a vise around his scrawny throat. "Chickenshit, you're only breathing because if you weren't you couldn't tell me where and what the hell I'm supposed to do down here."

His heels were skittering on the floor a little which was surprising. He couldn't have been much shorter than I am. On the other hand, I noticed I was holding him almost overhead as if my hand were the noose at his impromptu toilet-side lynching. When I looked back up his face was turning some interesting shades of gray or blue or maybe purple.

There were hints of all three as well as some lovely scarlet tones around the bugged-out eyes.

With a stifled profanity, I dropped him back to his own feet. He staggered and massaged his throat before whispering savagely, "Wot the hell man!?"

My lifted hand in his face and a sharp stare cut him off short. "You probably should have considered this kind of reaction when you lost my gear and got my ass beat raw and bloody by a bunch of friends of your motorcycle escort."

He probably knew I wouldn't follow through with a direct threat. At least he figured he was safe until I knew the job. Still, he tried to move a few inches to the safer side of my own personal shit list. "Hey, now Gringo! I had to get rid of her cousin, the Harley guy! The girl didn't need his kind knowing where to find her or Abuela. Besides if you'd had that duffel bag when we got pulled over the checkpoint guards would have had you. They got dogs can smell drugs, bodies, guns, shit man I think they can smell bad intentions."

I gave him a little shake to indicate that I wasn't entirely convinced then stepped back against the door with my not inconsiderable arms crossed across my chest. "And the orgy of leather and denim-clad violence?"

"Whoa, now Mouse." It was the first time I'd ever heard him pronounce my name correctly so I was inclined to believe he was either serious or trying really hard to make me believe he was being straightforward and trustworthy. "Hey, we probably should have guessed those bikers were gonna be mad. All brotherhood of the road an all ya know? I ain't a biker though so my bad. Still, they didn't get off scot-free."

He shook his shoulders to straighten his coat and then looked at me with an appreciative grin. "Damn man I wasn't very confident when old Lobo told me he was sending one dude to deal with El Patron. But you're bad-ass eh bro? One of those guys had to ride back in a car. In the *back* of the car. You messed him up bad. Three or four others were limping and wearing casts. I saw the police report. Eyewitnesses and everything. You know if you plan to stay all incognito you might not wanna get described in a lot of police reports. Anyway, by the time I got there, all the fireworks had settled down. I managed to search your room. Got your clothes and stuff. Used a little green paper diplomacy to get some info from my cop buddy. Hey, I even cornered one of your victims and persuaded him to tell me what finally happened to the stocky little gringo. Man, he was *muy* scared of you."

If nothing else, old Perro knew how to sell a story and pull his audience along. Then again most audiences hadn't been through everything I had. I reached for his throat again but he sidestepped it nervously and continued. "Anyway, I figured out just about where they'd left you. Called your own biker buddy that I call Mr. Lobo and told him he was gonna need a new Mr. Fixer. He just laughed and asked me if I saw the body."

"Well Hell man, I hadn't seen the body but when those guys dump someone they generally don't last long enough to make an ID. Lobo just laughed some more and told me to find you. Said if there wasn't a body then you were still around and owed him this one. Also told me you won't be able to reach him for a while. Said to tell you he's sticking to his promise. You won't need to contact him and besides, he's gonna be outta touch for a while to make good on your deal." He finished straightening up any damage I might have done to his attire and leaned against the wall of the dingy truck stop restroom like some worn-out version of James Dean.

"So yea, here I am. Been waiting around for some kind of clue about how to find you and poof there you are all lean and mean and ready to eat me whole. But hey! I got you some replacements. We'll have to get out to the car and get them though. I got us a little beater car near the gas pumps. I'll go first and you follow a couple minutes later so nobody gets suspicious." He obviously forgot that I'd been victim to his vanishing act more than once now. Before he got his hand on the doorknob, I had the nape of his neck in my somewhat stern grip.

"Nope. We'll go together. But I'm gonna eat first." He started to sputter some sort of protest but by then we were marching out of the john and towards the little diner that inhabited one side of the truck stop.

"Asshole, everyone's gonna think we were being queer in there!" Apparently the fear of being branded homosexual was more terrifying than my grip or the sheer mayhem I'd almost merrily performed on and about his person. Which somehow seemed far fetched. I mean human smugglers shouldn't be worried about a little thing like their private tastes being made public right?

Despite his protests, I kept a grip on a certain bundle of nerves near his elbow and helped my "friend" up the curb and into a booth near the back. To be honest I was almost eager for one of the cartel types to start some trouble. I'd had the worst of it for a few days now. Having someone not only willing but deserving of a little retribution seemed like a perfectly grand pursuit for the time being.

Maybe they had better sense than I assumed, or maybe they just saw that I was an unknown variable with either no fear of them or a level of insanity they didn't want to deal with. The better-dressed group of men at their long table and private section didn't interrupt us even when we practically brushed against their table.

In fact, they seemed to avoid really noticing us at all until we were seated at our own booth. Perro immediately sat with his back to them and the high back of the bench providing a level of concealment. That didn't stop one of them from seeming to recognize the little smuggler and making a comment to the middle-aged man seated at the head of the table. I saw the perceptive guard type make a comment and gesture towards us. A few other eyes probed our way after that, including the gaze of what I assumed was the boss of this particular group.

He not only glanced, but he also locked eyes with me for a few very long seconds. Neither of us seemed willing to be the first to look away yet somehow we both managed to do so simultaneously. Maybe we had similar levels of predator floating back behind our eyes. Pedro noticed the exchange and his bronze face paled to a noteworthy degree.

"Sonofabitch! Look jefe, you wanna commit suicide by cartel you go right ahead. But pick a time when I ain't sitting with you ok? That's one stone-cold badass boss of badasses sitting over there. Don't do anything else to get their attention ok?"

That particular phrasing drew my attention more than almost anything else he'd ever said. Was that accurate? Maybe I really was trying to punish myself; take some abuse and get killed to go back and face the worst Kara and One-eye could come up with. I focused inward and was confused to discover I didn't know for sure that he was wrong. I'd say being distracted is what allowed things to develop as much as they did.

Apparently, the muttered conversation at the far table had reached a conclusion. I saw the first guy who spotted us rise and start stalking towards our table with a demeanor that would pass for glowering at least. He might even be able to sell it as intimidating to most people. Me? I wasn't in the mood to be intimidated.

I turned to the hesitant looking waitress by our table. A quick look at the menu triggered my appetite. My Spanglish was pretty bad but a guy built like me knows how to order food usually. "Enchiladas with frijoles por favor. No pappas, just a couple of tortillas. Oh and lots more coffee."

I turned back to the table and saw the thighs of Mr. Doomy McDoomface standing almost against the table. I didn't initially react. Instead, I got some cream and sugar into my coffee and took a big gulp. It wasn't the best coffee in the world. But it had the necessary bits to make me fairly content with the world at the moment.

Only after I'd savored the brew for a moment did I look up to squint at the enforcer or guard or whatever he was. I had to squint because the asshole had situated himself so that the lowering sun was right in my face when I looked at him. "Did you need something bud?"

I saw Perro fairly squirm in his seat before he made a patting gesture with his hand and then looked over with barely any trace of his customary smirk. "Hey there Mateo."

He looked back at me with one eye fairly twitching. "Gringo you talk pretty to Senor Mateo. He is a very important man where it counts. Just play nice and answer his questions."

I took a longer glance at Doomguy. He was wearing black combat fatigue pants, the kind I myself used sometimes and had been wearing in my role as a paramedic. Above that though was a very nice polo under a lightweight sports coat. He wasn't even trying to hide the holsters. He had one on his hip and a strap that obviously belonged to a shoulder holster.

I was betting on some kind of magnum at his hip and maybe one of those mini uzis or a Skorpion in the shoulder holster. When he leaned over to give me the icy glare at eyeball to eyeball range his jacket parted and I grinned. I was right, it was a Skorpion. A really wicked looking gun but useless at anything over a few meters and underpowered with the .32 caliber round. By comparison, the high dollar colt Anaconda on his hip was brutal. It would stop a rhinoceros, and the guy behind the rhino, and the car the guy was sitting in.

I switched my view from the hardware to his cold stare. "Yea I'm not great at pretty. Kind of blunt and unrefined. You need something, Matty?"

I heard my "ally" suck in a breath and override my previous statement with his own nervous energy. "Hey hey, now Gringo. Senor *Mateo* is one muy malo hombre. You don't start acting right and I'll let him eat you for breakfast."

I turned just enough to keep the cartel guy in my peripheral vision. Taking another drawn-out slurp of the coffee I spoke to Pedro. "You think your friend would mind if I eat something myself first? I'm about starved and it's been a bad couple of days."

The oily little weasel who'd gotten me into this mess just stared for a minute then a frown furrowed his brow. He tilted his head back to Mateo so I looked over. Pedro was doing the patting thing in the middle of the table again. Despite his attempts, it looked like ole Mateo and Mouse weren't going to get along. He had a flush starting along his jawline and I saw a blood vessel pulsing almost hypnotically in the side of his neck.

"Coyote, you need to come to pay respect to El Patron

Achilles." He followed that with a staccato burst of Spanish. In a rapid-fire exchange, I could only keep up with tones and emotions. The errand boy of "El Patron" was insistent and more than a little condescending. Pedro seemed intent on placating and being absolutely spineless. I had figured he wasn't much of a fighter but this little show made me want to curl my lip and kick his cowardly face in myself.

It appeared to be exactly what was expected from the drug dealing contingent though. They were all cracking broad smiles and sneering at his display. Since I was with him that meant they were sneering at me too. In other circumstances, I'd probably have ignored it. But there was that whole bad mood and angry at the world theme I had going.

When I stood up senor Mateo had little choice but to back up a step. I guess he could have just knocked me back to my seat. Then again sometimes I take a lot of knocking.

I was restrained from any kind of violence when the smuggler grabbed my forearm and used it to immobilize any violent intentions I might harbor. He disguised the movement by acting as if he used my help getting out of the relatively tight booth. Once he was up though he didn't let go so much as he ignored his grip on my sleeve and practically apologized to the big doofus with his ever so manly gun. "Por favor jefe, the gringo he is not really responsible. His girl left him. Left him for an older man. We all know how something like that feels don't we?"

His words went a whole lot further to lock me in place than his physical hold could have. What the hell did he know and how did he know it? And was he right? Did she run off with Uncle Bill and his gleaming grin? A minute later I realized he was just improvising. He just happened to have hit a little close to home. If I found out any differently then there would be Hel to pay. For now, though I'd go with the simplest explanation. That moment of frozen introspection though was enough to break the tension between me and the gunman for the local establishment.

He and Pedro had said a few more things that I only partially caught due to linguistic issues and my half-hearted attention. But I noticed that Pedro squared his shoulders like someone facing a firing squad before he turned away in preparation for approaching the crime boss. I couldn't help myself. I had to give the pathetic little figure at least a little support. "If my compadre here needs to go pay respects I'll tag along and nod whenever he tells me to."

Maybe Pedro wasn't as grateful as I'd like, but he did get up and walk with only half his normal swagger to the cartel section. He didn't even have to clear his throat or stumble over the words when he addressed the boss man. He did, however, dip his head low enough that for a minute I thought the sniveling weasel was going full renaissance bow for a minute. "Patron."

What followed was a slower but heavily accented Spanish that allowed me to understand just a few words here and there. There wasn't enough for me to make sense of what either of them had to say though. Finally, though Pedro backed up several steps before turning away and hurrying past our table. He dropped a few bills by the coffee cups and yelled something about keeping the change.

I started to object about my highly anticipated meal but he just grabbed my arm and pulled along like a skinny tugboat towing a much thicker cargo vessel. Outside he shoved me at an old international jeep with windows dirty enough to be economy window tinting. "Your new toys are in the back. Take a look and I'll get you something to go."

He didn't give me time to respond or ask any questions.

He just trotted back into the building. With time on my hands and a more than average level of interest in the "toys" he was providing, I delved into the back of the jeep to investigate. Old Pedro Perro and I had widely different views about hardware.

I pulled out a revolver that would have made old Mateo in the diner swell with pride. It was thick, massive even. The barrel was probably six inches, and it was obviously larger caliber. I looked at the barrel and saw .454 printed in an italicized script along its side. So one of the largest and most powerful handgun rounds you can find. Ok, it would do for stopping the SUVs if they pursued. Reloading time was hell though. A second glance identified it as the beefed-up South American version of my own little .410/.45 revolver.

Unfortunately, the revolver was the grand prize within that gear. There was some oversized hunting knife made of Pakistani steel stuffed in a cheap imitation leather sheath. It was guaranteed to break if it hit anything tougher than tender roast beef.

There was a pump-action shotgun that had obvious soldering iron marks near the pump. I worked the pump back and forth a few times using the button under the action that allowed just such misuse. The pump of course stuck and had to be wiggled just right to feed another shell.

And finally, for armaments, there was a vintage-looking lever-action "repeating rifle" with the octagon barrel. It was chambered for .45 so I guess I'd be slinging large chunks of lead at anyone who annoyed me. At least if it was one of the vintage guns the thing was known for the kind of accuracy you rarely see today. A good bolt action or semi-auto would make me regret missing any first shots though.

Okay maybe there was one more weapon in the bag but I hardly considered it such. It was a copper looking predecessor to the tactical tomahawk I'd used in certain overseas locations doing things that it's best not to talk about. This one looked as old or older than the lever-action. It had a number of beads worked into some sort of wrap around mid handle. There were fetishes and beads and even a feather or two dangling here and there. So yea, I didn't really consider it an armament.

Still...I tucked it behind my back with the handle diagonally through a belt loop. It hung horizontally above my butt like an old seax except the blade was down instead of up. Sure it wasn't a weapon of choice but the thing just had a reassuring feel to it and kept those memories I had just uncovered from going back to sleep. I guess I can be a little weird and superstitious but hey...nigh immortal chosen warrior here. We're allowed.

While I was getting comfortable with the least impressive looking bit of some truly uninspired weapons, my guide made it back to the vehicle. He tossed two bags into the back seat and then swore steadily and with rising impatience at the jeep ignition until the thing finally started. We didn't quite spin the tires or sling gravel but I think that had more to do with the rusted block of an engine than it did Perro's restraint on the gas pedal.

All he finally said as we exited the parking lot was, "After you eat you can get out of those hand me down clothes. I couldn't get your other stuff back because it was held for evidence but I got your duffel full of clothes."

Right then he moved down several spots on my personal shit list. I could just imagine the sneak and apparent coward entering the blood-spattered shambles of that Hotel room. Even worse he might have had to go to his contacts in the police. I couldn't even imagine how much anxiety something like that would have caused him. I found the first few shreds of respect for him.

"I gave the housekeeper twenty bucks to get me the stuff the cops hadn't taken in yet. She found your duffel kicked behind the dresser." Somehow he just couldn't help bursting my bubbles.

"Does that mean you got a mechanic to fix my dinner?" I tilted the rumpled brown bag towards him so Perro could see the bag full of oil and dirt grimed cables.

"No those are SUV distributor caps. Your tacos are in the other bag. Got a six-pack of Amber beer too. Crack me one of those when you get a chance." He said it like sneaking around Cartel vehicles and disabling them was just no big deal. My head was starting to spin trying to figure out if the guy was a crawling coward or some kind of sneaky hero. I gave up the process and focused on feeding the metabolism that was burning extra hot with all of the necessary recuperation. Of course, as a responsible guest, I opened a beer and handed it to my driver.

After my first few tacos, Perro looked over with a quirk of that expressive brow. "Hey jefe, save one or two for your partner eh?"

A glance into the bag confirmed that I'd eaten almost the entire contents. Almost sheepishly, I handed over the bag with a couple of last tacos inside as well as a single container of hot sauce. "Sorry. They're pretty damned good by the way."

He grunted a nonanswer and fished in the bag with his free hand while he steered with the wrist that ended in a fist wrapped beer. Before he stuffed half a taco into his mouth he spoke once more. "Duffels in the floorboard behind me. Help yourself. It's your stuff after all."

"Okay Senor Perro," My voice was momentarily cut off as I pulled one of my own better fitting and much newer and cleaner shirts over my head. When I craned my head around to get thick arms into tight sleeves I caught sight of his scowl.

"Mr. Dog does not ring with respect and admiration my pale Yankee amigo." He deftly maneuvered the vehicle around a prodigious bit of broken asphalt that could only charitably be called a pothole. "And to answer your unspoken question. Yes, they are likely to connect me with their broke down luxury jeeps. Good thing there ain't no mechanic closer than a few hours away. They won't be able to chase us. Should be for long enough to escape. I just gotta give them a good long time to forget they're mad at me. Like maybe until most of those guys are dead. Good thing they live fast and die young eh? For now, though it appears that your business has cost me part of my business. Make sure you express my unhappiness to your shaggy friend when you talk to him."

I wasn't sure either of us was really considering the biker and immortal wolf Freke as a friend. I was willing to bet he had something to hold over Pedro's head just like he had something on me. Wolves don't tend to have many friends within their own pack. They usually had even fewer outside of the pack. On the other hand, the smuggler's comments opened the door for some of my own questions. I thought I'd start fairly easy. " So is that your real name? Pedro Perro? Sounds like a comic book character."

"Says the guy named Moose?" He quirked that eyebrow at me again but at least this time there was a grin at his verbal dig. "Besides, Pedro Perro is alot better than the opposite. I mean Peter Dog? Sounds alot better than Dog Peter don't it?" He chuckled and took a drink that emptied a good quarter of his beer.

With a shrug, I moved on to more important topics. "You're gonna have to tell me what the job is some time, chief. I looked over that gear and unless we're knocking over a gas station I'm not sure we're adequately equipped."

His further series of chuckles confirmed my suspicion that he knew what kind of junk he'd given me. "No big deal, man. You just gotta go into a cartel compound built around an old bunch of ruins like a mini-pyramid ya know? Avoid or eliminate a bunch of spooky bad-ass hired soldiers, find out what the hell everyone is hiding down there. Oh, and get your biker buddy's brother out of wherever he disappeared. No problem for a super merc and international man of mystery eh Mr. Moose?"

9

PERRO SURVIVED my initial reaction which was to shoot him full of large and debilitating holes. Ok, it was only a thought which I did not put into action. I did think about it for one brief and gloriously satisfying moment though. "Ok smuggler. Now that I caught my breath, you're going to have to give me a soupcon more info."

"Yea you really lost it there for a minute." He grinned sideways at me. "Your nostrils started flaring like a bull. This great big purple vein started pulsing all around your head. Oh and you pointed a hand at me and kept squeezing your pointer finger back and forth. I wasn't sure you were coming back for a minute there."

"I'm not sure I'm all the way back yet." To emphasize the point I carefully opened the cylinder of my shiny new quarter ton revolver and spun the cylinder. I pulled out one of the shotgun shells and considered it then slipped it back in. The beast ended up loaded with three of those small red plastic shells carrying a handful of small ball bearings each. After that went two old .45 long colt shells, and finally a single intimidating fat and ugly .454.

That last one was suitable for stopping cars, or water buffalo.

The familiar actions of weapon maintenance steadied my nerves and voice. "So, what kind of freaking suicide mission did you just describe to me? Don't leave out any details you know, got it?"

Good old Pedro didn't gulp or anything when he saw me loading the handgun. He did however carefully look at each round as it went in. It might have been safer watching the road. On the other hand, in the mood I was in, it might not have been safer after all. He did lose some of his smirk when he finally replied though.

"Ok jefe, it's like this." He paused to light a cigarette from the butt of his almost defunct smoke. "Your buddy Lobo's brother down there was doing some work for some pretty bad people. The same kind of people we just ran into and probably pissed off at the truckstop."

His grin was apparently almost irrepressible because it snuck back while he remembered disabling the trucks. "Anyway, everything was all hunky-dory until he found out about some of the uh...side business. Apparently, he don't mind killing or drugs or even some polite blackmail and leg breaking. Really progressive thinker Mr. Gary."

I noticed his name for the other wolf. It made me wonder if the wolf was being cute or if Perro knew more than he was telling. Then again I'm pretty sure Pedro Perro always knew more than he told. It also sounded just as arrogant as one of these guys to use his real name with just a little twist on the accent.

"So here we are with Mr. Gary doing a lot of work for the big Cartel boss. And then things go sideways. Mr. Gary, he finds out about the sex slaving. Turns out he got a soft spot for the ladies. Doesn't mind em whoring around if they

want. Got a problem with them being sold like cattle." Perro
shrugged and a look of distaste replaced the smirk for a
minute. "Don't really like that part myself."

He let his mind wander for the space of two or three
drags of the cigarette then got back to the topic. I decided
not to interrupt his thoughts since this was maybe the first
time I'd ever seen the little bundle of snark act anything like
a real person. "So there we are. Mr. Gary lost his taste for the
work. Sitting around stewing about all the little mamacitas
getting roped in and turned over to kinky old men without
any say in it. And he meets the boss's little sister. She wasn't
real old. Just out of her teens. But that made her older than
some of the girls getting sold. They get in an argument one
day at a coffee shop. He's mad because she's safe while her
brother sells girls almost half her age. She's mad because
he's yelling at her and she don't know why. They yell. They
calm down. They go to dinner. Next morning he sneaks her
back to her room."

The grin made it back suddenly. "Best way to get their
attention is to piss em off then turn around and make it up
to em eh?"

"Perro my friend. We'll talk about women and pissing
em off shortly. For now, let's concentrate on your info." I
hadn't forgotten his little tidbit about me and my girl being
at odds. We'd get around to that eventually. I wanted to
know how he knew about Maureen and what he knew that I
didn't. That might not get me killed though. Not knowing
about what I was heading into probably would get me
deader than a Klanner in Harlem.

He tossed me a weird confused glance then continued.
"Ok, so that's the first bit of trouble. Gary's being surly and
he's spending time with the boss's sister. That's bad. But
then he finds out there's some auction gonna take place.

Somehow the boss got hold of some weapon or weapons. I'm a little confused about that part. It's all hush-hush need to know and die before you tell kind of secret."

While he talked Perro finished his beer and fished another one out of the bag without bothering to look. "Well, Gary does some digging. The boss finds out and sends a few of these merc guys after him. He wanted to talk to Gary about snooping in his business. But the mercs never come back. So the boss, he calls in his personal troops."

He took a long drink then gave me perhaps the single most sincere look I'd seen in him. "The mercs are bad but not the worst thing the boss can do. He has at least a couple dozen of these guys. Real weirdos. Throwbacks to bygone days or something. They all get the tattoos and talk Nahuatl instead of Spanish, act like real Aztecas you know? Sneer at the white or blonde Mexicans. Look down their hooked noses at anyone not as brown as them, not as dark-haired or dark-eyed. Got real hard-ons for taking back "the empire". Crazy bastards ya know? Got no morals. Sell drugs, guns, women it don't matter. They don't just *tolerate* killing and hurting. Those bastards get off on it."

He shook his head and drank some more. "Any-way...these bastards go looking for Mr. Gary and he disappears. Nobody talks about it. Don't know if they got him and hid him somewhere or he lit out. The boss was mad enough about the mercs that nobody wanted to ask him. Nobody asks. Nobody talks. Nobody mentions Mr. Gary's name no more. And the sister, nobody seen her in a while either."

Neither of us had much to say for the next little while. He seemed unaccustomed to feelings of remorse, or sadness or maybe it was worry. I was busy processing information. A little voice inside me was clamoring to move onto the topic of my estranged lady love. That part got shoved back into a dark corner of my thoughts while I worked on staying alive for now.

After all, why worry about the girl if I wasn't going to be alive long enough to do anything about it anyway. From the information I'd just received, an angry ex-girlfriend was the last thing I needed to be concentrating on. Mercs were bad enough. I'd spent some time with them overseas while I got my feet under me after Vietnam.

Getting your feet under you when you wake up in a field hospital surrounded by people from another time and place can be...trying. The language barrier wasn't that difficult. Even before Kara found me I'd had a gift for languages. Maybe that was one of the reasons they left my noggin more intact than some of my brethren.

They also had a tendency to give us speaking primers to help us pass for normals in some assignments. So my English wasn't great but it was understandable beneath the accent. After "Nam" the folks I worked and fought with didn't seem to notice anything odd about my speech. They did notice what they called my "primal brutality man, just brutal".

That didn't mean I was nastier or more vicious than the others. There were some trophies that I found disgusting. Ears seemed a favorite. What they meant was, I had no problem going hand-to-hand with a variety of weapons as opposed to their clear preference for firearms and explosives. The mercenaries I traveled with though, weren't exactly lightweights in the martial arts. Some of them were good, very good.

If these fanatical cartel guys were supposed to be better than the professional soldiers of fortune then I needed to be very careful. Maybe in this instance, my old mercenary comrades were right. A sniper rifle and some hand grenades might be a better choice than an ancient tomahawk and a revolver. "Okay Pedro, if that's all true then we're going to have to get hold of some better gear. I'm not backing out. I made a deal and if I don't follow through then maybe nobody trusts me again. More importantly, I wouldn't trust me anymore."

"Buddy, we got worse problems than your trust issues." Pedro had gone from his introspective quiet to something much more tense while I was lost in my own thoughts. He pointed into the rearview mirror and then behind us. "Shoulda done something about their phones I guess."

When my head snapped around it took less than a few seconds to notice the large black helicopter coming down the road just fifty or sixty feet above the broken roadway. I didn't see any markings from our angle. "Cops maybe?"

Pedro barely managed to give me a scornful look of disbelief. "Even if it was the policia, half of them work for the Cartels. No that's our friends from the truck stop. And they're mad. Maybe I should have left the cars alone eh?"

For once he didn't bother smirking. Instead, he hunched over the wheel of the dilapidated old truck and stepped on the gas. I wasn't exactly surprised by the engine power in the beast. Okay, maybe a little surprised. The engine sputtered once or twice but then it gave a throaty growl and surged ahead. The speed seemed a little superfluous. There weren't many cars around that were going to outrun a helicopter, especially in broken desert terrain where they could go in a straight line and keep an eye on us from above.

But maybe I underestimated the little smuggler. He took off for the more rugged terrain in the foothills nearby. We left the road just a minute or two after he spotted the chopper. Once more, it didn't seem like a great option. Even if they lost sight of us they could follow the dust trail.

He thought of that too. Instead of going in a straight line Pedro pulled the wheel in a wide circle. The dry flat dust we were on clouded above us and came in through the windows thick enough to choke. He circled a dozen times in increasing arcs of travel before sliding to a halt.

I heard his door open, I worked my own seatbelt and abruptly jerked the door handle away in my hand. I was still choking while he scrambled away. Finally, I gave up on my broken door and shoved across the seat to wrench his door back open. I was half falling and scrambling from the car when I heard him. Unfortunately, I couldn't tell which direction it came from when he yelled "This way."

When in doubt, rush headlong into folly. That seems to have been my policy for a while now. I ducked back and got my bag of mayhem then headed into what looked like a wash or dried creek bed under the cloud of dust. He'd kicked up enough of the surface desert that it might hang between us and the aerial recon for a half hour. Or it might blow away in the next few minutes.

I slung the duffel and stuffed the revolver into my belt. It felt nice in my hand but I might need hands free for climbing or slapping branches out of my way as they appeared out of the dust. That was a real consideration as I started running into the crevice between two low ridges. My feet dug into the sand rippled from water flowing long ago. Now it was dry as old bones and just about as fun to walk on. It didn't snap underfoot but it certainly turned ankles and caught toes.

I was still looking at my toes when a series of holes appeared ahead of them accompanied by more puffs of dirt and rock. One particularly evil fragment of rock decided to embed itself in my shin as I stumbled to a halt. The pain was almost enough to make me ignore other things. Like the sound of automatic weapons fire that explained the holes in the dirt.

I spun around with the big revolver rising from where I'd snatched it out of my belt. That big-bore round would do terrible things to a helicopter. Rotors, tails, engines or even a good shot at the cockpit should deter the pilot or even bring the thing down. My hand was extended skyward while I searched with my ears for the incoming aircraft.

I should have been looking lower. At least three of them came out of the dust aimed right at me. The first one was stocky but shorter even than my own disappointing height. Instinctively I clubbed at him with the revolver.

It caught him coming in fast. His sturdy little legs were driving him forward like a little puffing steam engine when the butt of the revolver struck with a hollow-sounding thunk right above his eyes. Those same dark eyes rolled back in his head while he slammed into me. I half turned with the impact and saw another short silhouette holding some kind of carbine or machine-pistol. That one was lining up on me and yelling something in Spanish when my flailing arm brought the revolver sights across his chest.

The noise was horrendous. It hurt like hell in my unprepared wrist and forearm but the silhouette simply dropped like crumpled cloth. No time to worry about broken wrist bones though. I heard the third one coming in from behind me now. That was how far the first guy had spun me I guess. This one came in fast but once more my instinct kicked in.

Maybe I'd caught a glimpse of him or heard his breath coming out above me. Whatever the reason, I knew this one was a full head taller than me or either of his buddies. Instead of swinging, I ducked lower and drove back while turning my shoulder into his rush. I felt the impact of his thighs against my chest while his belt line hit me across the shoulder.

That made it seem like a dandy idea to toss him over my shoulder. So I did. From my bent position, it was easy to wrap a hand around his legs and straighten myself with his own momentum helping. I'd seen a move from some football player on the television back at the bar. He had a guy just like I held this one, and he just spun and held on while the other guy slammed into the turf.

This was no turf, and my guy wasn't wearing pads or a helmet. He got a kick into my ribs on the way down. If I'd been healthy it would have been laughable. Having recently had my ribcage kicked out of shape by bikers made it less humorous. I felt an ominous creaking and just maybe a snap down low on the left side of those ribs. It caught my breath I'll have to admit. I probably even winced a little. I know I winced when I heard the nasty sound of my wrestling buddy hitting the dry washboard dirt headfirst.

I looked up from the ground and saw that none of my three pursuers were moving. It seemed like a good time to vacate the area. Standing up hurt. Those same ribs were catching my breath although I didn't think they were broken anew. Just too sore from the last break to take the kind of abuse they were getting. So with a hand trying to splint that side of my chest, I stumbled in a random direction until I saw Pedro Perro waving at me from the end of the wash I was following.

The relief at seeing him was short-lived though. Another shot rang out. This one sounded like a shotgun and the pattern of flying bark and shredded tree to my right agreed with that assessment. An instant later a bullhorn echoed words at me in Spanish followed by what sounded like the same command in English. "This is the Policia. Halt or we shall shoot to kill."

I watched as Pedro faded into the shadows and underbrush ahead of me. Apparently, the cop behind me didn't see my guide. There were no more shots. I also decided that the tree was not collateral damage but a demonstration. They didn't miss me and shoot it. They were making sure I saw what kind of weapon I was dealing with.

I decided not to gamble. With hands in the air, I turned to face what looked like half a dozen guys in police uniforms complete with vests and helmets as well as AR rifles in most of their hands.

The one with the bullhorn was medium height but above medium girth. His face was flushed, probably from the exertion of climbing out of the chopper and following on foot. He looked like the type to enjoy his desk more than a helicopter. On either side of him were two of the cops not carrying rifles. They each had a large bore shotgun trained at approximately the middle of my chest.

"Senor, lift your hands, and do not move." His voice was almost petulant between gasping breaths. He probably blamed me for the stroke he seemed about to have. Or maybe he'd seen one of his men with a beer can sized hole where my .454 had exited his back. It seemed imprudent to test either his mood or the aim of his men. I raised my hands.

One of the closest riflemen approached and relieved me of...what the hel had I done with the revolver? He searched me and found a knife but that was about it. That didn't stop him from giving me a nice shot to the kidneys with his rifle butt before he returned to the chief cop on site.

"No ID eh Yankee? Why you gotta keep secrets?" He studied the knife and with a nod slipped into his pocket.

Somehow I didn't think it as going to make it to the evidence lock-up. When he was through examining my fairly meager possessions as well as my distinctly non-Latino face he nodded sharply and gestured with a pudgy hand. "Get him back to the cars. I'll get the pilot to drop me off at the airport and call a taxi."

With that, he turned away and started waddling back to where I assume the helicopter waited. That meant he didn't see the rifle take me in the kidneys again. Or any of the other assorted rifle butts, boots, flashlights and sundry other objects bounce me along from the scene of the arrest to the back of a fairly nice looking black and white SUV. I bled on the seats as a form of protest.

10

IF ANYONE SUGGESTS SPENDING some vacation time in Mexico, make sure it's nowhere near one of their famous correctional facilities. The scenery sucks and service consists of food that even the rats view suspiciously. At that, the rats are better company than the guards. At least where I was concerned.

In the States, prisoners are allowed some time in a courtyard or other open area for exercise and such. I discovered my exercise regimen consisted of two to four beatings a day. I must say all of that practice had made my guards fairly professional. They could dish out a great deal of pain without permanently disabling or even leaving that many marks on a prisoner.

Fortunately, they only plied their trade for a few days before I got my first visitor. It was odd because the guard came to pick me up and take me to the infirmary. Apparently, someone had begun to worry about the sundry and assorted damage and wanted to get me well enough to beat some more.

That sounded like both a very good idea and a very

ominous forecast for my future; except we never made it to
the infirmary. Instead, the guard took me straight to the visitors' room. He stepped between me and another guard
escorting a different prisoner. It looked like a natural adjust-
ment in the narrow corridor but it kept them from seeing
me, and vice versa. A few minutes later he looked through a
thick window in the middle of a door. With a nod, he
ushered me into a room with nothing except a table and
three or four chairs, and one Pedro Perro wearing his snazzy
leather coat and a smirk along with much more comfortable
looking clothes than my own.

"Hey, gringo! Thanks for inviting me. Love what you've
done with the place. You lose some weight or the bruises
just make it look that way?" He was already sitting at the
worn old table and gestured to the chair opposite him.

I couldn't help myself. I looked around astonished and
maybe even just a little alarmed "Are you crazy man? You
should be avoiding me like the plague. They find out we
know each other and it just leads to more questions."

He caught the glance over my shoulder at the guard who
had escorted me. The guard had turned around however
and was retreating outside to watch through the little
window in the door. Pedro's voice turned me back around.
"Don't worry. His English is horrible. Barely able to tell you
to come with him."

He gestured to the seat again and waited until I sat
down with my pulse barely slowing from the racing pace it
had achieved. "Like I said, don't worry. I'm not visiting you.
I'm on the books as visiting another guy. He's someone I
knew from other umm...jobs. So there's no record of us talking. The guard that brought you is the only guy I bribed a
little. I also got some info that might get him hurt so he
won't tell if I don't. So sit down and let's get this done quick.

We're good for a little while. Just don't need to push our luck."

If it had been anyone else I might have doubted them. But this little weasel had more tricks and twists than anyone I'd met. That was saying something when you consider that I spent a few centuries with not only some of the brawniest warriors but some of the sneakiest and most conniving divine beings. I sat and leaned across the table. "Hate to admit it but I'm glad you got away."

He looked over at me with a deadpan expression and replied. "Don't go soft and sweet on me Moose. We ain't got time for foreplay."

When I grinned he just chuckled and got down to business. "We gotta get you out of here. I've got some ideas but wanted to talk to you first. So whatcha think?"

I paused for a minute while I thought about the kind of plans this little bundle of chaos might come up with. The problem was my imagination probably wasn't big enough for some of his solutions. While I don't cry over unavoidable collateral damage, I do try and limit the chances it might happen. I'm pretty sure Pedro Pero never thought past the *"wouldn't it be cool if"* stage of planning.

"Smuggler I'm damned glad to see you. But we need to do this as discreetly as possible. I don't want to send out any red flags to our targets. So here's a number. Call this guy and tell him you need money. He's good for whatever it takes. Tell him I'll owe him one. If it gets me out of here I might even fill in some of those blanks he's curious about. Tell him that and then get the money and bribe my way out of here. The sooner the better. I can take a few more days at this pace but they might get tired of this pace and up the ante. I imagine they aren't too happy about a cop-killer." I scrawled Eachan's cell number on an index card awkwardly with my hands chained together but it was legible. Pushing the paper across I looked up to see a grim expression replacing his normal jocularity.

"You didn't kill a cop, Mr. Moose. If you think back you'll probably remember that the guys you put down weren't wearing uniforms. Not like the cops that arrested you. You killed one of the Cartel guys trying to get to us before you got arrested." For some reason the thought of a criminal dying to my shot was comforting. Not only did it mean I had shot what most people would consider a bad guy. It also meant I hadn't killed a cop.

He didn't give me long to feel that relief. "There's new players in the game Gringo." He got up and gestured me to join him at the small window on the outer wall.

Outside I could see one of the black SUVs just like those he'd disabled. "One of our old friends is already calling. They're probably searching your cell right now. They'll look all over the common areas and if they don't find you the alarms will go off."

I couldn't believe my ears at first. "Well, thanks for sharing that info as soon as possible. It's not like that's something I should be worried about eh?"

I barely had the words out before the aforementioned alarms started to blare. A PA system overhead burst into excited Spanish. Seconds later we heard boots slapping the concrete as the guards sprang into action. There were yelling and the sound of glass breaking, as well as doors, slamming shut.

"What the hell? All this for one Gringo without ID?" I looked at the windows to the outside. That was fruitless. Those apertures were all head high and too narrow for even someone like Pedro to get through. My head might have made it, or maybe just my neck. There was no way I was getting even one shoulder through though. He stopped me with a surprisingly strong grip above the elbow while I was looking around.

"This one ain't you. There's a riot in the cafeteria. They're going to lockdown which means we gotta get you out of here." Almost as an afterthought, he added. "Me too."

The door opened to admit my guard looking more frantic than I felt. He engaged my old smuggler buddy in rapid-fire Spanish and was answered in kind. I only caught a few words because of the pace probably. "Ok go with him. He's gonna get you to the infirmary. You had a sharp pain in your chest and couldn't catch your breath. Got it?"

Before I could answer the guard tugged me out of the room with an insistent grip on my upper arm. I didn't resist when he checked my cuffs then hustled me out. It took a few minutes of dodging guards running down the narrow hallways. We finally made it to the infirmary where the guard passed me off to a harried-looking older doctor. He had me chained to an old battered treatment table and turned away. His priorities seemed to center around getting the pair of females in the clinic out.

I couldn't really blame him. It didn't take a lot of imagination to picture what could happen to women in a place like this. Many of these guys had no hope of ever seeing the outside again. One of the two was relatively young and not unattractive. The other one had probably been attractive in her youth but she was at the point where middle age was leaning away from youth entirely. I doubt some of the prisoners would have even noticed. For their purposes just about any woman would probably do.

I stayed quiet and out of the way while the doctor helped them gather their stuff and slip down a hallway with one of the guards as an escort. I noted his shotgun with some caution. If I had that weapon I could probably make it out with the women. He never even came close to me though. I watched the gun and the potential victims escape out of sight and hopefully out of harm's way. At least I didn't hear any shotgun booms echoing off the stone walls.

The old doctor didn't leave. He probably figured he was safe compared to the women. Depending on what had set the prisoners off he might be right or he might be terribly wrong. Anyway, he managed to give me a thorough inspection considering the complete lack of equipment and generally shoddy environment. At least his English was good enough for us to communicate. His poking at my ribs got a few grunts and stunted breaths. I answered his questions fairly honestly. Apparently, beatings like mine weren't the norm. They even seemed fairly rare. He knew about it and didn't approve but we both knew there was nothing he could do about it. A doctor's note saying "Please excuse Magnus from beatings for three days" was unlikely to garner much respect.

He had just finished taping the tenderest part of my ribs when the door burst open and a handful of guards pushed in. Two of them leveled weapons at me, one shotgun and one AR. The third lifted an old fashioned walkie-talkie with its stubby black antenna and spat a rapid-fire string of Hispanic words into it. The beat-up black box spat right back at him only to be interrupted by the doctor working on me. His Spanish was slower but barely less incomprehensible to me.

I caught that he was telling them I'd been there and he was almost done. Something like "shut up and let me finish" came across even though I wasn't sure what the words actually were. It was close enough. The lead guard with his venerable radio spoke into it again a lot slower and with less spit and breathless excitement. I caught the reply from the crackling box. It amounted to "get him back to his cell ASAP."

It turns out that a big enough brawl in the exercise area of such an establishment is considered a riot. Even in sketchier Mexican facilities, such an event means a lockdown. Most prisoners are locked in their cells or other secure areas if it's deemed safer. I was moved from the infirmary to my cell quickly and just a touch furtively. It seemed like maybe they weren't supposed to be moving me during the lockdown. From a few words I caught, it also seemed they didn't want to take a chance on losing me. Someone thought maybe this was a distraction for a prison escape and nobody quite knew who I was or what to do with me so they wanted me nice and tucked away.

I found out later that all visitors had been rushed out. That must have included the guests arriving via Cartel SUVs. I never saw the guys looking for me. More to the point, they never saw me. Instead, I was back in the dark of my isolated cell. The best part was, due to the doctor, or the riot, or just random uncertainty, I didn't have any sadistic visitors that night. For the first time since I saw that chopper, I got some rest and just lay there thinking about my situation until sleep took over.

MAYBE IT WAS all of the stress or the injuries. Maybe I had just exhausted some of my normally limitless vitality. Whatever the reason, I slept the entire night until the metal grate slid open to deliver my meal. It wasn't even gruel this time. I mean it wasn't good. It wasn't even good for cheap food. But it had most of the required nutrients in one form or another.

You know you've had it bad when dry tortillas and runny powdered eggs seem extravagant and delicious. I was still sopping up eggs and some refried beans with a partially burned tortilla when a surprise visitor showed up. The door opened almost instantly with just the merest pause for unlocking. In filed a pair of the guards who had merrily pummeled me while I was either tied or handcuffed to a sturdy metal chair. Behind them, the fat police officer from the chopper waddled in. One of the guards grabbed my chair and held it for fats while the other pointed at the bunk with his unholstered sidearm.

"Please Senor, have a seat." The officer was much more pleasant while sitting than he had been after hiking around the sandy foothills near the border. He lit a slender brown cigar or cigarillo then offered me one. There are times that I think a good cigar or pipe enhances a situation. Sitting on a squalid and verifiably infested thin mattress in a dark and odorous Mexican jail or prison cell is not one of those situations. I shook my head and waited while he puffed a couple of times.

"Senor, I have come to negotiate. My men quite enjoy beating your Yankee ass. It's almost like a break or...what do you call? Entertainment for them. Yes, that's it. They find it quite entertaining. However, they have not been productive in their...entertainment. And I do not care one way or the other, except I want to be more productive." He gave me what was supposed to be an encouraging smile. It didn't do much to bolster my goodwill though.

He continued as if I was smiling back. "So I wish to ask you just a handful of questions, and then we will cease with the beatings for now if you answer truthfully."

This time he waited and appraised me while I considered. "Depends on the questions El Capitan."

"Very good. Now we are negotiating!" His smile was much more charming and perhaps a tad smug. "We must simply come to terms. So here are my questions. What is your name? Where are you from? What were you doing in my country? And who were you doing it for?"

He waited with that genial smile thinly covering a very intent awareness. I couldn't help but think he already knew something. I just had no idea what. That's one of the problems with changing your identification and paperwork several times in your life. It's not always easy to remember who you are and what your papers say.

"Ok Senor Capitan." I stopped when he waved a hand as if shooing away an insect.

"You may call me Senor Martinez or just senor. My rank

is of no consequence here." He beamed that friendly and oh so fake smile again then gestured with a rolling motion of his hand. I assumed he meant for me to carry on.

"Ok senor. My name is Magnus Gustaveson. I'm from Texas. Work in Austin as security at a bar. And I came down to drive with one of my boss's friends. The friend was cautious about some kind of errand he had to run down here. I was told his name was Armando but I'm not sure if it was or not." I kept it fairly simple and gave him just enough truth that he could verify. The untrue bits were going to be harder to track down. I happened to know that my boss Roy had gone out of town for a few weeks. Some kind of family emergency and he wasn't expected back for another few weeks. Normally I'd have been in charge during his absence. Now the bar was in the hands of the senior bartender and the senior waitress combined.

As for my own history, well I thought it was pretty well buried due to the considerable gifts my hacker friend Wild Bill had with computers and databases. Apparently, I missed something though. The officer shook his head with a sad look on his face.

"I'm afraid you are lying senor Guztav." The name probably reminded him of Guzman or some such. He pronounced it with a decidedly softer z sound than I would have used. "We know you were with a known smuggler and scoundrel. We have no record of you passing any of our border checks. And you ran like the wind from my men. This does not make you look like an innocent man."

"Hey, I can explain all of that!" My mind was racing and I had formulated about half a dozen possible answers to his accusations. He put a hand up to silence me before I got good and started though.

"Do not bother working on your lies today senor Guztav.

We will, of course, check into your story. I have no doubt it is mostly a thin tissue of lies that will fall apart under scrutiny. For now, the men will cease their entertainment as well. Our little bit of excitement in the recreation yard has brought visitors that must not know about some of our, little activities. So...you can remain here and be silent to escape their notice. Or I can have my men drop your body off near the closest resort. Another tourist lost in the bad part of town. Such a tragedy."

I looked at the floor and took a deep breath. Was it time to take a calculated risk? It didn't seem like I could hurt my position much. "Okay so I'll give a little and you think it through."

A little dramatic pause seemed in order so I gave it a few seconds. Gotta let the bait dangle a bit sometimes. "I might know more about what my "associate" was doing down here. I might. If you kill me, well you'll never know what I know. Will you?"

The silence grew heavy in my cell. Apparently, I wasn't the only one who put stock in the dramatic pause. But the old horse-trading rule is; never be the first to talk when it gets down to the final deal. He broke first. "You are very bold Yankee. We will give you a few days to think things over. In fact, I shall make sure you are fed well and get some time in the yard. Under close supervision with orders to kill no? You can see what your time here could be like. And you will think about what it would be like to have one of these men butcher you like a goat and dump the mess into the water eh?"

Martinez rose with a polite nod for me. His guards got more of a curt jerk of his head which had them scrambling. They hastily managed to get the door opened and their boss out in a manner to suit his apparently demanding nature.

They had both been loud and aggressive, beating me when I was restrained. With this portly little police commander though they seemed, perhaps not terrified, but at least very anxious to please. It made me wonder exactly what position he held in the law enforcement hierarchy.

It must have been a fairly exalted position. Martinez was true to his word and I received edible and basic nutrition for three meals that day. There was maybe an excess of beans and rice. From what I'd read though, beans and rice were just about as good as meat for a protein source. I ate everything they gave me. Once I got out of this hole I'd need to be in decent shape for what came next.

Whenever possible I'd been doing basic exercises alone in my cell. Leg lifts were always good on the occasions when my legs and feet weren't tied down. I'd managed some sit-ups and pushups a few different times. The day after Martinez and I had our talk though I was allowed out of the cell. It was an unusual time. First, two guards led me to the shower well before the sun rose.

Until you've been rolling around in filth and your own blood for a few days, you don't really remember how good it is to be clean. Hot water washing the grime away seems to take some of the pain and stress with it. I probably would have been happy with just that concession. There was so much more though.

I was handed baggy cotton pants in a nondescript gray. There was a shirt to match and a pair of cheap canvas slip-on shoes. Somewhere they even found a pair of clean socks that felt like two weeks of vacation on an exotic island compared to the stained tatters of clothing I'd been forced to deal with. Once I was dressed and my damp hair combed back, the same two guards cuffed me again. Then we went ever so warily out into the recreation yard. The front guard stuck his head out and took a long look before turning and gesturing for his partner to bring me up.

Right there in the doorway, they removed my manacles. Everyone else seemed to be eating breakfast and I had the yard to myself. With no idea how long it would last, or even if it was some kind of trap, I concentrated on two things.

Half of my attention stayed with the guards in their tower. Fortunately, I had plenty of muscle memory when it came to exercise equipment. I went through the free weights quickly. After ten to twelve repetitions of each exercise, I would switch to the next. In that manner, the full circuit got done then rinsed and repeated. Once I was pretty certain the guards weren't going to spontaneously shoot me to death, I could concentrate on my goals and results.

The same vitality that helped me stay alive was also good for helping me stay in reasonably good shape. Don't get me wrong, we can let it all go to waste. We can also beef up like an action movie star. All I was shooting for was strength without sacrificing mobility. That's the problem with putting too much muscle on. Not that I planned to be stuck in the place long enough to bulk up.

First off, it takes one of us a lot more effort to hulk out through exercise. After a few classes and a lot of reading, I'd found out how exercise and nutrition are supposed to work. When you exercise you effectively tear up muscle. As it heals it makes more of the same type tissue and you get bigger and stronger bundles of muscle. The problem was, we didn't wound like other people, and we didn't tear muscle down to be repaired and improved as fast as a normal person.

So while I appreciated a few days of respite and some toning up. I damned sure did not want to be hanging out in the Mexican correctional system long enough to build any excess muscle. Fortunately, I very much doubted that such a thing might happen.

I did not for a second doubt that Eachan would come through for me. Not only was he intensely curious about me, but he was also the closest thing I had to a real friend in many ways. He had never pried too much, but I knew he wanted to know my story. Like most researchers and educators he was pushed to uncover secrets. The fact that we shared some secrets, like rune lore and rune magick just made it more interesting to the professor. Eachan wouldn't let me rot in prison if it meant he might never learn some of my secrets. He also had more money than some national economies.

I finished my workout in a positive mood for the first time in days. Some decent nutrition would help me recover from any lingering effects of my multiple recent traumas. I was also willing to bet that Eachan would come through with the money before the local authorities could uncover my murky and well-hidden past.

Lunch that day was more of the beans and rice with shredded meat of some sort. It looked like pork, or maybe chicken. It was also drowned in enough spice to prevent identification by taste. Then again I'd had worse, I think. I mean yea I must have had worse in some of those locked up memories. What I did remember was no tea party in wonderland. I can only guess at the bits still missing.

I ate all of the protein and did the same for the evening meal. In the intervening hours, I'd paced off my cell until I could find every wall, corner, door, and piece of furniture in the dark. It took some more time to try and ascertain whether I was alone down in what I assumed was some cut-rate version of solitary confinement.

I called out in English. Then I tried my broken Spanish.

Finally, it came down to knocking on walls to try and get a response. At one point I even tapped out the whole dot-dot-dot dash-dash-dash routine. As far as could be determined, there was nobody within listening range. That fit with the theory that they were keeping me secret. I still hadn't figured that one out. What did they suspect that made me such an interesting case?

Maybe it was just the lack of identification coupled with being very obviously non-Hispanic. Or maybe Perro had lied to me about the body I'd produced with a very large and messy hole in it. Most likely they had been put on our tail by the cartel guys and just hadn't had the opportunity to get us all in the same room yet.

With nothing else productive to do, I decided to attempt some more of those memories on my own. Okay, so it probably wasn't a great idea. What can I say? Sitting alone in a filthy cell full of shadows does not make time fly swiftly.

I tried to force my mind into the framework of a deep meditation. Not too surprisingly, being surrounded by grim dark building stone is not the best way to ground with mother terra. I could, only with a great deal of effort, find my own nodes of internal energy.

The pulsing well at my core was the easiest. Even that was difficult to find when my mind was racing around concepts like imprisonment and impending torture. Once I located that well of vital energy though I was pretty certain I could do some rune work with just a few materials. It also helped me trace the pathways of the life force within myself to the other centers of energy and awareness.

That was my limit though. Maybe the "sacred drink" was necessary or I needed a shaman or at least a skilled hypnotist. Whatever the lack was, I couldn't venture into the other-world alone in that cell. After an hour or two I gave up. That gave me several hours of solitary darkness to think about what I'd tried unsuccessfully to avoid just about every other minute between beatings.

What had Perro known about Maureen? Was he right about the old medicine man moving in on my girl? Of course, that brought up the next thought. What right did I have to call any normal woman mine? Despite my every intention to ignore those thoughts, they seemed to stay waiting for any opening to spring back to mind.

I was made of sterner stuff than that though. I kept telling myself that Maureen and her disposition were trivial compared to staying alive and finishing what I'd promised Freke. It wasn't as much that he'd promised to "lose" me again after popping up on his radar. It was more apt to say that I could not break that promise I'd given in order for him to give me the deal. To risk becoming an oathbreaker was about as dire a fate as I could picture. So I would ignore the girl and concentrate on the job at hand.

That seemed to work almost every time. Occasionally I even forgot about her for as long as ten or fifteen minutes at a time. Once more I pushed the girl and the knot of worry in my gut out of mind and back into the recesses of my thoughts. At least as far back as they'd go. Sometimes it seems like the more you want to forget something the harder it is to make it happen.

As I lay there resolutely not thinking, it was tempting to rest and store energy until the morning. That was not going to help me with the rather impressive set of tasks I'd committed myself to though. Instead, I lay on the rough surface of the disreputable mattress and did my best to come up with some winning plans to address both known and unknown obstacles in this Cartel stronghold I had to infiltrate.

I went to sleep with nothing but half-formed plans and fully formed regrets about losing even the limited gear Pedro had gotten me. And a persistent ache of guilt that would not go away no matter how often I adamantly pushed it aside.

That was pretty much my pattern for three whole glorious days that felt like a vacation. No bikers, no beatings, no crazy Indian medicine men showed up to mess with me. The worst I had to deal with was boredom and internal conflict.

The boredom let up a little when they allowed me a brief quarter-hour or so to pick up a few books from the sparse library. Most of their material was in Spanish but I found a few old high school literature books in both Spanish and English. There was a stack of old true crime magazine that appeared older than the walls around us. I grabbed half a dozen of those and some L'Amour westerns before they hustled me back to my cell.

The reading helped pass some of the time. For the rest, I worked on simple healing rituals and exercise whenever I had the energy and inclination. There was rudimentary exercise equipment in the yard. Barring access to that, there were always walls and floors and gravity to help with some calisthenics and mind-numbing, energy-draining exercise.

I was in what one of the last trainers I'd had called "the dying cockroach". It's a fairly simple exercise that quickly becomes tedious. Simply lay on your back then extend both arms and legs straight into the air. It sounds easy. And for all of a few seconds it is. Shortly after that, you find out how heavy the muscle, bone, blood, and tissues in your limbs actually are. I held the position for almost three minutes before the walls began to echo footsteps coming towards my ratty little temporary domicile.

Just such footsteps very rarely heralded good news for me. If it had been one of the regular times for a meal or break from the cell I might have been more optimistic. This was well past any hour that they were likely to let me out of my cell though. Maybe that's why I was at least partially prepared for a bad time again.

My suspicions were further aroused when the rotund little Mexican officer Martinez showed up in what I have to assume was a disguise. Always before he wore a suit or a highly decorated officer's uniform. This time he was wearing the simple greys of one of the prison guards. I was betting that anything he was going to do that required a disguise would not be for my benefit.

He shut the door behind him and waddled over to me in all but a dash. "Ok senor Yankee. You're going to have a visitor. You will be polite to him and say nothing except how well you've been treated. He can not help you tonight and if you say the wrong things I can assure you, there will be an unfortunate incident before breakfast tomorrow."

My new "guard" bent over to fasten a chain around my waist to a ring in the floor just as the door opened. The first guard through the door was one of those I had a special place in my heart for. He had been most enthusiastic and jovial about beating on my tenderest bruises and abrasions. I was so fixated on my plans for his face that I barely noticed the person walking in behind him. When my intended victim spoke to the fat officer right beside me in rapid-fire Spanish it didn't seem that strange. His next words, however, gave me pause.

"I apologize Senor Andrews my guard does not speak Engles." The surprise was multifold. First, Martinez was no more this guy's guard than Kara was my backseat bitch. Secondly, Martinez spoke English better than anyone I'd met in the prison. And thirdly, Senor Andrews was not an Andrews. He was an *ANDREW*, but the proper name would have been Senor Dixon. I knew this because he'd carefully told me his name and given me some vague but convincing identification when he interrogated me about a murder back in Austin. He was also a member in good standing of one of the American "alphabet agencies" that employs spooky people like him.

"That's quite alright Sergeant Nunes. I'm here to talk to the prisoner and not the guards anyway. If you don't mind I'd like to interview him alone.

I made a special note of the name "sergeant Nunes" to go with the face I intended to pummel into various irregular shapes. That did not keep me from hearing his response though.

"Prison rules require one officer in the room or at the door when there is a visitor Senor Andrews." The poor guard was obviously ill at ease and had to visibly restrain himself from looking over to his "guard" for approval between words.

I saw Senor Andrews pause and take an exaggeratedly casual glance at Martinez as he agreed. "Of course Sergeant Nunes. If your man would wait at the door I would appreciate it."

Agent Andrew Dixon of the unknown spook agency sat down in the chair another officer hurried into the room as everyone else made their way out. Finally, the retreating footsteps told us everyone was gone except for Dixon, Martinez, and of course the unfortunate prisoner, me.

"Well, now Mr. Gustaveson. I can't tell you how happy I am to see you. You've led me a merry chase sir. I was very disappointed to miss you at your home. There are some more questions about the missing police officer from the last little incident you were involved in."

There was no reason to tip off the Mexican police, but the officer in question was Dixon's own uncle. That he did not mention that fact made me even more wary of the entire situation. There were too many people keeping too many secrets in whatever I was now part of. For once I managed to wisely remain silent.

"No comment sir? That's fine. I'm sure we can persuade you to be more communicative after I extradite you tomorrow. I would do it tonight but the Embassy seems to have gone native somewhat. They apparently are as fond of the word "manana" as the locals." Dixon neatly crossed his legs with one ankle atop the opposite knee.

In a pose of complete confidence, he continued. "I would almost be more content to leave you down here in this cell if I knew you would get the most *benefit* the locals could provide. Unfortunately, that would not get me the answers I want. I will, however, get those answers, sir. Now that I have absolutely identified that the prisoner in question is exactly who I have been tracking, the process to get you into my custody should not take too long. You might recall the level of pressure I can apply. That pressure is only slightly diminished across the border. I assure you that the people I will talk to can have you transferred faster than you would likely believe. Still nothing to say?"

Dixon nodded once to himself then rose with a satisfied or perhaps it was just a smug smile. "Rest well Mr. Gustaveson. We have a long trip and a great deal to talk about tomorrow."

His knock on the door got a mumbled reply in Spanish then the door opened and both sets of footsteps retreated to leave me alone once again. I took a minute to guess the purpose of his visit. Was it really a trip to ID me? If so then I had to assume that Dixon had gotten tired of waiting for answers about his uncle's disappearance. Alternately he had already jumped to his own conclusions about why the older man had abruptly disappeared just a year or two before his retirement.

I could probably answer some of those questions. But how do you tell a high-level intelligence official that their family member had helped kill an ancient animated tree creature and then been killed in turn by that creature's puppet master? Dixon was pretty open-minded as far as his type goes. I'm not sure he was going to believe the whole story behind that Bruja witch and the two creatures she had commanded in a short but brutal crime spree in the heart of Texas' Capital. No, if I were guessing, he had a different and very broad set of shoulders to pin that disappearance on. The sad part is, I would have almost traded places with old Officer Joseph Jackson to bring the old man back.

I was saved from my own recollections by the return of some of those footsteps. Several sets of them in fact. This time I had little doubt that the arrival of more visitors would be anything but soothing and pleasant. I was only wrong in the degree of anxiety I experienced when the door reopened.

"We have more visitors, Mr. Gustaveson. Old friends of yours from here in Mexico rather than the United States." Martinez was not pretending to be non-English speaking anymore. He hadn't changed from his nondescript grey uniform but that wasn't very surprising. What was more of a shock was the identification of my visitor this time. He still had on the fancy clothes and both holstered weapons from the truck stop.

While I digested what that meant, the guy I knew only as

Senor Mateo of a fairly nasty and powerful sounding cartel leaned over and gave me a toothy and less than reassuring smile. "Hola Gringo! Been looking forward to seeing ya ever since you shot my compadre and tossed me on my head in the desert."

12

I HADN'T REALLY THOUGHT TOO HARD about my adventures in the desert after Maureen had left. I'd like to say it was a humanitarian response with some guilt and grief about the guy I'd shot. I'd like to say that but I try not to lie to myself anymore than necessary.

The truth is that I was raised in a time where you couldn't call the police if someone was threatening you. So we got accustomed to dealing with those situations on our own. If someone pulls a weapon on me they have declared their intent. At that point, my only concern is whether I can do unto them before they do unto me. It may not be the Christian version of that old saying, but it works for me.

I hadn't thought much about the guy I shot or his buddies I'd dealt with less drastically for the simple reason that I didn't really care about them. I had plenty of other things to occupy my attention if I gave the thoughts room to crowd in. Maureen and our relationship woes were the most persistent pressure for my attention. No matter how often I told myself that we were both better off, the thoughts kept pushing back to gnaw at my feelings.

After her I had some concerns about my incarceration, my bribe assisted release, my reckless promise to do something about a situation without knowing how serious it was. And of course my attempts to come up with someplace to start working on that problem once I got out.

So really it shouldn't be that surprising that I'd failed to associate the half-seen presence in the desert with some guy I'd met for a few minutes in a truckstop. Maybe at the time, I had half sensed something familiar about the lanky individual I tossed around. Since then though I simply hadn't thought about that fight.

Maybe it wasn't in my thoughts, but my foe from that little disagreement had apparently spent some time dwelling on it. He barely took time to shed his fancy jacket and put on gloves. "They want me to ask you some questions tough guy. You so tough though, we just skip to softening up."

He obviously had as much practice as my previous experts in the art of prisoner tenderizing. That would have been good if he hadn't also possessed a certain level of passion for the job. He was certainly energetic and invested in my case.

The first couple of shots went to the better side of my ribcage. I'd have tried to answer some questions before he got to the other side but he didn't give me the opportunity. I couldn't so much as catch my breath before the next fist hit like a tight leather-clad rock. I lost count sometime after the third fist thudded into creaking ribs that were just barely healed. He worked over one side of my head and then did some rearranging of my facial features for a minute or so.

That's when I figured out that this was supposed to be it for me. Always before, my tormentors had left little visible damage. They pretty much avoided any serious blows to my face. He took things to the opposite extreme. I felt blood sheeting down one side of my face either from the cheek cut down to the bone, or maybe from the tear across that side of my forehead. There was also a nice burn in the eyebrow itself that told me he'd gotten through the skin there as well.

All of that visible and appalling damage could only mean that I wouldn't be seeing anyone who might notice. Couple that knowledge with my visit from the American spook earlier and you can come to some pretty grim conclusions. I was guessing on either a prison yard confrontation gone bad or the all too often used "attempted escape". Whatever excuse they came up with, I wouldn't be around to dispute their story.

It took a few seconds for me to notice that the steady impact of his fists had stopped. When they didn't resume I opened my eyes to see my current torture specialist in an animated argument with the rotund Mexican Federale. I caught enough of their heated and rapid-fire Spanish to breathe a hopeful sigh of relief.

The official was arguing that I needed to be healthy enough to answer some questions. The cartel thug seemed to think that any answers were immaterial to his desire for further personalized trauma to various parts of my anatomy. I was rooting for the official.

I guess he won that round at least. The thug turned away in disgust and strode over to lean against a wall. While he lounged I saw him pull out a rag and clean some of the blood from his gloves. Wouldn't want too much liquid to seep in. Nothing ruins leather like getting it too wet.

A light slap on the better of my two battered cheeks brought my attention back to the more official leadership amongst my visitors. "Oh senor Gustaveson, things they don't look good for you. My associate over there wants to enjoy himself beating you slowly to death. On the other hand, I need to know who you are that American spies and embassies are willing to get involved over. Are you by chance Central Intelligence Agency or NSA? Or do you work for one of the American agencies combating drugs?"

When I didn't respond to any of those suggestions he continued. "If it's not drugs then what is it? Counterterrorism? Arms trading? What is your interest down here and what have you discovered so far?"

He seemed both incited and frustrated by my silence. "You are protecting no one Yankee. I can save you much pain and trouble though."

I decided maybe he needed a few words as a reward for making the beatings temporarily cease. "What can you offer me jefe? We both know my life is forfeit. Not a lot of incentive there for my cooperation is there?"

"Forfeit?" For once his better than average English vocabulary stuttered. "Ah, lost? Yes, your life is over senor Gustaveson. But it can be over quickly and without too much pain. Or it can take much longer and be hell for you. We are men senor Gustaveson. Let there be truth between us. Who do you work for and what have you discovered?"

Maybe it was all of the beatings. Or maybe I was just feeling a tad overwrought about being sent back to Valhalla. If he wanted some truth I'd give him some. "Who do I work for? My day job is as security in a bar back in Austin. My temporary boss though is an immortal freakin wolf. I've learned not to trust anybody I've run into in the last couple of weeks. I've learned that half the people down here are nuttier than Aunt Sally's pecan pie. I've also learned that your corrections facility is full of sadistic bastards that I suspect are using violence to compensate for small dicks and homosexual insecurities."

I paused for a breath and how to phrase the final shot. "Oh, and I figured out that your big bad cartel thugs are easy to toss around in a desert or kill even when they have the drop on you."

That got just about the reaction I was expecting. Mr. Mateo came through the door in a dash. That was one hundred percent in line with my expectations. However, I'd been counting on him coming at me with fists and maybe a little rabid froth around his open maw. Instead, I got the thug in his natural reactions. Out came the hand cannon he kept on his hip.

In retrospect that was probably better than the machine pistol in his shoulder holster. The Skorpion would have sprayed little .32 caliber bullets all over the room and likely ricocheted jagged wounds into each and every one of us. The .454 revolver was just going to knock a large chunk of my anatomy off. Maybe my head or half my rib cage would go or maybe he'd start with a leg or something to prolong it briefly.

I'm not sure what he had in mind, but it became immaterial a second later. First, there was a hellacious bang and then the lights flickered. Everyone not chained in place froze like deer in the headlights. The guy chained to the floor, me, didn't move much. I did curl up a little bit since I recognized the sound of a shaped charge going off nearby. That first explosion was followed by half a dozen more rippling closer if the sound was any reference.

That initial bang had carried quite a charge. Even though it seemed the furthest away it also seemed the strongest explosion. It kicked hard enough to raise dust in my crappy little cell. None of the others did as much until the one that took out the wall behind me.

I felt the shockwave even before the chunks of masonry

began tumbling around the room. One melon-sized rock clipped my shoulder. A slightly smaller piece took out my would-be executioner before he got a shot off. The rock was flat on both sides but had ragged edges where it had broken free of the wall. One of those jagged edges hit him right along his jawline and instantly turned the dust around him pink.

From the spray, I figured it caught the jugular or maybe the carotid. Whatever was cut, it was a beauty. I gave him just minutes before the compromised blood flow to his head did irreparable brain damage. I mean more brain damage than he'd probably inflicted through years of pharmaceutical recreation. With all of that going on, he wasn't even the worst injured.

The guard standing behind me was probably the main reason I only got clipped by the one rock and enough noise to leave my ears ringing. His position had just by coincidence shielded me from the worst of the explosion and architectural shrapnel. I saw him lying to my side with his upturned face almost touching my leg. That wouldn't have been so bad if his chest hadn't been to the floor. The explosion must have been close enough to kill him almost immediately. His expression showed no pain, just surprise, and puzzlement.

The other cartel guy was stumbling across the room towards the door. He didn't even pause to render aid to his boss on the way out. I looked away from that mess and checked my six. My urgency increased several-fold almost immediately. I became acutely aware of the chains holding me in place when I saw what looked suspiciously like smoke and reflected flames through the now absent wall behind me. It only bothered me a little that I didn't hear the next explosion though I saw dust and smoke fly from somewhere further down the exterior wall.

All of those observations probably took no more than two or three seconds. The nature of an adrenalin rush though stretched that time out to seem much longer. That same adrenalin rush made me decide to take a gamble. Nobody in the room seemed concerned about me or even watching.

Bracing my forearms against my thighs I rose to a crouch and gripped the chains in either hand. In a slow steady surge of recently renewed muscle, I tried to stand erect and drag the eyebolt free of its concrete anchor. No doubt anyone taking the time to look over would think I was wounded or having a seizure of some sort. I could feel cords and blood vessels in my head, neck and chest strain with the effort. The strain in my chest translated to a searing pain in my ribs. It didn't seem like a time to baby myself though. Not if I wanted to avoid becoming a Mexican barbecue.

Spots started to swim in front of me as my breath ran out and the strain became too much to bear. I felt the chains slipping through damp palms until I fell back with a jerk of the manacles at my wrists. With the release of that effort, I dragged in a ragged breath and felt sound slowly start to return after the calamitous explosion.

Now I could hear several types of alarms. Bells, whistles, claxons, and gunfire were all prevalent once the ringing let up enough. That's also when I heard the hammer go back on that big revolver somewhere nearby.

I was amazed to see ole Mateo sitting up and giving out an A-plus effort to get that hand cannon lined up on my skull. With the limited amount of play in my chains, there was no chance of dodging a punch much less a bullet. I stood frozen for the first time in a long time while Valhalla loomed ahead. His A plus was downgraded to a B minus when the bullet burned past my arm and hit the Mexican intelligence officer behind me with an authoritative splat. A brief glance showed me that El Capitan was no longer a worry. The hole in his cheek was ugly enough that I didn't care to take a longer look at what was left of the back of his head. Another shot rang out from Mateo's oversized toy.

Bubbling Spanish profanities and the sound of rubble moving brought me back to the cartel gunsel. His second shot had knocked him off balance and kicked the heavy revolver out of his grip. Half reclined on his side, Mateo drug the little Skorpion out of his shoulder holster and aimed it in shaking hands.

That was just the incentive I needed to make a better effort at those chains. Stooping low I gripped them again and started straining as the low caliber bullets began spitting out of the machine pistol with angry whines. I had no cover and could only keep jerking against the chains as deadly little metal hornets swarmed all around me.

I felt at least two of them nick me somewhere in the torso. My left leg and the opposite arm both screamed fiery pain at me from their own wounds. For a wild spray of shots that was pretty good. It made me want to give up and lay on the cold concrete floor. It was not however enough to knock me down. I kept exerting every ounce of will and strength I could summon into those chains. It seemed hopeless though, right up until the eye bolt snapped off somewhere at its base.

The various small caliber holes and burns Mateo had given me all shot their own individual spikes of agony when I fell. I had been straining so hard I never saw the shots hit my chains or the one that weakened the bolt. That might have been the last .454 he fired. The unnoticed damage to restraints, in turn, meant I never expected the strain to release so abruptly and toss me on the floor. I was laying there partially dazed and in a red haze of pain when even more reddish or pink colors invaded my field of vision.

I followed the movement, as a vision in pink, white and purple stuck her head around the corner. I saw her eyes dart all around the room pausing briefly on each corpse or near corpse before she caught my return gaze. Studying me with her head tilted oddly, the girl with the blond ponytail and "muddy girl" camouflage fatigues blew a big pink bubblegum bubble before shouting. "Hey! Like, your name isn't Mr. Moose is it?"

13

I WATCHED motes of dust settle while I tried to reconcile the last few violent and tense minutes with the completely incongruous appearance of my apparent rescuer. She didn't wait for me to decide if this was reality or the effect of too many blows to the head recently. Blondie rolled her eyes like a teenager being lectured and leaned away from the opening in the wall.

"Hey, Mr. sleaze weasel! I think your dudes in this one! He's like deaf and stupid or something though." I was wondering if she meant deaf and dumb since I hadn't answered her. The other option was that she was a few apples short a bushel herself. She gave me a friendly wave and a big cheerleader smile before strolling blissfully down the exterior wall and out of my sight.

I had made it to my feet and was stumbling over the remains of my ankle chains when yet another visitor showed up through the new "door" in my cell. This one was at least familiar. Pedro swaggered through the dust with a self-amused smirk.

The expression of self-satisfaction barely altered when

he saw my sorry state. He hauled me to my feet with barely any hint of consideration for any trauma or wounds I happened to be suffering. When I hissed out my displeasure I got an eye roll almost as good as the girl. "Don't be a little girl Moose, we gotta get moving. You get caught in a cell with all them dead guys and I won't get another shot at getting you rescued eh?"

I guess bullet wounds just aren't worthy of concern these days. He leaned me against the wall near the jagged opening and wandered back to the dead people. The whole time he searched bloody pockets and torn uniforms I could hear a litany of profanity in both English and Spanish. Finally, he came back with the keys to strip off my mangled chains and restraints. "Ok there we go, now let's hurry up eh?"

He led me straight through the hole and towards a further opening ripped in the fence nearby. Behind it, I saw a big tan SUV idling with the front doors open. "You ain't in good shape for driving but can you sit upfront or do you need to lie in the back?"

"I'll take shotgun. Let the girl and whoever she's looking for ride in the back." I clambered into the front seat and jerked the door shut with a couple of feeble efforts. By the time I had the door shut Pedro was behind the wheel. He didn't give me time to buckle my safety belt before he shoved us into gear and started down the road in a surprisingly sedate manner.

"We got no shotguns or guns at all to get us in trouble. And they got their own ride." Pedro seemed calm and unfazed by the noise and chaos erupting behind us. He also seemed pretty nonchalant about the whereabouts or activities of the girl who had presumably helped him with the abruptly explosive evacuation of the entire correction facility.

We passed no few guards and prisoners alike stumbling through the dust and smoke as flames erupted from more than part of the rubble we were in the process of leaving. I kept an eye out for the vibrantly pink and purple fatigues but didn't catch another glimpse of her. "So Pedro. Why are we escaping instead of bribing my way out and what's the deal with Commando Barbie?"

He kept his eyes on the road and his voice level but without most of the amused-at-the-world tone he normally used. " Heh, I didn't much like those people enough to pay em. I got the money from your guy though. Damn, he must be made of the stuff. He was on a boat or something but got the message and emailed me back. Said he was sailing his new yacht. You got some nice friends to have there Moose."

Without pausing his visual sweep of the roads and alleys around us he dug into the back seat and handed me a bag. "Clothes in there. Also a few gauze and stuff. Those prison rags might get some bad attention eh?"

I had more questions but he was right. The quicker I got rid of the evidence the less likely I was to be "accidentally" shot for escaping or resisting arrest. Shot any more that is. Still, I could talk while I got rid of the clothes.

"Okay, so you had some kind of reasons. I guess they made sense to you. But what now? And you still haven't said anything about the blond in barbie-doll camouflage. My voice was muffled as I stripped off my prison uniform and taped pads of gauze over anyplace oozing from low powered .32 rounds. There was a hole above my collar bone that made lifting my arm a profanity-enhanced experience. A similar hole above my hip barely went through a couple of inches of meat before popping out on the side. Add a burn across my ribs and the little nick of meat taken from my thigh and you get the worst of the injuries. The grazing hit on my left bicep had already stopped bleeding. I put a small bandage on it anyway since it still looked alot like a bullet graze. With the worst of my leakages plugged I dug out my replacement shirt. The knock-off football jersey fit my chest and shoulders but that meant it hit me a little above the knees in length. It took a minute to get all of that excess material settled right.

Pedro looked over with a grin and shake of his head at my predicament. "Nice dress. We got a rendezvous. Hang on." He fumbled in his leather jacket for a cell phone and hit a speed dial number.

"Yea there's way more people around than I planned." He didn't even start with a greeting or normal pleasantries. "Forget plan A. We're gonna skip ahead. Okay so you told me so, but shut up a minute."

He took the phone from his ear to pinch his nose at the bridge. It looked like maybe he was dealing with his own headache. I couldn't feel too sorry for the guy who seemed to make me feel just the same every other time he spoke. I heard a teeth-grating giggle come out of the phone. It seemed an awfully odd time to be giggling, but who am I to judge? I was still trying to make heads or tails of what was going on most of the time. The giggles turned into a breathy and excited voice with a distinct accent from somewhere in Southern California. Finally, she had to pause for breath or had reached a stopping place. Pedro jumped in before she could resume.

"Yea. Plans B and C don't seem great either. Go with D. Don't call again, I'm ditchin' this phone. Just be careful until the rendezvous." He didn't wait for a response but turned off the phone and took a brief detour to toss it out of the window and into a barrel full of burning refuse in a nearby alley.

By that time we were out of town a ways. Most of the mayhem seemed behind us but Perro kept a wary eye all the way around us. I had also managed to get into some brightly floral swim trunks that were barely long enough to peek out from under the red and black college football jersey. At least the trunks had that mesh inner lining. I wasn't quite ready to toss on used undies from some stall in a Mexican flea market. To finish off my ensemble he'd picked up some canvas boat shoes with the rubber soles. Twenty years ago you saw the "cool" guys all over wearing em without socks. Now they pretty much just show up on boats. These were only a size or two bigger than my feet.

"So we have a plan for tomorrow? Some rendezvous with the raspberry beret bimbo. In the meantime, we have no guns and I still have very little idea where I am or what the overall plan is. Not to mention what we're doing until this rendezvous." I gave him my stern and foreboding look. Maybe prison had taken some of my edge away. He didn't even look aware of it much less intimidated.

"I got some friends out here. Just a few miles and we'll stop for the night. Probably have a different vehicle tomorrow and then we'll meet with the blonde you're so interested in and her people. Also might have a few others join us." He stopped talking to turn on the lights and veer off down a barely visible track in the thicker trees we had reached. "Hey when we get there, just be quiet man. I'll do the talking and you keep your head down. Try to look, how you call it? inconspicuous eh?"

I spared a glance for my brilliant swim shorts and dresslike college jersey. "Inconspicuous, right. I'll blend right in I bet."

14

PEDRO'S FRIENDS seemed to be simple farmers. At least they appeared that way until you noticed how many various and interesting firearms were worn or just laying around. I saw one guy with a brand new high-end SCAR-L assault rifle. Countering that super modern firepower was an old guy with what looked like a worn and ancient blunderbuss. There were at least a dozen other guns within sight and probably three times that many machetes.

Of course, the machete's might have been working tools. That didn't prevent them from being handy at removing bits of anatomy from offensive interlopers. As the newest interloper, I worked at being as inoffensive as possible. It's not easy being invisible and subservient looking in vibrant hibiscus shorts and an oversized basketball jersey. But I went with it.

The easiest tactic for reducing your annoyance factor always seems to involve speaking. To best remain inoffensive and thus unmodified by machete or gunplay, try to remain silent. I clenched my jaw shut and followed Pedro as he walked through and greeted half the people in the collection of worn old buildings. He slapped a couple of shoulders and even gave one old granny a big hug before we reached the largest adobe building.

The fellow that stepped out of that building was composed of sinew and leather. There was barely enough meat on him to round out the knobby orbs of his elbows and knees under the rainbow-colored serape. Despite the lack of muscle, he looked like one of those old men that would put a piano on their back and walk it upstairs by themselves. Whipcord muscle and more willpower than common sense. It was fairly easy to identify that last trait. Maybe because I've also been accused of being more stubborn than smart.

He stared me up and down with a cigar dangling from his clenched jaw. When I stood there and kept my mouth shut he nodded. "Good senor. I don't wanna know nothin'. Not even your name. Pedro is not a bad man. But he sometimes makes confusing decisions. We don't need to get involved. We got enough problems of our own no?"

He turned with a wave and mumbled something to the old Abuela Pedro Perro had hugged. She gathered the two of us up with a flip of her apron. "This way. We bring you some tamales and frijoles. Beer and tequila are in the hut. You eat in there, stay out of sight. Tomorrow you leave again. Si?"

Just like that, we were left alone in a one-room adobe building. There were cots with old military surplus sleeping bags and a crate with a sputtering lantern. More importantly, there was a box of first aid gear and a styrofoam cooler with beer. The tequila wasn't that intriguing. It might work to clean out some wounds if necessary but that was about my only interest in it at that point.

I found myself pulling the tab on a beer and fortifying myself for a more thorough first aid session. In the meager lantern light, I couldn't really read the beer label. It was dark, rich and more filling than anything I'd eaten since that helicopter landed, however many days ago. It also took just enough tension away to let me deal with the bullet wounds.

My "enhanced" hardiness had already taken care of the grazes and burns. There was little to see but raw skin and dried blood where the little submachine gun rounds had chewed at me. The wound above my hip was closed enough to take off the bandage as was the one in my shoulder. Still, it seemed like a good idea to clean them up and maybe touch up my thoroughly degraded runework.

"Hey People smuggler," I tossed Pedro a beer just to make sure I got his attention. "You got a sharpie or some markers or something?" I tried to keep the request light. There was little benefit in trying to explain to him how my runic tattoos and artwork could help with healing or even less believable endeavors. If I was lucky he'd just think I was crazy. It didn't seem very likely he'd embrace the whole idea.

"Nope Gringo. No markers or anything. If it's important we'll pick them up tomorrow. We have to meet some people a few hours away in a decent-sized little tourist town. Got ya reservations in a good hotel. Nice view, real luxury digs comprende? Anyway, we should be able to get just about anything ya need there. Real nice place and I got some good friends there." He finished his commentary by shoving a tamale in his face before handing me a warm cloth wrapped around half a dozen of the southwestern version of energy bars and a bowl of beans. "That's manana though. Eat up and then rack out man. Or do you need help patching up?"

I gave him a shake of the head as my own face was promptly stuffed with shredded pork and steamed masa flour. I didn't know if old Abuela out there had done these herself or if she'd just taught a daughter or granddaughter the goods. They were some of the best things I'd ever shoved down my half-starved throat though. Say what you want about this cuisine or that culinary tradition, when it comes down to revitalizing simple fare, it's hard to beat tamales and beans. Of course, they also induce a certain sedative effect when added to days of abuse and poor nutrition as well as multiple bruises, abrasions, lacerations, and wounds.

I might have wanted some answers to a lot of questions. What I got was a much-needed snooze.

I woke up feeling better than I had in days. The freedom from an all but inevitable beating probably helped. Or maybe it was the open door of the little hut. All that mattered was that I had managed to relax enough to truly get a decent charge on my batteries. As I sat up I heard the sound of the SUV moving away from the hut. I might have been alarmed about my possible abandonment by my erratic and potentially insane tour guide.

That would have required that I actually would have *felt* abandonment at his absence. That also would have required his absence. I couldn't be that lucky. As I was running a hand over the roughened contours of my face the familiar smirk came through the door with its customary cigarette smoke frame. "Buenos Dias senor Moose! It is good you are up. Our ride will be here shortly. There's a *cazuela* with Chilaquiles and tortillas in a warm towel on the crate."

He was gone before the words had fully penetrated my early morning bemusement. Still, there didn't seem to be a huge hurry so I pulled the jersey back on over my obnoxious swim trunks and shoved my bare feet into canvas shoes to saunter over and survey breakfast options.

It took approximately two bites to add Chilaquiles and scrambled eggs to my eclectic list of comfort foods. Based on tastes and textures, some genius had simmered tortillas in green chiles and tomatoes until soft, to this they'd added pulled chicken and some kind of farmers cheese. If you topped the mix with fresh scrambled eggs it came close to one of those rarely discovered perfect breakfast foods. I was sopping the remnants with a fresh tortilla when Pedro came back.

"Come on, we don't wanna make em wait too long. Some of the kinda people we're gotta see get skittish and disappear when plans change." I immediately noticed a contrast in our appearance. He had found an opportunity to at least don a fresh shirt though the pants were probably unchanged as was his leather jacket. I imagine I looked rather like an unmade bed covered in bristly hair. A brightly floral unmade bed at that, with hibiscus sheets.

Fortunately, breakfast had restored my spirits and the crude first aid was keeping various fluids from leaking in too many places. As soon as we got someplace with a little more in the way of time and resources I could probably all but erase the damage but for now, I had plenty of minor aches and pains. At least they were minor. Considering the abundance of bullets and explosions in my recent history I figure minor aches were something of a miracle.

I trotted outside to find an older but serviceable pickup in place of our nicer SUV. This one was a faded bronze with only a few small dents. Chances were it would pass inspection in almost any rural area or small town in the whole country. I quickly found out how much of that countryside we were likely to see.

"Ok Gringo, we got a couple of hours on this road. We'll stop in Mexico City tonight. The assholes you gotta deal with would call it Tenochtitlan but we'll stick with Mexico City eh Moose?" For a change, Pedro Perro was downright garrulous. It was enough to spark my natural sense of self-preservation and suspicion. When someone has avoided telling you anything for so long, you gotta start looking for their motivations when they do start doling out info.

I wasn't going to stop the flow though, not when I'd been starving for any kind of Intel at all. Of course, there were some more personal questions I wanted to ask. The stuff he was giving me now though might be the difference between life, and a fast trip back to the unpleasantness I expected from Valhalla. I just nodded to get the flow of information started again.

"Anyway, tonight we meet some people in the city. Some of em have things to tell you about your little quest. A couple of them will be bringing some better gear. You didn't gush approval of the stuff I got you so I used some of your rich old sugar daddy's coin to upgrade"

I was pretty sure he had no idea what a "sugar daddy" actually meant in normal conversation. Either that or he was trying to get a rise out of me.

Either way, I needed my own information more than I needed to correct his errors. "Damn he must have really come through on the finances. Remind me to write Eachan a very nice thank you note. At least if I die before I can repay him he'll know I appreciated the investment."

From the renewed smirk I decided maybe Perro knew what he was implying after all. But I let him continue uncorrected, as well as unharmed. "Anyway, you look over the gear and give me a list of anything else you need. We'll make some plans and get some rest. You should be able to get a look at the place the next day or so. After that we finalize your plans and bang, go in, defeat the blackhats and save the day eh?"

"Well, it's kind of hard to list any necessities if I don't have any idea what the plan is. I need to know the locations, targets, obstacles, alarms. Are there any targets I need to avoid? Are there any targets I need to make a priority. Right now I don't know if I need one of your buddy's machetes or an armored company with close air support." I was exasperated, but we still had some time to use during our ride and I hadn't gotten any answers from this little turd that helped.

"Fyi, Pedro Perro, I've been a pretty patient guy but you give me more details or I'm going to have to consider a little divination. Maybe I can read the future in your entrails after I haul em out through any handy orifice." For once I was not going to be diverted.

"Okay Okay, let me think a minute." It took maybe four or five minutes before he finally got his thoughts in order but a couple of glances my way seemed to convince him that I was serious this time.

"Here's the deal then. I told you the main boss here has some big plans rolling. Well, he's got a crazy idea these ruins he camped out in hold some ancient mystical technology. He's got some old anthopro-ology kinda guy reading the walls and telling him stuff. He thinks he can open the secrets with a blood sacrifice. But not just any chicken or goat. He's gotta use the blood of an ancient line of kings. So happens that his great grandfather s'posed to have been Mayan or Aztec or Olmec or somethin. He thinks he's descended from these old prehistory kings. Which means so is his sister. Got it?" He reached into his bag and pulled out a lukewarm cola.

Almost as an afterthought he offered it to me and reached back for another. I'm not normally a big fan of soda and even less infatuated with a warm one. But fluid is sometimes just fluid. That brown baking sheet of a landscape made me accept whatever hydration was offered.

After a quick drink, Pedro continued. "So that's what

your Mr. Gary found out. He was going to run with the girl but the boss man found out. Put out a hit on Gary and locked the girl up. Well, Gary ain't never been too afraid. He came into the compound that night. There was some fighting. A few bad guys got a bad case of dead and some of the others were close enough to count. But...those whack job Aztec guys joined in and turned things around. Gary was bleeding last anyone saw him but he was still on his feet. Next morning he was gone, the girl was gone, and the boss was mad as hell."

"So you're telling me I have to find a missing or possibly dismembered guy inside a quasi-military compound secured by both trained mercs and rabid psychos? That's not a job that's an abstract fantasy or a soap opera adventure." It was almost enough to make me turn around and find the quickest route back to Austin and my mundane job at the bar.

"Hey, you ain't gotta do it alone. I got you a weapons guy, some whaddya call it? Moral support? I even got a guy who knows the inside of the compound better than I do and I been there a few times." If I didn't know better I'd say he was getting a tad indignant as well as still keeping some secrets. But what do I know?

I shook my head and dug for more info. "Okay, and I get you're not telling me who any of these people are for security reasons or something. But I get a full briefing and a chance to work on more gear when we get into town later today?"

I was by no means satisfied but maybe if I gave in a little now I could push for more later. The last thing I wanted to do was get the little miscreant's nose out of joint so he would become even more close-mouthed.

He gave me one of his oily self-satisfied grins and

nodded an affirmative on more intel and equipment. As briefings go, it left a lot to be desired.

I grudgingly gave up on that chain of questions and got to something a little closer to the heart. "Ok fine, we'll do our planning tonight. In the meantime, what do you know about my girlfriend's abrupt disappearance? And how the Hel do you know anything at all? Are you friends with that damned old witch doctor?" I was disappointed when his response was just a quizzical glance.

"Mande?" His expression translated that for me into a profound *Huh?*

When he offered nothing more I expanded on my original question. "Back before I went to prison. You told that guy that my girl left me for an older man. How did you know she left me and what do you know about some older man? Was it that damned Tio Guillermo? Is he one of your weird friends or something?"

I expected surprise, or maybe guilt. He would probably follow those with a half-assed denial and explanation. What I got was totally different. The smug little bastard laughed at me. "OH! Haha, Gringo!"

There was little doubt that he was genuinely entertained by the news. My own response was icy disdain and silence. Or maybe he saw it as pouting incoherence. "Oh damn, that's the funniest..."

He lost himself in shoulder-shaking high pitched sounds that weren't dignified enough to be called laughter. I'd probably go with giggling, or maybe an unseemly titter. That's probably closer. He was tiggling like an evil git. "Oh Moose, you make my day eh? Ole Uncle Guillermo snuck away with your girl? You probably shoulda stayed a prisoner and maybe I would never know."

I was strongly tempted to fish around in the back for any

of the weapons Perro had managed to keep track of. If I hadn't been mad enough at the old shaman, my new embarrassment would have pushed the smolder to new heights.

"So the old fraud is your buddy eh? I should have known. You got my gear confiscated, my ass beat and abandoned. I was half killed and dying in the desert when your buddy Tio mysteriously shows up and steals my girl. Remind me to shoot the hell out of Freke if I ever see him again. It might not kill the bastard mongrel but it ought to hurt like hell and make me feel better."

This time he slowed down the hilarity to answer my accusations. "Whoa there Mouse, I didn't send Guillermo to find you. I was still looking for your dumb ass on the other side of the border. But I'm surprised the "old fraud" found you. That's not the kind of thing he used to be able to do."

He seemed to consider for a minute and then chuckled in a completely different sound from his earlier giggles and titters. "Yea I know Guillermo though. He don't like me much. Thinks I owe him somethin' I guess. He blames me for all those broken teeth."

"What the hell Perro? That old man has the most perfect teeth I've seen outside of a movie star's gaping maw." The vision of that old pervert's gleaming smile was still pretty fresh in my mind. It hadn't dimmed much at all prior to Pedro's comments to the Cartel gunnies. Once he planted that particular seed of suspicion though I'd found myself frequently revisiting the memory of Tio leering at my Maureen. Those pearly whites didn't seem very broken. I'd have been happy to fix that for him.

"Oh yea! I heard he got a new mouth." Pedro Perro still seemed particularly happy with both his story and my romantic shortcomings.

"Last time I saw him was right after a little jeep wreck.

One minute he was arguing with me, the next minute he was biting hell out of the dashboard while the dust settled. Man, there was yellow bits of teeth and red splashes all over that jeep. He was still breathing good enough to cuss the hell out of me though, so I just left. Haven't seen him since. And now you let that wrinkled leathery old man take your woman? Damn..." Once more he erupted into the sounds of an overly entertained idiot.

"Just chill out Peter." I let enough irritation into my voice to cool his enthusiasm. "I don't *know* that he stole Maureen. I woke up and she was gone. The old man said she got mad at me and left. So when you spouted off to embarrass me in front of your drug-running playmates I may have jumped to some conclusions."

I imagine the tapping of my fingers on the armrest was another indicator of my mood. Whatever the reason, he at least stopped laughing while I stewed in my thoughts. The smug little creep was right. I should have checked up on the story.

He interrupted me with an actual question that sounded more curious than amused. "So what did you do to make her run off...?" He considerately left the "with him" out of the statement.

"Aw hel, you know what it's like when you keep secrets for most of your life. We'd been getting pretty close, and I hadn't told her a lot of things about myself. I haven't spoken about some of that stuff in decades and for all I know it could dangerous for her to know." I suppose my own voice had gone from irritated to contemplative.

The smug little smuggler mulled it over for a minute. " You sure she didn't get tired of waiting for the big proposal thing? I mean some girls get mad and then stew about how they do so much for you and you ain't even put a ring on it."

I didn't even think it through before answering, or maybe I'd have anticipated the fresh peals of laughter as soon as I finished saying, "Naw we hadn't even hit our third month together yet when I left."

His laughter was enough to make the car weave a little and I assumed his vision was blurry from the tears as he struggled to regain control of his breathing and the car both.

"Not even a year? You seen this chica a few weeks and you're all tied up about it!? *BWAHAHA*!!" The car slowed and I thought he was going to pull over and get it out of his system. He managed to control his response enough to get the car going straight again and slowly gained speed as he wiped tears from the corners of his eyes.

"Man you ain't nothing like I expected. A big tough problem solver come to settle scores for old Lobo himself? Naw, you're the kinda softy that gets all mushed up over some chica he barely knows. Hell even if she left with the old man, left over something else, or got kidnapped by the cartel, what the hell does it matter to you? She ain't family. You need to get your head back in the game hombre." He slapped the steering wheel and then subsided to just the occasional chuckle accompanied by a shake of his head.

"Seriously brah, get your head on straight. A couple of these mercs or Aztecas will toss you out with the garbage and not even break a sweat." I could tell he was honestly concerned about my focus. The problem was, he irritated the hel out of me by being so dismissive.

I just chuckled back at him for the first time in this particular conversation and then replied. "Yea, there were a dozen bikers that felt the same way. How'd that work out for them?"

The worst of it was...he was pretty much right about putting Maureen on the back burner until we were all safely out of the current mess. If we didn't die in the attempt.

That didn't make me care any less. And for that matter, he was also correct in that she might have run into harm's way. That shook me to the core. I'd been jumping to tons of conclusions and not looking at the thing from other angles.

I had no idea if she was safe or not. It was just so disappointing at the time, and frankly? It was at least partially expected. I was all ready to believe that she left me for some shortcomings. All the old shaman did was give me a handle for my insecurities.

So, where did that leave me? On top of feeling lost and lonely, now I was worried and dealing with the kind of guilt I usually managed to avoid. Maybe I'd just spent too much time in this newer and softer era. The memories I still had of my early life didn't have this kind of guilt or even a ton of self-reflection.

That must have changed somehow. Guilt, however, was not something I could indulge in for the moment. Maybe after...after whatever this was, I could investigate those feelings.

"You should call her." My sketchy companion spoke up just ahead of my own racing thoughts. I looked over to see him still watching the road while he spoke casually at me. "You don't know what's up so instead of worrying, you should call her. There will be a phone when we stop. No cellphone signal out here even if you had one. But when we stop, call her."

He was right. I'm pretty sure I was about to come to the same conclusion even without his input. The answer was obvious though regardless of the source. Just like that, a number of knots in my gut disappeared. Now I had a plan so the rest of the worries could wait. That left me room to concentrate on more important stuff at the moment. Like stuff that might keep me or someone else alive.

"Yea, I'll call her. In the meantime, do you have any of my old stuff or the guns and such you'd scrounged last time?" I looked over the seat but there were no suspicious-looking bags. Nor were there even an auspicious package or two, just a small travel bag which probably held the smuggler's clothes or toothbrush.

He tossed me a look as if I had gone nuts. "Yea that would be a good idea eh? Blow up a prison and run around the country with an escaped prisoner and a car full of weapons and explosives and stuff just in case they missed the weird Yankee dog in prison clothes. We're innocent as babes jefe. Not a care in the world and nothing to declare to any authorities. Would be better if we had you some fake papers but I can talk us out of any real hassle I expect."

15

THE LITTLE WEASEL was true to his word. We only had one minor brush with a checkpoint. We were almost to the city when we were pulled over. I leaned back and feigned sleep. After the recent abuses, it was barely feigning. It would take at least one more good night of rest to get my reserves back, for now, though I was barely pretending fatigue. Maybe that made his spiel work better, or maybe he coughed up another envelope filled with monetary motivation. Whatever he did got us to our meeting well ahead of anyone else.

Pedro checked us into a five-star hotel in Mexico City under the name, Velasquez. Apparently, the credit card matched the name and paired admirably with several large denomination American currency notes. I did a mental double-take when the total cost for three nights came to more than some car prices. There was also a certain amount of skepticism about why we needed three nights.

I asked him in the elevator. "So, Senor Velasquez, is there a reason we'll be sleeping alongside movie stars and politicians tonight? Or a reason we need to be here for three nights?"

Pedro tossed me an irritated glance and then gestured to an elderly couple sharing the elevator with us. By gesture I mean he gazed rather pointedly and pursed his lips in their general vicinity. I shrugged and waited for three more hotel floors to get his explanation.

We exited the elevator with a casual smile from the gentleman and a pleasant nod in return. Before I could repeat any questions, Pedro gave me a palm-down gesture encouraging patience. I hate that kind of gesture. Patience is not my norm unless on a stalk or in an ambush position. I managed to bite my tongue and hold any acrid remarks until we were in the room.

"Okay, so we good for explanations now secret agent man?" In retrospect, I might have kept a little condescension and sarcasm out of my voice.

His response was an annoyed glare and another gesture to be quiet. This time there was a knock at the door which he opened to admit a bellboy pushing one of the ornate brass luggage racks. That was somewhat surprising since I had seen no luggage in the vehicle nor a place to hide the half dozen bags and trunks Pedro Perro tipped for. When the door was closed again, I helped the smuggler arrange the trunks on an incredibly comfortable looking king size bed that overlooked the terrace.

He tossed me a good-sized duffle and gestured to the bathroom. "Got some stuff delivered for you. Get cleaned up and dressed. We don't have anywhere to be for a couple of hours. As for why here? Nobody will expect any escaped prisoners here. Nobody is looking for you anyway since there is a mostly incinerated body in your cell with your prison greys folded on a cot nearby. Everyone who knew you were in that torture room is dead or not talking. That doesn't mean we take chances. And finally, people do not check into a five-star resort for a one night stay. This ain't a pay by the hour hooker hotel."

That much information delivered rapidly and with a shove to get me started towards the shower left me with a number of questions but I decided to think a little bit before letting fly. That self-restraint surprised me almost as much as the flood of info.

Maybe twenty minutes later I exited the shower in an outfit I might have picked out myself. Charcoal cargo pants, a navy sweater and combat boots over thick weatherproof socks seemed sinfully decadent after my recent wardrobe choices. The best part is that the boots weren't used but someone had very thoughtfully rubbed them with saddle soap or some other leather treatment to make them supple. Somehow they even felt broken in, though the tags were still inside and there was no sign of any use. In my eyes that was as impressive as any runework.

When I did come out of the bathroom, my guide pointed to a table bearing an assortment of gourmet offerings from room service. I immediately stacked together manchego cheese and mortadella with spicy mustard and sundry vegetables on thick rustic bread. There were hot coffee and a variety of sweeteners and even a tiny silver pitcher full of cream. This was perhaps almost as good as divine mead and roasted haunches served by immortal beauties. Ok, not quite as good, but almost.

I got one mouthful of gustatory inspiration before a quiet knock sounded on the door joining our suite with the conference room next door. I released the coffee cup I was about to raise and instead used that hand to palm a sharp-looking steak knife from the room service tray.

Pedro grinned and gave me a "stand down" motion with one hand while he turned the lock in the doorknob. As he did so a slightly harder knock rattled the door just enough for the barely engaged door chain to flop out of its track by itself. The door swung open to reveal a suspicious-looking visage that seemed familiar.

The suspicion lingered as he scanned the room before entering then marched around checking behind doors and drapes. He even ducked into the bathroom and might have looked behind the towels for all I know. He was pretty thorough whether that was the case or not. Finally, assured that we were alone, he whistled a short trill of notes that might have been some bird impersonation.

Right after that, a more familiar face came in. Her current makeup made her look old enough to be out of high school but too young to be in a graduate program. This time she wasn't wearing pink fatigues. Instead, she had on a white sleeveless dress with a bold red and black floral pattern. It was just long enough to swirl above some very appealing knees and calves. I saw her toss a speculative glance my way, but that ended when she stepped in and waved at Pedro and then me. "Hola sleaze weasel and Mr. Moose."

The fellow with her was dressed all in "Hollywood bodyguard" with a black turtleneck and a black leather bomber jacket over dark pants and dark sneakers of some sort. He pulled out a chair which she dropped into with a completely unselfconscious poise and ease at odds with her very youthful appearance. "Pass me a cup of java please gringo prisoner."

The mocking smile and her own barely tan skin made the "gringo" a joke. I was still thinking about that while my hands seemed to obey her of their own volition. I guess my hands are suckers for sundresses and nice legs.

Pedro seemed made of sterner stuff. His tone was flat

and matter of fact when he asked, "You found the adjoining suite and conference room without difficulty?"

She eyed him over the lip of her coffee cup and nodded. "I got lucky. We're set up in the conference room. Thought we'd take a chance and see if you made it in earlier than expected. Aren't we all glad I was right?"

What sounded vaguely like a low growl told me that her companion wasn't as glad as the rest of us apparently were supposed to be. He looked unhappy or perhaps annoyed. Then again the lines in his face indicated a pattern of frowning that had left its mark on him. He walked over and looked through the open doorway into the larger room that I assumed sat between two suites. Once he was satisfied there he adopted a stiff stance glowering from behind his female charge. When he crossed his arms I spotted the lines of a hidden shoulder holster as well as a couple of bulges that might be magazines or a knife at his belt.

Okay. That made him my top priority if the balloon went up. He was better armed, but I had a knife palmed and half ready for use. Given even a split second of warning, I figured I could have arterial blood spraying while he was still fishing for a weapon under his stereotypical costume. If the girl was armed I couldn't figure out where it would be in that short skirt and form-fitting dress.

A cough from the conference room abruptly dragged my attention away from our current guests. I let my best brooding glare slide from bodyguard to vixen to the smuggler. "Who's in the other room?"

It was Pedro who answered. "Ah, my merchandise specialist is here! I told you we didn't dare bring any weapons on the road with us. But I also told you I had saved some of the cash from your patrone with the yacht. We have some samples for you to look over next door."

He switched his attention from me to the girl while managing to act like the lurking guard wasn't even in the room. "You have the diagrams and everything else set up too?"

At her nod, he gathered us up with a glance and headed into the next room. Being of sound and paranoid mind, I palmed the knife and then jockeyed back and forth with the other guy in black to be the last person through the door. That was when I recognized him as the other prisoner that had been in the hallway when I was brought to visit Pedro in prison.

I pushed that to the back of my attention while I scanned the room for new threats and surprises. I got a surprise first. Not only had I now identified the bubblegum barbie commando, but another mysterious escapee from the prison. But the surprise was that I knew the other fellow in the room.

I hadn't seen Franco for years, maybe even a decade or more. He had of course changed but he was still recognizable. Maybe part of that was because he'd been one of the youngest guys in our group guarding Nigerian oil refineries. He looked like a very tough kid back then. Now he looked like an even tougher man close to my own apparent age.

That was saying something because he must have been in his forties at least and looked a decade younger. Of course, I look a thousand years younger than I am, so take that. Franco looked up and noticed me as quickly as I identified him. It was probably easier for him. I hadn't changed much at all.

"Mon Frere!" He stepped around a table laden with cases and boxes to give me one of those effusive "continental" greetings. Fortunately, he stopped just short of some awkward cheek kissing.

With his hands on both of my shoulders, he stepped back and gave me a quick scrutinizing glance. "Mon Dieu, you look magnificent! Especially for an old worn-out relic!"

I saw a tightening around the eyes of everyone else in the room. It seemed that perhaps they weren't comfortable with the familiarity of two newcomers to whatever conspiracy they had going.

I stepped back myself and offered Franco a hand to shake instead of a cheek to kiss. He obliged with a sideways smile for the others in the room. Compared to our dark and intimidating disguises, Franco was a study in alternative style. His waist-length coat was form-fitting and looked like it was made of reddish silk or something similar. He had on blue jeans and hiking boots. The carefully groomed vandyke and handlebar moustache showed just a sprinkle of silver as did the waved dark hair falling just short of his shoulders."So you are the unknown quantity, my old friend. What are we calling you today?"

"Let's stick with Magnus. Eh, mon ami. Et tu?" I wasn't a native speaker by any means but I could sling a little french to keep in step with an old friend. Of course, I had to concentrate to keep old or middle french terms from popping up. Then again he'd probably just assume I was mistaking a modern word.

"Moi? I am...as always, Franco. Franco the magnificent, the jovial, the lover and beloved. But why would I want to be anyone else?" His enthusiasm was almost as contagious as his sense of humor. Fortunately, I was inoculated against enthusiasm by a justifiable paranoia concerning my current "assignment".

"Why indeed? Perhaps to save money on antibiotics for a number of social diseases. I'm guessing you got used to nude women since we first met. I seem to recall some acquaintances mentioning a number of romantic exploits that sounded unlikely at the time. Weren't you a virgin in Nigeria?" We were grinning like war buddies in a bar. A cough from the other escaped prisoner in the room brought us back to the current situation.

"But of course! Business first my friends. Business always comes first." Franco cast a speculative look at the only female in the room. His glance also seemed to linger on what I had already appraised as very comely calves. "But we can discuss pleasure later, non?"

His business apparently consisted of the packages on the conference table. A second table had a number of folders and papers on it. From across the room, I'd guess several of those papers were maps. I didn't get a chance to investigate though. Franco guided me with an arm around my shoulders while he unlocked cases to show off his products. "They didn't give me much to go on so I brought along a variety."

I stopped at the second case he opened. Inside laying across padded racks were over a half dozen AR-style rifles. I recognized the FN, a trio of Heckler and Koch 416s, and a brace of Colt carbines. There were a couple of others that I couldn't immediately place. None of them looked in other than pristine condition. I picked up an HK and tried the action. It was smoother than twenty-year-old single malt whiskey. I put it down and moved on.

"The HKs are good non? But look here. If you want long-range I have some truly inspired choices. There is a Mcmillan in fifty cal and another in .338. For Creedmoor, I have a Springfield M1A and a Browning X-bolt. There is also an M24 in .300 Winchester." He opened a case with more rifles. These were longer and heavier looking than the deadly ARs. Beside it was a smaller box, this one revealed a number of optical accessories.

He pointed from one to another while listing. "Zeiss, Sig Sauer, Leupold, Vortex and a Hensoldt. You have low light and thermal options too." He flipped open two hard-bodied cases to show the bulkier powered scopes made for use in near-total darkness.

The others moved over to the separate table and began organizing maps, photos, and documents. The last to go was the bodyguard slash escapee. His glance at the weapons expressed both interest and longing. Maybe I'd be nice and get him a gift too.

After another half hour or so of looking over a master wishlist of mayhem, we were called to the other table. Our compatriots had gotten things organized enough to finally give me the briefing I'd been wanting for days now. A few minutes into it, I stopped wanting any briefing at all. For that matter, I didn't really want to be in Mexico City, or the country, or even Central America. Back home in Austin had never sounded so good after they started giving me details of the insane plan apparently cobbled together by Pedro and the young lady.

The layout was a nightmare. We could use jungle thick cover to get within sight of the ancient structures dominated by a ziggurat. If I just needed to knock off a target and fade away it was excellent. That wasn't going to find out if Gere was inside though. Nor would it get him out if he was indeed a prisoner.

That was the extent of the good news. Some bright tactician had trimmed the jungle back for about three hundred meters all around the buildings. That even included a wide space around a handful of parking areas. We had considered using vehicles themselves as cover. The problem with that was, satellite images showed quite a few vehicles from open-air jeeps to large cargo and troop transports. Unfortunately, it showed a lot more open space than it showed vehicles for cover.

That space was made doubly annoying by the excess of lights and a random disposition of guards. There were several guard towers, but only occasionally were all of them occupied. Just my bad luck that there was no set schedule or rotation to determine which would hold a guard at any given moment.

To top off the list of my woes, there were big freakin jungle cats walking the walls. They marched right around foot troops like a Doberman, but bigger, meaner, hungrier. I was never really clear on which was which. Jaguar or leopards were all but indistinguishable to me. All I knew was that both of them had similar fur and markings, both were capable of powerful blows with big meaty paws tipped with oversized claws, and both had large unsightly fangs that probably craved chosen warrior meat.

"Okay, how many snipers we got that can take out the cats or any guards that get too close." When I looked up all I saw were heads rubbernecking around to spot someone else volunteering.

"Okay, so no snipers. I take it I'm going in alone?" I was fully prepared for the bevy of agreements with that statement. Which is probably why I was surprised by an indignant voice from an unlikely source.

"Hey now!" Pedro seemed to have gained an inch or two of height and maybe even girth as he bristled with indignation. "Don't be a martyr Moose. We all gotta go in. I mean except for the gun guy. He's just here to get you outfitted. But I'm going in for my own job. I just gotta know that my people are in there for me to get out. By the same token,

Heather and her guy are going in for something she won't tell me. They'll be doing their own thing though. You and I, we stick together until we know for sure who is and is not down there. After that, you get your guy out and maybe start a diversion. If everyone is looking out then nobody will be looking in while I get my people out right?"

I wanted to enquire about "his job" but didn't get a chance. The barbie doll broke in with a voice that caught my spine in a wrench and jerked it around a few times. It wasn't just a spoiled little rich girl voice. It was all of that of course, but so much more. There was a hint of a whine to her nasal vocalizations, and smugness, condescension maybe? And above all was the unmistakable lilt of a "valley girl" in her words and phrasing.

"So like, we don't need to know your business dudes, and like you don't have to know ours? Capiche?" She looked like she started to cross her arms and thought better of it. I think there was an aborted foot stomp too. Finally, she settled for a suspicious glare though. "And what's this about not knowing who is down there? Didn't Luis tell you? He was in there just a week ago before he got picked up for questioning in that awful prison. If Luis said your folks were there then they're there."

Pedro started to respond. "Yea lady but like you said, that was last week and now..."

His cell phone went off and Pedro put up a hand to forestall anyone else from speaking.

"Bueno?" He spoke into a cheap-looking phone that came out of his jacket pocket. We could barely hear a response in Spanish even before Pedro waved and indicated he needed to take the call. With another vaguely circular wave, he suggested we carry on while he went into the other room and shut the door. I didn't like that very much.

Apparently, neither did anyone else. I saw Franco purse his lips and take a long look at the door before cracking the door into the hallway and checking both for anyone out there and a longer look at the stairwell near the end of the hall. He shut the door and strode over to look out the window from far above a swimming pool and Mexico city spread out all around us.

I might have done some checking myself but the girl and her guardian both stepped up to confront me.

"What the hell is that about?" His voice was deep, it was gravelly, and it was surprisingly free of any hint of a Latin accent that his appearance would have suggested. I was expecting at least a Banderas level of Spanish, what I got was the west coast America.

My shrug didn't seem to appease either the little enforcer or his mistress/handler. His scowl spoke volumes but her frown screamed libraries worth of dissatisfaction.

I tried for a little of that diplomacy that I had learned in customer service training. "Look I don't know any more about this than you people. I just met the little con artist a few days ago. He was referred by someone who I'm beginning to think might not have had my best interests at heart. But he's got me here. I've got a job to do. That's it. I promised to handle something for someone and they promised to take care of something for me. It sounded like a neatly balanced transaction. Nobody mentioned drug cartels, exploding prisons, weird ranger recon girls and most significantly, there was no mention of huge freaking man-eating jungle cat guards. You wanna know what the smuggler is pulling, ask him yourself. Good luck with getting a straight answer."

"Mr. Mouse! You wound me." Perro's voice didn't sound particularly wounded. In fact, he sounded positively pleased with himself. "If you have had a chance to look over the merchandise from your old acquaintance, is there anything else you would like for our little errand?"

I liked that. A little "errand" that involved psycho drugged-out cultists and professional mercs not to mention a few man-eating cats. But I did need some other things. "Yea Perro, let me write a list of what I'd like. I'm not sure where you can get it all but it's worth asking right?"

I sat down with a pad of hotel stationery and a very nice pen with the hotel logo on it. At the same time Bubbles, the enigma and her flunky scooted across the room and bent their heads to compose their own list. Pedro apparently had some needs too but he used the burner cell phone he'd produced to type in a list. The only one not occupied with writing was Franco.

He was making a round and repacking some of the weapons and gear that I had already rejected. That left quite a pile of stuff though that I approved or was still consider-ing. "So, Mr...Moose? Have you decided about the long-range guns or do I pack them all away?"

He chuckled and waved a hand to placate my glare when I gave him the annoyed look that occurs when anyone inter-rupts my sometimes tenuous chain of thoughts. Instead of answering I quickly finished my list to give the smuggler. After that, I joined Franco at his table. "Okay, give me the RAV soft armor, I think the heavier plates would limit mobility too much. I'll take the tactical tomahawk and the commando dirk with the boot sheath. Toss in the M4 with the grenade launcher. Maybe pack up a few smoke grenades and some flashbangs. I don't suppose you have frag?"

Franco gave me a mouse eating smirk and produced another crate. "Frag, incendiary and even a couple of flechettes. Of course, if you get caught with them you will be hung from the walls of the prison then flogged and shot for good measure. They might even be able to find a guillotine from good Emperor Maximilian's days. If there were anything left they would undoubtedly set it ablaze."

I had to shrug. Somehow incarceration paled in comparison to having my soft and tender bits pulled off and chewed by large jungle cats. "Okay, you've sold me. Give me three frags, a flechette and two incendiaries in case we want to make s'mores later."

I turned away from the purchase table and lifted the tomahawk while waving at Pedro with my other hand. I pointed to my list with an afterthought. "That reminds me, amigo. I'm gonna need a metal engraver. Doesn't have to be expensive. Just a little twenty-dollar toy or maybe a rotary tool with an engraving tip. Put that on your list with a star beside it or something. That's a fairly important piece to me."

A clap on my shoulder turned my gaze back to the widely grinning European arms dealer. "Very nice Mon ami. Are you thinking of putting your initials on the highly suspicious and illegal guns and explosives here?"

I grinned right back. "Naw, just need to do a little creative decorating on some of the metal. Don't worry about gift wrapping it either. I'll take it as is with just a duffel or two to pack it in for now."

Behind me, Pedro had his phone open again and was reading off the various lists to whoever was on the other side. My ears tried to swivel and understand everything he was saying when I faintly heard the word "bruja". It took an effort of will not to turn and stare or even shudder a little bit at memories of such a creature standing over me while I was paralyzed and vulnerable to her cutting blade. But that was weeks ago. And that particular bruja was dead and dealt with by the very being that had sent me down to Mexico on a fool's errand.

Unfortunately, intensity and interest don't make up for a lack of linguistic skill. I still only caught a few words of his conversation. It was enough to know that he wasn't ordering a bruja hit squad though. No, it sounded like some of my list might only be available at a new age or witch's shop of some sort. I guess that made sense. I was planning on using some of that stuff for purposes very similar to what any good witch would tell you she could do with her magic. The main difference was, mine almost always worked and they tended to be a lot more effective than most Wiccans or santeria practitioners.

Perro broke my train of thought by ending his call and pocketing the phone. In the same instant, he picked up the landline phone and barked some staccato Spanish into it as well. From across the room where they had been whispering with their heads together, the other guy turned and machine-gunned some more Spanish which added to the phone call. This time the language barrier wasn't so bad. I might not be great with the language but I am completely fluent in food. Old Pedro was ordering a large amount of room-service. Or more likely, someone else was ordering it with their credit card and the little con artist's voice.

Finally, he hung up the phone and turned to the rest of us. "Very well campaneros, we have a bare plan laid out. Everyone take some time to refresh yourselves. Dinner will be served at seven this evening in this very room. I will remove any papers that would be better kept secret. If you would be so kind as to clear away your extra merchandise as well Senor Franco. We meet back here at..."

"Got it." The black-clad tactical bodyguard was apparently very fond of short speeches and shorter replies. He snapped out the acknowledgment and then gathered up his boss, or wife, or little sister for all I knew. They went to the other side of the conference room and went into what I had to assume was a suite that mirrored our own.

Pedro offered me first chance at a nap, but I had other priorities.

"Yea amigo, I'll take a nap shortly. First, can I use one of those burner phones you seem to be stocked up on? I just want to call Maureen and I'd rather not use a traceable hotel phone to do it."

Pedro arched an eyebrow but dug into his pocket and tossed me the same phone he'd used for his earlier calls. "Use the international code, you're not in America now. Don't take too long. And if any other calls come in just ignore them. I'll call back later."

Just like that, he trusted me with the phone and left to pursue his own interests. He might be getting low on other people's credit cards or something. I figured it wasn't really my business.

Fortunately, I come from a time before calculators, computers, phones or cash registers. Numbers stick in my head pretty well. I dialed Maureen's phone and waited until the voicemail came on. Somehow I didn't want to just leave a message without knowing how things stood. The fact that she *seemed* to have left me alone with strangers in the desert made any message insufficient for my purposes.

On the other hand, I didn't want to leave my number on her phone with no explanation at all. "Maureen, I'd very much like to talk to you. A lot happened in the desert and I'm...Well, I don't know...Look, call me when you get this message, please? We need to talk. I'll try your number again later. If I don't pick up your call then I'm not free to do so. I'll also try to get another phone and get you that number."

I paused and drew a breath after that long rambling mess of a message. "Anyway, I hope you're safe and I...I just hope you're safe for now and we can talk soon."

I closed the call and put the phone on the tiny table by the door. Had I been about to drop the L bomb? Even rattled and uncomfortable I don't think that was very likely. However, I distinctly got the impression that a certain four-letter word had tried to slip past my lips unbidden. I was probably just tired. That's what that was. Fatigue and anxiety.

It took a stern effort, but I pushed everything from my mind and devoted myself to a soldier's primary mission. Sleep.

16

DINNER at one of the top Hotels in Mexico did not resemble warm tortillas in a towel with beans and chilaquiles. There's something to be said for woodfire grilled fish brushed with spices then served with charred citrus on a banana leaf. It definitely wasn't bland gelatinized lutefisk or the smoky hard dried fish of my youth. Old Pedro had spared no expense, of someone else's money. Al pastor shaved pork and thinly sliced carne asada vied with chicken breast prepared fajita style. There was an enormous shallow bowl full of grilled vegetables in a riot of bright colors. And of course, warm tortillas served in their own ceramic warmer.

He'd purchased a small buffet it seemed, although for just a handful of people it was enough to last for days. I'm not sure I didn't prefer the chilaquiles and beans though.

During the meal, I learned that the enigmatic female of our little conspiracy was named Heather. She was indeed from California although she seemed reluctant to talk about it. She mostly spoke of the foods and various touristy loca-tions she'd seen while down south. Compared to her companion Luis she was garrulous, despite keeping the conversation carefully steered away from herself.

Luis mostly spoke in terse phrases or monosyllabic responses. If nothing else it kept me from determining whether he was secretive or thick-witted. Personally, I was leaning towards a mix of the two; confused and covert or maybe dazed and deceptive.

While we were enjoying our choice of dessert and after-dinner beverages, there was a knock which Pedro leapt up to answer himself. The little man had been animated and charming during the meal. Nevermind that our perfect host was basically a con artist and thief as well as a smuggler.

After a low-voiced conversation through the door, he swung it open to reveal a luggage cart piled with packages. He stepped around it to tip the porter I supposed. As he pushed the cart further into the room I caught a glimpse of the delivery man. The face was familiar, but by the time I placed it, he was gone. I darted to the door and looked down the hall. The elevator was headed down, but there was also a stairwell not that far away.

There was no way to catch the elevator except by maybe racing it down. On the other hand, if he was on the stairs I had a decent chance of catching him there as well. I sprinted for the stairs and pounded into the enclosed space. There was a faint sound when I opened the door. It might have been my imagination, or might have been another door opening a floor or two down.

There was certainly no sound of footsteps pattering down the concrete stairs. I have no doubt my face reflected frustration as I went ahead and pounded down the stairs at a pace most would find foolish. At the worst, I was worried about a twisted ankle or maybe a bad fall. Either of those would be nothing more than a minor inconvenience for a day or so.

I managed to make it all the way down without mishap. I also beat the elevator. In a hotel the size of this one, I'd been willing to bet there would be others pushing elevator buttons at this time of night. I was right.

When the doors parted, I saw a very well dressed older couple step out. There was also a small family with two terribly polite and courteous children. There was not, however, a familiar face that had just finished delivering packages.

I had missed him leaving the stairs, or he'd gotten off the elevator on one of the other floors. Either way, there didn't seem to be much point in knocking on doors at dozens of rooms

I rode the elevator back up and pushed our door open to find a room full of tension.

"Where the hell have you been?" Was the longest sentence I think Luis had ever spoken.

"Well, let us see. I darted across a street full of mind your own business and bought a whole crate full of keep your nose out of mine." I don't know why, but this guy set me off just by glaring. It wasn't some testosterone competition as far as I know. We were just two guys that would have been happy to beat each other to pissed off pulp.

"Look, Moose," It seemed the girl was no happier than her minion. "We're all in a tight spot here and don't need anyone going off-reservation."

I idly noticed a sly grin develop on Pedro, but at the moment I had other concerns. Like two irate conspirators in a room with a pile of guns and explosives in nearby duffels. My first instinct was to toss her the same kind of sarcasm I'd dealt her sidekick. That wouldn't have gotten us anywhere though except maybe into a brawl that wouldn't help with getting this all over so I could go home.

"Okay, this once I'll answer. Don't get in the habit of expecting compliance." I tried to match her glare with my own. I doubt it worked. The girl seemed to have been blessed with some serious glaring genes.

"I thought I saw someone I recognized." That much was true. "I just wanted to make sure we hadn't been spotted and if so, well I'd have dealt with it."

It must have sounded thin to her just like it did to me. But one of the things I'd heard about a good lie is, stick with it no matter what. I was preparing to defend that flimsy deception when Pedro cut in and shut down the conversation.

" That was one of my associates, Mr. Moose. Even if he did recognize you he is unlikely to go to the authorities over someone he knows I helped escape from prison." He waved off any objections or concerns although it didn't completely erase the scowls from our "allies". I decided not to mention that I recognized that face at the hotel door from seeing it at another hotel. In fact, the last time I'd seen that face had been when I was slamming a forearm against his temple back in a parking lot in Arizona.

Franco had remained at the table and was content with a cigar and snifter of brandy while the rest of us either bristled or nonchalantly tried defusing the situation. My one-time squadmate gave the warm brandy a slow and deliberate swirl and then added his input.

"Come ma Cherie Heather. Ignore the uncivilized baboon and come enjoy an aperitif. I can tell you about Europe and you...can tell me anything you want my dear." He didn't actually enunciate the "H" in her name but the girl recognized her name and managed to convert her scowl into a weak smile as he continued.

"Perhaps after this whole distasteful affair is over we can see what kind of nightlife they provide in Mexico? Maybe the Mayan coast for a weekend?" Franco seemed pretty optimistic to me. I mean this valley girl was attractive enough. She was toned, tan, blonde and had almost model-like looks. So far though, she'd had little to say to anyone except her own companion. For all, I knew they were a couple.

Franco wasn't big on that kind of obstacle though. "You will be completely safe from ruffians with Franco. Your bodyguard can have the night off eh? No-one would dare risk the wrath of a legendary fighter and lover like myself."

She didn't seem as impressed by the European charm as he'd intended. "How about we focus on getting through the errands here before we start making other plans? It would be nice if all of us made it out alive. Or at least most of us."

I decided to let them work out their own issues. I had my own concerns to worry about. Like why was Pedro Perro employing one of the guys who had beat me half to death and left the other half for the desert to finish off? I was also a little curious about which of us Heather wouldn't mind losing during our foray.

I heard the damsel ask a question that put me on alert. "You say you knew Mr. Moose from a while back? Was it long ago?"

These people didn't need to know enough about me to start wondering. For that matter, Franco didn't need to start thinking about how long ago we had served together. I mean, yeah, he'd aged fairly well. He didn't look any older than I did now. But before, he'd been barely out of his teens and I looked just about the same as I did now.

"Oh, Mademoiselle! Are you trying to weasel my age or

sneak more information about the kind of chicanery we were up to in our misspent youth?" It seemed that Franco had learned some discretion too. Of course, that made sense. Gunrunners and mercenaries rarely got ahead by broadcasting their business. Which raised a sudden question of my own.

"Speaking of chicanery Franco, why are you hanging around? We've got the gear settled and packed up to go. So there isn't any real need for you to be here, unless you can't resist a girl half your age?"

The jerk didn't even bother to turn around to address me. With his eyes still on Heather, he tossed a barbed retort over his shoulder. "I had to receive payment. You've come up in the world. First-class digs in a fine hotel. Another sugar daddy footing the bill for your weapons. I'm just glad you finally gave up that thin disguise of chasing women."

Sugar daddy, I didn't have to guess where he heard that description. Pedro Perro shrugged off my glare with one of his smug little smirks and spread his hands as if to proclaim innocence. I'm not sure how he expected me to buy "innocence" from a guy that carried more credit cards than a small corporation, and each card seemed to have a different name on it. He must also have a ready supply of fake IDs to match some of the cards. Hotels tend to want identification as well as payment.

In retrospect, worrying about my sexual reputation probably shouldn't have been a top concern. I was about to try sneaking into a compound full of mercenaries, crazy cultists, and man-eating cats. Once inside I had to fight or stealth my way to find an immortal wolf in the human form and convince him I wasn't an enemy, preferably without revealing my origins and nature. For allies, I had a smuggler and con-man who employed people I'd already tangled with, and an enigmatic valley girl commando with her tight-lipped bodyguard. I couldn't forget the mercenary gunrunner either. Any minute now he might realize some things that would be awkward to explain.

I sighed and dug a fork into the sticky dessert on my plate. At least the tres leche cake didn't let me down.

After an awkward evening of suspicions and silent appraisals, we all made our way to various beds. I didn't pry or even really care where everyone else ended up. I was willing to bet that Franco ended up somewhere other than Conspiracy Barbie. I was also willing to bet that he'd manage to find company anyway. As I recall he'd been getting almost as good with young ladies as he'd been with weapons and explosives the last time I saw him. And that was before he grew into those ears.

I chuckled over those ears until I found my way into a deep sleep in the most comfortable bed I'd ever felt.

17

By the time Perro got moving, I was well into my own preparations. My list of requested materials had probably not made a lot of sense to him or whoever did the shopping. As usual, there was method to the madness, even my madness.

Then again Pedro Perro was crazy enough to think blowing up chunks of a prison was reasonable, so maybe my suggestions didn't sound mad at all to him. That was uncomfortable when I thought about it. I'd hate to think my logic might actually align with the people-smuggler and amateur saboteur.

When he wandered into the outer room of the suite I had done some rearranging. I had a smaller table moved over beside the dining table. Sitting in the angle provided, I had laid out my materials and several of the weapons.

"Stop right there smuggler." I didn't have to look to know he was close to causing some issues.

I pointed down at the entire cowhide I'd spotted in the market earlier. At least they didn't cost as much in Mexico as I would have paid in Texas. Some Americans put almost as much value in cattle as any bull-stealing Irish king of bygone ages. "Don't step on the new rug. You'll break my circle and slow everything down. Might even contaminate the work I've already started."

I saw him narrow his eyes and take a look at the "rug". Clearly visible were the lines and runes I'd marked into the hide with a Woodburner. Less noticeable were the sprinklings of various earths, metals and other sundries. It was by no means some greater magic circle you'd expect from a Gandalf or Merlin. It served much the same purpose though.

"If you break my circle a lot of work gets wasted. I could either keep going and hope to get lucky, or I would have to start over on the hide and hope I had enough material left over. We don't want to call up your sketchy associates for more errands do we?" I still hadn't forgotten that my "guide" associated and even employed at least one of the guys who'd come as close to killing me as anyone had since 'Nam.

For once Pedro took a hint and ran with it. Without a word he waved and shot me his cocky grin before moving into the conference room between the two suites. Maybe half an hour later I heard them start setting up brunch on the same tables he'd put a feast on the previous night. I was too busy to worry about it though.

The tactical tomahawk was my current project. The vinyl handle felt good, was shock resistant and it had a great grip wrapped in paracord. Those artificial materials were not as good as leather or other natural materials for holding runes though. I compromised by adding a coil of leather that wrapped around the handle after I had worked it with runes that I had chanted while burning them into the material.

The blade was good quality steel. It wasn't professionally

stained or polished like many others. Instead, it was rough looking, heavy and brutal. The handle was shorter than others and the blade thick and rugged. In short, it looked like a descendant of something I'd have found hanging on some blacksmith's wall in my youth.

I'd already carved a number of runes and runebinds into that steel with the engraving tool. Prominent amongst the runes sung into that steel were Teiwaz, Uruz, and Algiz either singly or bound together into a more complex runebind. I wasn't entirely sure why, but at the end, I had meticulously added Kenaz plus Sowulo for fire hardening and finally that chaotic powerhouse Thurisaz.

I had come to respect Thor's rune Thurisaz even more after it effects in the mist world of my shamanic journey. It might not work the same in the real world but apparently, it was much like setting off a small nuke in the dreamworld. I just had to hope it didn't have some random trigger waiting in ancient MesoAmerican ruins.

Pedro and Franco both took a minute to poke a head into the room and inform me first of breakfast's arrival, and later about lunch. Each time I pointed to a coffee pot sitting on the smaller table at my side with a cheese danish, a sandwich and some fruit on a plate. Breaking a circle like mine wasn't disastrous by any means but I had no idea how long the work might take. So I had planned accordingly.

By afternoon, my back was starting to hurt. I could stand and stretch but there was no room to walk around inside the small circle. The last time I'd really walked about was while I tried to get in touch with Maureen again by way of Pedro's burner phone. Again she didn't answer. Maybe she was just screening her calls? I left a message and then got down to work.

Since that call, I had barely moved after adding the

energy that "powered" the circle. On the other hand, I got a lot of work done. The combat dirk was about as good as I could make it with such limited time and material. The same could be said for enhancements I'd put on the vest and a couple of baubles I'd made. The bulk of that time had gone into the tomahawk. In the end, I'd found myself singing Ansuz into the steel without remembering a decision to do so.

That was alarming. Ansuz is the rune of communication but it is also a "God" rune. It is used to communicate with higher powers, spiritual matters...Gods. Many people associate it with Odin himself. Had my dream journey triggered something? Was my subconscious trying to get the attention of the great Cyclops in the Sky?

That didn't seem to matter at the moment. I had too much else to worry about.

Once the runework itself was done I gathered everything and went into the conference room. Everyone else was sitting and talking at that point. I don't know what kind of preparations the others required but they seemed in no rush to go about their business. The only exception was Franco. I finally got the idea that he might be more than a weapons courier. He had pulled a chair up to the weapons table and was working on a couple of guns as well as a satchel that closely resembled his demolitions bag from back in the day.

Fumbling together some rough fajitas in lukewarm tortillas, I made a meal to carry me over while I worked on things that didn't require a protective circle.

"So you're going in with me or got something else cooking?" I directed the question in a voice that wouldn't carry past out table.

"Hmm?" He didn't lift his eyes from the disassembled gun in front of him. "Oh, I will be going along part of the way. Your handler over there seems to want some distractions scattered around in case extraction becomes a problem. A few bangs and some flashes should do the trick no? Of course, I also have a couple of new additions for you. He said you might need to provide an opening where otherwise there was none. There's a bandolier with a handful of shaped charges. Beehives, amatol, quick snap fuses should do the trick, my friend. Just press the fat side to a surface and trigger it then make some room. Shaped or not they are dangerous. You could expect at least a headache and loss of hearing if you stand too close."

I just grunted agreement while I was loading extra magazines for some of my own choices. It seemed we were both getting our game faces on. A minute later I cleared my throat and broke character. "Hey, and thanks, Franco. I appreciate you offering me the best you had."

His grunt had a hint of laughter behind it. "Your Sugar Daddy had a good credit rating Moose."

"It's Mouse dammit. And he's my friend, not a sugar daddy. Eachan just happens to have a great deal more accessible financing than I did from inside a Mexican prison." I made a note to punch the hel out of Pedro when time and circumstances permitted. For the prison and the "sugar daddy" both.

Franco's happy chuckle interrupted that thought. I looked up to see him beaming a wide gleaming smile of pure joy. "So he is your friend, with benefits?"

I was saved from answering that by an urgent knock at the door. Franco and I seated magazines and chambered rounds as if orchestrated. That was good. We hadn't even been that well-coordinated when we worked together every day.

I saw the gunsel with the blonde produce his own

weapon. He was toting a revolver today. It was some type of magnum since it said so in bold letters along its vented barrel. For her part, the girl flipped her hair back behind her ears and then picked up her phone of all things.

Pedro gave us all a disgusted look mixed with amusement as he opened the door to show his "associate" leaning weakly against the frame. There was blood all over his shirt and he seemed to be gasping for breath. Pedro leaned forward to give him his complete attention. I guess the rest of us were more or less following suit.

That was probably why we didn't immediately notice the side doors open from each of our suites. The sound of a cleared throat drew our attention though. These guys were professional. No pumping a shotgun or sliding a bolt back to startle us. He just gave that one almost apologetic sounding cough.

"Gentlemen, please put your weapons down. If you do not I shall have my men cut you down like the dogs you undoubtedly are." His voice was as steady as the shotgun in his hands. No pump action for him. It was a fancy enthusiast's gun. I'd seen them before. Turkish made toys that looked like an AR-15 on steroids. I saw two more of them in the hands of characters not carrying either an AK or the ubiquitous Uzi.

All in all, there must have been close to a dozen guns in that room all of the sudden and ours were the only ones not pointed someplace productive. Only two people moved in that first instant. The bloody guy at the door produced a sleek looking pistol and stuck it in Pedro's ribs, and the girl smoothed her hair back again and with an air of complete nonchalance started to plug her earphones in.

I saw Pedro go pale. Apparently, close contact gunshot

wounds bothered him. "Hang on. Nobody gets excited here. Right compadres?"

His voice was for all of us but I saw him make brief eye contact with our own people starting with the girl who got a longer look. He probably wasn't sure she was paying attention. Her nod was at least reassuring. He didn't seem as concerned with the rest of us noticing. I guess our complete focus on all of the guns was plain enough.

To our uninvited guests, his tone wasn't deferential as it had been to the cartel guys at the diner. To these guys, he reacted with more confusion and frustration. "I messed up trusting the wrong guys didn't I?"

A prod of the gun in his ribs got Perro to move into the room so his bad decision could shut the door behind him. "Yea I guess you shouldn't have trusted me so much. Once they had Mr. Gary though it seemed prudent to switch sides, Pedro. I'd apologize but I don't think it would matter for very long at all."

"Shut up, dog" The command came from the previous spokesman who also seemed to be the leader of the gunmen. He detailed the two other guys with shotguns to a guard position just by waving them towards the door with his own weapon.

"The rest of you keep quiet and cluster up in the corner over there. No moves towards a door or window and no sudden moves at all. It would be nice if we could handle this calmly and quietly." He used his gun barrel again as a baton to herd us into a secure little knot of victims.

"Two Uzis to watch, don't get in anyone's line of fire. You two take their guns and search them." That took care of half the invading troops. It didn't take long to find out what the others would be doing.

None of us felt suicidal enough to resist as they removed our weapons and patted us down for further things we'd failed to use when it mattered. While our closest new buddies did that, their allies began packing everything up in both suites as well as anything in the conference room that didn't belong to the hotel.

18

"WHAT CAN I SAY, Perro? With the boss in their hands it was join, run or die. I'm too lazy to run and I like being on the winning side." The little weasel's name was Porfirio and he was apparently very pleased with his betrayal and performance at the door. Porfirio was interrupted by the barrel of a sleek Turkish shotgun that broke off a couple of teeth and bloodied his lips.

"I said shut up, cur." The guy in charge of our captors would bear watching. Even after some creative violence and amateur dental work he didn't show any emotion. His tone was flat and he hadn't even drawn a deep breath or anything before delivering the brutal blow. A side glance told me I wasn't the only one that noticed. Franco pursed his lips considering the man while the Latino bodyguard turned a flat gaze that said pretty much the same thing about both captor and captive. This is not someone to take lightly.

It didn't take long at all before the entire set of rooms had been sanitized of our presence. Bossman did a walk-through himself to make sure. While he was out of the room we had no less than six assorted weapons trained on us.

Either these guys were extremely professional or someone had been telling them stories to make us sound dangerous.

Finally, the chief bad guy came back. "Okay, you three with me. We will all walk down with the luggage and our friends here. The rest of you get the cars and meet us at the side entrance."

I saw Pedro give the girl an almost unnoticeable shake of the head. For her part, she still had her earphones in and was chewing gum. She returned a tiny nod before going back to gently bobbing her head to whatever music she had queued.

"Here is how we will do things. You may call me Jefe. We are all old friends now aren't we?" He tossed his shotgun to one of the retreating troops and pulled out a big ugly revolver.

"I will walk with the lovely lady on my arm." He grabbed her and wrapped one arm around her waist. Then he turned to flash a broad and toothy smile at her while his other hand held the revolver almost against her side between them.

"If any of you become bold, I am afraid there will be a terrible mess. Blood and gaping holes in her fashionable dress. That would be tragic no?" He stopped to chuckle as she gave him a brief but fairly icy stare.

"Don't worry chica." I'm not sure what Pedro thought a good time to worry was if that wasn't one. "They won't hurt you right now. We just play nice eh? The cars will be here soon then we can see what kind of trouble we're in."

Good ole Jefe laughed out loud at this. "Oh dear no. We do not hurt young fashionable women with stunning blonde hair! They are too valuable. We know people that would pay a great deal to claim you for their own dear. Who knows? Maybe you will get one of the good ones who treats you well between...sessions."

I didn't like the direction he was going. But that was nothing compared to her little guard. Luis took a step forward with both hands clenching and unclenching in time to the throbbing blood vessel on his forehead. He spat out a fairly filthy word or two before switching to what might have been even more imaginative obscenities in Spanish. The tirade only stopped when one of the uzi stocks hit him behind the kidney hard enough to steal his breath.

"Very good." Boss-man nodded his approval. "I hope you got that out of your system. It always becomes tedious paying off authorities when you spray bullets at people in a crowded hotel. Hopefully, nobody else is going to be loud then. No?... Good, you two husky gringos can push the luggage cart. If you take your hands off of it, she will be shot."

When nobody took him up on the opportunity to vent a little hostility he nodded again. In a fairly quiet clump, we went down the hall, and into the elevator which was packed enough to prompt thoughts of resistance. Jefe had thought of that though. As soon as the doors closed he moved the pistol from her side to point it under her chin.

By the time the elevators were open again, the gun was back in Heather's side and we walked through the lobby with the only sound coming from the pistolero with the lady. He was telling some entertaining story and laughing at his own wit enough that nobody noticed any of the rest of us.

That got us to the side entrance where the cars were waiting. By cars I mean large and sturdy looking SUVs and a hummer. "My old friend Pedro will ride with me. Put the little Mexican with one of the gringos. Make it the tall one. The short fat one will ride with the girl in the hummer. I thought I saw Heather almost smile at the "fat" comment.

That didn't make sense though. She was looking at being our insurance for now and somebody's sex-slave later. That didn't seem like anything to be taken lightly.

In short order, we took off. Heather and I were in the middle, in the military-grade vehicle. We were bracketed between the two merc types in the front truck and Pedro with his previous employer and current captor in the rear car. I could only guess how unpleasant that conversation was. Our own car was no laugh fest. The guy in the rear with us kept turning to brush up against Heather while making comments to his buddies in front. He was sitting in one of those little fold-out seats behind the shotgun guy in the passenger seat.

Just to make it more hilarious, he would switch from Spanish to English every once in a while so she could be sure to understand his innuendos and filthy suggestions for her. That finally came to a halt when he reached over and slid a hand up her thigh to push the dress up well over her knees.

"Okay, that is *totes* not cool." This time she pulled out one of her earbuds and let it hang down her chest while she thumbed a new song to play. I heard a synthesizer or electric organ start playing a long low note with hints of church service in it.

She turned to me and said, "You should like, brace yourself."

And then her hands moved almost too fast to see. One came up to smash up into his nose. The other hand dropped to his offending paw on her thigh and closed with a distinct sound of cracking bone and cartilage. Mr sexual offender let out a gurgling scream and pulled the trigger on an Uzi that was pointed at my middle from no more than a foot away.

I tensed my stomach muscles because that was going to

stop a stream of nine-millimeter bullets right? Except there were no bullets. The submachine gun went click. Somewhere in the process, I must have closed my eyes because I had to unscrew one to see what happened next.

Heather, still with one of his hands in hers, reached across and struck him in the throat, this time with her hand held like a knife's edge. I heard the delicate bones at the front of his larynx break. Breathing was going to be something of a problem after that. He seemed to realize it too. The malfunctioning gun hit the seat between us. I didn't bother going for it though. It might have made a decent club but that wasn't a fair fight against the guy leaning between the seats to level his own weapon at us.

I grabbed the barrel of the shotgun and wrenched it forward only to drive it back into his shoulder. The tactical stock hit with a heavy enough impact to twist him in his seat. That gave me the leverage to force the gun barrel down. He released that gun and went for the handgun in his belt. There was little chance to beat him. The shotgun was unwieldy and trapped between the seat and the gurgling fellow in the back with us.

I was still reversing the longer weapon when his barrel lined up with my left eye. In that limited space there wasn't a chance in Hel of dodging that shot. I was about to have my disorganized memories scrambled more thoroughly and spread all over the back of the hummer. Then the Uzi burped a handful of rounds that took out his gun hand, then smacked into his chest, and finally, a round went in over his left eye to spread ugly scarlet and off-white on the windshield.

One of the bullets must have gone astray because there was the nasty whine of a ricochet followed by a breathless grunt from the driver.

"I told you to brace yourself." Heather's voice was light, almost cheerful as I looked over to see her wrapping her free hand around the safety bar above her window. I barely got hold of my own safety bar when the Hummer abruptly spun to the right and hit a curb. I felt the vehicle start to tilt under me and had to hope we didn't roll too many times. We were in the outskirts of Mexico City by then so we weren't traveling at a crawl but we weren't speeding along either.

The speed was enough for a roll though. Between the sudden turn, no brakes, and the lift of the curb we went over in a fairly slow tumble. I managed to brace myself with a foot on the transmission hump and my shoulders pressed against the corner of the rear seat. I'm not sure exactly how Heather managed to control her own tumbling so that she barely had a hair out of place when we came to a grinding sliding stop.

She was on the underside laying back against her door. Since there was no exit that way she made one for us. I heard the silenced gun burp again and felt rounds whip past my face to remove the window above me. Falling glass dropped on my neck and down my shirt but managed to fall all around her without actually touching the girl. She gestured me through the window with the little automatic and I took her suggestion to heart.

Somewhere below me was a shotgun and at least one other handgun. I regretted not stopping for one of them when I got through the window to sit on the door. Armed people were spilling out of the car ahead of us. The car behind us had spun out of control as well when it tried to avoid our surprise acrobatics. That one was all tangled up with some entrepreneur's carriage and donkey. At least the donkey and his driver looked alright. The SUV and the carriage were an intermingled wreck. Thankfully there didn't seem to be any carriage passengers.

A slap on my leg got my attention. I looked down to see Heather's well-manicured hand waving imperiously to demand my assistance. "No good ma'am. There are a lot of busy bees piling up out here with guns. They look pretty pissed off."

She slapped my leg again and I looked back down to see her smile. "It's all okay Moose. I've left the guns in the car see? They don't know what happened just yet. I'm just an innocent unarmed girl to them. So give me a hand."

With no better response, I helped her out while I tried not to think about all of the weapons that would be pointed our way fairly soon. I don't know why it was right then that I noticed her song had gone from hymnal sounding organs to an energetic electric guitar. I lowered her to the ground and start to extricate myself the rest of the way as I heard the first words of the song start low voiced but growing louder. "Bawitdaba da bang da dang diggy diggy"

The sound was muted when she replaced the dangling earbud. "Stay here Moose. I'm gonna go get Luis."

I barely had time to get down from the car before she was moving at a slow but steady pace into the oncoming gunmen. I started to scramble back up the car and get some firepower of my own. It would be too late for her but I could at least pile some of the bastards up for her before I went back to Valhalla.

I needn't have worried. The first two guys to reach her were shouting and gesturing with their AKs. She just ignored them and moved in close enough to start dancing. I mean she was literally within hand-holding, arms around each other, dancing distance without being shot. That was a bad mistake. The first one was taken by surprise when she spun into him and used her leverage to point the rifle at his buddy. That seemed like a bad time to pull the trigger to me, but he reacted to the surprise more than his aim I guess. Holes stitched their way up his buddies legs with loud bangs from the weapon.

One of the guys behind them tried to shoot but had no clear angle with Heather cuddled up against the rifleman. She spun to keep her living shield between them while she snagged a knife from his belt and dug it a good two inches into his side. Maybe he didn't have good trigger discipline, but his posture got a ton better while he tried to keep straight up on his toes to avoid the pain pressing in near his innards.

The approaching gunmen were still circling when I popped back out of the car with the handgun. I couldn't find the uzi and there was no time to free the shotgun from where it was wedged under seats and a body or two. I was just about to even the odds for her when I felt a hard metal object slam against the side of my head.

Somebody must have gotten out of the carriage and SUV pileup. I was down but not out. Which turned out to be fortuitous. Since I was on the ground I barely felt the rush of air as something blew on the other side of the Hummer. It didn't make a lot of sense. I mean *maybe* the friction of the car had thrown some sparks, and *maybe* there was something combustible there. There *might* have even been some impact to cause a fuel leak. But the chances of enough leakage to cause the gas tanks to go up were astronomical. The odds must have been with us. I felt a rush of hot air above me and actually heard the passage of some metal banging off the road around me. None of it came close to hitting me though. Maybe that was because most of the flames and metal seemed to have found their way to the guy standing over me.

I rolled to my feet with the handgun leveled. The guy with bits of glass and flaming metal in him fell to take my place. One of the two guys facing Heather had turned to face the explosion. That meant he wasn't an immediate threat while he blinked away the spots. I shot the other one four times with two steady evenly timed shots to center mass and two to the head as I advanced.

His buddy was just beginning to switch his aim from Heather to me when a different gun spoke out from the other side of the burning car. I went ahead and shot him twice myself before I saw the mess that the other shot had made of one side of his head. I swung around to point my gun that direction as Franco came around with his pointed towards me. We both lifted identical eyebrows and then swung to face the other vehicle.

We were just in time to see "Jefe" step into view. He had made it out of the same accident that Franco and the shish kabob at my feet had.

"Senorita, you will release my man, or I will have *your* man castrated! Domingo bring him out!" We'd managed to get past that icy reserve. Jefe sounded very angry and very confident of his control of the situation.

"The same goes for these men. If they do not lower their weapons they will be shot, if they survive that, I will make sure they see you raped repeatedly and thoroughly *puta*." The anger was gaining an upper hand, he practically spit the last word at her. I wasn't sure if that was good or bad. But I was sure that I didn't intend to just drop my gun because we'd hurt his feelings.

The arrival of a guy I assumed was Domingo changed the dynamics. He had Luis by a cord around his neck. The

bodyguard was also bound with zip ties but at least his
hands were in front of him. The problem was the machete
held up between his legs from behind. It must have been
really sharp. There was already a cut in the pants and a
sheet of blood oozing down the material and exposed thigh.
If that blade moved much at all it would make a mess of not
only Luis' junk, but probably his femoral artery leading to a
very real chance of bleeding to death in mere moments.

I wasn't sure how Heather would react to such a threat.
Not many people would take that kind of chance with a
friend and there had been some indications that the two
of them might be much more than buddies. I was
expecting her to release her gunman which would put
Franco and me in an ugly three-way crossfire. I misjudged
her.

She rolled her eyes and blew a gum bubble while she
took her next step. Without any real effort, she pushed the
blade to the hilt in her hostage's ribs and watched him slide
off the knife to the ground. That left us at a stalemate of
sorts. We didn't have a clean shot at Domingo with his
machete. But if either of the baddies did anything, then Jefe
was going to spring a whole bunch of painful leaks.

"So now what Mr. Jefe?" The girl's voice was almost
syrupy sweet as she stood with her fashionable shoes in the
scarlet puddle she'd made with her knife. "If you like do
anything, I like smile and ask my posse over there to like
shoot you like a whole lot and it's totally gonna hurt almost
as bad as your haircut, and like if your little friend slices so
much as an inch more of my friend, I will ask these
gentlemen to totally shoot lots of holes in you and your
cheap wardrobe."

I saw the head kidnapper stifle his rage with a supreme
effort. He took a minute to control his breathing and tamp

down the fires of his anger then barked an order over his shoulder. "Bring him."

This time the hostage was Pedro Perro himself with his traitorous ex-associate. The smuggler was walking carefully as the rat behind him scurried to stay in the cover of his charge while pointing his own handgun at the back of Pedro's skull.

"There is no play. Only a deal." Jefe had regained his composure and went so far as to lower his own weapon. "We take the car, and we take your friend over there and the short Americano. The rest of you leave. Run and get out of Mexico before I can get back with enough men to paint this whole street in your blood."

It was Heather's turn to get red from her neck up. Her grip tightened on the knife and I was pretty sure that "Jefe" would have his guts for foot warmers if he'd been within reach. She had to settle for stamping a foot and splashing gore all over her legs. "I'm not leaving Luis. Take the sleazy smuggler and his buddies or whatever but you don't get mine."

That got the first smile Jefe had displayed since the wreck. "Now that would be stupid of me. Why take a hostage that your foes find without value? Let us be clear. The only way you leave here with your "friend", is carrying his lifeless body as the blood leaks out. I have seen such a death. If the cut is high like Domingo is holding it, then the blood vessels they snap back up into his crotch. Blood pours out by the bucket. Only a very good surgeon can fix it. If, however, you take your friends and leave, then I will let your precious Luis go unharmed when we are through with our business tonight."

Out of the corner of my eye, I saw the girl fight the urge to stomp her elegant shoe into the blood puddle again. Her fists clenched and unclenched for a long three count before she spoke through locked teeth. It wasn't the right time for it, but I couldn't help being amused that even with her jaw locked tight she still had that valley girl accent from the eighties or nineties. "O, M, G, You already have *one* hostage. So like *why* would we give you another one?"

Somehow the cartel guy could make a shrug almost as irritatingly smug as his smile. "I need two hostages for two different purposes senorita. Your companion is coming to make you and your associates behave. The short and wide Yankee is coming because there are Americano spies asking questions about him. We do not need the Americanos interrupting our operations tonight. By tomorrow none of that will matter and we will be gone. The gunrunner knows where to find us. He provided many of the weapons for my men. Have him show you tomorrow so you can pick up your friend."

Heather had shown impressive patience during his long-winded speeches. I was starting to think maybe there was a sharp brain working behind the bubblegum and blonde bimbo vibes. That all came crashing down with her next move. She dropped the knife and walked over to Jefe who kept his gun trained on her while his own eyes tightened. "Please do not be stupid little girl. It would be terrible to put a bullet hole in such a lovely creature."

"Like, I totes hope my dudes are simpatico" She let out a sigh as she turned her back and slowly walked the last few steps with her hands in the air until her back was almost against him.

"Ugh, I guess You're gonna have to like take me too. I'll go and like keep an eye on you and your bargain haircut and cheap clothes. I don't trust you to play nice behind my back."

Which probably explains why she had deliberately put her back to him with her hands up. My impression of her mental capability took a sharp turn from upwards to precipitously falling.

The boss kidnapper was nothing if not swift thinking and adaptable. He took one long step and hooked a hand into her hair as the other brought his gun up along her jaw.

"Very admirable little girl. And you Perro? Do you see how things have changed?" His one visible eye glittered with an eager hate behind the girl's head. "You will come with us now too. Everyone but the businessman with the guns is invited to the party now."

Franco looked around the tableau making up his mind. Other than my weapon, his was the only one not pointed at one of our supposed allies. With a shrug, he changed even that. His aim switched from Jefe to my head in one swift smooth motion.

"Magnus was it? Please drop your weapon. I assume the Latin gentleman would be just as pleased with your death as your captivity. This way I get to go back to Corsica and eat mamma's manicotti one more time." He had dropped that joyful banter finally. I had little doubt that he would shoot me if it came to that. We had been brothers in arms once, but that was a long time ago. Who knew what he'd seen since then? Or how it had changed him?

I didn't do anything stupid and dramatic like let the weapon loose to swing from the trigger guard. I simply pulled my trigger finger out and very gently put it on the ground. Nothing else seemed prudent. Then again surrendering to these assholes didn't seem particularly prudent either but sometimes you take the lemon with the least bitter suck to it.

"Very good senor Franco. You may keep your weapon,

but please, back away to that cafe behind you. Once you are inside we will acquire another vehicle and be on our way. Please stay inside. Have a cup of coffee. Maybe eat something. Do not come back out for half an hour and we will be long gone. After that, I think perhaps you should sell your weapons elsewhere." I idly wondered if Franco wanted to put a bullet in this windbag's teeth as much as I did.

If so, he didn't show it. After a curt nod, he backed away with his weapon trained on Jefe despite the likelihood of hitting the girl. If I was guessing he would shoot her and keep firing even as she fell. Eventually, some bullets would get past to the target behind her. Franco didn't seem jovial and harmless at that precise moment.

Once he was out of sight, orders came spitting out from behind Heather's head as Jefe ordered his men. Two of them with AKs showed up from behind the wrecked donkey cart. If the situation had devolved we would have all gone down in a shitstorm of bullets. Maybe the girl wasn't as stupid as I thought. Or maybe she was just lucky.

It took the heavily armed criminals less than five minutes to get us back on the road in their one working vehicle and a great big pickup they "borrowed". A glimpse at the guys they took the truck from told me this was probably not the first time this truck had been borrowed. It might even have been the second time in twenty-four hours.

It probably would have been smart to separate us again inside the two vehicles. I think el Jefe was more pissed than smart though. He had us all zip-tied at the wrist and ankle then all three of us were tied to the cargo rings inside the pickup bed. He gestured at one of the guards to join us and traded that guy a shotgun for his own little uzi. The shotgun made sense. If we got rambunctious he could probably get us all with minimal effort and only incidental damage to the vehicle.

We were on our way along fiercely uneven cobblestones before Pedro finally spoke up. "Well, that was a real cluster fuck. What the hell happened to your car?"

I don't know why he glared at me. When it came down to blowing things up and wrecking everything from prisons to hopes and dreams he was way ahead of me. I hadn't blown up anything.

"One of those.." Heather paused to find the right word, "*Assholes!* Put his hand up my skirt."

Apparently, that was all she deemed important about the previous scene. I decided to clarify for those who hadn't been part of it. "She smacked him and his gun went off. One of those little full autos. Ricocheted around and got the driver. Flop goes the weasel. As for the explosion, it beats the hell out of me. Maybe a fuel line or something."

Our guard grunted a command in Spanish and gestured with his gun. We all four shrugged at him in unison despite at least two of us understanding whatever he'd said. The gunny glared at us and then lifted a thick and filthy looking finger to his lips.

"Damn man, I don't know that I'd put that ugly nubbin anywhere close to my mouth. I mean maybe you know where it's been and all but that digit is nasty." Pedro didn't sound too upset by our turn of fate. Instead, he seemed delighted to antagonize the guy with the face-chewing buckshot in his gun. Which earned him another glare and grunt that had to mean "*shut the hell up*" in Spanish.

"Good, we can talk now." Pedro turned to the rest of us and completely ignored the guy tasked with guarding us,

"How do you figure that? Just because he didn't respond to your insults in English you think we're safe?" Sometimes his train of thought went a little too quick for me. Sometimes it just seemed to derail whether I was paying attention or not.

"No, I figure we're safe because I defied him and he did not make a mess of my brains on the rear window of the truck. Besides, I already knew he doesn't speak English. This muchacho doesn't even really speak Spanish. I believe he is only truly fluent in grunts and bodily function. So if he has not shot me, it is because he has instruction to *NOT* shoot us." He was awful smug for a little guy restrained and tied to the back of a truck bearing ugly men carrying ugly guns.

"So you risked getting shot to death, to see if he would shoot you to death? Pedro, you really scare me sometimes." I didn't even know where to go from there. Maybe I was off my game from being on death's door so often lately, not to mention being blown up repeatedly.

"Hush warrior," For the first time I noticed that Luis had a very pleasant and calm baritone voice. Then again those two words were one of the longer sentences he'd said in my presence.

"Oh my god, preserve me from testosterone." Heather interrupted to toss her own two cents worth. "Sleaze meister, your plan is sooo screwed right now. You heard right? They're like ready to go *now, tonight.* You totally need to work on your minions. The four-one-one they give you is like totally just craptastic."

Pedro Perro's shrug was almost eloquent. "True, but they *are* cheap. What did that old white guy say anyway about plans and battles? How one of them rarely survives the other or something like that right? Besides, we're gonna be there right on time. It is a couple days earlier than I expected, but we're still gonna be there. The problem is, I probably won't get to do my job. They'll have me where their patrone can keep an eye on me. So...I propose you and I change tasks. I do yours and you do mine."

Luis rolled his eyes but Heather's lips quirked in a little smirk. "You wish, weasel. You do mine? Lawl. But, like, deal. You like, take care of our little problem and We'll totes go in and get your peeps."

Things starting clicking together about then. "Wait, you meant, to come along? And this jerkoff just wants to save a bunch of his folks? Do I even want to know what your little problem is? For that matter do I even know what the Hel I'm actually here for?"

All sorts of things were starting to make sense to me. There were a ton of images and moments from the last few days that suddenly took new meaning. "You little son of a bitch. Half the crap I've been through was about timing, wasn't it? You had to slow me down to get us all here at just the right time for your own purposes."

Again with the eloquent shrug, this time Pedro added a smug grin with just a hint of embarrassment. "Si Senor Mouse. It took some doing. I could tell you were the type that would just keep going straight ahead. Like the bull in the dish stall no?"

"A bull in the china shop?" I growled but truth be told, he wasn't that far off. I've noticed and often been told that I can focus a little too much on goals and a little less than necessary about the route. Of course, the last person had said it differently. *Boy, you ain't got the sense to go 'round a wall, do you? But I ain't never seen a wall that would stop you either.*

"Damn it was impressive seein you work though. That old Lobo knew what he was sendin', didn't he? Little hard on the detainees here and there, but those guys don't exactly play nice either. It was really bad luck that got you in that particular prison and you got a right to be pissed about that one. I mean damn. But you come through still tickin' and pointed at the job. I don't think anyone coulda found a wall to stop you this side of the grave eh? That must have been some favor you owe him." While he was talking, Pedro wasn't watching.

I started to mention how mad our guard looked. It was very hard not to say anything when the guy stood up in the bouncing truck and gripped his weapon in a manner I knew well. But then again I figured I was due a little rough fun of my own at this point. Don't ask me why Luis didn't say anything either when the not-so-bright guard cold-cocked Pedro with the butt of his shotgun.

That left me and the girl to communicate with an occasional grunt or monosyllable from her sidekick. They weren't exactly fountains of information. But I felt like just maybe I could trust their spoken word a pinch more than the conniving smuggler.

19

WE DROVE through a lot of empty space once the city was behind us. Parts of central America are great and other parts are open, dry and mostly desolate. We drove through the afternoon in one of those desert-like environments. We could see mountains near the horizon and closer to our route were some of the large ziggurat structures that tourists flock to.

Our "hosts" skirted just within sight of the Pyramid of the Sun and its attendant buildings without going in. Instead, they angled away down a dirt track that looked rough but rode as if it was newly graded. It seemed a good guess that someone had set this road up not too long ago and prepared it for some fairly heavy equipment. The track led towards the mountains in the distance.

With Pedro unconscious for most of the way, the talk was quieter and much less frequent. The occasional grunt and scowl from our monosyllabic guard limited the conversation even more. To be honest it seemed like my other two allies weren't too keen to talk to me anyway. They reluctantly gave me a little more information.

For instance, they were there to stop the head honcho from acquiring some nasty sound WMDs or "weapons of mass destruction". They were a little vague on the type. I got shrugs in response to questions about everything from nukes to bio or chemical weapons. When I asked who was selling the things they got even more noncommittal.

By dusk, we were in the shadows of whichever Sierra Madres Mountains this one was. I never could keep it straight which was the oriental range and which the occidental. Not that it really mattered when you're zip-tied in the back of a truck with sketchy allies and a single neanderthal toting a shotgun. Someday I'm going to take a long hard look at how I get into these situations.

It was deep night by the time we rounded a hill to find a sprawling complex surrounded by spotlights. The topography immediately snapped in my mind to the maps we'd been using to plan our operations. The guard towers were all occupied rather than one or two. Their spotlights weren't on any casual random table either but were constantly sweeping the perimeter of the area carved out of rough trees and rock.

We passed through a manned gate surrounded by barbed wire fences. There was even a set of the heavy concrete crash barriers and the huge steel "jacks" or giant caltrops you see in old WWII movies. These folks didn't seem to be very hospitable. I have no doubt that we would have been in serious trouble without el Jefe leaning out of the window as identification.

The cavernous muzzles of twin Russian-made anti-aircraft machine guns tracked us from either tower near the gate. Only after a brief conversation with Jefe did the guards wave us through and the nasty old machine guns swerve away from our vehicle. I happen to know what those guns could do. Maybe my companions didn't because they never even looked at the beasts the whole time I was imagining being reduced to a wet and slimy coating on the junked pieces of a truck.

"Look, like we totally told you our roll down here." Heather all but hissed the words.

When I turned towards the malibu militant I could see the intensity of her look as she continued. "So who, like, sent you and what the Hel for?"

I shook my head and chuckled. I've tried before, to explain the little things about being a centuries-old chosen warrior. It rarely goes well. "Lady, you wouldn't believe me if I told you."

She turned that intense gaze up a notch and cocked her head to one side before snapping out two terse words. "Try me!"

Her voice was insistent and I found myself answering despite any reservations. "I was sent by an immortal wolf to rescue his brother from some vague problems down here."

Her eyes went from intense to wide and shocked as she did her own mystifying mental gymnastics. "Mr. Gary...Gere!? You're down here to rescue freakin Gere? How would he be involved in this kind of thing?"

A sudden buzzing started behind my ears and radiated all the way into my teeth to distract me. From the looks of Heather and Luis, it was doing something similar to them. A weak but very persistent headache began developing almost immediately.

It was distracting enough that I barely heard Perro speak for the first time in hours. "By accident. Mr. Gary got sucked into this by accident. He was just hanging out with biker buddies he called his pack. They did some side work for Achilles and the Cartel. With just a little luck he would never have heard of the chamber under the ruins and he would have never met the girl much less become involved with her."

The buzzing sensation lightened up until I could feel my jaw muscles relax and the tension headache eased up.

Pedro must have felt it too because he spoke again. "Amateurs, they're using it all wrong. The thing is essentially a high powered radio broadcaster. You just don't need a radio to hear it. And he's using it to fog people. What an idiot."

Maybe it was just an after effect of whatever that buzzing had been, but it seemed like most of Pedro's accent had changed. His diction seemed more precise and whatever accent remained was exotic and almost primal in the tones and guttural sounds.

I shrugged and tried to concentrate on what had happened just prior to the sound show. Something the girl had asked me, Mr. Gary, Gere, she'd put those two names together really fast for someone who was on a different mission altogether. I didn't get to finish that chain of thoughts before the truck rocked to a stop and our mexican-derthal guard dropped the tailgate and gestured the rest of us out.

Pedro landed with perfect balance, the girl did almost as well and Luis only needed to steady himself with the help of the smuggler. By comparison, I was a rodeo clown. I landed off balance and immediately fell heavily to roll twice before struggling to reach my knees. Luis got both of his tethered hands under my bicep and helped me up while the guards around us laughed or in a few cases stood around looking bored.

Laughing guards got barely a glance compared to the lean and well-dressed figure that descended ancient steps to step out of shadow into the bright light around us. I recognized El Patron Achilles from our previous encounter days ago and just this side of the border. He looked calm and entirely in command. It took an effort not to smile though as I noticed the empty spot where his enforcer should be standing.

The memory of Mateo spraying his life's blood into the dust around him was fairly heartwarming. It reminded me that these guys had captured me more than once and I was still kicking. Maybe there were zip ties, but they weren't the best restraints. Give me a minute of solitude and I'd be out of them and ready for mayhem.

The spectacle that was our chief captor paused for effect a few steps from the bottom of the stairs. He had judged the spot perfectly to capture the best light with the widest audience to see him. Achilles was wearing some conglomeration of costumes. The shirt was french silk in a Byronesque look. Instead of pants though he had on an odd loin cloth that wrapped around his hips and was knotted to hang almost to his knees in front. The cloth looked like good quality cotton, maybe the Egyptian stuff women love for their sheets. It was dyed in a rainbow of bright colors and trimmed with what I suspected was real gold and gems.

His feet were covered in sandals that had ties wrapping up his calves, while atop his head was the most discordant and ornate note to the odd costume. His headdress sported the multitude of feathers and flowers one would imagine an ancient Aztec or Mayan king would wear, but the centerpiece of all that color was a conch shaped helmet that looked like it was made of horn or abalone. It definitely looked organic in origin but had been shaped cunningly by nature or artifice to perfectly fit the megalomaniac noggin.

"Shit, he has a control helmet." Pedro's displeasure

devolved from English into a number of words that fit no language I knew but were probably still curses and profanities.

Finally, he paused for breath before continuing. "That stupid looking shell on his head means he can control the machinery from anywhere within a few miles. Even worse it's bulletproof. How the hell did he get down into the chamber again? I hid his key."

Pedro turned to look at the rest of us as if all of his newest ramblings made any sense at all. "Ok, promise me you will get my people out! He will bring me up next to him and make a spectacle so I will be able to take care of Achilles. You three have to save my people though. So swear it!"

For once the little charlatan was agitated enough to startle me. I saw the other two with me nod in agreement before chiming in unison. "Of course. We promise."

"AH Pedro Perro!" El Patrone's voice pulled us back to the moment. "You have brought guests to view our special night!"

He stopped a few feet away to look us all over with long penetrating glares. "The girl and her little friend I do not know. This must be the Yankee with the spies no?"

His glare for me seemed touched with more amusement than fear or anger. "Well, you are here Yankee spy. Let me show you what you are too late to stop."

To the guards around us, he snapped a phrase in what I assumed was the ancient Aztec tongue, Nahuatl. At a guess, it was "Bring the dogs." Because the guards were none too gentle in prodding us along with antique-looking weapons. Mostly they were the obsidian-toothed wooden clubs or swords that had proved almost a match for conquistador armor. Almost a match but not quite, because the Spaniards had left the vast and fairly advanced Aztec empire in ruins. Then again a lack of immunity to European bugs had played its part in that demise.

When Cortes descended on Tenochtitlan it had been larger than any city in Europe except possibly Constantinople. Within a short time, he had decimated that city through a mix of siege, allied Indian tribes, and disease. The fellows prodding us along would have felt entirely at ease alongside the warriors and priests that had fought,(and rumor said *eaten)* Spanish invaders. All of them wore the same odd loincloth as their leader, though instead of anachronistic silk shirts they wore short triangular cloaks and a number of tattoos. Most of them had some kind of spotting or feline camouflage tattooed along their arms. At least one had covered his entire torso in jaguar spots.

They got us to the top of the low pyramid where we were able to see all around. There were a few more buildings but they were too ruined to be identified as to use or function. Below us was a broad amphitheater with stone seating about twenty feet above the sandy floor of an arena. A fight below us was just ending as we topped the pyramid to get our first look.

A large but lean man was standing over the body of a jaguar while two more circled around him. In addition to the cat, there were several other corpses. I recognized the leather jackets and denim from my previous encounter at a hotel in Arizona. Apparently so did the odd man out in our gathering.

Out of all the guards and captors still, with us, the only one not dressed as some sort of Aztec was our betrayer and Pedro's sometime associate. He audibly gasped when he saw the gruesome spectacle of his former biker buddies.

Achilles responded with a turn of his head. "Oh yes,

your packmates were proving to me that they were tough. I was very disappointed when I heard they were so defeated by a single gringo that half of them had to be hospitalized. They are allaying my suspicions that they were part of some conspiracy. I fear they were truthful. They truly were too weak to fight well. I even let them have the dogs from your fighting pits. The dogs did no better than the bikers. Except for your Mr. Gary. He is a warrior. Two cats down and two to go. Also two dogs. Not pit bulls though. One is some sort of lion dog. The other I do not know."

He might not know. I did though. I registered the identity of the "man" below us. Mr. Gary, Gere the immortal wolf that did Odin's bidding and sat at his side. Like many residents of Asgard, he was able to take human form. His brother was an oversized biker at least six and a half feet tall when I had last seen him. Gere was only a few inches shorter but built more like a swimmer or runner than a brawler like Freke. He was all lean muscle and long limbs. There was enough muscle there to casually toss a charging jaguar twenty feet though.

I saw all of that in the instant before I recognized the golden-colored dog circling opposite a giant canine around the second remaining jaguar. The larger dog charged and the cat spun to meet him. It had given Grimmr his chance though. My Catahoula charged in and ripped at the cat's back legs. He drew blood and a snarl from the jaguar, but he missed any crippling damage to the tendons.

The cat's response was instantaneous. He spun almost too quick to see and slapped my dog rolling across the sand with a spray of blood. I knew that Jaguars fought and killed prey much larger than themselves. Their typical kill was a leap that ended in a single bite that could penetrate skull and brain alike. That didn't mean their four-inch claws and powerful forelimbs were a joke. Such a blow might very well snap a dogs neck even if the claws did not open an artery.

I don't remember any decision to act. One minute I was listening to the bragging megalomaniac in a shell helmet, the next I was pushing my forearms down on either side of a shard of hyper-sharpened obsidian. Mother Nature's response to surgical steel cut through the zip ties like they were thread. The black rock also opened a long incision down one wrist, but I was already moving and too busy to notice how bad it might be.

I sprang down the steps in rapid bounding leaps that covered three or four steps in each awkward jump. I saw the cat dodge the larger lion dog's rush and ride him to the ground with paws locked over the dog's shoulders. The jaws of the jaguar opened wider than seemed possible then shut on the dog's head and the fighting canine went limp with a yelp. The already dead meat continued to spasm for several seconds as the cat climbed off and oriented on my dog who was limping and side-walking away from the gore covered hunter. I saw the other cat limping in a circle around Gary but that was barely a consideration.

Somewhere in my core, a beast was rising. I could see the surge and tide of red in time to the pulse beating in my head and heart. "Grimmr!"

The roar was in response to a sudden rush of the cat. I couldn't make it in time. Limping and unable to avoid the larger cat, my dog didn't stand a chance. All I could do was charge forward and watch as my oldest companion had his skull and brain turned to jelly.

Except he didn't. At the very last split second, Grimmr spun on his "injured" leg and drove forward to grip the cat's foreleg. I heard the feline spitting its surprise, but above that, I heard the snap as Grimmr rolled, still with the lean limb locked between his jaws. Eighty pounds of dog going one way, and two hundred pounds of cat going another, all multiplied by the torque of his rolling, added up to one broke bone.

Grimmr rolled one way, the cat rolled the other, and I exploded into the air above my pet and his attacker. The cat's claws raked at my shirt and tore it as well as the flesh underneath. I got my forearms around its neck though so it couldn't deploy that devastating bite. The damned cat felt like it weighed as much as I do and seemed considerably stronger than a man of similar size.

That didn't really matter much to whatever was raging inside me though. I straddled the back of the beast while it batted air with his forelegs and tried to gain purchase with his rear claws. All of that stopped when I tightened my arms and jerked the dangerous head upwards and sideways. For the second time in as many seconds, the sound of bone breaking and separating cracked across the arena.

I wanted to sprint over and check on my dog, but there was still a dangerous predator in the arena with me. I turned in my tracks to see that deadly predator catch the remaining jaguar in mid-air. Gary ducked under the jaws and claws of the cat but came up underneath it almost too quick to see. He caught the back legs as they were almost overhead and brought the beast crashing down.

Without losing his grip, Gere stood and began to spin, he lifted the cat off the sand and with a guttural snarl slammed it headfirst into the stone wall surrounding us. The impact of a particularly large melon splattering was the closest I could find to what sounded out over the stadium and ended in a sudden and profound silence.

The spectators and guards all around us stopped and stared as my dog limped over and joined me in walking up to the long lost end of my personal quest. Now all I had to do was get Gere out of here and I could go home. Easy right?

The three of us turned towards the sound of an altercation above us. I had a moment to wonder *how in Hel's decayed dugs had my dog gotten here*. And if he was here what did that mean for Rafe and most importantly my Maureen? The shock of that thought drove down the tides of red rage that had fueled my fight with the jaguar.

Maureen wouldn't just abandon my pets. No matter how annoyed, irritated or plain pissed off she was, she would take care of the animals. If Grimmr was here then something had happened to Maureen. Rafe, I wasn't as worried about. If he saw so much as a cracked window he'd make a break for it. Then everything from a kitten to a bobcat might be in danger but Rafe would probably be fine. He really didn't like cats. Except maybe for dinner.

Grimmr must have sensed my mood. He trotted up and thrust a gore spattered nose under my hand. Out of the corner of my eye, I saw his tail wave just enough to let me know it was moving. I guess fighting felines twice your size can be exhausting for an old pup. I gave him a pat and wished more than anything that the beast could talk. That he could tell me where the girl was and what had happened.

My wishes and musings were brought short by a shot fired from above. We all looked up to see Achilles standing behind his warriors who were in turn behind Heather and Luis. Pedro and his treacherous henchman were towards the middle of that formation.

"So, the dog belongs to the gringo Yankee. I see we were right to be suspicious of spies." Achilles' voice attempted to portray confidence. I was sensing a current of fear under that pose though.

For the moment I remained silent and let him continue.

"And to think my own dear ally Senor Perro brought this intruder across the border and all the way to my doorstep so to speak. What should I make of that? Perhaps Pedro Perro is not as loyal as I would wish. No?"

He punctuated that statement abruptly and in a final manner. His hand came up with a heavy pistol just like his enforcer Mateo had favored. With the barrel practically against Perro's head, it thundered once and the smuggler fell with his strings cut as his head was momentarily obscured by a spray of blood and bone and worse. I wasn't inclined to take a closer look when he rolled down the stone stairs.

The trail of blood for the first dozen steps spoke volumes. After that, his heart must have stopped. The blood trail faded away but his body continued to roll until it landed at our feet. I knew what a round that size would do, not to mention the muzzle blast at such proximity. There was no need to check vitals, though I did spare one quick glance at the surprised expression on what was visible of his face.

That burning rage started to rise again. Maybe we weren't blood-brothers or anything but Pedro and I had been through a lot in the last few days. He was a conniving little weasel but he was *my* conniving little weasel. That didn't give someone like a pompous asshat in a poet shirt and mesoamerican skirt the right to end him.

Apparently, Achilles did not agree with or even acknowledge my feelings on the matter. He all but ignored me and the dog, and the wolf. Instead, he barked some of those exotic sounding orders at his archaic bodyguards and watched with satisfaction as they shoved the remaining prisoners to fall down the steep steps. The rat-like biker hit first followed by Luis.

Above them, Achilles clarified the situation for all of

us."You have killed the pets of my loyal servants. For that, I shall give you to them." He finished his little speech with a snarl of more orders in Nahuatl.

The half dozen tattooed and skirted men atop the pyramid began stalking down the steps. As they walked each began limbering the arm that held his obsidian weapon. The soft thud of several more feet on the sand heralded the arrival of more Aztec wannabes. At least half a dozen extra primitives jumped down from the twenty-foot wall to join the ones coming down the steps.

As they started down the steps I saw a particularly muscular and grim looking warrior point his club at me and then at the cat I had killed. He snarled and gave me a glimpse at teeth that were filed to points and stained red.

When he spoke, the word sounded guttural and foreign to his tongue. " Cub was Mine! Now you, Mine!"

Luis regained his balance on the second roll. Instead of continuing to the sand he staggered to his feet three steps from the floor of the arena. He started down to help Heather to her feet but never got the chance. One of the descending warriors made an impressive leap that cleared half a dozen steps before he swung his club at the back of the body-guard's neck.

Luis ducked that slashing attack and clipped the Aztec's legs just enough to send him headfirst into the stone steps with an audible snap of what was probably facial bones and vertebrae. We could count that one out for the time being.

The Aztecs responded with a new attack of three on one, with Luis being in the minority for this fight. He handily evaded two of them but the third obsidian sword seemed to catch his shirt just above the beltline.

The blades were sharp enough that we didn't even hear the tearing of cloth, instead, we saw a scrap of shirt flutter down with a perfectly clean edge, while Luis stumbled and fell back with a loop of purple-grey protruding from his exposed belly.

The incision was surgically perfect and opened him for a length of at least six or eight inches. Somehow, despite the injury, he managed to cut his own bonds on the dropped weapon of the foe he'd dropped. He pressed a hand against the bulging intestine and held it in place while his free hand struck the offending attacker across the bridge of his nose. That one went down for a second. A one-handed fighter is at a distinct disadvantage though, even more so when facing three opponents and holding slippery guts in place. A well-timed kick sent him down the last few steps. He lost his grip and more innards spilled out along with a spray of blood as Luis landed on his back.

The third member of our party, betrayer of smugglers and gang-member weakling, was less concerned with approaching doom than he was focused on the head of his "pack" of mostly deceased buddies.

"Sangre de Cristo Senor Gary! I am so glad to see you!" His voice quavered and broke as if on the verge of tears. It was the kind of voice that went with clasped hands and kneeling pleas. It was, however, apparently not the kind of voice to present to a gore spattered Alpha male standing in the ruins of his pack that you had turned your back on.

Gere leaned forward and I kid you not, snapped his teeth in the guy's face. For a minute it almost looked like his face was elongating into a muzzle, but the moment passed and he was fairly normal looking again. At least normal looking for a guy that could dash a hunting cat's brains out with his bare hands and a handy wall. He finished his response by backhanding his ex-associate with a casual power that sent the other guy rolling.

Snitch-ferret got shakily to his feet and licked his lips as his eyes darted from Gere to the approaching jaguar warriors. With a low moan of fear, he backed away to circle around and put Grimmr and I between him and the approaching Aztecs. Of course that put his back to the ones coming from behind. The little guy was apparently too terrified to think of that though.

Gere and my dog weren't as stricken with abject fear. Almost like a single unit they bounded towards the leading Aztec. Gere reached him first and drew the lightning-fast swipe of razor-sharp obsidian. The weapon never struck, as the wise old wolf spun on a heel and rolled back and to his left even as Grimmr came in from the right and ripped at the back of his target's calf.

There was a whining snarl and their victim fell to a knee just in time for Gere to bounce back with a jaw-breaking punch into the side of the kneeling warrior's face. Count that one out as well.

A rush of feet behind me brought me around to face the other attackers. They had surprised the snitch and he rushed past me with his wide-eyed stare devoted to the ones who had nearly got him from behind. That, of course, left him not watching the *new* threat behind him. All of the warriors still functioning went past him without notice, except for the last fellow who fetched a dandy of a shot to the back of the traitor's knee. The leg seemed to all but come free at mid point. A scrap of meat held the leg on while the wounded weasel shrieked in surprise and agony.

His cries died out when the two wounded Aztecs pounced on him. The one with the broken jaw lashed out with a hand curved into a claw. He used his free hand to pound on the one embedded in his victim's chest until ribs and sternum cracked. Out came a pulsing squirting bunch of purple gray and red. The warrior forced his broken jaw open and squeezed blood from the beating heart into his mouth along with a good-sized piece of meat. The rest of the organ he gave to his brother with the wrecked face and flopping neck.

Almost instantly their wounds closed and bones snapped back into place. Even the apparent neural damage was erased as the awkward and broken jaguar warrior regained his posture and suddenly began moving with feline grace again.

"What the Hel?" I wasn't aware that I had stopped breathing until I had to draw a breath to exclaim and question what I had just seen. "Are they freakin' vampires?"

Gere's answer was not as reassuring as I would have liked. He responded by charging at the nearest warrior while grinning over his shoulder. "Don't know, I'll tell you in a second."

20

THE NEXT FEW seconds got pretty busy. I had my hands too full to see exactly how Gere was going to determine the undead status of our adversaries. I was keeping three of the warriors off of us by a series of feints and an occasional actual attack using various hand to hand skills I'd picked up here and there.

The cat warriors were ok with some basic karate and even krav maga. The American style Kenpo kept them off balance though. Three guaranteed disables had been returned for a refund. All three of my targets had slowed some but none of them were out of the fight. With just enough breathing room to check, I gave a swift glance for my allies.

Heather had pressed both of Luis' hands over his wound and dragged him back into the limited protection of Gere and I. While she did so Grimmr showed an unusual level of teamwork and harried the warriors while they tried to get to the wounded gunman.

Gere had downed three of the ones behind us but wasn't

able to finish any of them before their buddies joined in. He
had, however, managed to accumulate a pile of broken
wooden bats with obsidian shards. Even as I glanced he
grabbed one of the broken bats and with a single savage
rush battered aside two of the warriors to thrust the jagged
wooden "stake" into the chest of one of the healthiest
jaguar-men.

I spun around to deliver a rapid-fire flurry of low kicks
and short punches which pushed my latest attacker back
again. With a break in the action, I looked back to where
Gere's staked foe shuddered and fell still. His nearest ally,
however, didn't accept that verdict as final. He grabbed one
of the weakly crawling bikers from an earlier brawl and
once more ribs cracked and a pulsing heart was pulled free.

The still operational warrior pressed the warm flesh into
his downed comrade's mouth and squeezed until the other
shuddered and took a weak bite of the flesh. Almost
instantly his color began to improve, his weak struggles
became purposeful and with a gasp of shock, I saw the stake
in his chest vibrate with the beat of a strong heart that
pushed the wood out of a wound that closed itself in
seconds.

"Nope, not vampires." Gere didn't sound as thrilled as he
had before. His voice wasn't exactly despondent but it had
lost some of the thrill of battle that had been there earlier.
Now he just sounded serious and very intense.

I felt my own hopes drop a little as I saw some of our
more wounded foes eating hearts freshly ripped from some
of the bikers that had not already expired from their battle
with actual felines. Each of the Aztecas shed every sign of
injury with the gulping of fresh cardiac muscle. By
comparison, I sported at least half a dozen wounds ranging
from what felt like a separated shoulder to a scratch that

came within inches of disemboweling me as Luis had been.

Gere was bleeding from twice as many places as I was. His immortal nature was even tougher than mine though. He didn't seem to even notice the deep slash running down the outer side of his left thigh. At least he moved on it as if it was nothing more than a minor inconvenience.

Grimmr was dragging a leg and heaving with the exertion. I wasn't sure how much of the gore on his chest was man, cat, or his own, but there was plenty of blood for all of the above.

I looked over to Heather and her patient just as one of the obsidian weapons made it past her and buried a trio of razor-sharp shards in Luis' chest. From the angle, I thought they missed his heart, but his right lung would be a mess. In either case, it was a mortal wound. Not that he'd been that much help anyway.

I saw Heather glare at the smirking warrior standing over her. When he jerked the blade out of Luis I started to try and intercept him. It was quite apparent that he wanted the girl next. I could easily picture her head rolling across the sand as he stood over her. Except I never got there, and he never got to swing. Instead, the girl threw what looked like a punch at him; if a punch could travel three feet farther than the lady could reach.

In that instant, several mishaps occurred at the same instant. The blade had been stuck in Luis' ribs. It snapped free with unexpected violence even as the warrior holding it slipped in a puddle. He fell backward to land on a similar weapon that was improbably lying with its edges upwards. At the same time his own weapon came down to land on and half sever his neck.

Everyone stopped to stare at the impossibility of the

moment. And that's when Heather's voice rang out with a steely. "NO!"

What followed was my own ancient Norse language, except colored by a heavy valley girl accent. Runes flared from invisible to brightly glowing around Luis chest and belly. I felt my own runic tattoos flare and pulse warm rolls of healing energy that snapped my shoulder into place and knitted flesh together as if it were whole and new.

I looked over to see Gere nod his approval to the young Valkyrie before turning back to the fray with his own wounds disappearing faster than he'd got them. Behind me, I heard Heather's indignant voice.

"Who like totally *runed* a dog, like, I don't even know what to...like, OMG." Apparently, she was at a loss for words.

On the other hand, I couldn't help but think of an accident years ago when Eachan had helped me use a little runic lore to take care of Grimmr. I usually took care of minor injuries with a rune or two myself. That time though, it had been a severe accident. The vet said my pup might never walk again, so I called the only non-medical friend I had that might be able to help.

It would be a surprise but not entirely unbelievable that the old professor was a true adept at rune work. I looked over to see if the runes near my dog's hips and spine were glowing as Luis had. What greeted me was a canine spectacle.

He didn't have a glowing rune, or two, or three, or even a dozen. He was literally covered in glowing nordic runes that might have written a novel. If so it would be a novel about dozens of minor or major wounds and accidents that I had casually helped my dog with over the course of our life together. Suddenly his ability to fight Jaguars and hunt me down across a desert wasn't half as mysterious.

I saw another Aztec pull the weapons out of Heather's downed warrior while the rest of them formed a loose cordon around us. Luis got up and helped Heather to her feet while she watched with narrowed eyes. The one she had dealt with was brought a fresh gibbet of bloody fresh valentine's meat. Like the others, he mended completely within seconds and stood up to take his weapon back despite the smear of his own blood along its length.

Gere backed up to the rest of us and bent down to ruffle Grimmr's ears with a grin. He handed me one of the broken weapons. This one was mostly handle, with only a trio of obsidian shards left in the bottom half of the bat. The rest had been broken off, leaving me a handy little stone-age handaxe of razor-sharp perfection.

I faintly heard Heather behind me echoing an idea I'd heard days ago in the dreamworld. "Looks like we aren't, like, a monopoly. These guys are totally, like, holy warriors too."

I flushed at the memory. Hadn't Hugin told me as much? That there were things in my memory that might help me stay alive. And I hadn't stopped to consider that we might meet enemies as steeped in their own mythos and lore as we were. I heard Gere growl as another of his downed bikers was ripped open for consumption. There were still a few weakly struggling to get out of the arena. Once those were gone, or dead, we might face a decent chance. Then again how often could Heather repeat her little trick with the Valkyrie magic?

From her appearance and demeanor, I'd guess she was born in the seventies or maybe eighties. Just old enough to have experienced the Breakfast Club firsthand. The fact that she was openly traveling for days on end with just one Einherjar told me she was new to the gig.

I shrugged away my doubts and noticed my shirt was torn to shreds. That was nothing new, but from previous experience, I knew that tattered rags could become inconvenient handles or restraints in a fight. I ripped the hazardous material away to expose more of my runes and tattoos than most people ever get a chance to see.

I heard Gere grunt and speak to me with a name I hadn't heard in ages. It wasn't the name I was born with, but rather a badge given me my Kara "the tempestuous" herself when I was still loyal to my Valkyrie. "Strombjorn, get ready. They are about to charge."

I heard Luis and Heather both gasp behind me. Luis breathed out his own earthy phrase and a question that didn't make a lot of sense initially. "Oh, shit Mija. You see that?"

"O.M.G. Oh HEL no. Like, this is totes some BS." Heather sounded almost as scared as indignant. "WTF is Kara's like, berserk enforcer, doing on our mission!?"

Enforcer? Berserk? Those didn't ring any bells for me but then again I was still coming to grips with what I remembered versus what I had apparently lost. Was I the stormy one's wetworks guy? Considering Wounded Knee, I couldn't give that an absolute *No*. But I didn't want to believe it either.

I was shaken from my reverie by the sound of a collective shout in Nahuatl as the prelude to an Aztec charge. And just like that, it crystalized. Aztec priests were known for sacrifice. The sacrifice was usually via removal of a heart. During such a ceremony they often blessed the best of their warriors.

I met the charge halfway. The big ugly fellow who had it in for me was in front. Apparently, he'd decided it was time to get revenge for his kitty cat. I ducked over the thunderous swing he tried to decapitate me with. Coming up with an underhand blow, my makeshift axe parted his belly a few inches below his sternum. The black shards continued up to rip into his sternum and ribs, while my free hand followed it.

I buried my hand to the wrist in his wound. From inches away I saw his eyes first widen, then close in agony. Meat and bone and worse parted around my questing fingers. I pushed harder, the corded muscles on my forearm standing out and starting to glow with the power of my own runes rather than the energy of Valkyrie. Suddenly I felt the throbbing muscle in my palm.

With a savage wrenching motion, I jerked the heart from my chief Aztec adversary. He fell without a sound. Bonelessly, limp, and without any semblance of life, he collapsed into an untidy pile at my feet. The other Jaguar warriors stopped in stunned silence.

For one long breathless moment, we all stared at each other. Then I dropped the weakly fluttering meat in my hand to the sand and crushed it with one filthy tactical boot.

I called out to Gere over my shoulder. "Don't stake the heart. Remove it. Now we are a little more even. You want to do this kitty cat boys?"

That last line was directed right at the suddenly hesitant Aztecs. The first three to recover charged me together. One swung low, one went for the decapitation, and the third brought a crushing overhand blow down at my face. There was no way to avoid them all. So I decided to go for the two I could avoid at once. I stepped back and down to the side. With luck, the overhand and the headshot would both miss completely. I was hoping the leg wounds wouldn't be debilitating, but whatever happened I was taking the middle guy with me.

The upper decker was jerked to my left by the force of

his swing, but the middle fellow was pushed forward by his own momentum and the downward blow of his weapon. I ripped him open from crotch to sternum with my now feeble axe so someone could give him the same treatment their dead hunting pack brother had received.

Tensing one's thigh muscles is probably not a proper defense to super-sharp ancient weaponry. It was, however, all I had left in my bag of tricks at that precise moment. I saw Grimmr ride the wannabe headsman to the ground. My dog had his jaws locked at the nape of his victim's neck. A surge of those shoulders would probably snap the neck bones and render said Aztec at least temporarily paralyzed. I couldn't help but wish he'd gone for the one about to shorten me by a foot or two.

My worries were for naught. A barely audible shot rang out and I saw a hand gripping one of the brutal archaic swords fly past me to land harmlessly in the sand. Gere let out an almost joyful laugh from somewhere in his belly and bounded towards his own clump of warriors.

In the next breath, another shot filtered down to us and one of the warriors near Heather went down with the back of his neck gone in a spray of blood. We already knew that such a wound slowed them down and made them clumsy. Heather took advantage of that vulnerability.

She took the spasming warrior's weapon away and neatly opened him from behind. I had a glimpse of the vicious Viking torture called the blood eagle as she spread the exposed ribs and pulled a beating heart out to pulp with her newly acquired weapon.

Just like that, the charge broke and Aztecs fell back to regroup. Heather helped steady Luis but I could tell he was still disoriented. If I had to guess, he'd been more dead than alive when she brought him back. That can take a while to adjust to. The brain doesn't always keep pace with the body during magical healing.

"Hey, Moose, or *Bjorn* should I say?" Luis' voice was husky but very intense. It looked like the hamsters were starting to stretch their legs in his cerebral wheel.

"Yeah Luis, or should I say *Chosen*?" It couldn't hurt to remind him that I wasn't the only one keeping secrets.

"Right, well one chosen to another, can you promise me you're not here to foil us or fuck up our job? We've heard stories, man. We know what Kara has used you for before." His voice was steadier and he was standing on his own at least. Worse for me, he seemed to know more about my past than I did. Maybe Wounded Knee wasn't the nastiest thing I'd perpetuated after all.

I decided not to convey that particular thought, or even to share my little amnesia problem. Instead, I replied with an innocuous assurance of sorts. "Chief, I promise you that all I am here for is to help the big bad wolf over there not get his house blown down."

"Oh, My, Gawd" Heather was all relief and hesitant smiles. "You promise? Like for reals?"

Here we were still facing more than half a dozen sacred warriors almost as tough as we were, on their home ground, with a boss who was presumably meaner than *they* were, and this girl was worried about what tricks I might play on her? I had to chuckle and shake my head at her. "Yea you got my word miss Val girl."

"Val girl?" Her eyes flashed with a touch of the pure arrogance I remembered in Kara. She shrugged it off though and then looked with distaste at the weakly fluttering heart in her hand. With a grunt of effort, she closed her fist and various fluids squirted between her fingers.

Heather looked up at me with a coolness that reminded

me, young she might be, but she'd had whatever it takes to be chosen as a Valkyrie, chooser of the slain and battle maiden. Her voice even dropped the valley girl accent and spoke in icy, aloof intensity. "You have this in hand then. Luis and I made a promise. We will go free Perro's people and then see about finishing off Achilles since the coyote can not. Good luck, Chosen of Kara."

She turned on her heel and stalked towards the trio of Jaguar warriors between her and a ground-level exit out of the arena. I got to see exactly what she meant by "good luck". Two warriors managed to get tangled up and sprawl all over each other trying to get to her. Another caught a sudden random swirl of sand blown up from the arena floor just in time to blind him.

Heather simply walked through them while Luis followed, walking backward to face us while she led the way behind him. "She's good no? No interest at all in weapons or runes but three black belts and that whole luck in battle thing. She does battle fortune with the best of them."

He punctuated his statement by pulling a knife off the belt of one of the dead bikers. With that in hand, he carefully opened up the blinded Aztec and cut his heart out before pulping it with the handle of the borrowed WWII vintage Kabar marine corps knife.

The remaining Aztecs were a little heartened by the sudden change of odds. They regrouped and charged as one. Gere and I rushed to meet them with their own weapons. On the outskirts of our fight, Grimmr circled to slash fangs at opportune ankles and calves. And for the entire short battle, shot after shot cracked down with each sounding closer than the last, and each shot finding a weapon, hand, or semi-vital target in one of our enemies.

In less than two minutes Gere and I stood in the middle

of the sand, covered in the gore of heart-blood while Grimmr bounded around, overjoyed with this new game he got to play with dad. From the top of the same steps we had descended, Franco tossed a small duffel down to land at my feet. "I couldn't bring everything. But they forgot that bag and the M2010 sniper system."

His grin was infectious enough that I returned it even before I opened the duffel to find a few of the toys he had sold me at good ole professor Eachan's expense. I pulled out the tomahawk with its inscriptions as well as the combat knife. There was also a suppressed .40 cal semi-automatic pistol with four loaded magazines.

I stuck the knife in my boot and the pistol behind my belt. Without really thinking about it, I tucked the blade of the rune enhanced tomahawk through my rear belt loop and secured the handle with a loop several inches away. It left the weapon hanging almost exactly like I used to wear my seax ages ago.

"I'd say you were a little late. But it's hard to argue with results." I grinned and thrust out a hand to grip his forearm in the ancient tradition of a warrior's handshake. "Let me introduce you to Mr. Gary."

A sudden thought brought me up short as I introduced the two and they exchanged names and wary glances. This normal everyday mortal mercenary and gun-runner had just engaged in a firefight of sorts with supernatural creatures while we ripped their hearts out and disposed of them. Where exactly was the fear, the revulsion, the gibbering insanity?

The sound of approaching footsteps put all of those thoughts on the back burner. All four of us, dog included, turned to face the newest threat. What we got were a few dozen women and girls being gently shepherded towards us by Heather while Luis watched the perimeter. The modern Einherjar was moving better, and more importantly, was absolutely loaded down with weapons. Multiple handguns were in his belt or holstered on borrowed web gear while he carried an AR and had a grenade launcher slung over his shoulder.

"They had a few guards. It wasn't even fair with my Chula watching my back." He tossed Heather a delighted little smile for her help in assassinating or at least defeating several men. She returned the smile with a blush and a half-curtsy.

"They said Achilles has gone into the tunnels." Heather paused and pointed to where some recent excavation was barely visible behind heavy digging equipment. "He has some little lady with him that he said he needs for blood sacrifice."

"Elena, his half-sister." The growl was barely distinguishable but very accurately portrayed Gere's rage at the plans for exsanguination.

I mentally slapped a hand on my forehead. "Elena? Pretty little thing, with caramel and cream skin, melted butter eyes? Has that innocent purity you usually associate with schoolgirls, nuns, and librarians? Calls a lady named Dolores her Abuela."

He tempered his rage with a quickfire and very self-satisfied smirk. " Its Princesa Dolores and Elena's not all *that* innocent."

I had forgotten Pedro's story that part of the trouble Gere was in had to do with dating the evil villain's sister. So maybe she wasn't as innocent as she seemed. I couldn't forget the pure and chaste kiss she'd bestowed on my cheek as thanks for a ride though. She might have fallen for the old wolf's tricks, but she was still pretty unbesmirched in my books.

"Ok, so let's go get her and punch his teeth in while we're at it." My statement seemed pretty obvious as I double checked my meager collection of weapons compared to Luis and his walking arsenal.

It took a minute for me to register the awkward silence. When I looked up, Gere and Luis were shaking their heads somberly while Heather cleared her throat before answering. "As if! No can do Kahuna. Like, holy ground, it's totally off-limits for us. It would have been like a spoonful of bad for sure taking this bitch outside. He answers to tres different bosses from us. But if we go into the tunnels to fight him. Like totes different gods and stuff. Rival holy man, totally rival holy ground, the one-eyed wonder would totally wig out if we like pissed-off in two different sets of divine wheaties at once."

"Gods on gods on gods huh?" I couldn't stifle a groan. *As if worrying about a divine comeuppance from Odin and a vengeful Kara weren't enough.*

For once Heather looked less than blondely oblivious. She simply nodded and then shrugged with her palms up. "Sorry BearMoose. Our hands are like, tied to the max. Odin would be royally pissed."

The thought of a sweet and cute little girl lying on some cold stone altar started to bug me. I could still remember the clean soapy scent of her as she bestowed her simple thank you. It wasn't like that was even my job. I'd signed on to get Gere out. We could leave right that moment and I would not be forsworn. My part of the bargain was complete. Right?

Gere cleared his throat. "The all-father would not easily forgive this Strombjorn. Would that it were different. The girl is dear to me. But I can not even set foot in those eldritch chambers. My link to the one-eyed would stop me as effectively as Gleipnir chains Fenrir."

I sighed and racked the slide back to make sure there was a round chambered in my pistol. "Pretty sure he's already pissed at me."

21

ALL THREE OF the others tried to dissuade me. It became evident that Kara had not put out a bulletin about my escape from her fold. They all seemed to think I had been working on some project of hers or else had been put in cold storage for a while. Nobody was advertising that I'd gone off-reservation. Which meant all of them assumed I was worried about Odin punishing me when we all went to Valhalla after this thing was settled. Good thing I didn't plan to return until somebody caved in my head enough to send me back.

Upshot was, they had to give up their arguments or follow me down. I went through some recent construction, or maybe destruction? They'd torn a hole in the side of the hill and bored a tunnel down to where the bedrock made them curve a good ninety degrees in a gentle arc.

I came to the end of the tunnel and found myself in a cave. The half of the cave directly before me was all recent work. Tools still lay around. The other half, however, was dominated by a large vault-like wall of stone. Along its border ran carved figures of fanciful creatures and people

wearing exotic outfits. There were irregularly shaped buildings and more of the weird conch like helmets on a few of
the humanoid carvings.

"You must be better than most Yankee dogs. My warriors
would have eaten most such with ease. Yet here you are."
Achilles strolled into view with Elena clasped tightly by her
bound wrists.

The only way I knew it was Achilles was from his headdress and voice. The rest of his features were hidden by an
elaborate costume. The cloak was made of vibrant flowers
that had dried and become bedraggled after a long time in
storage somewhere. His own face and hair were covered by a
pale leather mask and a scraggly dark wig.

As he continued speaking, his voice changed. It took on
a totally unfamiliar accent and became heavier, more
primal."You can not stop the ritual though. I have worked
for thousands of years for this moment. Now wearing the
face of Yaocihuatl and with the blood of ancient royalty. I
shall open the chamber and retrieve the riches we barely
touched before the little sister here escaped."

"Thousands of years eh? Damn you look good. I
wouldn't have placed you a day over eight hundred." I edged
into the chamber and with the gun hidden in my hand
behind one thigh, I sidled a few feet closer. "But who the
Hel is yowie hottel or whatever you said?"

Even through the mask, I felt the heat of his anger. "Yaocihuatl, the Culhuacan princess we made into a Mexicah
goddess. Her sacrifice would have opened the chamber of
the ancients had we not been forced to flee!"

Again his eyes flashed and his teeth actually gnashed
behind, what I now realized with a tightening of my stomach, was the skin of an ancient princess. "But now I have
another princess. Dear Achilles' little half-sister whose

mother bore the same ancient blood as Yaocihuatl before her. A bloodline that I have traced from tens of thousands of years ago to make this day possible!"

He struck such a heroic and proud pose that I just couldn't stand it. With a shrug, I raised the pistol and put a cool half dozen rounds into his chest and the mummified mask he wore. I almost expected the result.

Achilles stumbled back and roared a curse before ripping the now tattered mask down around his neck. "A hundred different faces have I worn. Kings and queens and presidents have heard my voice in their ear and brought the world to a moment when I might put my hands on treasures and mysteries from so far in ancient prehistory that most scoff at even the names. Yet you expect to stop me with a few pitiful shots from a mundane modern weapon? Your firearms are like straw to me. I can heal this flesh package with a thought. It will only fail when I find a new package that I prefer. Perhaps something like this shapely young girl? After all, I only need a little of the blood."

A cruel laugh accompanied his slice down Elena's wrist to splash her blood into a cup on the side of the wall. As if on greased tracks, the wall parted in the middle and slid open to reveal a room that looked more like an army quartermaster's storage than an ancient cavern. Rows of shelves towered opposite racks and cases that contained things that looked like everything from a fantasy gaming spear to a biotech suit and helmet.

Achilles, or whatever was wearing Achilles, turned with widespread arms and a deep breath of satisfaction. That seemed like the perfect time to try and disappoint him. I grabbed the tomahawk from my back and shouted an ululating cry to power more runes than I had ever attempted before.

Desperation gave me fuel for that willpower. I wasn't sure what I was looking at, or where it came from. But I knew I didn't want this Mr. Mysterious Asshat to have whatever he was looking for. I triggered runes in my legs to enhance my leap. The muscles seemed to be tearing. I had no doubt that there would be a physical price to pay for what I had done. Some things come with a cost though.

A second surge of willpower and personal energy channeled whatever had been stored with the Thurisaz and Kenaz runes. Lightning crackles and flames licked over the axehead in tendrils of blue, white, scarlet and gold.

The Achilles guest creature sensed my attack at the last minute. He spun and lifted a hand to bring up some sort of ward or shield of his own. Thunder crashed and lightning spat, flames detonated to spread around the evil villain to the wall beside his impossible automatic door. Soot-blackened and charred feathers exploded in a spray of blinding color and fluff.

Whatever he did was at least partially effective. When the shock of my explosive attack started to clear, I could see what damage was done. A wooden case flickered with sparks where it had burst open and tried to catch fire. One whole section of shelf fell with a crash.

The Achilles puppet though stood back up from where he sprawled a dozen yards away. His costume smoked and gaped to reveal reddened flesh beneath. Whatever protection he had, might have kept him alive but they hadn't stopped the unpredictable energy added with the rune of Thor's hammer and chaotic Jotun or giant power.

I found myself bellowing in a roar that fitted a name like StromBjorn, the storm bear. "Dthu tapar! Gefast upp!"

In retrospect, I might have gone with English. But "You Lose! Give up!" seems a pretty easy concept to convey, particularly when pointing a weapon sheathed in flames and lightning.

He probably understood me because he yelled back what I suspect was a centuries-old version of "Bite me small fry." His language was as incomprehensible to me as mine must have been to him. His gesture, however, was clear.

He produced his own silenced pistol and pointed it at Elena where she had been thrown several yards back from the arsenal opening. He learned quickly too. This time his challenge was in plain English. "Move again and I splatter her brains on the stone. Without her living blood, this door remains open and all of these things are released to whoever finds them first. Let me assure you that there are things in here that would not be safe in any hands in the entire world."

I barely dared to breathe. It wasn't so much the threat of releasing doom and mayhem. I'd seen mayhem advertised a time or two before. It was usually horrific, but I wasn't convinced it was apocalyptic. We had failed to destroy mother earth so far despite some pretty concentrated and sometimes stupid efforts in that direction.

My dilemma was the girl. She had been the main reason I was down in this cave to begin with. Alright, maybe there was a little grudge to settle for Pedro too. But mostly it was the girl, or the mission, maybe. Hel maybe I wasn't even sure why I was down there at all. I didn't intend to see a sweet fairly innocent girl slain for nothing more than the blood that had flown to her from an ancestor in the dawn of time.

"So where's that leave us, Senor old and ugly?" Maybe I could just make him mad enough to empty the mag into me. It looked like one of the sleek concealed carry pieces. Probably didn't have more than six or seven rounds in it. There was at least a decent chance that I might survive anything but a headshot or a couple in my ticker.

He seemed confident of the situation though, while his gun was on the young lady. He sneered around his reply. "Take her and leave. By the time you can return I will have what I need from in here. Given thirty seconds I don't think you could stop me with the whole of your Yankee spy agency behind you. So take her and go."

I hadn't forgotten what he'd said about leaving the chamber open though. "Yea? And leave the door open to Pandora's sweater closet there? That doesn't seem like a great trade to me. What's your second offer?"

"Child! Idiot meat monkey!" His color really did interesting things when he got mad and started to spray some of Achilles' spittle around. "You only live at my whim! Take the girl and go before I decide you are a better mask than this sheath I now wear. If you are worried about the chamber then have some bombs dropped down the hole or something. They should at least close the tunnel even if they can't damage walls built by ancients more powerful than your wildest imaginings."

"Don't listen to him Mouse." The voice was familiar, but the accent softer and more refined. Pedro Perro stepped out of the shadows of the tunnel behind me.

His brains and blood still stained the shirt and dapper leather jacket. Other than that, there was no sign of the wound that had consumed a quarter of his head just minutes ago. All I could do was stare. He wasn't Einherjar. I could feel an unknown aura around him now. In fact, if I looked out of the corner of my eyes he even glowed with a very faint sparkle of warring vibrant colors.

Noting my deer in the headlights pose, a little of my old smuggler peeked out. The irascible rogue grinned his crooked smile. "You didn't think you had a monopoly, did you? There are more things in Heaven and Earth Horatio..."

He turned back to the other stunned and unmoving figure in the cavern. Achilles' spirit kidnapper glared back with a hint of his own confusion. "How? I killed you myself."

Pedro let out a tired sounding chuckle. "Says the guy that claims to be a thousand years old and able to move from one body to the next. By the way are you demonic? Fallen angel? Maybe something from the middle east or the Hebrews?"

With another of his weary laughs, Pedro Perro shrugged off his own question. "No matter. Hell vato. I told you. I told all of you. Even thick old Mouse over there. Didn't I tell you I was a Coyote? Okay maybe just Coyote, or if you prefer, The Coyote. Sometimes the Crow called me Old Man Coyote or the First Maker."

While he talked, Coyote walked closer to the exposed storehouse. His movements were easy and casual and he held his hands out empty and plain to see. "You two aren't all *that* special. I been around for longer than both of you put together."

Pedro Perro, Peter Dog, the God Coyote, shrugged and smirked again as he leaned on the wall just beside the opening and the offering bowl that required Elena's royal blood. "Even her people knew me, back in the *before times,* when I still danced with maidens and snuck into the bedchambers of queens and princesses."

He turned and winked at me where Achilles couldn't see. At his wink, I felt the power-wrapped weapon in my hand twist and change. Instead of my modern sleek tactical tomahawk. I held the venerable museum piece he had given me near the border. Bone, wood, copper, and feathers were all stained with various dyes and rough stick figures.

Though I could no longer see the flames and electrical energy on my weapon, I could feel a deep thrum and pull as if the earth itself pushed awareness and purpose into my hand.

"Come to think of it, maybe that royal blood came from me instead of those ancients." Coyote reached behind him blindly. I threw the tomahawk even before he began that move. Copper blade and immortal flesh met a scant foot from the bowl. Dark, thick spools of blood splashed out and along the wall. A small portion, perhaps a few ounces at most, splashed into that stone bowl as Coyote threw himself on the fallen angel or whatever it was that possessed Achilles. Both went down with a haunting supernatural scream of fury, fear, and denial ripped from one of their throats. The hiss of those invulnerable ancient doors shutting cut the sound off as if it had never been.

22

THE EARTH BEGAN TO SHAKE, at first gently. That didn't bode well for people trapped down in a new and rough excavation. Elena barely gasped when I jerked her up and tossed her over a shoulder. "Hold your wrist above the wound. Use your other hand and hold as tight as you can. It would be pure Hel if you bled out after all the effort that went into saving you."

We made it halfway back up the tunnel before Franco and Luis met us on their way in. They were smart cookies though. When they saw me running with the girl in tow, both hardened gunmen paled and turned to race ahead of us. At the entrance, we all stopped.

Luis and I stood with our hands at the small of our backs and drew deep breaths to steady our heart rate and nerves. Franco all but fell to the ground to gasp in large volumes of air himself.

I found myself watching the gunrunner while unworthy speculations bounced inside my head. I wanted to trust him. But a treasure trove like we'd found? It was worth a fortune and he seemed a perfect mercenary these days. For that matter could I trust Heather and Luis not to run off and tell the Odin and the other Aesir where to find some doomsday level weapons?

"Magnus!" A sobbing cry caught my attention and forestalled that decision. I don't remember running to meet her. It had to be me though, Maureen couldn't do any running from where she was lying on a makeshift stretcher with stained bandages on what must have been fresh gunshot wounds. I didn't lift her, though my arms went around the lady who tied my guts in knots.

"Maureen! What in the nine worlds are you doing here?" I barely whispered the question but she heard it.

"Those idiot nephews of Guillermo. They tried to kidnap me when I asked for a ride to fetch the car back." She winced and had to catch her breath as my arms tightened both in concern and anger. I knew two boys that would do very well to avoid any place where I might accidentally show up.

When she caught her breath my lady love continued, "When they found out I wasn't a real American doctor with millions of dollars they changed plans. Would you believe I was given as a gift? They sold your damned dog to some Cartel guys for pit fights, and when the drug lords commented on my red hair, I was given away to curry favor for the little snots."

I kissed Maureen and straightened her hair before lifting the thin blanket to survey some of the damage. At least two bullets were somewhere inside her. There was probably some intestinal damage and internal bleeding. Depending on the angle they might have nicked a liver or gallbladder. As much juice as I had slung already, I doubted I could heal a hangnail of my own much less serious damage on another person.

"This isn't horrible elsket, but it ain't good." I wasn't going to lie, but I wasn't going to tell her anything to drop her morale either. "If I had a fraction of my own power right now I'd see what I could do."

I swayed and almost fell against her. After a steadying breath, I looked her in the eyes and frowned along with a sigh of regret. "You're going to need a hospital."

Looking around showed me others in sorry shape. There was everything from more bullet wounds to long term malnutrition and neglect. "We'll get some people down here. A little humanitarian aid. But we can't let them see what's down that tunnel."

Maureen's questioning gaze and a skeptical eyebrow demanded answers. I gave them to her. I gave her all the answers I could about the current situation. Maybe there wasn't every little detail about my own past. Then again I didn't know that many details about my past. I gave her some of it though. Mostly I tried to explain how dangerous I thought the newly revealed chamber might be if anyone ever discovered it again.

Throughout my story, Maureen listened wide-eyed. She didn't reject any of it though. Maybe she had doubts but she heard me out. Finally, it was her turn to comment.

"Magnus Gustaveson. You go close that tunnel. Close the tunnel and then get away from here. Some of the captives are already using radios out of the criminal's vehicles. Who knows when officials might show up. You need to deal with that cave and then vanish before someone starts asking questions about undocumented Americans and prison escapes."

I tried to argue with her but she shushed me with a gentle kiss and a caress of my cheek. "Nae, my bonny lad. You do what you ought. I'll be fine. There are enough Americans in this lot that we'll all be fine. Someone even said they could reach the embassy and have all non-citizen names recorded just to avoid any "accidents" to shut up witnesses. She said they might have UN troops here to help evacuate us all if her husband can arrange it. It's some kind of ambassador or politician he is."

Franco tapped me on the shoulder with an almost apologetic smile. "Mon ami, she is quite correct. I heard the other Mademoiselle on the satellite phone. Troops should be arriving within the half-hour. If you would trust an old brother in arms, I will guarantee her safety. If we still had the explosive I could insure that the tunnel would take years to open if it was ever possible. It is but modesty that prevents me from saying I could open one of the magma tunnels underneath us and flood the whole thing with an impossible barrier. Had I my explosives of course."

I didn't want to trust him, particularly with a young and vibrantly beautiful woman. The sincerity in his voice was inescapable on that subject though. The rest might be questionable, but I had no doubt that he would die before he allowed harm to Maureen now.

Something else he had said begged for my attention though. "Magma tunnels? How close?"

Franco gave me a blank look for a minute. "Close. I do not know the exact direction or how many meters. I just know that Achilles' engineers were arguing about the route when I delivered the Russian machine guns for their towers."

One of the few remaining bad guys cleared his voice from where they were sitting with their hands tied. Luis was standing over a few of them. This time however he was the guard and they were the prisoners. He certainly seemed to handle a battle rifle with poise and confidence, and maybe a teaspoon of relish. He quirked a questioning expression at me, which got a nod of agreement.

Luis helped the suddenly helpful cartel merc to his feet and pointed the fellow at us without bothering to remove his handcuffs. They were probably the very same handcuffs that were missing from his belt pouch.

"Hey, this wasn't anything personal." The guy spoke perfectly accented midwest Americana. "It was just a paid gig. Now it's gone south. I never hurt any of these people or even knew about them. We were just perimeter guards. If you let us go, I'll show you where they kept their survey maps and excavation records."

Maureen regarded him with narrowed eyes. "He's a proper scoundrel, but we never saw him down by the cells. I'd have to say he's most likely being truthful mo chroí. The local authorities are likely to stretch out any of these fellows and blame the Americans for the whole brouhaha if they catch those fellows down here. I say take his help and let him go. But what are you able to do with some old maps and ye can barely stand on your own two feet? again I might add. It's almost as bad as the last time I had to find you and patch everything back together."

I had to think about it, but not too long. The truth is, these guys were no better or worse than I have been. They used certain skills professionally and were paid for their services. The fact that those services were sometimes repugnant to the very people you helped, or even the people you had protected while learning those skills, didn't matter that much to me. I'd been in his shoes. Of course, our Valkyrie generally insured we weren't ever captured, but there had been rare incidents.

"You've got a deal. Show me those records and then you guys get out of here. No weapons. Take one of the cargo trucks and make yourself scarce. Maybe you can find enough spare clothes to look like workers or something instead of a bad recasting of the dirty dozen."

I forestalled him with a raised hand when the merc started to introduce himself, a real rookie mistake. "Nope, no names. Just do your side of the bargain and get out of here."

Maybe ten minutes later those of us with immortal or at least semi-immoral natures were standing maybe thirty yards from the excavated tunnel. Here there was another half-carved hole that led down at a different angle. Warm and foul-smelling gasses wafted out of the hole.

"It's not poisonous, just rank with sulfur and maybe some methane. El Patrone had some scientists check it to reassure his men." The unidentified merc took a step back. Whether it was the stench, uncertainty about El Patrone and his scientists, or just a hurry to get out ahead of the authorities wasn't certain.

"Go ahead and get out of here. If you want to help finish loading those last stretchers onto trucks you could do that. Just leave room in each vehicle for medical folks to get in and work. I think everyone is stable enough to transport as far as Mexico city though." I barely finished talking before he turned on a heel and darted away.

I heard Gere rumble a question out behind me. I had to turn around to clarify. "What was that, Wolf?"

"I asked what the plan was. I don't care what the scientists said. I can smell enough bad air down there to knock even one of you guys out in just a minute or two. Give it ten minutes and you're blue-skinned, cool to the touch, and then your meat starts to rot."

I had an uncomfortable mental image of how exactly

Gere knew when a human being started to rot. Somehow I imagine a taste test was involved.

"So you take the end of the safety rope." I wanted to say please, and sir, to show some respect. Somehow being deferential to a supernatural wolf on two legs didn't seem smart. I couldn't help remembering teeth and blood spraying all over the sand when one of Gere's own packmates came over all blubbering and beseeching.

"Got it. Three tugs and I reel you in like a fish." He took a few turns around his formidable wrist with the rope attached to a safety harness we'd found to fit my chest. It was a little long in the torso but we'd tightened it down by knotting a strap here and there. The best part was, it fit down over the RAV armor we'd found with the rest of my gear.

I might not need flechettes or flashbangs but that armor with my own runic enhancements went a long way to helping me stay calm. I idly wondered if a few of the HE grenades might help me out, the problem would have been with firing them inside a tight tunnel without blowing myself into potted meat.

"Three tugs, right, just don't clean and gut the fish once you get it out chief." I turned away on my last statement, but not before he flashed me a grin with those uncommonly large and sharp-looking teeth.

Heather and Luis were off to one side talking with Franco while he "secured" a number of weapons and gear into a hummer he'd claimed for his part in the great Jaguar hunt. They all turned for the briefest of instances to give me various versions of thumbs up or good luck type gestures. I waved back and started into the hole.

The stench was several times worse in the confined hole. I found myself taking in a deep breath anyway. If this was as good as the air got, then I wanted enough of it to last a little while once the deeper air became too bad to inhale.

We'd measured about forty-five yards on the survey map before the tunnel approached that previously unknown volcanic tube. It was the closest point we could find to the lava field somewhere below us. Which meant that it was the thinnest section of rock between me and a painfully intimate demonstration of flash cooking.

The tunnel had several smaller side tunnels. A very small miner might have gone down them, but even then he probably had to crouch or crawl. The only reason they were important to me was, Achilles had used them as ventilation tunnels to circulate air out of the main cavern in front of the ancient portals. If we were right and there was a tube full of hot magma coursing near this tunnel, then letting it in here, should also drain it through the ventilation holes and into the cave around the weird gear in its ancient storehouse.

That was my goal. I got close enough that the air was steaming as well as stinking. The heat coming off the tunnel wall was horrendous. I had to think that it had increased since the excavators gave up. I doubt anyone could have worked for more than a minute or two, tunneling in this kind of heat.

When I braced myself on the stone wall I had to snatch my hand right back off. That rock was frying pan hot. I'd found my spot. Now all I had to do was magically detonate the wall, with just a fraction of my own energy and willpower left, while timing it so that my whimsical immortal ally could get me out of danger if he was so inclined. I had to recall that Gere's usual place was at Odin's hand or feet. If he was so moved, then all it would take was inaction to make sure I found myself back at the not so tender mercies of old Ygg and Kara.

What the Hel? I was living on gravy time as it was. With one hand I gripped the tether that stretched behind me. The other hand held my runed tomahawk as high as the rough tunnel would allow. It took what seemed an eternity to focus in that steaming, foul tunnel. But I dug into everything I could think of.

Memories from the shamanic world, my first wife, the hatred I felt for Lorcan all added fuel to make the runes of destruction and power glow. Kenaz for fire and understanding. I jerked the tether for the first time.

I tossed into the runes my fears and longing for Maureen, my pride and love for Grimmr and even Rafe. And then I jerked the tether again.

Finally, I touched recent feelings. Wonder, sadness, admiration for the trickster god and his sacrifice. Thurisaz took on a muddy swirl of random colors while another barely visible rune just weakly flickered.

It was that last part that did the trick I think. I felt the tomahawk shift again. When I looked closer, it was flickering with the spectral image of feathers and bone fetishes. On a whim, I shouted as I threw the weapon. "*ANSUZ!*"

As the tomahawk flew I began running and jerked the tether the third time. This time there was no resistance. About fifteen feet of rope whipped towards me with an end that was visibly frayed after being jerked around a rough rock corner twice already.

I heard the detonation behind me, as well as the scream of some giant bird and the baying of a coyote in the thunder. The explosion was enough to throw me off my feet. I was still lying there when the heat began to build and a rush of even hotter air began to billow.

This was not a good place to be. I saw the air do that blurry invisible effect you get off of superheated air. Behind it, ropes of painfully bright scarlet and gold snaked out of a man-sized hole in the rock. They came rushing into the tunnel not like a river but like a flood of something thinner than syrup but thicker than coffee. If syrup and coffee were liquid fire that is.

Already it was hot enough to make my lungs ache when I drew a breath. It didn't seem likely that I could escape the rise of that broiling superheated air. But odds rarely figured into my calculations. I rose to a crouch and started thundering down the tunnel in an awkward stumbling jog as jagged corners and uneven walls snatched at my clothes and tore my skin.

Heat hammered into my shirt and I thought I felt sparks where the cloth began to ignite. The next thing that hammered into me though was teeth, or a beak, or maybe teeth inside a beak. Whatever it was grabbed my smouldering shirt between the shoulders and lifted me off my feet again.

I was carried forward as another blast echoed behind me. Maybe the earth was responding to the weakness or maybe the increased pressure of hot air had done something deep within the rock. This detonation was several times stronger than my own puny strike. Gases and heat rushed down the tunnel with me as I was carried like a cannonball to bounce off the rough-hewn walls.

I saw the weak light at the end of the tunnel. Then I saw Gere's expression of surprise. Finally, I saw his chest from just past the end of my nose. An instant later, I hit him hard enough to carry us both flying into the air behind him. That was the last thing I saw.

23

THE BED WAS MOVING when I woke up. That seemed like a good sign. It might mean there was someone in said bed with me. Without opening my eyes I reached a hand gingerly to either side in search of a shapely redhead. All my hands encountered were fine down comforters and expensive cotton sheets.

Cracking open a single eye showed a small bedroom I'd never seen before. A tiny table and chair sat facing a small round window. Above the window in flowing letters were the words. Arr Guile below a framed painting of a crafty looking pirate cutting a coin purse from someone's belt.

A porthole meant I was on a boat. In the far distance, I could almost see the waves cresting. So a boat at sea. That would account for the motion of a bed bereft of a sleeping companion. I sighed and started to sit up.

That proved to be a mistake. If I had to guess, there were probably a few dozen broken bones underneath the spectacular full body bruise that slid into view as the sheets fell off my torso. Even if there weren't *any* broken bones, there was plenty of pain to go around. I stumbled out of bed and made it to the head, or what landlubbers call the toilet or facilities.

When I returned from the tiny cubicle that held the necessities, there was a fresh tray on the small writing desk. I found coffee, juice, a whole ewer of cold water, and a double meat club sandwich on thick rye bread. Bacon is, as far as I can tell, one of the greatest culinary advancements in the last thousand years. I ate the sandwich, drank the coffee, juice and about half the water.

By then I was well enough to limp out into the passage-way. I walked down impeccably polished maple decks to find a huddle of crew-folk all dressed casually. There was no distinct uniform except for rubber-soled canvas shoes. Most of them had on knee-length beige or khaki shorts and a polo style shirt. I counted five men and two women who all seemed very unprofessor-like.

I know Eachan. He might not be a lecher or world-class pervert, but the old man did enjoy watching beautiful women. I'd never seen a male chauffeur or butler working for him. Instead, he tended to hire students and young people looking for temporary work. The only rule he ever admitted to was that they couldn't be in his classes. I suspect there was an unwritten rule or guideline involving lovely women though.

"I'd ask permission to come aboard but someone already put me here." My voice seemed to catch them by surprise. All seven crewmates turned to face me as one.

"Welcome aboard Mr. Gustaveson. The professor told us to take care of your every need. He had to make an emergency flight back home but thought you would appre-ciate the voyage to, "heal and unwind" I believe were his words. " The fellow who stepped forward to shake my hand wore a plastic name tag that said "Sanders" on his shirt.

He was a decade too old to be in one of the prof's classes. But his physical condition was almost as good as some of my bouncers back in Austin. The rest of the crew seemed cut from a similar mold. Not all were as fit and muscular as Sanders, but all were in what some of our old trainers called fighting trim.

Before I could respond with any questions, Sanders was leading me into a salon with a good selection of liquor visible on the teak bar. The others all dispersed to whatever duties they were required to perform.

I sat and pondered while enjoying some of Eachan's excellent taste in whiskeys.

That's how it went for almost a full week. The crew was professionally absent. Whenever I needed a meal or a drink it was conveniently at hand. The food was a major shift from the simple beans and tortillas I'd gotten used to. The small library of books and videos was perfectly entertaining, and the scenery was enough to help even a numerously blown up mercenary grow fat and lazy.

But there was nobody to talk to or defuse with. The crew was only available when I needed something. None of them sat down to share a glass or discuss their day. As far as I could tell, the boat was on some kind of auto-pilot. I couldn't figure out where the radio was, much less make it function. The people were of no help. They just maintained the boat while it made its merry single-minded way wherever we were headed. Whenever I asked any questions I got no real answers. They'd just shrug, smile and excuse themselves on one pretext or another.

On the sixth day, as I was sprawled in a deck chair with some fruity alcohol enhanced concoction, one of the crew members sat down beside me. This was the first time any of them had initiated any contact so I was surprised.

When he spoke I was even more surprised. "Not bad Moose. Not bad at all. Your sugar daddy sure travels in style."

I tried not to jump too much when I turned to find Pedro sitting beside me in the shorts and polo of a crewman. There wasn't even a scar or thinning of hair where he'd been missing part of his skull a few days past. It made my own healing power seem a little shoddy.

"My friend, not my sugar daddy." I stopped and poured a drink to hand my new companion. "So why aren't you languishing away or cooked to a crisp in some ancient barrow?"

I settled back facing the sea but kept him focused in the corner of my eye. Pedro, or Coyote rather, grinned that mischievous smirk of his and replied. "It might be inde-structible, and foolproof protection from everything but a nuclear strike. Damn man, they even made it impassable to demons and angels and ghosts for all I know. Nobody knew how to make it immune to a god though."

He tossed back his drink while I digested that before asking. "What about Achilles?"

While I refilled his glass the trickster explained. "He lasted a couple of days. The heat didn't get him or even when the oxygen got low. He was telling the truth about keeping a body alive. I don't think he would have died at all, except he got tired of my singing and stories. Hell, he ain't a god. Just some semi-angel or demon creature. Never did figure out who he answers to."

He took another appreciative sip of Tequila sunrise before continuing. "Anyway, along about the third morning he just let the body fall dead. Tried to take my body."

I heard a new voice from over near the deck railing. "Dumbass"

"Dumbass indeed." Coyote nodded an agreement at my pet Rafe. "Anyway, "Achilles" went a little nuts when he figured out he couldn't push me out of the meat. Went even crazier when he figured out the walls were impervious to spiritual energy. Almost made me feel sorry for him, knowing that he'd be in there until the next time it opened. Could be another twenty or thirty thousand years before anyone gets through all that volcanic rock and rubble."

We both sat back and digested that for a while. The self-satisfied sighs were almost simultaneous when we let them out.

"Oh by the way. I found your old cell phone when I went back for one of the cars." He never explained how he got out of a box that kept in demonic or angelic beings. I was just glad to know that I wouldn't have to watch for Achilles or whatever that was in addition to the various other supernatural heavyweights that might be looking for me.

He handed over the cell phone and looked around the deck for a minute with a content smile. "Yea your guy really knows how to live. I wonder where the old man is and why they won't let you call on the ship to shore. Anyway, enjoy the phone and the sarcastic bird. I saw him circling around when I got out of the mountains, thought I'd deliver him to you. And I had your loyal blonde buddy shipped back home for you. Those Austin people are weird. You know they got kennels that cost more to stay in than some hotels? He was good an' loyal though. I thought he deserved a little vacation so put it on a card. I mean c'mon. A jaguar? That damned dog fought a jaguar and walked away."

That was just the first part. I forgot he'd missed some of the middle after having his head blown half off. He missed the whole fight with the Aztec-wannabes I guess. I looked up to brag about Grimmr's part in that mayhem. The only one to tell was Rafe though, and I didn't feel like being called a dumbass again just yet. At least I had the phone. I flipped it open and picked out a number from speed dial.

24

"WAIT, *that's* why I could get nowhere with you?" Franco's voice was all but swallowed by the guffaws that erupted. His acceptance of such inconvenient concepts as wolf demi-gods and immortal warriors with beautiful handlers had been extraordinary to Heather and Luis. He'd absorbed the information with a large amount of calm or sangfroid and a few keen questions.

Which is possibly why they were surprised by his outburst at what seemed a fairly minor admission on their part. He barely got the next question out around another deep belly laugh. "You're a virgin. Heather the heathen and virgin valley-girl Valkyrie?"

One of the youngest of the Choosers of the slain glared at him but nodded. The mortal gunman had earned some leniency by saving her the trouble of killing everyone at the ulama arena. Her glare indicated that he was using that leniency up rapidly.

"And you? You are a chosen warrior of Viking gods but you just happen to be gay?" He had to lean forward to look around the Valkyrie at her wiry gunman einherjar.

Luis nodded with a self-confident smile of his own.

"And Mouse, aka Strombjorn, Magnus or Eric back when we fought together before, he is probably back in Valhalla right now having a big party and orgy starring his own Valkyrie this Kara?"

Even the name of the tempestuous one was enough to make Heather and Luis look uncomfortable. Luis was the first to recover and answer. "Yea, all of the older warriors talk about it. The stories, man, the stories about Kara are brutal."

Heather nodded an enthusiastic agreement which popped the gum bubble she'd blown. "She's like, Oh my god, she's just so not cool. Everybody knows better than to like, get on her crusty side. The betch is crazy fer shur. Even the other Valkyrie, like, walk around. But she totally screws all of her guys. Like when she's not flippin' out on them. I wonder where she hid him. You know, for like years? We never, like even saw him before. Just, you know, like stories? They were *sooo* intense."

Everyone stopped and pondered that for a while. Finally, Franco grinned and looked at her again for a little clarification. "So...how does that afterparty thing work with a virgin and her gay warrior? How do you guys celebrate?"

Heather's expression went from dark and serious to something more like a cheerful valley girl talking about her favorite rockstar. "Oh, that's awesome! We do, like, mani-pedis, shoe shopping, totally munch out on Ben and Jerry's, and stream old John Hughes movies!"

The End

ALSO BY STEVE CURRY

For more in The Saga of Mouse, aka The Valhalla AWOL series.

Start with book one

Austin Wyrd, Book One

Wyrd Gere, Book Two

Freke Wyrd Voodoo, Book Three

Yule, Have a Wyrd Christmas, The holiday Novella.

APPENDIX OF WYRDNESS

(MORE OR LESS IN ORDER OF APPEARANCE)

Freke and Gere are the wolves who sit at Odin's feet at times. Otherwise they are out and about in the world. They are curious, wild animals, duh. But their main purpose is to teach mankind about teamwork, family, packhunting, that kind of thing.

Ia Drang is a valley, by a mountain, in Vietnam, where a bunch of Americans rounded up way more vietcong than their daily limit. One of my uncles was there. He suffered from some pretty severe social effects but towards the end I got him to talk about his time in the service. Troyce Ray Stacker was the seed for much of Magnus' backstory. The battle was made into a movie "We Were Soldiers".

Runes The runic alphabet of the Norse has several variations. Magnus uses the elder futhark of twenty-four runes. It can be used to write a message, carve a marker stone, or depending on who you talk to they are tools to divine information, or cast magical effects.

Valkyrie There are a number of "choosers of the slain" named in various stories. Kara, Brunhild, Gondul and more. Alternately called Swan Maidens or Wolf Maidens, they are under the direction of Freja rather than Odin. Odin does have control of them when attending to his warriors in Valhalla though.

Skaldic Poetry, Hugin and Munin Not for the first time, Magnus enjoyed a visit from one of Odin's ravens. Hugin or thought, and Munin or memory, are the eyes ears and solid state storage drive of Odin in our world. In AWOL they speak in dreams and always in Skaldic Poetic verse. The main skaldic verse is alliterative rather than rhyming. It is an imabic meter with stress on every other syllable. The alliteration occurs in the first syllable of every couplet and the next to the last syllable in the first line of every couplet. I know, it's confusing, and challenging, and I can't help myself.

The Dream world, Yaqui, The Bone-Lady etc. A large chunk of this book takes places in a dream sequence initiated by the Yaqui shaman. The yaqui are related to both Aztecs and Apaches. The stories of their conflict with Mexican officials are epic. Tio Bill uses a version of Ayahuasca to achieve the mental state for the dreamwalk.The bone lady Magnus ends up with is a staple of many shamanic beliefs. She welcomes new shaman to the dreamworld and usually ritualistically kills them and then imparts the knowledge of other worlds before sending the initiate back as a shaman in his own right.

The Angel of Mons During World War One a story appeared in newspapers. It told of an isolated group of British soldiers trapped by a much larger force of Germans. Just as things looked hopeless, an Angel appeared in the heavens and opened a gateway through which ancient warriors with obsolete arms appeared and drove the enemy away. The respite allowed British troops to escape the impossible situation. The good christian lads attributed their survival to divine intervention. I just theorised that maybe they got the divine agent wrong. Later the story was declared a hoax. But who really knows?

Draugr Norse vikings were known as fierce foes. So their terrors had to be just as fierce. A draugr was the norse equivalent of a zombie, ghoul, rampaging undead and vengeful spirit all rolled into a super powered threat. You can read about them in several sources or fight them in the game Skyrim by Bethesda.

Ogham Just like the norse had their mystical and magical alphabet and divination tools, the Celts had a version of their own. It was most often associated with various plants and trees but was supposed to have been comprehensible as a written code to certain nobles and warriors of Celtic legend.

Wounded Knee It was hard finding a suitable place to illustrate that Magnus was not always the "nice guy" that he seems to be some of the time. Wounded Knee was one of the most brutal and well documented atrocities to occur in the old west. I apologise for any offense or discomfort the scene might cause. Most of the "facts" are true down to weapon and equipment descriptions as well as certain names. I can't testify to the presence of Einherjar, Valkyrie or holy Mandan warriors though.

Weapons speaking of weapons above, everything from the field artillery pieces to the high-tech scopes and weapons later are real and researched equipment. In some instances I've even managed to fire a few of them.

Chilaquiles, Tres Leche and more Robert B Parker was well known for putting food and cooking front and center in many of his books. It rubbed off. Of course a decade of Culinary and Hospitality service probably had it's impact too. All of the food is real and you can find recipes. Or wait for me to get the cookbook together and some of the recipes out on MyWyrdMuse.com

Tenochtitlan was what we now call Mexico City. At the time of the Spanish conquest this city of Aztecs was larger than anyplace in Europe with the possible exception of Constantinople. Even London or Paris would have suffered from a comparison.

Yaocihuatl The daughter of an important Toltec chief was given in marriage to the chief of the Aztecs as they moved into central America. They managed this by telling the Toltecs that they would make her a goddess. It was never mentioned that they meant they would sacrifice her to Yaocihuatl, their goddess of weather and beauty, for fertility and abundance. Nor did they bring up the part where she would be skinned and worn as a talisman for rituals.

ABOUT THE AUTHOR

Steve Curry is a fledgling author just beginning to use a spread of experiences and careers. His current forays into writing are Urban Fantasy infused with Culinary tidbits from a decade as a Le Cordon Bleu chef. Military weapons and protocols plus realistic medical and physical descriptions abound from his work with Uncle Sam's Army NBC branch and time as a Licensed Respiratory Therapist in ICUs across the nation. Toss in lots of mythology, new age religion, supernatural goodness and real world history along with a soupcon of Jim Butcher's humor, and a few pinches of Robert Parker's character building traits to see how he'll entertain you. He currently resides in West Texas under the management of a yellow hound dog with claims on most of a large bed. Others in the hierarchy are an imperial princess and rainbow unicorn riding granddaughter, his wife, the imperial queen and mistress of eyerolls, and an uncountable horde of invading mongrel cats. The author enthusiastically accepts reviews and for such a favor will praise you to your ancestors or whatever higher power suits you. You can join others interested in his work at Steve Curry's author pages linked below.

www.MyWyrdMuse.com
https://www.facebook.com/MyWyrdMuse/